Jane Toombs, with seventy published books in print and pixels to her credit, lives in Michigan's beautiful Upper Peninsula from May to December. Jane, the Viking from her past, their calico cat, Kinko, and her laptop flee to sunny Florida from January to April. She writes in all genres.

NIGHTINGALE MAN

During World War I, Luke is recruited by the British Secret Service from the American pilots flying with the French Air Force. His mission is to rescue Nurse Edith Cavell, captured by the Boche, imprisoned in German-occupied Belgium and doomed to be shot as a spy. All too soon it becomes a challenge to stay alive. Who's double-crossing him? Can it be the English gal he's falling in love with? Or is it the spymaster back in England who's set him up as the fall guy?

Books by Jane Toombs
Published by The House of Ulverscroft:

HARTE'S GOLD

JANE TOOMBS

NIGHTINGALE MAN

Complete and Unabridged

ULVERSCROFT
Leicester

First published in Great Britain in 2002

First Large Print Edition
published 2003

The moral right of the author has been asserted

All characters in this book have no existence outside
the imagination of the author, and have no relation
whatever to anyone bearing the same name or names.
These characters are not even distantly inspired by
any individual known or unknown to the author, and
all incidents are pure invention.

British Library CIP Data

Toombs, Jane, *1926 –*
    Nightingale man.—Large print ed.—
    Ulverscroft large print series: adventure & suspense
    1. World War, *1914 – 1918* —Secret service—Fiction
    2. Adventure stories
    3. Large type books
    I. Title
    813.5′4 [F]

    ISBN 0–7089–4940–1

Published by
F. A. Thorpe (Publishing)
Anstey, Leicestershire

Set by Words & Graphics Ltd.
Anstey, Leicestershire
Printed and bound in Great Britain by
T. J. International Ltd., Padstow, Cornwall

This book is printed on acid-free paper

1

Luke Ray peered through the taxi's windshield into the enshrouding mist. The 1911 Dodge slowed and then slowed again as its headlights probed the damp grayness. A building, low, dark and insubstantial, materialized in front of the taxi, a dim light glowing in a window. The driver sighed with relief before he turned to Luke with a smile.

'*La escadrille.*' His voice was triumphant.

Luke paid the fare he'd negotiated hours before in Chaumont, shouldered his duffel bag and walked slowly along the flagstone path, his heart hammering in anticipation. At last! The tinkle of an out-of-tune piano grew louder and louder, stopping abruptly when he opened the door to what he saw was the lounge. Heads turned, eyes evaluated him.

'*Fermez la porte,*' a lieutenant told him.

Luke shut the door behind him. Immediately the men resumed talking, playing cards, and reading. The piano-player started up again. Luke, duffel bag at his side, gazed from one group to another, waiting. No one made a move to greet him. He frowned, puzzled and disappointed.

How could they be so sure he wasn't one of them? With his dark hair and eyes he might be French — would they treat one of their own countrymen so coldly? It was clear, though, that they knew exactly who he was — the American who'd volunteered for the *Service Aeronautique* by way of the Foreign Legion. He hadn't expected a brass band but what the hell, what was wrong with being an American?

Yet he didn't sense hostility in the room, more an uneasiness.

One of the men reading, short and round-faced, closed his book without marking his place and stood. He walked to Luke, extending his hand.

'I am Felix DuFour,' he said in English.

'Luke Ray.' They shook hands.

'We expected you to arrive yesterday,' said DuFour.

'I was delayed by the fog.' Again Luke glanced around the room. 'Did I miss a patrol? A fight? Is that why — ?'

'We show a lack of enthusiasm?' DuFour shook his head. 'No, we did not fly yesterday. But what can you expect, considering the circumstances?' He met Luke's gaze and shrugged. 'I will take you to our captain.' He nodded toward the door.

Outside, the afternoon mist dampened

Luke's face again and he blinked drops of water from his eyelashes. DuFour strode ahead, becoming an indistinct gray form.

'Such strange weather, this, for August.' DuFour's disembodied voice came from the mist ahead of Luke. 'If the wind changes and the weather clears, we fly in the morning. Three of us — you, myself and Henri Passard.'

'Was Passard in the lounge?'

There was a silence. 'No,' DuFour said finally, 'he is absent, confined to his quarters. As your M. Thoreau would say, perhaps it is because he hears a different drummer. Ah, but such an aviator. If he were not, he would have been dead many times over by now.'

So Passard was a maverick, Luke thought. Not exactly the flyer he'd pick to go with him on his first patrol with the escadrille. A maverick and an American. It made him wonder about DuFour.

Through the mist he saw a light over the doorway of a camouflaged building. Increasing his pace, he pulled up even with his companion. 'Why were you chosen?' asked Luke.

DuFour shrugged. 'After all, I am a Jew.' He opened the door and led the way into a room where men and women worked at desks covered with ordered piles of documents.

'I don't understand.'

'What is there to understand? We follow orders, we kill the Boche, we flight for glory and for France. We don't inquire into reasons.' DuFour passed through a door on their right, Luke on his heels.

As Luke shook his head, giving it up, a pretty black-haired young woman behind a railing to his left caught his eye. As he passed, she glanced up from her typewriter and smiled at him. He smiled back, grateful for the first spontaneous sign of welcome.

DuFour led him into the next room, telling a corporal that Sergeant Luke Ray was reporting for duty. The corporal nodded and left them.

DuFour's dark eyes appraised Luke. 'Yvette smiled at you.'

Luke grinned. 'In Denver we'd call her a right pretty gal.'

'We in the *escadrille* call her the Angel of Death.'

Luke stared at him.

'She has an unusual ability,' DuFour went on, 'of offering her affection to those who are about to die or be maimed. Some men might say it was worth the price. As for myself — '

The corporal, returning, interrupted. 'You will report to the captain, Sergeant,' he told Luke.

4

Captain Trenault's blue tunic accented the gray of his hair and the sallowness of his thin face. As Luke saluted, he found it difficult to keep his gaze from following the track of the scar curving along the left side of the captain's chin to his ear.

'We expected you yesterday,' the captain told him.

'My train was held back to wait for a troop transport, sir, heading for the front. To Verdun. Then the weather — '

'The weather will be better tomorrow.' The captain spoke in a monotone, bored and weary. He looked at Luke, yet beyond him. 'Have you been told of your mission?' he asked.

'No, sir.'

'In the last week we have lost five planes and five aviators north of Verdun. Over the German lines, behind the German lines. Some of the *escadrille's* best pilots. They flew north and they disappeared. The Boche, we are convinced, have a new and powerful weapon. A new aircraft? A new anti-aircraft gun? We do not know.'

Luke nodded. Despite his own self-confidence, he felt a crawl of unease.

'Three of you will fly north tomorrow at dawn,' the captain went on. 'You and two of our best aviators, DuFour and Passard. You

5

are to cross the German lines and discover why our aircraft have not come back. I expect that at least one of you will return with the answer.' He focused directly on Luke for the first time. 'I understand you've flown the Nieuport 10.'

'Yes, sir. I have twenty hours flight time, five in combat.'

'A magnificent machine, the best we have.'

'She handles well. She can turn on a dime.'

'A great improvement over what we flew at the beginning of the war. Is it only a year ago? It seems much longer.' The captain pinched the bridge of his nose between his thumb and forefinger, then turned his gaze to photographs of aviators and aircraft on the wall beside the desk. 'Those machines were little more than kites with motors.'

'The Nieuport's a hell of a machine, sir,' Luke said. 'Except for the wings.'

'The wings, the wings, that's all I hear, the wings. Can a plane be built without a flaw? Do you want speed or do you want strength? Do you want maneuverability or do you want a plodding gun platform?'

Luke didn't reply. 'There's no sense talking,' his father, T.J., had always told him, 'when nobody's listening.'

'Aircraft are like men,' the captain continued. 'They are all flawed, they must be flawed. An imperfect human cannot create a perfect machine. Even Americans are flawed. You agree, sergeant?'

'Yes, sir,' Luke said. T.J. would have agreed as well — at least as far as Luke himself was concerned. Luke remembered his father shaking his head over Luke's twenty-dollar loss to a three-card monte dealer.

'You're going to keep losing until you stop seeing just what other folks want you to see,' T.J. had warned him.

'You'll be awakened at three in the morning.' The captain nodded his dismissal.

Luke saluted and about-faced.

'Sergeant.'

Luke, at the door, turned and saw that Captain Trenault was standing, leaning forward with his hands on the desk. 'I wish you the best of good fortune.'

Surprised, Luke hesitated. '*Merci, mon capitaine,*' he replied.

★ ★ ★

Fading stars shone from between cumulus clouds as Luke, wearing his flying suit, strode toward the dark shapes of the three Nieuport 10s waiting on the field in the gray light of

7

pre-dawn. A good flying day, warm with a breeze from the south. Anticipation quickened his step.

Passard, whom he'd met briefly the night before, stood beside one of the planes, pulling a flying suit over his thickset bulk. 'Myself, I understand,' Passard said as Luke came up. 'And DuFour. But why you?'

Luke shrugged before turning to walk slowly around his plane. He examined the stays, ran his fingers lovingly over the fabric. He wasn't going to worry about why he'd been chosen, it was enough he was flying again.

He climbed up beside the cockpit to check the alignment of the machine-gun. A godawful place to put the Lewis gun, on top of the upper wing. Firing it was like shooting a pistol held over your head. The only worse spot for the Lewis would be on the fuselage. Metal bullet deflectors or not, props always shredded when you fired fuselage guns.

Luke lowered himself into the Nieuport's cockpit, breathing in the familiar smells of gasoline, castor oil, and dope. He locked the webbed belt around his waist, kicked the rudder bar left and right, heard the cables and the pulleys creak, checked behind him to make sure the rudder snapped from side to side, pivoting the ailerons.

He raised his hand and a waiting mechanic grasped the propeller. '*Coupe! Plein gaz!*' the man called. Ignition switch off, gas cock on.

'*Coupe! Plein gaz!*' Luke shouted back.

The mechanic rotated the prop to draw fuel into the cylinders. 'Contact!'

Luke switched the ignition on. 'Contact!'

The mechanic snapped the prop and the 80-horsepower Gnome rotary engine exploded to life, smoke belching from the cowling. After a few seconds the engine settled into a high-pitched roar.

DuFour's Nieuport jounced across the field, its tail came up and the aircraft rose into the brightening sky. When Passard's plane rolled forward, the mechanic yanked the wooden chocks from in front of Luke's wheels and his plane bumped over the grass into the wind. The tail lifted from the ground, he eased the stick back and the horizon dropped away underneath him as the Nieuport soared skyward.

Climbing, he took his position above and behind DuFour with Passard to his right. Luke breathed deeply, exulting. He was free, the bonds of earth broken, with only the limitless sky above and around him. He dipped his right wing and looked down at the French trenches zigzagging ahead of him on the near side of the desolation of No-Man's

Land. Beyond that treeless, cratered waste, German trenches scarred the countryside west of Verdun. Observation balloons floated serenely above the German rear.

Verdun was a killing ground. Luke pitied those poor bastards in the trenches — mud-coated, hollow-eyed, deafened and driven half-mad by the shelling. Thank God he was up here, flying. This was the way wars should be fought, man against man, airplane against airplane. Just as in T.J.'s day when two men, Colts on their hips, dueled on a dusty frontier street. Just as centuries ago knights rode to battle. The only knights left in the world were aviators and their battlefield was the sky.

Luke grinned at his fancy even as his fingers fumbled inside his flying suit, reaching for the red rose Yvette had given him. She'd run up to him last night, smiled and handed him the flower, her hand brushing against his. Smelling the rose now, its sweet scent recalled the promise in her dark eyes as she looked back at him over her shoulder.

After fastening the rose stem to the side of his map case, he looked overhead to search the sky. Nothing. Except for the other two Nieuports, the sky was empty of aircraft. Clouds floated above him, the sun was rising off his right wing. As he crossed the German trenches, Archies puffed below him.

Pulling back on the stick to avoid the shells, Luke grinned at the quick response of his plane.

The Nieuport 10 was twenty-three feet from prop to tail with a wingspan of less than thirty feet — small and feisty. She'd fit nicely into the front room of T.J.'s Denver house, the one on Tremont that T.J. had been so proud of before losing it to the bank. Luke burst into song. Unable to carry a tune, he sang when he was alone, preferably in the sky where there was no danger of being overheard. Even he couldn't hear himself over the engine.

'It's a long way to Tipperary
It's long way to go.
It's a long way . . . '

Tac-tac-tac.

Damn.

Kicking the rudder, Luke leaned his body from the plane's turn, the maneuver getting an extra kick from the torque of the rotary. He pulled back on the stick and began to climb. Ahead of him DuFour veered to the left with a Fokker on his tail. Luke couldn't spot Passard.

He glanced behind and to the right, blinking when he looked into the sun. The tan monoplane climbing in pursuit of his Nieuport sported black Maltese crosses on its

11

wings, fuselage and rudder. A Fokker.

Luke saw holes in his upper right wing. He looped, bringing his Nieuport around to fly in the same direction as before. Except that now he was behind the Hun. Far below he saw DuFour's plane angling earthward trailing a long plume of smoke. The poor bastard.

Fritz in the Fokker looked back at Luke. Smiling. A cocky son-of-a-bitch.

The range of two hundred yards was too great but Luke pressed off a burst for luck and to let the Hun know he was there. The Nieuport failed to gain on the Fokker. Luke climbed, losing more distance as he flew deeper into German territory. Into what he knew was a trap. Searching the sky ahead he saw only the billows of cumulus clouds.

He looked back. At first he couldn't see Passard's Nieuport. Then he found him, in a steep dive, a Fokker following him down. The dive steepened and the plane plummeted. Fragments spun loose from Passard's Nieuport to flutter in the air. *My God!* The wings, the damn wings had sheared off. Luke winced.

He looked ahead. Fritz was circling to face him. Something was different about his Fokker. What was it? The machine-gun. The Spandau was mounted behind the propeller. Didn't the Boche fear a shattered prop?

The Hun plane was a mile away and closing. Excitement roiled Luke's gut, blood pounded in his ears, a shiver of fear ran along his spine. He caressed the butt of T.J.'s Colt .45 Peacemaker in the holster on his belt. For luck. The Hun's machine-gun winked at him. Too far, much too far. Fritz held his fire after the get-acquainted burst.

The planes roared directly at one another. He'd be damned it he'd be the first to turn aside. Three hundred yards now. Closer. Luke pulled the machine-gun cable and his bullets sought out the German. The Hun fired. There were ropes of fire binding the planes together. Why didn't the Fokker's prop shatter? Had Tony Fokker found a way to synchronize gun and prop?

The new German weapon!

New German weapon or not, Fritz stopped firing. Luke smile grimly as his tracers slammed into the other plane's fuselage. The German refused to yield. Luke braced for the crash, murmuring the only prayer he could remember from his childhood. 'Now I lay me down to sleep . . . '

The Fokker veered, the Maltese crosses, huge and black, swept over Luke's head. He rolled the Nieuport in a half inside loop, following the Hun. The Fokker was in trouble. Fritz struggled with his gun.

The Nieuport gained on the lagging Fokker. Still Fritz worked at his jammed gun. Luke dove and came up under the German plane's tail, his hand ready to trigger the Lewis. Fritz glanced down at him. Luke saw helmet, goggles, white scarf, impassive face.

He roared past the other plane without firing, leaving the German staring after him. He'd be damned if he'd shoot an unarmed man. He'd found the new German weapon, his job was to get back to the aerodrome. Putting the sun on his left wing top, he flew south, leaving the German behind.

He took one last look at the Fokker. Fritz raised one hand in salute. Luke saluted back, the slipstream tearing at his glove. He felt a strange kinship with the German. They were both flyers, both faced the same dangers of flimsy wooden planes, the turbulence of storms, the lurking threat of fire aloft. They both flew in open cockpits without parachutes.

Only one thing lifted them above the beasts of the jungle. Their chivalry, their code. Like T.J.'s code of the West. T.J.R. Theodore Joseph Ray. There'd never be another man like his father.

The hairs on Luke's neck bristled in warning. He jerked erect, glanced right and left. Nothing. The sun blinded him and he blinked, peering through slitted lids. The black outline of an airplane appeared in the glare of the sun. He threw the Nieuport into a vrille, a falling, twisting dive, heard the tac-tac-tac of machine-gun fire follow him down.

Remembering the death dive of Passard's plane, he pulled back, the Nieuport groaning her protest, and saw a yellow biplane lumbering above him. An Aviatik, crew of two, reconnaissance, slow as a lame horse. Luke smiled, his lips tight as he maneuvered to come up behind in the German plane's blind spot.

He shook his head. His job was to return to France. Again he flew south, leaving the Aviatik far behind. He wasn't yet over friendly territory when his engine hiccupped uncontrollably and died with a wheeze. The silence was complete. Awesome.

Luke clicked the switch, throttled. Nothing happened, nothing at all. He choked as he inhaled the sweet panic odor of escaping gas. The Fokker's bullets had found their mark after all. *Don't burn. Please God, don't burn.*

He glided toward France, observation sausages hovering above the horizon ahead of him, wind humming faintly in the Nieuport's wires. He must be five miles from the front. Had he flown that far behind the German lines? His altimeter read zero but Luke judged he was at a thousand feet, guessed he could glide a few hundred more yards at best.

Green treetops drifted past below, a forest untouched by a year of war. He glanced at his map. The *Bois de Forges?* A spire thrust above the trees to his left and he turned the Nieuport in that direction. As he neared the church, the trees slipped beneath him and Luke saw a small village with fields on both sides.

He glided toward the nearest field. The odor of gas lessened and he drew a deep breath while he studied the ground. A road curled from the woods below him, straightened to pass through the village, bisected the far fields and entered another wood. Far ahead a motorcycle crawled along the road with his Nieuport's wavering shadow following what he guessed was a German courier. The motorcycle vanished beneath the trees.

The first of the houses passed under him. The village streets were empty and he realized with a shock that the houses were burned out and deserted. The church was a ruin, its roof gone, one wall rubble, the tower with its spire intact. The Huns must have spared the tower to use as an observation post.

A field of grass rippled in the breeze ahead of him.

He eased his Nieuport down, the plane handling well, refusing to guess what the tall grass might hide. His wheels whispered beneath him, touched down and the plane bounced across the field. Luke was breathing a sigh of relief when he saw an obstruction jutting ahead of the plane. A stump? A boulder? He tried to wrench the plane into a turn. Too late.

The Nieuport jolted to a halt, whipping up on its nose and hurling Luke forward. Held by the strap, he clutched the side of the cockpit with one hand as he unbuckled with the other. He climbed down between the upended wings to the ground where he leaned against the fuselage, shaking his head to clear it. Gas dripped from a ruptured fuel line onto the grass near his feet.

He looked back over the lower wing and saw that his undercarriage had struck an oblong stone, knocking it flat. Other stones reared in the high grass around him. The shell-torn church was a hundred yards away at the foot of a gentle slope. It took Luke a moment to realize the stones were markers in an untended graveyard.

Sliding a small metal box from his pocket, he opened it and took out a match. Climbing clear of the wings, he struck the match on the sole of his boot, tossed it toward the dripping gas and backed quickly away. The fumes exploded with a roar and heat seared his face. His throat tightened and his eyes stung with more than the smoke as he watched the flames lick up the sides of the Nieuport's fuselage. He felt almost the same wrench of pain and loss he'd known years before when he had to shoot Ivanhoe after the bay gelding broke his leg in a prairie dog hole.

Luke strode away from the burning Nieuport, passed between stone pillars at the entrance to the cemetery and headed down the hill. Sensing movement in the distance, he looked past the ruined church to the woods on the far side of the village. Soldiers in gray-green uniforms and *pickelhaubes*, spiked helmets, trotted from the trees into the field.

Huns. A squad of Huns.

Crouching, Luke ran to the church, keeping its remaining walls between him and the approaching soldiers. From the cemetery behind him he heard the crackle of the blazing Nieuport and, glancing back, saw the flames and smoke rising like a beacon. With luck they'd think it was his pyre.

The church's rear door gaped open. Unholstering his Colt, he entered cautiously, his gaze darting over the confusion of charred beams and shattered stone from the collapsed wall. Unable to spot a decent hiding place, he finally climbed across a fallen timber and dropped to one knee behind a pile of rubble. Sunlight glinted red from a triangle of crimson in the broken stained-glass window beside him.

He looked at the front door, at the open rear door, back to the front. He weighed the Colt in his hand. Time passed. He heard a German shout commands from the direction of the burning plane and hoped they'd think he jumped to his death before it crashed.

No such luck.

'*Du schau in der Kirche nach*,' a voice ordered. Look in the church.

Damn German thoroughness.

He tightened his grip on the revolver. If they searched the church they'd find him. The only question was how many he'd take with him. He had five rounds in the Colt, another six in his belt. Most airmen downed behind German lines surrendered. The hell with that.

A shadow crossed the stained glass fragment as a soldier trotted past the window on his way to the rear door.

'*Mon ami*.'

Luke jumped. The whisper came from a few feet away. He looked around. No one.

'*Mon ami.*' A thin, white face appeared amidst the rubble.

Luke hesitated.

'*Dépechez-vous!*'

Luke did as he was told. Hurriedly pushed himself up, Colt in hand. Scrambled to where the face had been. He saw nothing but rubble.

'*Ici.*'

A pale hand reached from beneath a burnt timber.

Luke knelt and saw a black hole at floor level leading under a pile of debris. He lay flat and levered himself backward. A rock fell, striking the floor, the sound like thunder in his ears. Dust choked him.

Running feet. The Germans were in the church. The running stopped. There was a long silence and then he heard footsteps approaching his hiding place. Jolting thuds told him a stick or rifle butt was probing the debris above him. He held his breath.

More footsteps. Receding. German voices from a distance, from outside. Thank God. Fingers tugged at the heel of his boot and he levered himself deeper into the warren. The hole broadened until he was able to sit up and turn. In the dim light he saw a shadowed figure.

His French friend disappeared into the

earth like a prairie dog scuttling into its hole. Luke, on his knees, felt along the floor and discovered stone steps leading down. He followed his rescuer into the darkness, heard a door open ahead of him. The room beyond was pitch dark and smelled of damp rot. Once inside he stood, bumped his head and swore. The flare of a match made him blink. He heard something — a rat? — scurry away into the gloom. A candle on a rough table threw a circle of light. Beside the table was a black-haired boy, his brown eyes huge in a wizened face. He might have been twelve, was probably younger.

'Are there others?' Luke asked in French. Thank God T.J. had hired French governesses.

'I'm alone.' The boy studied him, staring at his gunbelt, at his flying suit. 'I heard the Boche searching for someone but I didn't know you were an aviator.'

A corner of Luke's mouth lifted at the awe in boy's voice. 'My Nieuport lost its fuel and I landed in your cemetery. I set the airplane afire so the Boche wouldn't get it. Or me.'

The boy nodded as though having to burn an airplane was an everyday occurrence. 'You're English.'

Luke shook his head. 'American.' Holding out his hand, he added, 'Luke Ray from

Denver, Colorado.' He always thought of himself as being from Denver even though he hadn't lived there for years.

'Jacques Cambon.' The boy's hand was small and limp in Luke's

'Your mother? Father?'

The boy's silence made Luke want to kick himself.

'They were murdered by the Boche,' Jacques said finally in a tone conveying no emotion. 'Last year, when the enemy burned our village.'

What was there to say to comfort the boy when in war there was no comfort. Luke sat on one of the two chairs drawn up to the table. 'I have to get past the German lines to the aerodrome. So I can fly again.'

The boy pushed a strand of hair from his forehead with a dirt-smeared hand, 'So you can kill the Boche.' Now his voice quivered with feeling. 'I, Jacques, will help you. Tonight. We will wait until dark and then we will see what can be done.' His smile was grim, not a boy's smile.

★ ★ ★

They slipped from the church a few minutes after ten and crossed the fields to the woods. The night was dark, there was no moon.

22

When they came to the road, Jacques tied one end of a wire to a tree before crouching behind bushes with the rest of the wire coiled in his hand.

'We must be patient,' Jacques warned when Luke settled beside him. 'Perhaps one will come tonight, perhaps not. Who can say?'

Five mule-drawn ammo carts rumbled past their hiding place shortly after midnight. Again the woods quieted. Time crawled. Luke closed his eyes and conjured up a mental picture of Yvette smiling at him, a promise in her dark eyes. Angel of Death? Not likely! He wished he'd remembered to rescue the rose before burning the Nieuport.

Jacques tensed. Luke listened but heard nothing. At least a minute passed before he made out a faint sputter in the distance to his right. Jacques dashed across the road and fastened the other end of the wire to a tree on the far side. He returned and taking Luke's hand, led his fingers to the wire. It was chest high and taut. The cycle's sputter grew to a muted roar. The German was riding hell bent for election, T.J. would've said.

Luke crouched at the side of the road. He pictured the courier's neck hitting the wire.

Jesus.

*   *   *

On August 4, 1915, Sergeant Henri Pinkoff of the *Geheime Politische Polizie*, the German Political Police, was driven to the training school for nurses on the rue de la Culture in the Brussels suburb of Ixelles. He arrested the school's matron, Edith Cavell, an English nurse.

Miss Cavell was taken under guard to the *Kammandantur* in the rue Delaimot where she was accused of sheltering British and French soldiers in her school and helping them escape from German-occupied Belgium to England and France by way of neutral Holland. The penalty for conducting soldier to the enemy, she was told, was death by firing squad.

★　★　★

Major Charles Cunningham spread the morning *London Times* on the drawing room table. Good, there was no mention of Churchill. God, how he detested the man. Now that Churchill was no longer First Lord of the Admiralty, his slide to a being of nonentity should be swift. Yet one could never tell. The man had a way of returning from the most obscure dustheaps.

Major Cunningham turned the page, intently read a story, all the while tapping his finger on the paper. 'Read this,' he ordered his colleague, Asberry, 'and give me your opinion.'

As Asberry leaned over the table, the major walked to the window where he stood with his hands clasped behind him staring past the potting shed down the lawns of Boling Hall to the field of hops and the roofs of Maidstone in the distance. Stiffly erect, he looked like what he was, a professional soldier, a graduate of Sandhurst, a veteran of the Boer War.

Major Cunningham, known as C to his subordinates in MI-6, was of middle height. His thinning hair and neatly trimmed mustache were gray. His face was kindly, a doting grandfather's face except for the eyes. The eyes were an icy blue, cold, cunning and unforgiving.

Yet he was a grandfather, having married for money and heirs, not passion. His passion was gardening and, before the War, his fuchsias had won several blue ribbons at the Coventry Fair. He was a crack shot but prided himself on not carrying a weapon. 'My job's to deceive the enemy, to out-think him,' he often said, 'not to outshoot the blighters.'

He succeeded at that job nine times out of ten. C, as everyone in MI-6 was well aware, had been responsible for 1914's the Russians-are-in-England hoax. Hearing an idle rumor, started by the arrival of a Scottish regiment from Ross-shire at a remote railway station, C had expanded it, given the story credibility and spread it until the Germans, believing a Russian army was on its way to the battlefields of Belgium and northern France, withdrew sorely needed troops from their advance on Paris. C was a master of deception.

Asberry looked up from the paper. 'You're considering his twenty-two-year-old American sergeant for Nightingale?'

'I am, though the code name's been changed. Nightingale's too obvious.' C walked to the table and went through the ritual of filling his pipe. 'The new name is Dark Storm.'

'The man's a hero in the States,' Asberry said slowly. 'If he works for us it might make that holier-than-thou Wilson sit up and take notice.'

'I can't help but admire the sergeant's initiative. His bloody cheek.' C lit his pipe. 'He crash lands his Nieuport behind Hun lines, commandeers a Boche motorcycle, and makes his way to safety in France disguised as a German courier. Splendid. Perfectly splendid.'

'I'm surprised the French sent him into combat. Being an American.'

'I'm not. An American who gives his life for France is much more impressive than one who merely fights for her.'

'He *is* in hospital,' Asberry pointed out, 'with unspecified injuries. He may not recuperate in time to serve our purpose. How long do you expect we have?'

'Two months, no more.'

'This aviator does possess a certain élan.'

C folded the *Times* precisely and set it exactly on the corner of the table. 'Of course, being an American, he may be completely unreliable. He did lose his aircraft. We'll have to find out.'

'A preliminary inquiry might be worthwhile.'

'I agree. Will you see to it, Asberry?'

'At once.'

Asberry had reached the door when he heard C grunt. He stopped to look back and saw him relighting his pipe. 'On the other hand,' C said, 'I have a hunch he may fit our bill of particulars exactly.'

Asberry, familiar with C's usually accurate hunches, nodded. *If you do fit in, Sergeant Luke Ray,* he thought as he opened the door, *God help you.*

2

Luke heard a flurry of raised voices at the nursing station at the far end of his ward in the hospital on the outskirts of Bar-le-Duc. He hunched himself up and saw Yvette, dressed in black in mourning for Passard and DuFour, walking toward him between the two rows of beds. Her face was flushed, she carried a bouquet of yellow roses in her hand. The soldiers stared at her in admiration as she passed, sitting up straight and smiling hopefully.

'That woman,' Yvette said to Luke, her lower lip pushing out in an enchanting pout. 'That new nurse, that Englander. She tried to stop me from seeing you.'

Luke held the roses in his lap while he admired the angry rise and fall of Yvette's breasts below the white lace trimming her bodice. 'I haven't met her yet,' he said.

'I told her I must see you, it was a matter of life and death. Still she refused to let me pass.'

'It sure looks like you outmaneuvered her.'

'I told her I brought you a message from *Capitaine* Trenault. She said I must give the message to her. She promised you would receive it. I told her I would not, that the message was private as well as oral.'

Yvette took his hand and raised it to her lips, kissing the tips of Luke's fingers. She inserted his little finger into her mouth and teased the end by circling it with her tongue. When she closed her lips, he felt her mouth tighten, heard a soft sucking sound as she slid her lips from the end of his finger.

'You see,' she said, 'I spoke only the truth. Except it was my message, not the *capitaine's*.'

Luke shifted his position in bed to hide his urgent arousal. He glanced around but the men's eyes were all on Yvette, not him. Except for Edmond, the French officer in the next bed who was reading *Le Figaro*.

'They have removed your bandage.' Yvette nodded at the shaved patch behind Luke's left ear.

'This morning. I'm supposed to leave the hospital tomorrow.'

Yvette smiled at him. She looked past Luke at Edmond who, glancing at her, nodded before returning to his paper. She leaned over Luke's bed until her lips brushed across his hair. He breathed in the lilac scent of her, felt her breath tingle in his ear.

'Tonight,' she whispered. 'Meet me in the

hallway past the next ward.'

'I'll count the minutes until I'm with you.' He meant what he said, couldn't wait to take her in his arms, hold her, kiss her. 'Ten-thirty?'

'*Oui, cheri.*' Her tongue teased a path along the curves of his ear.

He turned his head, kissing her quickly.

'I must leave,' Yvette said. 'If I don't, *Capitaine* Trenault will be very angry.'

'Damn the captain,' Luke said in English.

'Damn the captain.' She giggled at her use of the English words. 'Damn the captain.'

Luke looked past her. A nurse was bearing down on them, a tall auburn-haired young woman in a white winged cap and a starched blue uniform.

'Damn the English,' Yvette said so softly only Luke could hear.

'But not the Americans?'

'No, no, never.' Yvette's eyes gleamed with mischief as she whispered, 'Tonight.'

He'd never known a single word to promise so much and he smiled in anticipation.

Yvette blew Luke a kiss. As she walked away he noticed she glanced at Edmond once more. The French captain turned the page of his newspaper, making no sign he'd seen her. When Yvette passed the new head nurse, she raised her chin, ignoring the Englishwoman.

The nurse stopped at the foot of Luke's bed and took his chart in her hands. 'I'm Miss Kezia Faith,' she told him. Luke nodded in acknowledgment, his attention on Yvette walking away from him, her derrière wiggling enticingly. It reminded him of Pegoud, squadron leader in his old *escadrille*, signaling by wagging the wings of his Nieuport. Both signals had the same meaning.

Follow me.

A hand brushed the blanket covering Luke's legs. 'I will place the flowers in a vase,' Kezia Faith said in schoolgirl French.

Reaching to stop her, Luke's hand closed on the stem of a rose, a thorn pricked his palm and he winced. Kezia took the flowers from him and laid the yellow roses on the stand next to his bed. She left, returning with a blue vase and a thermometer.

'I'm perfectly okay,' Luke protested. 'I shouldn't even be here.'

She thrust the thermometer in his mouth, taking his pulse while she waited, not speaking or meeting his angry eyes.

He should have been out of the hospital two days ago. Anyone with any gumption would have ignored the doctor's orders and walked out. Teddy Roosevelt would have. Like the time in Milwaukee during the 1912 campaign when a madman shot Colonel Roosevelt at close range.

Brushing aside offers of help, the Colonel rode to the auditorium and walked onto the stage where he was scheduled to speak. When the audience saw blood on his shirt, the men shouted in anger, the women sobbed.

'I'm going to ask you to be very quiet.' Roosevelt said. 'You see, there's a bullet in my body.'

He pulled his manuscript from his pocket and stared at it as though surprised to see the bullet holes. Again the crowd urged him to stop, to see a doctor.

'I'll make this speech or die,' he told them, 'one or the other.'

That's the kind of man I mean to be, Luke told himself. Kezia took the thermometer from his mouth, wrote on his chart and walked away without a word. A damn poor bedside manner. Why, then, did he hope she'd come back?

'That one, she's a woman,' Edmond said from the next bed. The French officer, thin-faced, moustached, urbanely handsome, had been an aviation instructor at the *escadrille*'s aerodrome.

'Yvette?'

'No, our new nurse. Yvette is a girl. A

delectable girl, to be sure,' he added hastily, 'but still a girl.'

'Yvette seemed to like you.' Admitting it made Luke feel better.

Edmond shrugged, putting aside his *Le Figaro*. 'Kezia,' he said. 'Oddly named. Yet surely she's English despite such an exotic cognomen.'

'She acts like she's got ice water in her veins.'

'Not that one, my friend. I'm something of a connoisseur of woman, or so I've been told. My instincts tell me Miss Kezia Faith is far from cold.' He lowered his voice. 'Have you seen how she notices you by making a point of not looking at you?'

'She's not my type,' Luke said. 'She's too tall, too English, too starched. Putting your arms around her would be like hugging a cigar store Indian.'

Edmond smiled. 'I will make a wager with you, Sergeant Ray.'

'I've never turned down a fair bet.'

'I will wager twenty francs that before you leave this hospital you will have, at the very least, kissed our new nurse with considerable passion.'

Luke raised his eyebrows in surprise. 'You're on,' he said in English. It'd be the easiest twenty francs he'd ever won. When

Edmond frowned, Luke said, 'I accept the wager,' in French. 'Remember I'll only be in the hospital until tomorrow.'

The captain shrugged. 'Events move swiftly these days. *C'est la guerre*. Women are drawn to men like yourself, aviators who have been wounded fighting the Hun. Unlike myself, injured when my Maurice Farman crashed on landing. One of my best students was the unfortunate pilot. Can the truth be I'm not the instructor I thought I was?'

So that's what had happened to the captain. Edmond had been moved next to Luke only last night and they'd said little to one another until now.

'We were both lucky to walk away,' he told Edmond, wanting to end the talk of crashes. The memory of Passard and DuFour plummeting to their deaths was all too vivid. 'When I get out of the hospital,' he went on, 'I have two weeks' leave.'

'Paris?'

'Where else? How about you?'

'I must remain here three more days, four at the most. But Paris isn't for me. I'll go home to Mimizan, a village near Bordeaux.' Edmond closed his eyes for a moment. 'It's very beautiful there.'

'You're married?'

34

'No, no. Before the war I raced automobiles. Bugattis. In France, in Italy. The Grand Prix. I had no time for marriage. A man with a feast spread before him doesn't settle for a single course.'

The English nurse walked into the ward pushing a wheelchair, positioning it beside Edmond's bed. He used his arms to push himself up. As Luke stared, he levered his body from the bed into the chair, his movements awkward, his face reddening from the exertion. The legs of his pajamas were folded and pinned a few inches below his knees to cover the stumps of his legs.

Kezia tucked a blanket around him. 'That was excellent,' she told him, smiling warmly.

Edmond propelled his wheelchair into the aisle. 'Just as in the old days,' he said to Luke, 'I'm in training. I estimate I've attained a speed of fifteen kilometers an hour.'

Luke watched him roll down the aisle between the beds to the nursing station where he narrowly avoided a doctor. The doctor laughed and shook his finger warningly at the captain. Luke's throat tightened and he wanted to cry but he couldn't. What a hell of a thing. And, damn it, here he'd said they'd both walked away from their respective crashes. He banged his fist against the mattress. He hated the war, hated the

Germans. He wanted revenge, to fly again, to kill the Huns who'd started this war by invading innocent Belgium. He regretted letting the Fokker escape.

He forced himself to think of Paris. He'd eat in the sidewalk cafés, drink a toast in the Ritz bar, meet a pretty *mademoiselle* with sparkling eyes who'd stroll arm in arm with him along the wide boulevards and beside the Seine . . .

That evening Luke ate supper from a tray while Edmond spoke wistfully of the countries he'd seen and the women he'd known in the years before the war. It seemed another world, that time before the war, a well-remembered sun-drenched summer that would never return.

The setting sun glinted on the ward windows. Lamps were lit and the men talked softly, played cards or read. A few stared silently above them at the darkness gathering at the top of the high-ceiling room.

When the lamps were put out at ten, a tingle of anticipation ran along Luke's legs and up his spine. Edmond's breathing deepened and the Frenchman slept. Still Luke waited, finally swinging from his bed and pulling on a robe. On slippered feet he approached the circle of lamplight at the nurses station.

Nurse Sorrell sat with her graying head bent over a desk as her pen inked notations in a ledger. She didn't look up as Luke tiptoed past her. He walked past a latrine smelling of disinfectant and along a dimly lit corridor. When he paused, he heard a man snore loudly. Another groaned in his sleep.

Luke pushed through swinging doors, turned left and walked quickly past the facing doors of the two adjacent wards, turned into a dark hallway. The odor of lilacs made him smile.

'Yvette?' he whispered.

There was no answer.

'Yvette, I know you're here.' He heard suppressed laughter in the darkness in front of him and stepped forward eagerly. He struck a match on the wall. The flame blinded him for an instant, then he saw Yvette standing a few yards away, her black hair spilling onto the shoulders of her gown. Her eyes gleamed.

Luke swore under his breath as the match burned his fingers. He stepped toward Yvette.

Footsteps sounded in the corridor behind him and Luke stopped with one hand outstretched. The steps were the rapid snap-snap of a woman's leather heels. Light shone along the hallway. Yvette's warm fingers closed on his hand and she led him through a doorway into a small room. He smelled soap, his hands touched sheets piled on a shelf.

The woman in the hall walked toward their hiding place. Light slanted through the partly open door. Luke held his breath, Yvette's hand grasped in his. Suddenly the woman increased her pace, the rectangle of lamplight shifting, shining brightly for a moment before receding as the steps faded into silence. Luke eased the door shut and turned to Yvette.

She came into his arms and his hands held her to him. When she pressed her body against his, he kissed her. Yvette's mouth opened, her tongue meeting his, entwining with his. Excitement surged in him as his hands trailed up from her waist to cup her breasts. His fingers found the buttons at the front of her dress, undid them, slid the dress from her breasts. She wore nothing underneath. His kiss deepened and she twisted her body deliciously against his, her hands at the nape of his neck.

Gripping him tightly, she leaped up to encircle his thighs with her legs. Luke knelt, holding her, his pulses pounding, easing her onto her back on the floor in front of him. Light flooded the room.

Kezia Faith stood in the doorway with a lamp in her hand. Her gray eyes snapped with

38

anger as she glared down at them. For a moment Luke thought she meant to hurl the lamp at them.

Yvette squealed, scrambling to her feet and pulling her dress closed to cover her naked breasts. Luke pulled his robe together and rose with as much dignity as he could muster, little enough considering the circumstances.

Kezia thumped the lamp down on a table and faced them with her arms folded. She spoke in English, her voice trembling with outrage. 'This. Is. Not. A. Brothel.'

Luke's face reddened. He started to speak, stopped. Yvette, one hand holding her dress together, pushed past him and shook her finger in Kezia's face, her voice rising in a volley of French that contained idioms Luke had never before heard. From the blank expression of Kezia's face, he knew the English nurse understood less than he did.

As far as he could tell, Yvette expressed the opinion that Kezia was in the habit of engaging in sexual intercourse with four-footed creatures, that she'd never slept with a man in her life, that her ancestry was misbegotten. Luke marveled at Yvette's fluency and her passionate illogic.

Kezia pointed to the door. 'Get out,' she told Yvette. 'Leave this hospital at once. Before I summon the *gendarmes*.' Her voice was as icy as the North Sea. In February.

Yvette looked at Luke with a plea for help in her brown eyes. He started toward her, stopped, glancing at Kezia. 'They use you,' Yvette told Luke. 'Don't you understand that?'

Kezia grasped the French girl's arm and propelled her to the door.

'Even now, without his legs,' Yvette screamed at Luke, 'Edmond's more of a man than you'll ever be.'

Kezia shoved her into the hall. Luke heard the rapid click, click of Yvette's heels growing fainter and fainter. Kezia, in the doorway, turned back to Luke. Her chest was heaving; her face was flushed.

Yvette's parting words had thrown Luke into confusion. Who was using him? And Edmond. What had Yvette meant by that. Had she and Edmond — ?

'Get back to your ward, Sergeant,' Kezia snapped.

When he made no move to obey, her eyes flashed angrily. 'You should be ashamed of yourself. You're no better than a — a — ' She searched for a word. 'A Hun,' she said.

Their eyes met and held. The lamplight warmed the high cheekbones of her shadowed face and glinted from her auburn hair, loose and nestling on her shoulders. Kezia

40

blinked and drew in her breath.

Without thinking, Luke leaned to her and kissed her on the mouth. Her eyes closed. For an instant her lips responded, then she jerked away and hit his face with her open hand.

The slap stung. Luke half-smiled. 'That's adding insult to injury,' he told her. 'You've already cost me twenty francs.'

'I would have thought it more likely I saved you twenty. If she charges that much.' She grabbed the lamp, swung on her heel and left him in darkness.

Luke, anger mingling with admiration, stared after her until she was out of sight. On his way back to the ward he saw no sign of Yvette.

He shook his head. What had she meant when he said they'd used him? What had made him suddenly want to kiss Kezia? Tossing his robe on a chair, he settled into bed, staring up at the darkness. He didn't understand women, never had, never would.

★   ★   ★

Kezia sat at the table in her small room, her hands trembling. As soon as she'd calmed enough, she dipped her pen in the ink well and printed a message on a sheet of tablet paper.

'Subject is completely recovered,' she wrote with slashing strokes. 'Subject is rash, unpredictable, naive, susceptible to women.'

After reading what she'd written, Kezia stood and walked to the window where she stared into the night, trying to remember all she learned of Sergeant Luke Ray since coming to Bar-le-Duc. Be objective, she told herself. Someone had said the first casualty in any war was the truth. How very true. Returning to the table, she took her pen, crossed out 'is rash' and wrote 'has initiative' above it.

She crossed out 'unpredictable' and replaced it with 'is aggressive.'

She crossed out 'naive', put the end of her pen in her mouth, wrote 'naive' again. She left 'susceptible to women' unchanged.

C hadn't asked for her recommendation and she debated whether he expected her to make one. If she recommended Luke Ray and anything happened to him she'd share the responsibility. She didn't trust C even though, for reasons of her own, she worked for him.

She should recommend the American sergeant. Why did she hesitate? She wasn't sure. She didn't like him, his sort had never appealed to her. He was arrogant, believed himself superior to women, irresistible to women. But despite herself, she wanted no harm to befall him.

Kezia forced herself to put personal feelings aside. They were unimportant. All that mattered was winning the war, saving England from Hun 'Kultur.'

After rereading what she'd written, she added one word. 'Recommended.'

Though she was still uneasy, she began to encode the message.

3

Byron Macneeley, book in hand, walked up the winding path leading from the cottage to the cliffs. When he reached the highest point he left the path to approach the edge of the precipice, the wind off the Atlantic tugging at his cap. His thoughts were fixed on Cynthia.

When he'd first brought her to the Cornish Heights four years ago, she'd been charmed by the village of St. Agnes and had fallen in love with the cottage at first sight. And with him? He nodded. If not at first, certainly later. Still, he sometimes suspected it might have been the view from these cliffs that convinced her to leave Exeter and come to Cornwall to live with him.

He smiled nostalgically. They'd had a good four years. In many ways he regretted their time together was coming to an end.

He forced himself to look down where, far below, the surf sent spray high over the dark rocks. He stepped back at once. Despite the cool breeze, sweat broke out on his forehead. Great heights unnerved him. When he stood on a cliff edge or at the window of a tall building and looked down, vertigo gripped him. A sensation far worse than his dizziness as a boy in Southhampton playing the game of who could spin around the most times before falling to the ground. Worse because of the expanding knot of panic in the pit of his stomach.

A fear of heights was one of his secrets. One of Byron MacNeeley's lesser secrets.

He followed the path westward along the top of the cliffs. When he came to a declivity angling inland, he climbed down to its bottom and walked between the rock walls, finally finding a patch of grass where he sat with his back to a boulder and opened his book. *The Return Of The Native*. He enjoyed reading authors who, like Hardy, seemed so English.

The August sun glaring from the white pages soon made him drowsy and he closed his eyes. He always took a book with him on his afternoon rambles and yet, though he read a great deal at the cottage in the long evenings, he read little on his excursions. He liked the idea of reading in the out-of-doors far more than he enjoyed the uncomfortable actuality.

Byron dozed and the book fell from his hands to the grass. An hour later he awoke with a start and opened his pocket watch, angrily shaking his head. Book in hand once more, he retraced his steps to the cliff where, standing well back, he breathed deeply of the damp tang of the sea. This would be the last time he'd stand here, at least until the war was over. No, he corrected himself, the next to last time. He planned to come here once more. With Cynthia.

It was 4:30 p.m. when he returned to the cottage. Going into the bedroom, he placed the book in the open suitcase on their bed. He'd packed earlier in the afternoon, leaving space for both *The Return of the Native* and his traveling kit.

He shaved and put the kit in the bag, snapped it shut and buckled the two leather straps. He placed the bag on the floor inside the bedroom door next to the locked portmanteau containing his work gear.

In the kitchen he opened the icebox and, after a glance at the bottle of Mumm's and the two long-stemmed glasses, took out the beef steak and laid it on the counter next to the stove. He glanced at the greengrocer's calendar on the wall and, for the first time, noticed Cynthia's penciled check beside today's date, August 12.

His orders were to report to London on the fourteenth for his third assignment since the war began the year before. He'd been in Antwerp during the retreat, helping to destroy more than thirty merchant ships trapped on the Scheldt. And to Havre during the winter on an aborted mission to invade the German island of Borkum. All indications were that this new assignment would be different. This time, he suspected, he'd be sent behind the German lines.

Walking into the main room of the cottage, he lit the red candle on the table he'd set for two and tossed the blackened match into the cold grate. The logs Cynthia had piled in a pyramid on the hearth for decorative effect reminded him how snug they'd been in the small cottage in the damp of winter and also how difficult wood was to obtain in Cornwall. They'd used peat for the most part but Cynthia insisted on a few logs for effect.

At first he feared he'd become bored, would tire of her. That hadn't happened. Quite the opposite, in fact.

Byron opened the door to Cynthia's studio and stepped inside. With his thumb and forefinger to this chin, he studied her unfinished oil in the soft light of the late afternoon. The scene, painted on the cliffs near the spot where he'd been walking an hour before, was dark and disturbing, unlike anything she'd ever done before. And better, in its way. Waves lashed the shore, clouds roiled above a stormy sea at dusk, two lights gleamed faintly from a freighter fighting its way into the gale.

Byron nodded. The painting was an integral part of his plan. He glanced briefly at the sketches of himself propped against the wall. Cynthia hadn't been satisfied with her work.

'You're such an anonymous man,' she'd complained but quickly apologized, saying she didn't mean it. 'The fact is, darling,' she'd added, 'I'm a rotten portrait painter.'

'I am and you're not,' he'd told her.

She was certainly a far better artist than he could ever hope to be. Byron readily admitted he had little artistic talent, at least not in the usual sense. He'd chosen the name of Byron in a spirit of ironic amusement rather than because of any poetic aspirations. Yet he appreciated the arts in all their forms and was instinctively drawn to painters, musicians and writers. He respected them, stood in awe of their gifts. Especially when the artists happened to be women.

He knew his frank admiration attracted them to him in turn.

He left Cynthia's studio, poured himself a brandy and sat sipping his drink by the front window where he'd be able to see her as soon as she reached the turn in the lane. He waited fifteen or more minutes before she came into view, walking with her brisk stride as she returned home from the village where she worked four afternoons a week as the volunteer at the free library.

Cynthia tucked in a strand of her reddish-brown hair as though she was aware of being watched. Byron smiled fondly. She was a petite girl, scarcely five feet tall. With her hair in a bun and dressed as she was in a wide-brimmed hat, a white shirtwaist and long black skirt, she appeared demure. Deceptively so.

Placing his empty glass on the table, Byron walked into the bedroom. Even now, after four years, he felt a heightened awareness, a sense of anticipation whenever she returned to the cottage. The contrast between the public and private Cynthia fascinated him as much now as it had when he'd first become aware of her two selves. The contrast between shadow and substance, appearance and reality, intrigued him.

He remembered a night years ago, before he met Cynthia, when he'd watched a dancer in a private men's club in Soho. The woman, a jet-haired Levantine, danced with veils writhing about her body now offering a glimpse of the pale flesh of her thigh, now of the arm, now of her breast. The performance had bored Byron.

49

Later he saw the dancer — he was positive it was the same woman — walking rapidly along a street in Mayfair. From her feathered hat to her black leather pumps she was smartly and conservatively dressed. Intrigued, he followed her until she entered a many-columned house. He stood for many minutes waiting for her to reappear but she did not. Though he never saw her again, he'd never forgotten her.

He shook away the memory as he hastily removed his clothes. For a moment he stood naked, running his hands down his lean body from chest to hips to thighs. Not a trace of fat. He slid into a purple silk robe and, as he walked to the front hall, tied the sash in a bow.

Cynthia sang as she hurried up the path. He couldn't recall the name of the song but a few of the words came through to him — 'life' and 'found you.' He opened the door abruptly and, startled, she held, staring at him, her eyes wide. Then she smiled.

'You have a lovely smile,' he told her. 'Your whole face comes alight when you smile.'

He took her in his arms and kissed her gently. Lifting her, he carried her into the cottage, kicking the door shut behind him to shut out the prying world.

If only it could always be like this, just the

two of them. He pushed the unexpected and dangerous thought from him. He'd lived in England too long, that was the trouble, he was beginning to think like an Englishman. A man's sense of values eroded here, he grew soft.

Cynthia's fingers slid down the back of his robe. 'My God, By,' she said breathlessly, 'you — you're — you haven't anything on. Not a stitch.' Her voice rose on the last word.

He smiled at her.

Looking past him she saw the table. 'A red candle. And our best napkins.'

'Later I'll put on the steak. Nothing's too good for you, not today.'

'I'm impressed, I really am.' Her eyes misted and she pressed her head against his shoulder, dislodging her hat. 'Damn,' she muttered. 'I promised myself I wouldn't cry.'

He kissed her damp cheeks. 'I know it's been beastly rotten for you,' he murmured.

'I shouldn't have gone to the village today. I didn't want to. I wouldn't have if Mrs. Jamison hadn't come down with the grippe. And if you hadn't said you thought it would be best. I never expected to come home and find you wrapped like a Christmas present, bow and all. In the middle of summer.'

He lowered Cynthia to the sofa, saying, 'Wait. I'll only be a second.'

After returning with the two glasses and the now open bottle of Mumm's, he poured the champagne, then sat in a chair facing her and raised his glass. 'You propose the toast,' he said.

She considered a moment before raising her glass. 'To the two of us. To peace in the world. To a long life. For us to be together always.' They touched glasses and she began to drink.

'Champagne is meant to be savored,' he chided gently.

'Sorry.' She held her glass for him to refill, then drank more slowly. 'I don't know why your leaving seems different this time. I behaved properly the other times, didn't I?'

'You've always been splendid.'

'I'm afraid, By. This time, for no good reason, I'm frightened. For you. I know I should keep a stiff upper lip and all. I know it's no more dangerous than what a lot of other men are going through. I'll do my best.'

He sat beside her, gathering her close and she rested her head on his shoulder for a few moments before finishing her glass and bending forward to refill it. Then she sat up, pushing a long strand of her reddish hair from her forehead as she stared at the rising bubbles.

'You're wearing only a robe.' He could hear

the deliberate lightness in her tone. 'That *is* all you have on, isn't it?'

He nodded, smiling.

She set her glass on the table and stood up. 'I'm going to change. Be right back.' She started for the bedroom.

'No.' He got to his feet. 'Don't, Cynthia. Stay here where I can see you.'

She hesitated in the bedroom doorway. 'Please.' He felt a stir of excitement.

'I don't know. I've never — ' She broke off, blushing. 'Please,' he said again.

'You must sit down first.'

He obeyed.

Cynthia returned to stand an arm's length from the sofa, facing him but keeping her hazel eyes averted. Removing the pins from her bun, she shook her head and her long hair fell around her shoulders, looking redder than usual in its release. Slowly and hesitantly, she unbuttoned her shirtwaist and slipped it off. Reaching behind her back, she undid her skirt, let it drop to the floor and stepped free. She faced him, smiling uncertainly, wearing a short chemise and a ruffled cambric underskirt that came to just below her knees.

Charming and enticing. Byron rose, approached her, then knelt to untie her shoes and slip them from her feet. His breath came faster as he slid his hand up her leg behind her underskirt and removed first one garter, then the other. He rolled her stockings down, caressing the smooth flesh of her thighs and calves and feeling her tremble.

He stood and undid the sash at his waist, letting the robe slide from his shoulders to the floor behind him, revealing his nakedness.

She drew in her breath, staring at his arousal. 'Oh, By,' she whispered. 'Kiss me.'

'Not yet. You've still too many clothes on.'

She eased off the chemise, undid the undershirt and let it fall to the floor, then unbuttoned and stepped out of her drawers, once again averting her eyes.

His gaze roved down her body from her unbound hair to her small, firm breasts, to the white curves of her hips and legs. 'You're lovely,' he murmured. 'So very lovely.'

No longer able to postpone his need, he reached for her and she sprang into his arms, clinging to him as they kissed, both straining to touch, to feel the other. His arms held her close and she wrapped hers around his neck, then encircled his legs with hers, raising her body as she searched for his sex. He braced his feet apart and let her hand guide him inside her.

She shuddered, her body trembling uncontrollably against his. 'Hurry,' she whispered, then kissed him, mouth open, her tongue meeting his. 'The bed,' she gasped. 'Carry me to the bed.'

He made it into the bedroom still inside her and sprawled on top of her on the bed. The came together passionately, joining again and again.

For a long time afterwards, they lay intertwined as the room darkened. All at once Byron realized she was crying. Lighting the lamp by the bed, he took the edge of the coverlet and brushed the tears from her wet cheeks.

'I refuse to become maudlin,' she assured him. 'I'm a self-sufficient sort of woman. Always have been. I've never needed anyone but myself and I don't now. No one. After all, I'm not a child any longer, I'm twenty-five years old.

'I won't miss you for more than two or three days. A week at the very most.' She paused. 'By, know what?'

He shook his head.

'I'm a most God-awful liar.'

He smiled.

'You never laugh, do you?' she asked. 'I never really thought about it until now. You smile, more lately than you used to when I first met you, but you never laugh. Sometimes I have the feeling you're lonely, that you're one of the loneliest people I've ever

55

known. And I suspect you could be a bloody son-of-a-bitch if you wanted to be.'

He raised his eyebrows in feigned surprise. 'You've changed, too. I don't recall you using words like that four years ago.'

'I didn't say them but I thought them. I was raised to 'always be a lady' and that's hard to overcome.'

'I suppose I could be what you suspect. But never with you.' He was, he often told himself, a compassionate man. He didn't always understand the feelings of others but he respected them. Within the limits imposed by duty.

Cynthia kissed him quickly before easing from the bed and disappearing into the bathroom. After a few minutes he heard her pouring water into the tub. When she came into his sight again she wore a long green dress.

'Must you leave tonight?' she asked.

'I have no choice.'

'I know better than to ask where you'll be. Or when you'll come back.'

'I actually haven't the foggiest myself. You know how close-lipped the powers-that-be are about these things. With good reason, of course.'

She knelt beside the bed and cradled his face in her hands. 'I'm so terribly proud of you, By. I understand how it must hurt you when they stare after you in the village because you're not in uniform.'

'They can jolly well think what they please.' He tousled her hair. 'I'll do up the beef steak. After we eat we'll take an evening walk on the cliffs.'

'I'd like that.' She sat back on her heels, her hazel eyes finding and holding his. 'You will come back, won't you? You do mean to come back to me?'

He sat up, draping a sheet across himself as he swung his legs over the side of the bed. Leaning to her, he took her chin between his thumb and forefinger. 'What on earth makes you ask that?'

He remembered waking in the night a month before and turning on the light to find her in the chair by the window staring appraisingly at him. He'd wondered then if she'd discovered something, guessed at least part of his secret. He'd been right to be concerned. She did suspect, he was certain of it.

'You're hurting me,' she said.

He let his hand fall from her chin, murmuring that he hadn't meant to.

'It's a feeling I've had these last few days,' she went on. 'That this time isn't the same as before. That you don't mean to come back to me. Ever. 'That — ' she hesitated. 'That there's someone else. Or maybe something else.'

'There's no one else and never has been.' He kissed her. 'As long as you're here waiting for me, I'll come back.'

'You'll come back,' she echoed without conviction.

Annoyed by her doubts, he got up, dressed and went to the kitchen to prepare the meal. They ate, speaking little. The candlelight glinted from her hair, highlighting the red. Her face looked vulnerable in the soft glow. When they finished eating, she smiled at him.

'Sorry,' she said.

He leaned across the table and kissed her. 'My fault. We'll go for that walk now if you'd like.'

'I would, ever so much.'

While he cleared the table, she walked to the window and looked into the darkness at the distant lights of the village. Byron came up behind her and put his arms around her waist and she leaned against him.

'I love you, By,' she said.

'You know how I feel about you. How I've felt about you from the very first.'

She nestled her head against his shoulder. 'I had so many doubts when I first came here four years ago. We're so different, you and I.

And your work, I didn't know if I could get used to having you around the cottage all day.

'Most men go to work in the morning and come home at night. You go away for days or weeks at a time and I never know when you'll be back. And when you work here it's with all those fuses and wires that you refuse to talk about.'

'You've never mentioned my work have you? In the village, I mean.'

'You know I wouldn't. Not after you asked me not to.'

He believed her. That wasn't terribly important, of course, for his work was easily explained. It was the letter that worried him most. The letter Schwartz forwarded from London before Byron insisted there be no communication with him, none at all. At other times he wondered what words he may have mumbled in his sleep. And in what language, because she had mentioned hearing him talk in his sleep but insisted what he said made no sense. Maybe so, maybe not.

He could take no chances.

Because he was a compassionate man, he asked, 'Are you happy, Cynthia?'

She sighed. 'Oh, yes. I've never been happier.'

'Good.' He cleared his mind, keeping only the knowledge of what he had to do. He eased away from Cynthia, raising his hands until they gripped her throat. Expertly and dispassionately, he broke her neck.

He carried her over his shoulder to the door, opened it with one hand and, looking out into the dusk, stopped to listen, hearing nothing but the usual night sounds. Very few people ever visited the cliffs and no one ventured there after dark.

He climbed the path to the cliff. When he reached the highest point he approached the edge with care and eased her body down until her dangling feet touched the ground, then he hurled her over the side. Though he listened long and carefully, he heard nothing but the surf far below.

Byron MacNeeley returned to the cottage and, after burning every sketch she'd done of him, he washed and put away the dinner dishes. Then he carried Cynthia's easel, the canvas and her paints to the cliff where he arranged them as he'd watched her do so many times. After that, by the light of the stars, he hurried down the path toward the village to sound the alarm.

4

Luke Ray crossed Marylebone Road carrying a copy of *Trilby*. The London traffic was heavy and he had to dodge honking taxis and a bus with playbills and other advertisements on its side. He stopped in the middle of the street while lorries rumbled past him heading toward Piccadilly.

This was asinine. All he lacked was a cloak and a dagger. Yet excitement tingled along his spine.

When he reached the sidewalk he headed for the shield-shaped sign in the middle of the block. The Red Rose Tea Room. Lord Kitchener pointed at him from a poster on the hoardings: 'Your King and Country need YOU.' Luke climbed the short flight of stairs and went through the open door into the tea room. A fan whirling lazily over his head barely stirred the humid August air.

Foolishness. He was needed in France where the Fokker Scourge was giving the Germans control of the skies above the trenches.

He glanced around the room. He counted

five other customers, two middle-aged women with parcels piled beside their chairs, a British lieutenant gazing into the eyes of a girl with marceled blonde hair, and an old gentleman whose mustache was stained yellow.

Not for the first time Luke asked himself why he'd agreed to come to London. He could have refused, couldn't he?

'You're being placed on administrative leave to serve with the British,' Captain Trenault had told him.

'As an aviator? Sir.'

The captain raised both hands in a Gallic shrug. 'When dealing with the English does one ever know what to expect?' The headlong retreat of the British Expeditionary Forces from northern France the year before still rankled Captain Trenault.

'Do I have a choice, *mon capitaine?*'

Luke much preferred serving with the French. They had élan, appreciated the well-turned phrase, the heroic gesture. As for the English —

'The bloody English,' T.J. always called them. Of course T.J.'s mother was a Scot and Scots had fought the English for hundreds of years. Luke wasn't interested in ancient history, though. That was one of the troubles with Europeans. They were too interested.

They had such long memories, such well-honed hates. The Scots and Irish hated the English, the English hated the French, the French hated the Germans, the Germans hated the Russians. Even the Belgians hadn't escaped the disease. They hated one another.

'The English request has been approved by General Auguste Hirschsuer himself.' Trenault was obviously impressed by the Aeronautical Service commander's interest. 'I would say you have no choice.'

Luke shrugged. 'When do I leave, sir?'

'At once.'

Yvette came into the room and Luke's eyes met hers for a moment before she looked away. After placing a document on the captain's desk, she left the room.

'Your orders.' Captain Trenault looked after Yvette, his finger tracing the scar on his cheek. 'Do you know the men call her The Angel of Death? Nonsense, of course. I have a staff car waiting to take you to Havre. From there you'll sail to England.' The captain came around the desk and embraced Luke formally. 'You performed heroically while you were with the *escadrille*, sergeant, may God go with you.'

The childish games began soon after Luke arrived in London. Luke shook his head in disgust as he crossed the tea room to sit by the window. He carefully placed his book on the table with the title showing. The waitress, a pale, thin girl wearing a frilly white apron over her black dress, hovered expectantly.

'Tea,' he ordered. 'And scones.'

The waitress disappeared through a door at the rear of the shop. Luke waited. Traffic slowed on the street outside. Horns blared, men shouted. Over the rooftops across the street a lone biplane droned south. An Avro? He'd heard the British were converting them to combat the Zeppelin raids on London.

'Would you mind awfully if I joined you?' The man standing beside his table was fat. More than fat. He was huge, balloon-like, three hundred pounds at least. His black suit and vest failed to adequately cover his bulging body. He wore a broad foulard tie, carried a briefcase in one hand, his bowler in the other, an umbrella hooked on his arm. His breath came in wheezing gasps and his face glistened with sweat.

'Not at all,' Luke told him.

When the fat man sat down across from him, the chair groaned. He took a large handkerchief from his coat pocket and mopped his face, saying, 'I don't believe I can recall suffering through a more ghastly August.'

Luke glanced outside and saw that the

traffic was moving again. 'It's hot as hell,' he agreed.

His companion frowned.

The waitress brought Luke's tea and scones. The fat man ordered tea and Danish pastry. Shifting heavily in his chair, he placed the brief case in his lap, his face flushing from the effort of opening it. He removed a book and laid it on the table beside Luke's.

'What a truly astonishing coincidence,' he said. The book, like Luke's, was *Trilby*.

'Amazing.' If they wanted to play children's games, Luke was glad to oblige.

The fat man talked inanely of the weather and a sporting event he'd attended the day before. Scrums, line-outs, scissors movements made Luke guess the game must be rugby. When the fat man finished his tea, he reached across the table and covered Luke's hand with his.

The pinkish skin on the back of the man's hand was stretched as tight as a sausage covering. Repelled by the sweaty touch, Luke eased his hand away.

'My dear boy,' the man said, 'do be careful. It's a shame but these days there's no one you can trust.' He struggled to his feet, the effort seeming to exhaust him. He stood there wheezing, leaning on the table with one hand while dabbing his face with his handkerchief.

'Do be careful, my dear boy,' he repeated.

After putting Luke's *Trilby* in his brief-case, he waddled from the room, leaving his own copy on the table. Luke left the tea room and walked to Regents Park where he sat on a bench and opened the fat man's du Maurier novel. He turned the pages, finding a message on a small slip of paper between 88 and 89. He was instructed to take the grey Jowett parked on Portland Place and drive to Boling Hall near Maidstone in Kent. He was given the route to follow, told to make sure he wasn't followed, and instructed to destroy the message.

Luke lit a Goldflake cigarette, using the flaming match to ignite the slip of paper on the bench at his side. After watching the paper burn and curl, he touched the blackened remains with his finger. They crumbled into ashes. He wondered who was masterminding this hocus-pocus. Wondered why whoever it was had nothing better to do. Especially in wartime.

The grey Jowett looked like a shoebox on wheels. The day was clear and the sun hot so Luke put the top down before cranking the automobile. He drove across the Thames and followed the Kent road west. Kent, he'd been told was the 'Garden of England.' The wind tousled his hair, the earth smelled of sun and summer and ripening grain. He laughed aloud, feeling on top of the world and glad to be living in these times. The war made a man appreciate being alive.

He missed not having a girl in the seat beside him. Missed not hearing a girl laugh. Sing. He liked girls who sang, liked talented girls, intelligent girls, chic girls, laughing girls, all manner and kinds of girls. He wished Yvette were here. Or did he? Let Edmond have her, he decided, she'd be out of place in England.

Kezia popped into his mind, making him wonder once again how she'd come by such an exotic name. It sounded foreign, perhaps African? Or Eastern. Did she have a father serving in India? He pictured her as she'd looked in the linen room with her auburn hair tumbling about her shoulders and her eyes flashing in anger. He smiled. She'd give a man a run for his money.

Why was he thinking of Kezia of all people? He hadn't seen her after that night. She'd come into his mind, he supposed, because he was in England and she was English.

He'd never see her again, he knew, and he felt a twinge of loss. The same feeling he'd had as a boy after watching the lighted windows of the night train flash past him on its way to Denver. A longing as clear yet as elusive as the echoing sound of the train's distant whistle.

A quarter of a mile ahead, a Model T Ford had stopped, halted by a Tommy standing in the middle of the road with his rifle at port arms. He wore a visored hat, khaki uniform, puttees. The soldier's motorcycle leaned on its kickstand near him. As Luke stopped behind the Model T he saw, fifty yards past the Tommy, a crossroads with a second soldier posted another fifty yards beyond.

Luke left his car and sat on the bank next to the road, watching the driver of the Ford drum his fingers on the steering wheel. Overhead, clouds drifted west to east across the cobalt blue of the sky. Luke remembered his father taking him to a baseball game between two town teams, remembered lying on his back on the grass while he listened to the thwack of bat on ball and the cries of the outfielders.

He heard the throaty roar of trucks. Standing, he watched the Army vehicles approach the crossroads, a cloud of dust in their wake, watched them lumber past, the shilling-a-day Tommies sitting in the open truckbeds bored and silent. As soon as the last of the trucks cleared the intersection, the two road guards mounted their cycles and sped after them. Luke sat on the bank again, waited until the Ford was out of sight, then started the Jowett and slowly followed. Savoring the day, he whistled, then started to sing:

> 'There's a long, long trail awinding,
> Into the land of my dreams.
> Where the nightingales are singing
> And the pale moon beams.'

Listening to himself, he wondered if his voice was as much of a monotone as they claimed. He might not make it as a soloist for any glee club on the Victrola but he wasn't all that bad.

He drove the Jowett into a sharp curve where breaks in the high hedges on both sides gave him glimpses of rolling hills and widely scattered farm buildings. As he accelerated out of the curve he saw a touring car pulled to the left side of the road a hundred feet ahead. A young man sat on the grass verge behind the car fanning himself with his straw hat. The car, a Vauxhall, was up on a jack and one of its wheels rested on the grass.

The young man looked up at the sound of Luke's car. He had reddish-gold hair and wore a blue blazer and white trousers. He jumped to his feet and waved at Luke to stop. Luke slowed and pulled to the side of the road behind the Vauxhall, noting that the motorist wasn't as young as he'd thought. His face was scarred, as though from smallpox, a ferret face. Both his face and hands were smudged, though there wasn't a spot on his white trousers, at close look, rather cheap and shiny. His blazer was a bit too blue, as well.

'Thanks for stopping, governor. The name's Sid.' His manner was both diffident and cocky. 'The tire punctured and I've come away without my bleeding repair kit. Your stopping was a bit of all right.'

Luke nodded. 'Could happen to anyone.' He swung his legs out of the Jowett and unlatched the tool box on the running board.

'I've been stranded here a bleeding half hour or more without seeing a soul,' Sid told him.

Luke wondered what had become of the Model T. He hadn't seen the Ford parked at any of the farms and there'd been no turnoffs. Frowning, he started to turn from the tool box, saying, 'Didn't you see — ?' He stopped abruptly, staring at the spanner in Sid's upraised hand.

Luke tried to raise his arm to block the blow. Too late. The wrench struck him a thudding blow behind the ear. Light exploded and then darkness swept over him . . .

Luke heard a drone. His eyelids, when he tried to open them, seemed extraordinarily heavy and his head ached with a drumming throb.

'Sid, he's coming around,' a man's voice said.

The steady drone pulsated around Luke, through him. His body swayed. He must be in the Nieuport, must have blacked out flying over the lines. Who were these men? He wanted to sit up but felt he'd cross the cutting edge of pain if he did. He waited, then slowly opened his eyes. The swaying motion, he realized wasn't the soar of flying and the sound wasn't the roar of an airplane engine.

A black-haired man he'd never seen before sat a few feet from him, watching him over the Webley revolver he held in his hand. Luke pressed his arm against his shoulder holster. Empty. The Peacemaker was gone.

A second man stood a few feet away with his back to Luke. He seemed to be steering. Not an airplane, a boat. A wave slapped against the side and threw spray into Luke's face. He licked the water from his lips and tasted salt. What the devil had happened? He tried to remember.

He'd been playing baseball. T.J. had been

71

there. No, that wasn't it. He seemed to recall driving an auto, a Jowett. Yes, that was it. Suddenly the entire sequence of events returned. Before the auto, there'd been the fat man. After he was driving — stopping at a roadblock, the lorries, stopping to help the ferret-faced man with the flat tire.

He looked at the helmsman again. Red hair. Sid, the bastard who'd been driving the Vauxhall. Gone were the blue blazer and white pants, Sid now wore brown workman's clothes. *Okay, Sid, I owe you one.* He started to push himself up. The man with the revolver leaned forward, placed his hand on Luke's chest and shoved him back. He waved the gun in front of Luke's face.

'I wouldn't if I was you, Yank,' he said, 'or you'll really find yourself in a cock up.' He turned to Sid. 'How much longer?'

'Ten minutes. Fifteen. Steady on, Alfie, don't be such an impatient bugger.'

They meant to kill him, Luke realized. Why? Who were they? He glanced around, wincing as pain stabbed into his head. He lay on a wooden seat on the port side of the powerboat near the stern. Alfie sat across from him. On the boat's deck Luke saw chains, a coiled rope, a can of petrol and black, truncated pyramids that appeared to be weights. Sid stood with his feet braced apart in the boat's open cabin gazing ahead through a glass windshield. Maybe a mile in front and to their left was the dark bulk of an approaching freighter.

'Would you take a gander at that, Alfie,' Sid said. 'She's painted all in stripes like a brown and green zebra.'

'Camouflage, Sid. I read about it. The U-Boats can't see her good when a ship's been camouflaged. It's supposed to make them look like clouds or something.'

'I suppose the blighters know what they're about.' Sid sounded unconvinced. 'Those bloody blokes are taking their half of the river in the middle, damn their hides.' Sid steered to the right, enabling Luke to see the low-lying shoreline over the gunwales.

'Why not here?' Alfie asked.

'If I'd known you were going to have a fit of nerves, I'd've brought some Phosperine Tablets.' Sid's tone held scorn.

'But ain't this as good a spot as any?'

'Can't you use your head for something more than a hat rack? We don't want anybody on that ship seeing us. We'll wait till she's well past us. Five minutes more won't kill you.' He snickered. 'It might him but not you.'

So he'd been right, Luke thought. They meant to shoot him and throw his weighted body in the Thames. Though his head still throbbed abominably, his mind was clear enough. 'Mind if I smoke?' he asked Alfie.

'Can Yank here have a fag, Sid?'

'Why the hell not? You just keep clear of him.'

'Who wants to get chummy? Not yours truly.'

Luke took the Goldflakes from his shirt pocket, jogged up a cigarette and put it between his lips. He reached into his pants pocket for his tin of matches, opened it and took a deep breath.

He waited until Sid looked from the looming freighter toward the shore off their starboard side.

Feigning terror, Luke shouted, 'Watch out! The damn freighter!'

Sid jerked his head to look forward, reactively spinning the wheel farther to starboard. The boat lurched. Alfie's mouth opened, his glance flicking from Luke to the ship bearing down on them.

Luke slid onto his knees. He grabbed the petrol can in one hand, twisted off the cap with the other, and threw gasoline into Alfie's face. Alfie yelled and stumbled back. Luke dropped the can top, gathered a handful of matches in his fist, scraping them against the boat's side. They flamed. Tossing the burning matches onto the gas-covered deck, he scrambled to his feet.

Fire leaped around him. Alfie, his pant's leg blazing, screamed. He beat at the flames with his hands, still holding the revolver. Luke kicked the gun and it spun free, skidding forward along the deck. Flames roared between Luke and Sid at the wheel. Sid swung around with a gun in his hand.

Luke leaped onto the stern and dived into the Thames. He swam under water, heading in the direction of the nearest shore. At least he hoped so. Prayed so. His lungs were bursting but he swam on until he had to come up. Surfacing, he gulped air, looked back. The boat was circling fifty yards behind him. Black smoke poured from the stern but he saw no flames.

Luke struck out for the shore a hundred yards away. Being fully dressed hampered him, but he managed to kick off his shoes, and the swimming grew easier. Soon he lost his socks as well. He swallowed water, coughed it up. Glimpsed a black wharf jutting over the water ahead of him, saw huddled buildings, a parked sedan, two women in long skirts and wide-brimmed hats bicycling on a road that wound along the side of a green hill.

A roar came from behind him. Twisting his head, he saw the powerboat bearing down.

Alfie stood topside holding the damn Webley in one hand as he braced himself against the windscreen with the other. Flame shot from the muzzle of the gun. Luke shallow-dived into the murky river, swimming under water again, making for the wharf.

He came up gasping, gulped in air, found the boat on top of him, the prow knifing through the water. Alfie raised his gun. Luke plunged. Thrust himself far below the surface. The boat roared over him.

He lost his sense of direction and had to come up to see where he was. The boat was circling for another pass. The wharf was less than fifty feet away. He swam on the surface, refusing to look back, telling himself a hit from a moving boat was next to impossible. At least he hoped so.

Reaching the pilings he saw beneath barnacle-encrusted piers, he swam between them until his feet touched bottom. He waded toward shore with pebbles biting into the soles of his now bare feet. The boat slowed when it came alongside the wharf. Alfie stood at the bow waiting for a clear shot between the rows of pilings. Spotting a wooden ladder on the side of the wharf away from the boat, Luke thrashed his way through the water to the ladder and started up, hand over hand. A shot snapped. He didn't hear the bullet's impact.

Luke flung himself from the ladder to the planking on top of the wharf, pushed up onto his knees. The boat droned below the far side of the wharf but he couldn't see it. Crouching, he ran in stocking feet toward the shore. When he was halfway to the first of the clustered buildings he changed his mind. Damn it, those thugs had his Colt. He turned and raced back along the wharf until he was opposite the boat.

The top of a ladder showed above the side of the wharf and he heard the boat stop. Crouching low, pushing wet hair from his forehead, Luke approached the edge. A head appeared. Alfie. Luke sprang forward, his fist smashing into Alfie's nose. Alfie screamed, swung away from Luke and the wharf, the Webley swinging wildly in his right hand, his left hand clinging to the ladder.

Recovering, his nose streaming blood, Alfie braced himself against the ladder at the side of the wharf. Luke grabbed his right wrist and twisted. The revolver spun away and thudded onto the planking. Luke locked his hands around Alfie's throat and squeezed, hearing the other man gasp and choke. He was vaguely aware of Sid below, trying to position himself on the boat for a shot that wouldn't hit his companion.

Luke shoved with all his strength, at the same time releasing his hold on Alfie's neck. Alfie gave a strangled cry and fell, twisting, pushing away from the wharf with his feet. Luke threw himself to the planking. A shot. He heard a splash as Alfie cleared the boat and plunged into the river.

Jumping to his feet, Luke ran along the wharf, grabbed Alfie's Webley from the planking and spun around in time to see Sid coming up over the side. Luke snapped off three quick shots but Sid kept coming, raising his gun. Luke, a dead shot, couldn't believe he hadn't hit him. He fired twice more. Sid kept coming. Luke's revolver clicked. Empty.

Sid, only a few yards from him, aimed pointblank at Luke's chest. Luke hurled himself at the ferret-faced man. Too late. Sid fired. Luke felt nothing. He stumbled toward Sid, who sidestepped.

'That's quite enough, gentlemen,' a voice said. 'That is really quite enough.'

Luke whirled. A grey-haired British major walked briskly toward them, pipe in hand. Field glasses hung from a strap around his neck. A taller man in mufti and two Tommies hurried after him. The major ignored Sid to stop in front of Luke, jabbing at him with the stem of his pipe.

'You were warned in London, sergeant,' the

78

major said. 'You obviously didn't listen. In fact, our man was most disappointed by your attitude. Supercilious, he called it. Your behavior at the disabled touring car was careless in the extreme. I expect you realize that now.'

Dumbfounded, Luke stared at the major. The major's civilian companion looked over the side of the wharf and motioned the Tommies to help him.

Sid started to edge past Luke. Luke stepped into his path. 'I owe you,' he said.

'Blimey, Yank, I was just — '

Luke hit him, his fist stinging from the blow. Sid sat down hard. He made no move to rise, looking at Luke and rubbing his jaw.

'Wasn't no bloody need for that, governor,' he muttered.

'We've had quite enough,' the major repeated. 'Sid was merely following orders. My orders. Instead of indiscriminately lashing out, Sergeant Ray, you should blame yourself for not being prepared. Still, after the debacle at the Vauxhall, you behaved splendidly. At least as best we could tell through the glasses.'

The Tommies helped Alfie climb to the wharf where the dripping man held a handkerchief to his bloody nose as he limped toward them. His trousers legs were both seared. Glancing at Luke, he smiled wanly.

'We'll get MacGregor to the aid station, C,' the tall civilian told the major.

'That young man has only himself to blame.' The major turned on his heel. Sid rose and scurried along at his side. When Luke made no move to follow, the major looked back at him, saying, 'Come along, Sergeant Ray, come along. You needn't worry. Overall, I was quite satisfied with your performance. Hurry. The Huns aren't likely to wait while you twiddle your thumbs, you know. And, as you must already know, they aren't in the habit of using blank cartridges, either.'

Luke let out pent-up breath and followed the others from the wharf to the waiting cars, glowering at the major's back. 'Bloody bastard,' he muttered, just loud enough to be heard.

5

In the planning room of the main house at Boling Hall, Asberry tapped his pointer on a black rectangle superimposed on the over-sized wall map of Brussels. 'This is your elective,' he told Luke Ray.

Luke hunched forward at his table to study the map. 'St. Gilles Prison?'

Asberry nodded. 'Presently being used by the Germans for political prisoners. Your group's assignment is to rescue Miss Edith Cavell from St. Gilles and transport her across northern Belgium into Holland.'

Luke let out his breath. They'd hinted at the mission's objective but this was the first time either C or Asberry had come right out with it. A moment of self-doubt plagued him. Could he do it?

Damn right he could.

'You'll have three men in your group besides yourself,' Asberry went on. 'You've already met Sid Jordan. There's not a lock he can't open, one way or the other. Sergeant Dennis Manion is on his way from France where he operated behind the German lines during last year's retreat. And we've an explosives expert from Cornwall, a chap by the name of Byron MacNeeley.'

Luke nodded. He liked Asberry. Even though the man was too much of a nitpicker. C was another story. Not that C wasn't good at what he did, he probably was, but Luke didn't trust him. Didn't like to have C behind him as he was now, watching from the depths of a leather chair.

'They're all good men,' C said. 'The best we could gather on such short notice.'

Luke shifted uneasily, hoping Sid was better with locks than he was with power-boats. He listened to Asberry and tried to ignore C but had to wrinkle his nose as the smoke from C's pipe settled around his head.

'Your group assembles at our Dover facility tomorrow for a week's intensive training before you sail for Amsterdam,' Asberry said. 'Weaponry, tactics, a review of the situation in Brussels by one of our chaps just back from there, procedures for communicating with the Belgians and with England if that ever becomes necessary, a plan for your attack on the prison.'

C coughed. 'Let me talk to the young man,' he said.

Asberry nodded, laid his pointer in the tray below the map and left the room. Luke turned his chair so he faced C.

'I understand you speak French,' C said.

'I do. And a smattering of German.'

'Flemish? Dutch?' At Luke's head shake he shrugged. 'French will have to see you through then. As you may or may not know, Flemish/Dutch is the language of the northern half of Belgium. The country has the misfortune of having the Flemish in the north and the Walloons in the south, each cordially hating the other. I find the Belgium coat of arms rather amusing. At the left there's the motto, '*L'Union fait la Force.*' On the right, '*Eendracht Makkt Macht.*' One in French, the other in Flemish, both meaning, 'In Union there is Strength.''

Luke didn't smile, he frowned. Something was amiss but he couldn't put his finger to it. Did it have something to do with the fact that in some twisted way C reminded him of T.J., his father? They didn't look alike, not in the least. Both, though, were men driven by their appetite for power. Only death had been able to halt T.J.'s lust for success. He'd been different from other men, right from the start, at least from the day he arrived in Colorado to do land surveying, then decided to settle down, open a store and do a little prospecting on the side.

Luke had read somewhere that success had

a thousand parents but failure was an orphan. It had seemed that way with T.J., men flocked to him in the good days, abandoned and condemned him when his luck soured. Yet T.J. hadn't changed, not a whit. He was the same through bonanza and borrasco.

Luke's musing was interrupted when C spoke again. 'The Hun happens to be an incredibly foolish creature. Think of Bethmann-Hollweg wondering in public why England went to war over what he called a 'scrap of paper.' Meaning our joint guarantee of Belgian neutrality. Consider the way they've flouted civilized tradition. Didn't their U-boat sink the *Lusitania?* Didn't their troops set the torch to Louvain with its priceless Medieval library? Didn't they massacre more than six hundred Belgian civilians at Dinant — one a baby three weeks old? Capturing Nurse Cavell is the latest atrocity.'

Luke regarded him warily. 'Nurse Cavell hasn't yet been sentenced to death. What if she isn't?'

'You're to proceed with your mission regardless of whether the death sentence is passed or not. Miss Cavell as Miss Cavell is unimportant.' C struck a match to relight his pipe. 'She's a symbol. She represents courageous, virginal English womanhood in

84

the clutches of the barbarian intent on rapine.'

Despite the irony in C's words, Luke couldn't help feeling an urge of pride that he'd been chosen to save Nurse Cavell. To hide his elation, he said, 'England could sure use a success right now.'

'You're entirely correct. Now that Mr. Winston Churchill's been forced to step down as First Lord, and none too soon to my way of thinking, the Gallipoli campaign will be abandoned as soon as our troops can be evacuated safely from the peninsula.'

'I've always admired Churchill,' Luke said. 'He's clever, a man of ideas.'

'True, Winston has ideas by the hundreds, even the thousands. Perhaps one of them magnificent. The question always is which one? Which one? But whatever we think of him, sergeant, we do need a success very badly. There's more to it than that, though. I'll be completely honest with you. Public sentiment in the States is important to us. More than important, it's crucial. And you happen to be an American.'

'And proud to be one.'

'Most of you are.' Luke thought he caught a smile on C's face, quickly repressed.

'We must do all we can to hasten your country's entry into this great struggle,' C went on. 'Individuals don't matter, I don't, you don't. Winning the war does. We have to save civilization as we know it, save England, preserve the Empire.'

'To hell with your Empire.' As he spoke Luke sprang up from the chair and strode toward the map. 'Almost a hundred fifty years ago one of my ancestors fought to free us from your domination. I don't like being a pawn in any battle for the preservation of the British Empire.'

C didn't move a muscle. 'A pawn? You mustn't think of yourself in any such servile capacity. Consider yourself not a pawn but a knight. A modern St. George preparing to sally forth to slay the dragon and rescue the fair damsel in distress.'

Luke remembered thinking of aviators as modern knights but C made the idea seem like a young boy's fantasy. Luke shook his head, his sense of unease increasing. The feeling was as real yet as insubstantial as the smoke from C's pipe.

'Another question.' Luke turned from the map to face C. 'Has any of my group ever been to Belgium? You know I haven't.'

'You've no need for concern. We'll arrange for a guide who'll also act as your liaison with the Belgians. Any other questions, sergeant?'

Luke assumed the answer had been 'no,'

that none of his group had been to Belgium. His frown deepened. Something was wrong, hellishly wrong.

'You make it sound so damn simple,' he said. Yes, that was the trouble. It was too simple. In some way, C wasn't leveling with him. 'Like a cakewalk.'

C raised an eyebrow.

'It'll be anything but,' Luke argued. 'It's like riding against a thousand Comanches with four men, trying to break into their guarded Indian camp where a white woman's tied to a stake, rescuing her, then spiriting her back to civilization without losing a man. Or the rescued woman. An expedition to hell and back would be simpler.'

Both of C's eyebrows elevated. 'I never meant to suggest your mission would be easy. Are you beginning to have second thoughts?'

'Not on your life. I think I have a right to know what our chances are of making it back, though. Especially since we'll have Miss Cavell with us. What are the odds?'

'One never really knows about that sort of thing — there are too many variables.'

'You expect me to lead this mission, C. Maybe you don't owe me much but you owe me your best guess.'

C nodded. 'I agree. To be frank, Sgt. Ray,

we estimate your chances for a successful mission at no better than one to two.'

★ ★ ★

After dinner, Asberry found C reading in his office on the second floor with a Scotch and soda on the stand beside him.

'Hammond called from the Yard,' Asberry reported. 'The constable at St. Agnes in Cornwall has reported the death of a young woman. She appears to have fallen from a cliff sometime late yesterday. While painting.'

'I fail to see how this concerns us.'

'She was the woman living with our Mr. MacNeeley.'

C's face was expressionless. 'Is there any evidence of foul play?'

'No, though the constable's not completely satisfied. He has no hard evidence, just doesn't like the smell of things. When the locals discovered that MacNeeley was under Army orders, they reported the circumstances to London. Hammond wants to know if we have any suggestions on how he should proceed.'

'MacNeeley must be allowed to report for duty as ordered,' C said.

'Very good, sir.' Asberry stood waiting.

'I didn't think he'd kill the woman,' C said

at last. 'I wonder why he got the wind up this time? He never has before.'

'Perhaps he suspected she was on to him. Or that we were.'

C shook his head emphatically. 'I don't see how he could possibly think that about us. We've made no move at all since intercepting the letter. No, the strain's beginning to tell on Mr. MacNeeley. He's becoming edgy. The man undoubtedly intends to bolt for home as soon as he has the opportunity. Good riddance to him, I say. Saves us the trouble.'

'And the Nightingale — the Dark Storm mission? Any revisions?'

'We'll proceed as planned, of course. Nothing's really changed from our point of view, nothing at all.'

★　★　★

Later, Luke followed Asberry down long corridors past rooms of men and women working at ordered ranks of desks, through doors guarded by stiff-backed Army sentries in parade uniform, into a crowded antechamber. Asberry left him sitting with a colonel of artillery on one side of him, on the other a young man wearing a frock coat with silk facings, a winged collar and black bow tie.

A sergeant major entered, called a name.

A major rose, straightened his uniform, and followed the sergeant-major. Asberry returned and sat beside Luke without speaking. They waited. The colonel and a captain were called and left with the sergeant-major. Luke began to sense an air of tense expectation in the room, of men who brought the results of months of work here to be praised or damned.

'Mr. Asberry, sir. Sergeant Ray.'

They followed the sergeant-major to an inner room, stopped in front of a lieutenant sitting behind a desk beside a paneled door. They presented their identification and the officer noted their names and the time in a log. 'Good to see you again, sir,' the lieutenant said to Asberry when he finished.

The sergeant-major opened the door and ushered them in. Asberry led Luke into the room, an office with a row of high windows along two sides, a room of dark leather chairs with trophies and photographs on the walls, a moustached officer sitting at a mahogany table, writing. With a start, Luke realized who the man was.

Lord Kitchener glanced up. Horatio Herbert Kitchener. Kitchener of Khartoum. Field Marshal, Secretary of State for War. Luke stood at attention and saluted. Lord Kitchener nodded without rising, motioned them to chairs. His face was brick red. He looked older than in his pictures, more tired. He had a paunch.

Luke gazed at him expectantly, trying not to be awed. Kitchener's blue eyes stared at him, blinked.

'You have been given a most important task.' Lord Kitchener paused to glance at a note on his desk. 'You will need courage, energy, and patience.' His voice was cold, oracular. This must have been, Luke thought, how God sounded to Moses.

'You're a citizen of a great nation, the United States,' Lord Kitchener went on. 'You are a stalwart representative of your nation fighting in the service of another great nation. Do your duty bravely, fear God, and honor the King.' Asberry shifted position. Taking the hint, Luke saluted once more. Without another word, Lord Kitchener turned his attention back to the papers on his desk. As Luke followed Asberry from the room, he found himself vaguely disappointed. What had he expected? Kitchener was only a man, after all. Yet he'd expected more. Perhaps heroes shouldn't live to grow old.

Asberry took Luke to an elevator and they descended slowly into the depths of the War Office where they walked along a corridor with their footsteps echoing hollowly. The passageway, Luke was certain, must lead to the basement of another building. Asberry stopped at a closed door and held his hand out to Luke.

'I hope you have a bloody good show,' he said.

His grip was firm. 'Go this way.' Asberry nodded at the door. 'You'll be driven to the rendezvous. You'll find your luggage already there.' Instead of making motions to leave, Asberry stood staring at him.

What is it you're not telling me, Luke wanted to ask. He knew it was futile, so all he said was, 'Thanks.'

He opened the door to a cavernous room. Lights shone from behind wire mesh covering brackets spaced at regular intervals along the walls. A chauffeured black Vauxhall waited for him at a loading ramp. The chauffeur ushered Luke into the back, returned to his seat and, without a word, eased the touring car up an incline to the street.

It was half before six in the evening and traffic was heavy. After twenty minutes of stops and starts they pulled up in front of a hotel, the Manchester. The driver sprang out and held the door. Looking at him, Luke noticed only one of the man's eyes moved, the other stared fixedly ahead. 'Sir,' the chauffeur said, 'you're expected in room two-thirty-eight.'

Luke left the Vauxhall and walked through the lobby, taking the steps two at a time. After a wrong turning, he found 238 and knocked. He waited, shifting his feet, wondering if the circular pattern on the door concealed a peephole because he was positive he was being observed from inside. The door opened and Luke started in surprise.

Kezia Faith stepped back, staring uncertainly at him.

★ ★ ★

A guard led Edith Cavell into the small gray interrogation room at St. Gilles Prison and seated her at a table. Sergeant Pinkhoff, grim and punctilious, sat down across from her. His assistant, Bergen, sat at a smaller table to her right, a pencil in his hand and a notepad on the table top in front of him.

Pinkhoff: I believe you told us the other night that you had been taking men into your nursing home since last November. Is that correct?

Nurse Cavell: Yes, you already know that.

Pinkhoff: We should be correct in saying, then, that you took these men in, fed them, and provided them with money.

Nurse Cavell: Yes.

Pinkhoff: They were mostly English and French soldiers, men who had been cut off from their regiments?

Nurse Cavell: Yes, to the best of my knowledge.

Pinkhoff: In addition to these soldiers, did you also give aid to able-bodied Belgians and Frenchmen who wanted to get to the front?

Nurse Cavell (after a moment's pause): Yes, there were a number of such men.

For the first time since the interrogation began, Pinkhoff smiled.

6

Kezia wore a pleated green gown with white trim on the high-necked bodice. Her auburn hair had been cut short and waved. Without her nurse's uniform she appeared soft, almost vulnerable, except for the cool gray eyes that appraised him. He hoped he'd concealed his surprise at seeing her here. As soon as she closed and locked the door behind him, he asked, 'You're our guide?'

'Do you have any objections, Sergeant Ray?'

'Why should I? It's just that I thought — ' What *had* he thought? Hadn't Asberry told him their escort into Belgium was to be a man? Or was that his own assumption? Luke frowned. Women shouldn't be involved in this business. A memory flashed into his mind of Captain Theroux telling him of the French female spy who'd been honored by her government for her 'heroic weakness,' in the presence of the enemy — French shorthand for her using sex to elicit information. Distaste tightened his lips.

'You thought your guide would be a man,' Kezia said crisply. 'Should be a man. That's what you were about to say.'

'I'll admit I didn't expect a woman.' He was annoyed at the defensive tone in his voice.

To collect his thoughts, Luke glanced across the hotel room at the billowing curtains letting in the none-too-fragrant London evening breeze. He moved closer to look through the open window at the small park on the other side of the street before glancing at Kezia again. She was self-possessed, cool. He couldn't help being attracted to her. Not just because she was a looker, more because she was a challenge, and he couldn't resist a challenge.

She indicated a table with a bottle of DeWars, siphon and glasses. 'Would you care for a drink?'

'No, thank you, not now.'

He watched with some surprise while she mixed herself a whisky and soda, recalling the last time they'd met at the hospital in France. He'd thought of her then as a prig, probably a teetotaler. He wondered if she was also remembering their angry confrontation.

'And how's your friend?' Kezia asked sweetly as she sat in a chair covered with rose-patterned fabric.

'My friend?' He knew very well who she meant.

'I believe her name is Yvette.'

He shrugged.

Kezia sipped her drink, glancing at him over the rim of the glass. 'You don't even care what became of her, do you?'

Angered, he crossed to her, stood over her. He took the glass from her hand and thumped it down on the table.

'Don't touch me,' she warned, stiffening. Her eyes sparked with defiance and a hint of apprehension.

'At night in the French trenches,' he said, his annoyance edging his words, 'they post the *poilus* on the fire steps to watch for enemy patrols in No-Man's-Land. Every so often, usually when the soldiers take their posts or just before they're relieved, they fire off a few rounds. As a warning to the Huns. Sort of to keep them honest.'

Her unblinking gaze never left his face.

'Is that the way it's going to be with us?' he asked. 'If it is, I say the hell with it.'

'We're not enemies, sergeant.' She reached up and touched his sleeve. 'We're on the same side.'

'You don't act like it.' Slowly the anger drained from him. He was tired, wanted the drink she'd offered but he was damned if he'd ask for it now.

'I promised myself I wouldn't utter a word

about what happened at the hospital,' Kezia said. 'We have a job to do, I told myself, the gallant sergeant and I. We'll do it and that will be the end of it. Personal feelings shouldn't matter in wartime. And now, five minutes after you knock on the door, I've broken my promise.'

Luke eyed her appraisingly. 'T.J., that's my father, always said it took a mighty big man to know when remembering what happened in the past did more harm than good. Maybe we'd both do better to start over.'

'I'd like that, Sergeant Ray. Really I would.'

'I'll get myself that drink now,' he said.

She shook her head, got up and walked past him to the table where she poured whisky, squirted in soda and handed the drink to Luke. He nodded his thanks.

'We leave Victoria Station for Dover at ten-thirty tonight,' she said. 'We'll eat dinner here at the hotel.' After a moment, she added, 'If that suits you.'

It did. So did the change in her attitude toward him. After they were seated in the hotel dining room, he noticed that Kezia Faith was by far the most attractive woman in the place. Luke said little, content to watch her. He enjoyed having other diners glance sideways at her when they passed their table, the men admiring, the women evaluating.

Kezia had, he decided, more than physical beauty. She had another quality, a radiance he could neither define nor tell where it came from.

Kezia treated him warily, like an opponent in a lull between battles. She seemed to surround herself with a privateness, impalpable yet real, like a Keep Out sign. Whenever he thought she was on the verge of revealing a part of herself she drew back, talking instead of the war or the weather or London.

She had no reason to like him, he knew that. He should be grateful she'd stopped sniping. But there was more to her reticence than dislike. It was almost as if she felt sorry for him and wanted to protect him, wanted to care for him whether she liked him or not. Perhaps it was because of her profession. Unless she'd lied about that.

'You are a nurse?' he asked.

Surprise crossed her face. 'Of course. What makes you ask? If you need credentials, I took my training at Battlesea Hospital and I nursed at the clinic on the rue de la Culture in Brussels for almost a year before the war.'

'Then you knew Nurse Cavell.'

'She was our matron. The head of the clinic.' Kezia glanced around the room. 'We shouldn't speak of such things in public. Besides, it's time we were on our way.'

The food had been nothing special, something one ate to satisfy hunger rather than enjoy, so Luke wasn't sorry the meal was over. He hailed a taxi, and soon it turned onto Buckingham Palace Road.

'This is where I was arrested,' said Kezia.

His eyebrows shot up. 'Arrested? You were arrested? What for?'

'Smashing shop windows. It was more than three years ago. My small part of the Suffrage Cause. Votes for women. The government betrayed us with one false promise after another.' Kezia sat straighter, her eyes flashing. 'The time for talking was long past so Mrs. Pankhurst had us scatter all over London, to Piccadilly, Regent Street. Whitehall, Downing Street, Chelsea, here, and at precisely the same time we all took our hammers from our handbags and began smashing the shop windows to force those in authority to take notice.'

'I didn't realize you were one of them.'

'Didn't realize that I was a woman, you mean? Oh, yes, I am. As it stands now, I'm not a citizen, not really, and I have no more rights than criminals and lunatics. But I'm glad and proud to be a woman nevertheless.' Her voice softened. 'I was at the Derby two years ago when Emily Davidson ran onto the course and forced the King's horse to stop.

She was killed. What courage! What devotion! Oh, yes, I'm proud to be one of them.'

'You know I meant Suffragettes,' Luke said. 'I've noticed we don't hear much from that group these days.' He didn't add his feeling that it was just as well.

'We believe that winning the war is more important at the moment. I don't mean the 'Woolies for Soldiers' campaign, I mean this, what I'm doing now.' She paused, looking away from him. When she spoke again, her voice was lower. 'I was sent to jail, of course. I joined the others in a hunger strike so they'd turn us loose, no food, no water. When they force-fed us with tubes going into our stomachs, I became sick. Seriously sick. That was when I decided to go to Belgium as a nurse.'

Luke frowned. Kezia a Suffragette? He'd always thought of them, when he bothered to think of them at all, as mannish maniacs dressed in purple, white and green gowns who threw stones, disrupted political meetings, slashed portraits in art galleries, and chained themselves to the railings outside the House of Commons.

Sirens began to wail and their cab accelerated. Luke noticed the cabby looking about apprehensively. The London night was dark, cloudy. The city was dimmed out with the street lights extinguished but not the lights in the buildings.

Traffic came to a halt in front of them. Muttering the cabby slowed. Luke saw a bobby in the next block motioning autos to the side of the street. Their taxicab pulled to the curb. Police were herding pedestrians into buildings. A bobby rode past on a bicycle with a placard hanging from his shoulders: 'Take Cover.'

'Bloody Zepps,' the cabby muttered.

Luke reached across Kezia, opened the door and they climbed down to the sidewalk. Men and women were hurrying into nearby buildings. He took Kezia's arm.

'Wait,' she said. 'The suitcases.'

He stared at her.

'Bring the suitcases. We mustn't risk losing them.'

He turned back to the cab, undid the strap holding the two suitcases to the roof and lifted them to the ground while Kezia waited in the shadows in front of a bookseller's shop. By the time he rejoined her with the suitcases all traffic was stopped on the street and only a few hurrying people remained on the sidewalks.

An explosion crumped several blocks away. Flame glared above the rooftops. The first blast was followed by another and another.

'Look!' Kezia pointed over the roofs on the other side of the street. Above the glow from the fire, searchlights probed the undersides of the clouds, swinging to and fro in graceful arcs. Seeking but not finding the raiders. The lights began darting impatiently from cloud to cloud.

'I thought I saw — ' Kezia drew in her breath. 'There,' she whispered.

A giant airship slid silently from behind the clouds. Huge, gray, serene, and deadly. The searchlights converged below the great ship, failing to reach it. The Zeppelin seemed untouchable, a monstrous nightmare being let loose upon an innocent world. Anti-aircraft guns barked. Shells exploded in white bursts. Too low, all too low. Shrapnel from the shells rained down onto London streets as the airship glided on above the tumult.

'The Zeppelin wouldn't be so frightening,' Kezia whispered close to his ear, 'if only it made a noise. A roar like an airplane.'

The airship, over six hundred feet long, slowly slid out of sight behind another cloud. 'She must be at least ten thousand feet up,' Luke guessed.

'Why don't our planes shoot her down? She makes such a big target.'

'They can't,' he told her. 'Actually, many of our planes are little more than animated kites.

It takes an Avro almost an hour to reach that height. By that time she'll be well on her way back to Belgium. Zepps go more than sixty miles an hour.'

They heard more explosions in the distance. A blue-helmeted bobby shouted at them to take cover so they entered a building two doors from the bookshop. Black cloths covered the windows but a faint blue light led them to a stairwell. Luke, carrying the two suitcases, led the way down the steps. Men and women huddled on the basement floor along both sides of a candlelit corridor that appeared to run the length of the building. A woman told a story to two fair-haired children, a baby cried despite its mother's hushing, a man in slippers and nightshirt pulled his robe close about himself.

As they continued to walk along the corridor, the way grew darker and the sheltering crowd thinned. They found a place to sit against the wall apart from the others and Luke eased down the suitcases. Hearing the steady pom-pom-pom of the anti-aircraft guns above them, Luke suppressed his urge to march from the shelter into the street where he could feel he was defying the raiders instead of fleeing from them.

As though she were reading his mind, Kezia said, 'I feel like I'm running away and hiding. I realize we couldn't do any good up there but I wanted to stay on the street.'

Luke glanced at her shadowed face. She continually surprised him. In this, at least, they were alike.

As they sat, their shoulders touching, he breathed in her faint aroma. At first he couldn't place it, then he did. Lilies-of-the-valley. He remembered walking with his mother across a sun-drenched field toward a stand of cottonwoods along a creek where the flowers grew in the shade. T.J. waited for them there, waving.

'Your father must have been someone quite special,' Kezia said, 'from the way you sounded when you talked about him.

Again he felt a slight shock, the feeling she could read his mind.

'T.J. was,' he told her.

The people sheltering at the other end of the corridor starting singing 'Tipperary.' Everywhere he went in London, Luke heard 'Tipperary.' The banner on the sheet music called it 'The song the soldiers sing.'

As the words ran, it was a long way to Tipperary — and also to Colorado. 'T.J. was one of the first prospectors to find silver in Leadville,' he told Kezia. 'That's a mining town in the Rockies in Colorado. It's near the Continental Divide. T.J. was lucky. Ray's luck,

105

the miners called it. Besides surveying, he ran a store with my mother near the Arkansas River and one day he grubstaked an old Dutchman and the prospector struck pay dirt.'

'Grubstaked?' she asked.

'That means my father gave the old prospector food and supplies in return for an interest in the mine if he found one. T.J. was always open-handed, big-hearted, that's why the store never made any money. My mother tried in vain to stop him from being so free with his cash. Charity should begin at home, she said. He always agreed with her since he didn't like to argue, but the next time one of the boys came along, down on his luck, T.J. was ready to give him a grubstake. He wasn't educated except for survey work and his talk was sort of rough and ready but there wasn't a better-liked man in the territory.'

'You sound as though you loved him very much.' Kezia's voice was wistful.

'I suppose I did. I didn't think about it. I just knew that when I grew up I wanted to be like him.'

Luke paused, remembering. 'By the time I was born, T.J. was one of the richest men in the state of Colorado. He built an opera house in Leadville, then decided to move into a mansion in Denver. My mother didn't want

106

to move, but she did. She said it was a foolish waste of hard-earned money. He bought a cable company and there was talk of him running for the Senate.' He paused again.

'And did he?' Kezia prompted.

Luke shook his head. 'When I was seven, my father and mother were divorced. She wouldn't talk to me about him, not a word. My mother and I still lived in the mansion with the peacocks on the lawn and my father used to come and see me and take me riding in his carriage, but it wasn't the same.'

Kezia touched his arm. Though she quickly withdrew her hand, the gesture warmed him.

'Later on T.J. married again,' he said, 'a divorced woman named Linda May Lowe. She was a lot younger than my mother, pretty and blonde. The Statehouse crowd told T.J. he was cutting his own throat as far as politics went if he married Linda May — because she was a divorced woman. My father wouldn't listen. My mother hated her. I once saw her tear a newspaper to shreds because Linda May's picture was in it.'

Kezia sniffed. 'Women should have as much right to get divorced as men do. What if your mother had wished to marry again? After all, she was divorced, too.'

Luke decided it was best not to get into a discussion of the difference between a woman who'd been divorced by her husband through no fault of her own and a woman who instigated a divorce. To him, it was the difference between his mother and Linda May but he knew enough about Kezia by now to be sure she wouldn't view it in the same light.

'For a while I hated all of them,' he went on, 'T.J. for leaving me, mother for, as I saw it, making him leave, Linda May for keeping him from coming home, ever. He cares nothing for me, I thought. He wouldn't have married her if he did.'

'If two people aren't compatible it's better for them to go their separate ways. Sometimes I wish — '

'You wish?' he prompted when she didn't go on.

She shook her head. The singing had ceased, the corridor was quiet. They no longer heard the slam of the guns.

'In the 90s,' Luke said at last, feeling a compulsion to go on, 'the price of silver went down and T.J.'s company failed. The bank repossessed the new mansion he'd built for Linda May. My mother took me there on the day of the auction. 'Serves him right,' she said. My mother should have been the business man in the family. She still had our house in Denver and was investing in land around San Francisco. I don't know how happy she was without T.J., I can't remember seeing her smile much, but she sure knew how to hang onto a dollar.'

'And your father?'

'The final straw was when his partner, a man named Irvine, was caught defrauding the company. Irvine killed himself rather than go to prison. My father lost all the money he'd ever made. And more. An old friend at the Statehouse got him a job in the Denver post office. One summer, my mother took sick with a fever and I lived with T.J. for six months. He took time off from work and taught me to ride and to shoot, to hunt and fish. I didn't want to go back home when my mother recovered but I had to.'

He smiled. 'The funny thing about that summer was, I found I liked Linda May. She acted awful young and she giggled a lot but I could tell she loved T.J. I saw why he liked her, why he married her.'

'Your father sounds like a man worth knowing.'

Luke sighed. 'He died the winter after I lived with him. Had a heart attack one morning when he was walking to work at the post office. He died the next day.'

'I'm sorry.'

'No need to be, it was almost ten years ago.

Truth to tell, though, I still choke up sometimes when I think about it.'

'Is your mother living?'

He nodded. 'She's in San Francisco. Linda May's still alive, too. She's back in Leadville. T.J. had one mine left, the Eureka. No one wanted it. He told Linda May never to sell the Eureka and she never has. Though it hasn't produced any pay dirt since the '80s.'

'Linda May sounds a bit foolish. Perhaps heroic, too, in a way.'

'T.J. always warned me not to be fooled by her feminine ways. 'That girl's got steel in her spine,' he used to say.' They sat in silence with Luke reflecting that maybe the same could be said of Kezia. After a time he felt her head drop against his shoulder. Her regular breathing told him she slept so he put his arm protectively around her and dozed himself.

The sirens awakened him. Kezia remained asleep and he didn't wake her. She confused him. He wanted to protect her from harm and she did attract him, he couldn't deny that. If only she acted more like other women . . .

She came awake with a start, gazing about her at the almost deserted shelter. She looked at Luke and he took his arm away. 'Where is everyone?' she asked.

'The all clear sounded. Maybe fifteen

minutes ago.' Kezia got to her feet and brushed off her green dress. 'We'll take the next train to Dover,' she said, picking up one of the suitcases. 'You bring the other one,' she added.

Luke started to protest, reaching for the suitcase in her hand. He held, sighing to himself. If she wanted it to be share and share alike there was no point in arguing.

He followed her up the stairs to the street where people milled about, many wearing robes over nightclothes, others fully dressed. Broken glass crunched under their shoes as they checked to see what buildings had been hit by the bombs.

England's island fortress suddenly seemed very vulnerable. Luke, though, worried more about Kezia's vulnerability than England's. While he couldn't help but look forward to being with her during the next weeks, at the same time he was afraid for her. This wouldn't be like tossing stones through shop windows. She was letting herself in for more than she bargained for.

In ten days or less they'd finish the training at Dover and cross the Channel to Holland. From Holland they'd travel to the Belgian border. There, they'd be four men plus Kezia matching wits with the German Army.

7

Anthony Mills scooped Trafalgar into his arms, opened the rear door of his semi-detached house, and lowered the cat gently onto the stoop. The black Manx glanced reproachfully at him before ambling down the steps and across the small fenced yard.

Anthony closed and locked the door, walked through the kitchen to the hall where he put on his bowler before going out to the street. He was small, neat and unpretentious as the Maida Vale houses he passed on his way to the tram stop. And as drab, as though the soot that drifted down to coat the porches, windows and walls of his London neighborhood had left a gray residue on him as well.

He arrived at the stop at ten minutes before eight, giving him ample time to discuss the hotter than usual September weather with Mr. Linden. When they heard the clang of the tram, both men automatically looked back along the sidestreet. Yes, there came Springer-Hall, late as usual, tightening his tie as he hurried toward them.

Cecil Springer-Hall, flushed and panting,

climbed aboard and made his way to his customary seat at the rear, ignoring the other two men. Anthony secretly hoped that someday Springer-Hall would miss the tram, arrive at work dreadfully late and be cashiered from his position. He had no patience whatsoever for men who failed to plan.

Anthony left the tram a block from his office. He paused, as was his custom, in front of Day and Son, Books New and Used. The window display had been changed overnight and copies of a recently published book describing life in the trenches were arranged to spell B.E.F.

When Anthony pushed the door open, a bell tinkled inside the shop. Horace Day sat on a high stool halfway along one of the narrow aisles between shelves that rose floor to ceiling from the front of the shop to the rear. Day looked up from reading the book in his hand, saw Anthony and inserted a marker between the pages. He closed the book and slid it back into its place on the highest shelf, tilting it slightly toward him.

'Ah, Mr. Mills.' Day scrambled down from his perch and hurried to the front of the shop. A short, balding man, Day, like his shop, smelled pleasantly of dust and yellowed pages. 'I was hoping you might stop by today, sir. The book you've been waiting for arrived this very morning.'

The shopkeeper knelt behind the counter, his back to Anthony, and scanned a row of books. Names were printed in small, precise letters on pieces of paper fastened to the books' spines with elastic bands: 'Addams, Clayton, Farquhar.'

'Ah, here we are. Mills.' Day pulled a book from the shelf and laid it on the counter. '*The Portrait Of A Lady*. A most engaging tale, although Henry James can be a trifle shocking at times. Or so my customers tell me.'

'You've never read it?'

'Only the first few chapters. I find myself starting books, putting them aside and then forgetting to finish them.'

Looking down the aisle between the shelves. Anthony saw that Horace Day had left dozens of books titled outward, each like an old friend extending his hand in greeting at a door, anxious to draw you inside.

'I've always suspected I entered the wrong profession,' Day confessed.

'But you love books. I've never known a man who loved them more than you.'

Day ran his fingers over the gilt letters on the cover of *The Portrait of A Lady*. He sighed. 'That's the very reason I maintain I'm in the wrong business. I should collect books, perhaps, not sell them. They say that a man who's overly fond of his whisky should never own a pub.' He grimaced. 'I can't abide the taste of liquor so I suppose I become drunk on words instead. I suspect Thomas might have been right, after all.'

'How is the boy?' Anthony asked. Thomas, the son of Day and Son, had left the shop under unpleasant circumstances ten years before, had failed at a variety of jobs, become an automobile mechanic, volunteered in 1914 and was sent to France. Horace Day had never changed the name of the business. The sign over the door was, Anthony suspected, Day's invitation to his son to return, his expression of hope for the future.

'What with the censor, you're never certain how they are,' Day replied. 'Or where they are. As you certainly must be aware, sir.' Day smiled, almost conspiratorially. 'Yet he seems to be doing as well as might be expected. Thank God he's with a repair battalion and not in the trenches.'

'Where he'd most likely be if he'd stayed on with you here in the shop.'

'Exactly. I suppose everything works out for the best in this best of all possible worlds.' Day glanced at *The Portrait Of A Lady*. 'Shall I wrap it up for you, Mr. Mills?'

'No, thank you, I expect I'll read a few pages during my lunch hour.' Anthony took the book, nodded to Day and left the shop, the bell tinkling behind him. When he glanced back, Horace Day was once more perched on his high stool, reading.

Anthony crossed a side street and climbed the marble steps of a great gray building, walked through the ornate, high-ceilinged entrance hall and entered the lift. Floyd Lewis, a veteran of Balaclava, now old and stooped, slid the door shut, pulled a lever and they made their way by fits and starts to the fourth floor. Anthony left the lift, walked along a gray corridor to his office and went in.

Parkington looked up.

'Tony.' Parkington was the only one who called him Tony. He hadn't been Tony since he was a boy. 'Tony,' Parkington said again, 'the Old Horror is in a terrible pet. I've never seen him this angry. He's positively livid.'

Anthony raised his eyebrows slightly but said nothing. He passed Parkington and put *The Portrait Of A Lady* on his own desk, then laid his hat on the shelf along the far wall. Parkington swung around in his chair, picked up the book and opened it. He flipped rapidly through the pages. A tall, thin young

116

man, Parkington was quick as a humming-bird, darting from subject to subject without warning. Quick and curious. No secret was ever completely safe when Charles Parkington was about.

'Whoever owned this book before,' Parkington said, 'should be drawn and quartered. Literally. He positively desecrated it.'

'Let me have the book,' said Anthony.

Parkington swung his chair away, keeping the book in his hand and his back to Anthony. 'He underscored whole passages,' he said. 'I can't abide reading a book with under-scorings in it.'

'You don't have to read it. The book's mine, after all.'

Parkington leafed through more of the pages. 'This doesn't make one iota of sense,' he said. 'Not one. Underscoring a novel is peculiar enough but these underscorings were made at random. Or so it appears.'

'Give. Me. The. Book.'

'You're getting as nasty as the Old Horror. Why the next thing I know you'll actually snatch the book from my hands.' He peered slyly over the top of his half-glasses. 'One would think you had some deep, dark secret you're guarding with a purple passion. Tony, you're acting positively demented. For you, that is.'

'I've nothing to hide, Parkington. What would I have to hide? I'm merely telling you the book's mine.'

'Listen to the first passage he's under-scored. Here. ' . . . she should be so. But she nevertheless made . . . ' You realize, don't you, that there's no earthly reason for someone to underscore those particular words. And here, further along. 'Well, said Henrietta, you think . . . ' Could this unhinged underscorer be playing games with himself? Let me try reading the passages consecutively. 'She should be so but she nevertheless made well, said Henrietta, you think.' There's no rhyme nor reason to it.'

'After my father was pensioned from the railway,' Anthony said, 'he used to sit at the kitchen table in his flat with the *Times* and blacken the loops of letters on whatever page happened to catch his fancy. He blackened all e's, o's and a's, never the b's, g's, nor p's. He was bored, that was his only reason. I have some of those papers at home still. I'll bring one to the office and see what you make of it.'

'What about the d's, old chap?'

'The what?'

'The d's, the d's. Did your father blacken the d's?'

Anthony reached out and snatched his

118

book from Charles Parkington and placed it in a drawer of his desk. 'I don't remember about the d's,' he said.

'It's five past nine. He wanted to see us at nine sharp. Both of us together.'

'Who did?'

'The Old Horror, of course.'

'Why didn't you tell me before?'

'You so intrigued me with your ciphered volume of Henry James that I quite forgot.' As he spoke, Charles Parkington rose, straightening his rust tie and fawn vest.

He led the way from the room along an interior corridor leading to the section chief's office where he tapped three times. A resonant voice told them to come in.

Though Anthony didn't approve of Parkington's calling their chief the 'Old Horror,' he appreciated the reason.

They stood uneasily in front of Ashley-Smith's desk, looking down at his bountiful mane of white hair. At last Ashley-Smith looked up, lifting bushy white eyebrows. His eyes were a pale and watery blue. 'Questions have been raised,' he said ominously.

Charles Parkington and Anthony nodded, expecting the worst. They were used to the telegraphic tempo of Ashley-Smith's pronouncements.

'Serious breaches have occurred. The

minister is alarmed. Changes must be made. New brooms will sweep clean. Heads may have to roll.'

'Were the questions about the Spanish desk?' Anthony asked. Parkington supervised Spain. 'Or the Portuguese desk?' Portugal was Anthony's responsibility.

'Inefficiency abounds. We haven't enough thumbs to thrust one in every dike. All of us will be tarred by the same brush. Don't ask me for whom the bell tolls. Make certain your houses are in order before you throw stones. We don't want it to be every man for himself and the devil take the hindmost. Do I make myself clear?'

Anthony heard Parkington let out his breath in a sigh of relief. He suppressed his own sigh.

'Then there's no indication of where the information is slipping through,' he said.

'None. None at all. You should consider that the tocsin has sounded and act accordingly.' Ashley-Smith waved his hand in dismissal. 'Carry on. Vigilance is the price we pay for freedom. Thoroughness. Application. Dedication to the tasks at hand.'

'You may rely on us to do our very best, sir,' Parkington said.

Once they were in the corridor, Anthony said, 'That wasn't as bad as I feared.'

'Routine.' Parkington mimicked Ashley-Smith's deep voice. 'All in a day's work. Diligence is next to Godliness. Hail Britannia.'

When, at half-past twelve, Parkington invited Anthony to accompany him to the Golden Boar, Anthony begged off, pleading a backlog of work. As soon as Parkington was well away, Anthony opened *The Portrait Of A Lady*, thumbing from one underlined section to the next.

He smiled. The underlined words, of course, meant nothing in themselves. The number of letters was the key, telling him how many words to count forward or backward to the words or letters that combined to form the message. The message was brief: Britain had dispatched a small unit to Holland with orders to cross the Belgian frontier near Kapellen, travel to Brussels, and attempt to rescue Nurse Cavell.

Anthony took a sheet of paper from his desk drawer, wrote rapidly in his small, precise hand, sealed the message in an envelope, and addressed it to a number on the Rua Augusta in Lisbon. He pulled a rubber stamp from its holder in the rack on his desk, pressed it onto an ink pad and stamped the front and back of the envelope: PASSED BY OFFICIAL CENSOR.

He dropped the letter in the basket of outgoing mail.

★   ★   ★

The Batman wakened Justin Graham at precisely one in the morning. Justin walked to the window and smiled as he thought ahead to what the day held. Words from a poem danced in his head, 'Proud, then, clear-eyed and laughing, go to greet death as a friend . . . '

After shaving and dressing, Justin walked along the muddy path to the officers' mess. The cool, damp night air warned of the approach of winter, the second winter of the year.

'Tea, sir?' the mess attendant asked.

'Please.'

The mess was empty since the pilots had come and gone, leaving their tea-stained mugs on the tables.

He sipped his tea, waiting. Aston arrived first, then Tryon and Seymour entered the hall together. Kingman was last, as Justin had expected, bleary-eyed, his hair tousled. 'I say, chaps,' Kingman said, 'do you think this is going to be a bloody good show? I do.'

The others nodded, saying little as they

drank and smoked. The time for talk was past, they were ready, the result depended on skill and the whims of the gods. When they finished their tea, the five men walked to the door where they paused to study the sky. Dark clouds drifted across the face of the moon, alternately silvering and darkening the aerodrome.

Major Mannering was waiting for them in front of the first of the hangars. He stepped forward, acknowledged their salutes, shook Justin's hand and nodded to the others. Engines roared to life behind the major. Justin saw the sleek silhouettes of three Avros, listened as their pilots revved them up.

'I only wish I was going with you chaps,' Major Mannering said.

Justin nodded without answering, knowing he'd feel the same in Mannering's place. War, after all, was a man's testing ground. More lines slipped into his mind: 'Now God be thanked who has matched us with His hour and caught our youth, and wakened us from sleeping.'

Justin's stomach knotted with the same anticipation and excitement he'd felt before a match. He glanced around the aerodrome at the hangars looming above the dark field, pictured another field, a rugby field with its tiered stadium, the crowds, the flags snapping, the blue sky, the players trotting across the turf . . .

'Ready for boarding, sir.' The mechanic shouted to make himself heard above the Avro's whine.

'Quite so.' The major turned to Justin. 'Good luck, Graham.'

'Any word of the decoy?' Justin asked.

'None. It's a bit too soon, of course. I'm confident they'll do their bit and then make their way back to Holland as planned.'

Like hell they'll make it back. Justin turned to his men, wondering if he should say something, a last word of caution, of encouragement, knowing he wouldn't. He didn't believe in the empty gesture, the jaunty remark, the false bravado. He looked at each of them in turn. 'Board your planes,' he ordered.

Kingman stepped forward to join him, Tryon followed Seymour to the second Avro, Aston to the third. Justin climbed onto the wing and dropped down into the converted observer's cockpit. Kingman squeezed in behind him and they strapped themselves in. The pilot turned in his seat to give them a thumbs up sign, then settled into his cockpit and raised his hand.

A mechanic ran to the side of the airplane,

yanked a rope pulling the chocks from in front of the wheels. The Avro jounced ahead. They gathered speed as they raced across the unlighted field, the Avro's tail came up and the plane rose into the night sky. They circled until the other two Avros were airborne, then the pilot pointed his plane's nose eastward and climbed slowly as the other Avros formed the tail of a vee behind him.

The clouds scudded away to the north, the sky cleared and they flew beneath the full moon toward the trenches of northern France. Justin breathed deeply. Exhilaration pulsed through him, the sense of daring the unknown that lay in wait for him behind the German lines. More of the poem came to him: 'Proud we were, and laughed, that had such brave true things to say — and then you suddenly cried, and turned away.'

Without warning, he thought of Kezia.

8

The five of them finished their supper in the kitchen of the Van Horn farmhouse a quarter mile from the Belgian frontier: Kezia Faith, Luke Ray, Byron MacNeeley, explosive expert and Luke's second in command, Sid Joerdan, thief and picker of locks, and Dennis Manion, sergeant in the Irish guards, veteran of Mons and the heavy fighting at Ypres. Manion called Ypres, 'Wipes.'

Luke put his cup of coffee on the plank table and glanced at his wristwatch. Before the war he would have thought it unmanly to carry anything but a pocket watch.

Five minutes to go.

'Check your arms and ammo,' he ordered. 'Your ammo pouches.'

Each of them carried a six-shot Webley .455 Mark VI revolver with ammunition and three hand grenades. The four men also packed a persuader and a knuckle knife. The persuader was a club two feet long, thin at one end and thick at the other, the thick end studded with steel spikes. The knuckle knife was a dagger, the blade eight inches long, with a heavy steel-spiked guard over the grip.

'Are there any questions about the hand signals?' Luke asked.

In the darkness of the night, they planned to communicate by touch. One tap meant advance, two taps, wait, three taps, you're on your own. And so on. Each signal would be confirmed by being relayed back to the sender.

There were no questions.

'Manion takes the point,' Luke said. 'Followed by Sid and me. Then MacNeeley and Kezia.'

Luke glanced at MacNeeley, aware the other man thought that he, the only one of the group to speak colloquial German, should lead them across. Probably thought he should be in command as well. Not a follower, MacNeeley, not at all like the mortally wounded French soldier who'd told his commanding officer, 'How fortunate it was I who was hit and not you, *mon capitaine*.'

MacNeeley, though, said nothing.

Two minutes.

The red-haired Manion grinned. 'The way I look at it, there's naught for me to fret about.'

'Christ,' Sid said, ignoring Manion, 'I wish I had a fag.'

Luke worried about Sid. No longer the

confident scoundrel who'd struck an unsuspecting Luke with a spanner, the lockpicker was pale, wound tight.

'I'll either get through the war scot-free,' Manion persisted, 'or I'll get shot. If I get through, I've naught to worry about. If it happens I do get hit, one of two things can happen. 'Tis either a scratch or 'tis bloody bad. If 'tis a scratch, I've naught to worry about. If I'm hurt bad, I'll either pull through or I'll click it. If I get better, the war's over for me, I'll get a free ride back to Blighty, so there's naught to worry about. If I click it and cross the Great Divide 'tis all over and too late for me to worry. So — '

Luke and MacNeely repeated the refrain with him. 'I've naught to worry about.'

2 a.m.

'Let's go,' said Luke.

Van Horn limped into the kitchen, his steps surprisingly silent despite the wooden *sabots* he wore. Without speaking, he shook hands with each man and bowed to Kezia. After filing from the house, they gathered around the pump in the courtyard between the farm buildings.

'Blacken yourselves,' Luke ordered.

They scooped mud from the ground and smeared their hands and faces. Wearing the dark clothing of peasants — Kezia dressed as a man — with their black caps pulled low on their foreheads, they left the courtyard, shadows in the cloud-darkened night.

If they were intercepted and captured by the Germans, they'd be shot as spies, Kezia included. Not for the first time, Luke wished she were safe in England.

He followed a path through a grove of oaks, the night quiet. There were few birds in Belgium, he'd been told, because the farmers assiduously netted and trapped them for pies. When he reached the last of the trees, he paused, the others stopping behind him. Peering into the darkness ahead, he pictured the terrain as he'd seen it a few hours before.

A canal paralleled their route some ten yards to his right. A flat and empty field lay directly ahead, a moor of sparse grass, of broom and heather. There was a second stand of trees, firs and pines, beyond the field. Their objective, the road to Kapellen, a Belgian town five miles inside the border, was a few hundred yards past the woods. Brussels was thirty-five miles to the south.

At the Dutch-Belgian frontier, fifty yards in front of Luke, the Germans had strung a double row of barbed wire, one on the border and the second ten yards inside Occupied Belgium. Border guards patrolled the corridor between the wire. The nearest

129

guardhouse was a mile to the west.

Luke glanced at the illuminated dial of his watch. A pair of German sentries should have passed this point fifteen minutes ago, not to return for an hour and three-quarters. With a tap on the shoulder of the man behind him, Luke signaled his group forward. They dropped to the sandy ground and crawled into the field.

They reached the first barrier in ten minutes, halting while Manion and Sid crawled ahead to the wire. The entanglements, fastened to metal stakes, crisscrossed the open ground. The two men took wire cutters from sheaths at their belts, the cutter handles coated with rubber to deaden the noise if they struck one of the iron stakes.

Among the many things Luke had learned at Dover was the fact that there was only one way to cut barbed wire. Grasp the wire about two inches from a stake and cut between the stake and your hand. An improperly cut wire twangs like a snapped banjo string.

He waited, sweating, for the night was damp — there'd be a ground mist before morning. He heard a muted snip several feet in front of him. Saw a man's form hugging the ground. A hand touched his arm and he started. It was Manion. They'd cut a path through the first barrier.

130

Luke gave the hand signal to advance. They crawled through the gap in the wire and into the patrolled corridor between the entanglements. He heard a voice. Footsteps. His heart leaped in alarm. He signaled the man next to him to stop.

The footsteps came closer. A man's voice began to sing, 'Deutschland, Deutschland uber alles.'

Luke saw a figure outlined against the lesser darkness of the sky. The German was an arm's length away from him. He pressed his body to the ground, listening to the man's slurred singing. The German lurched as he walked and Luke realized he was drunk. The soldier disappeared into the darkness to their left. Luke waited five minutes before signaling the wirecutters to crawl to the second barrier. He glanced behind him, thought he saw MacNeeley but couldn't see Kezia. He pushed his worry about her away. They'd soon be past the last of the barbed wire and on the road to Kapellen.

A wire twanged ahead of him. Sid's wire. Luke froze, the sound echoing and re-echoing in his mind. Wait, he signaled. Time passed, time where he scarcely breathed. No sound came from the darkness.

He thought of Colonel Roosevelt and his Rough Riders in Cuba, advancing along a trail from Siboney, being ambushed at a barbed wire fence, the Mauser bullets making a 'z-z-z-z-z-eu' sound as they whipped through the jungle thicket. How many times had he read and reread that account of one of the newspapermen accompanying the expedition?

Perhaps a dozen of Roosevelt's men had passed into the thicket before he did. Then he stepped across the wire himself, and, from that instant, became the most magnificent soldier I have ever seen. It was as if that barbed-wire strand had formed a dividing line in his life, and that when he stepped across it he left behind him in the bridle path all those unadmirable and conspicuous traits which have so often caused him to be unjustly criticized in civic life, and found on the other side of it, in that Cuban thicket, the coolness, the calm judgment, the towering heroism, which made him, perhaps, the most admired and best beloved of all Americans in Cuba.

What, Luke wondered, awaited him beyond this barbed wire? He was about to signal the wirecutters back to work when a light exploded in the sky to his left. A German star shell. Damn, damn, damn.

Luke and the four others huddled at the edge of the thirty-yard-wide circle of glaring calcium light. The scene was etched white on black. The tangle of barbed wire, the path worn in the grass parallel to and between the two barriers, Manion and Sid lying motionless a few yards in front of him.

He counted the seconds. An eternity passed. He listened, heard nothing. No challenge, no command, no warning shot. Nothing. Thirty seconds. The light glared as brightly as ever. No footsteps. If the Germans watched from beyond the far side of the exploding light, they wouldn't be able to spot the five of them. But if his group was outlined between the light and the enemy . . .

Forty seconds. Forty-five. The light faded. Went out at his count of sixty-three. Darkness closed in. Protecting, comforting. Blessed darkness. Luke crawled to Manion and whispered into his ear. 'Let's get through the wire. Fast.'

Manion and Sid started cutting their way through the second barrier. Again the night was quiet except for the chirping of cicadas. A sound came from behind him. Luke twisted around, heard breathing, sensed it was Kezia. Afraid she was about to break the silence, he reached out to warn her.

A whistle shrilled in the distance off to the right, to the west. Another whistle. Lights bobbed. A half mile away? Closer? He couldn't be sure.

The lights blinked out. Silence again. A hand touched his shoulder, tapped four times. Manion and Sid were through the wire barricade. He passed the message back to Kezia. When she touched him, signaling that both she and MacNeeley had been alerted, he signaled the group forward. Crouching, Luke pushed his way between the first of the severed wire strands.

Suddenly a dog barked. From the west, where he'd seen the lights. A short, sharp yelp. As though he'd found a scent. The sound of men running, still some way off. The running stopped.

'Go ahead of me,' Luke whispered to Kezia, then to MacNeeley.

Kezia moved up to crouch beside him. He grabbed her arm and pushed her forward.

MacNeeley knelt, touched Luke's shoulder, put his lips to Luke's ear. 'What do you intend to do?'

A star shell burst with a plop above and to their left. They were caught between the harsh light and the approaching Germans that he could yet see. Both men froze. Luke held his breath. He saw the tangled wire, three dark and motionless shapes ahead of him, almost through the barrier. Time stretched into an eternity. He waited for the crack of machine-gun or rifle fire.

He wondered if the drunken German had been a ruse. Whether the Germans had been forewarned of their crossing. By the Dutch? By Van Horn?

After an agony of waiting, the light died.

'They must have spotted us,' Luke whispered to MacNeeley 'Take charge. Go ahead. I'll hold them off.'

'The rearguard's my job,' MacNeeley whispered back. 'I'm not so sure they're on to us yet. Go ahead with the others.'

His anger rising, Luke said, 'Follow orders.'

MacNeeley hesitated. Finally he crawled forward, leaving Luke alone. The Germans must have seen them in the second light. Must have spotted their path through the barbed wire. MacNeeley was wrong about them not being spotted.

Luke crawled back to the strip of land between the two rows of wire. Another star shell exploded overhead. He was a fraction of a second slow in freezing. A rifle cracked. The bullet struck the wire beside him and zinged off into the night. Luke held, motionless, resisting the impulse to drop flat on the ground.

Rifle fire cracked from his right. Wild, thank God. As the light over his head dimmed, he pinpointed the direction of the flashes of the guns. A dog barked. The light went out. Luke turned and ran toward the Germans, unhooking a grenade from his belt. He heard a command whispered in German a short way ahead of him.

He stopped, grasping the grenade's lever with his right hand as he pulled the firing pin out with his left. He paused, holding the grenade behind him. Heard a sound to his right. He lobbed the grenade in the direction of the sound, hurled a second grenade to the right of the first.

Turning, Luke threw himself to the ground. The first grenade exploded with a whomp. The second exploded a heartbeat later. A man screamed in pain. Luke sprang up and dashed away from the Germans, realizing he'd never find the break in the wire in the dark. Afraid of completely losing his bearing, he slowed.

Rifle fire cracked from behind him. A star shell burst over his head. In the sudden glare he spotted the break in the wire and raced toward it. A soldier shouted in German, rifle fire snapped. Wire snagged his pants, tore them. He ran on. The light faded and vanished but by then he was beyond the wire, running for the woods.

Luke cursed as he ran. Everything had gone wrong. The Germans were alerted. From the beginning? It seemed a possibility.

Now he'd lost contact with his group.

Shouts erupted ahead of him, to his right. Germans. He slowed, heard the pound of boots. Close, closer. He dropped to one knee, threw himself to the ground. Scrub underbrush rose a few feet in front of him. He crawled beneath its scanty cover.

Men trotted past his hiding place. Three soldiers, he thought, from the sound of their boots. Through the brush, he tried to make out the woods, their rendezvous if they became separated. He thought he saw the dark mass of trees in the near distance.

More steps. Receding. When he could no longer hear them, Luke pushed himself to his feet and trotted forward at a crouch. The figure of a spike-helmeted soldier loomed in front of him. Luke yanked his knuckle knife from his belt, then realized the soldier's back was to him and held, waiting, hoping not to be discovered.

The soldier started to turn. Luke heard a gasp, the startled beginning of a shout and lunged forward, swinging the knife. The steel spikes on the grip guard smashed into the soldier's face. Bone crunched and the German staggered back. Luke pulled the knife back close to his body, thrust it forward, felt the blade plunge into flesh, glance off bone.

Blood, warm and wet, with its characteristic metallic odor, surged onto his hand. The German swayed toward him, trying to cry out, his words lost in a gurgle. Luke pulled the knife from the soldier's body and sprang to one side. The man hit the ground hard. Luke stood stockstill, listening. He heard shouts in the far distance, saw the beam of an electric torch at least a mile away.

He ran, holding the knife, his hand sticky with drying blood. Trees rose in front of him. He slowed to a walk and entered the shelter of the woods, followed what might have been a path. A twig snapped a few feet in front of him.

He tensed and held.

'Louvain.' The word was spoken so softly he almost missed hearing it.

'Mons,' Luke answered.

'Hurry,' MacNeeley told him. 'The others are deeper in the woods. Kezia says she knows the way from here.'

They trotted along a path until they came to a wide swathe cut through the trees. Luke started ahead but MacNeeley held him back. 'The Germans might have planted — ' MacNeeley began.

An explosion flashed twenty yard in front of them. A voice cried out in shock and pain.

'A mine,' MacNeeley said.

Moans guided them forward. Luke stumbled into a figure in the darkness. Kezia. He held her by her arms. 'Are you hurt?' he asked.

'It was Manion.' Her voice was a whisper. Taking a deep breath, she let it out and then led him to Manion's side.

Luke knelt, touched the other mans' chest with his fingers, felt the wetness of blood. There was no heartbeat. He reached for Manion's face, picturing his grin, his red hair. Blood again. Pulp where his face should have been.

'He's dead,' Luke muttered.

Someone said something behind him. 'What?' he asked, his ears still ringing from the explosion.

'Naught to worry about,' he kept saying. Luke recognized Sid's voice.

'A tripwire mine,' MacNeeley said. 'With the wire running to a grenade.'

'Get into the woods,' Luke told the three of them.

'We can't leave him here,' Kezia said, taking his arm to hold him back. 'We can't let them find him.'

'We've no choice.' Luke shook off her hand, went on.

As soon as they were in the woods again, Luke stopped to listen. 'Hear anything?' he asked the others in case his ears weren't working normally yet.

They hadn't. Neither did he. Good. No pursuit or at least no sounds of pursuit. Not yet. He led them on until he reached the verge of the trees where he halted again. The road was only a few hundred yards from here according to their maps.

'This way,' Kezia said. She led the way from the woods, across an open field, into and out of a ditch and onto the dirt road.

'We'll go across the fields,' she told Luke. 'It's safer than the road.'

'No, we don't have time. How far to the house?'

'About two kilometers,' she replied.

He still had to translate kilometers into miles in his head. A mile and a quarter. 'We'll stay on the road,' he said.

They trotted along the left side of the road, Kezia, Luke, Sid, MacNeeley. Four now, instead of five. The Colorado Utes believed four was their magic number.

After what he estimated was a mile, Luke saw beams of light ahead of them. The lights brightened and he heard a harsh rumble, recognized the sound of motorcycles. An unlighted farmhouse sat off to their right.

'That's the place,' Kezia said. 'I'm sure of it.

The roar of the cycles grew as Kezia led them from the road and along a lane beside the house. They crouched behind a hedge as the cycles, three of them, sped past. The helmeted outlines of the cyclists labeled them as German soldiers.

As soon as the cycles were gone, Kezia walked rapidly between the two buildings into a courtyard. There were no lights, the farm seemed deserted. A dog barked and Luke tensed. The dog barked again and he heard the rattle of its chain.

Kezia knocked at a rear door, three quick taps. She paused and repeated the sequence. Through a curtained window, Luke saw a light moving inside the house. The door opened slowly. A short man, a candle in his shaking hand, peered out at them. He was a farmer, moustached, gray-haired, a worn robe hanging loosely on his body.

'Friends,' Kezia said in Dutch. 'Anton sent us.'

The farmer stared at them from frightened eyes. He drew a ragged breath before shrugging and stepping back. Kezia entered, the three men crowding in after her. They found themselves in a kitchen with pots and kettles on shelves along the walls, a fireplace opposite them, a pump next to a sink on one side. Carefully, the farmer placed his candle on the table.

'*Halt. Ihr sind meine Gefangenen.*'

Luke whirled. A German soldier stood in a doorway off the kitchen, a Mauser pistol in his hand.

9

The German soldier with the Mauser was young and blonde with pimples on his face. Luke's group had trained together long enough for him to be able to guess what should happen next. When the time was right, Sid would cause a distraction, MacNeeley, closest to the table, would knock the candle to the floor while, he, Luke, wrested the Mauser from the soldier. The German might have time to get off one shot. If he was damn quick.

The young soldier glanced from Luke to the other two men. He stared, surprised, at Kezia, who, even in her masculine garb, was unmistakably feminine. Though obviously tense, the German's pistol never wavered.

Find a way to lull him, Luke told himself.

Sid began to cough, a wheezing smoker's cough. The German glanced at him suspiciously. Luke kept his own eyes on the soldier's gun hand.

A gun roared, the sound reverberating in the small room, the noise loud and startling. As the soldier's jaw dropped in shock, Luke sprang forward, grasped the man's wrist and twisted. The gun thudded to the wooden floor. Sid flung himself forward and retrieved the Mauser.

The German dropped to his knees. Luke, wary, suspecting a trick, kept a firm grip on the man's wrist, letting go when the German fell away from him, sprawling on his back on the floor. He mumbled words Luke couldn't make out. A spasm shuddered through his body and he lay still. The crotch of his pants darkened as his bladder let go.

Out of the corner of his eye, Luke saw MacNeeley gesturing toward the room behind him. He whirled to stare into the room, saw a bedstead outlined against the pale rectangle of a window. MacNeeley, his Webley in one hand, carried the candle to the doorway. A boy, his fair face ashen, stood just inside the bedroom holding an oversized pistol at his side. He looked ten years old at the most.

'Cornelius.' The farmer pushed past MacNeeley and dropped to his knees in front of the boy. Cornelius handed him the pistol. The farmer embraced him, enfolding him in his arms.

'He's dead,' Kezia said.

Luke looked down. Kezia, kneeling at the German's side, was, with Sid's help, rolling him over onto his stomach. Blood stained the lower back of his gray-green uniform jacket and oozed to the floor.

'Check the other rooms,' Luke ordered.

MacNeeley and Sid flung open the other two inner doors leading from the kitchen. The rooms beyond were silent. Warily, guns drawn, the two men left the kitchen to search the rest of the house.

The farmer, who'd been murmuring to the boy, rose and carried the pistol into the kitchen where he offered it to Luke, then slumped onto a bench at the table. Seeing it was a one shot, Luke still checked to be sure no bullet remained in the barrel, then tucked the pistol under his belt.

Kezia spoke to the farmer in Dutch. Catching the name of Cornelius, Luke decided she must be asking if the boy was all right. When the farmer nodded, she went on talking to him. After a time she looked up at Luke.

'He says there's no other Germans here. Only the one soldier. He doesn't recognize the man, he wasn't one of those stationed in the village. He says the Germans have been searching all the farms in the area, not just his.'

'He and the boy live here alone?' Luke asked.

'Herr Van Pelt's wife is dead. The boy's his

son. His only son. Cornelius.'

'Ask him if he has a canvas or old blanket we can roll the body up in. Then he'll need to scrub the blood from the floor.'

Kezia spoke to Van Pelt. At first he didn't seem to understand. Kezia spoke to him again. Finally he gestured toward the outer door and mumbled a few words.

'There's an old horse blanket in the barn,' she translated. 'No horse, the Germans confiscated it.'

Van Pelt got up, shambled to the sink, lifted a bucket into it and worked the pump until the bucket was half-full of water. He carried it to the dead German, knelt, and began scrubbing the dark stain next to the body with a worn brush. MacNeeley and Sid returned to the kitchen.

'There's only the lad,' Sid told Luke. 'He's tucked up in bed. Not asleep. Scared.'

'I found this chap's bicycle in front of the house,' MacNeeley said. 'Wheeled it around to the rear.'

'So we have one dead German and one bicycle on our hands,' Luke said.

'We can't leave them here,' Kezia said. 'The Germans will ransack every farm in the area searching for the missing soldier. Herr Van Pelt will be shot if the body's found here.'

'I wasn't planning to leave the body,' Luke

146

said curtly. Did she think he was an idiot? He glanced at Van Pelt who was scrubbing in aimless circles.

'He'll wear a hole in the bloody floor,' Sid said. Looking more closely at the farmer, Luke saw tears coursing down Van Pelt's cheeks. 'Tell him he doesn't have to worry,' Luke said to Kezia. 'We'll dispose of the body and the bike.'

She crouched by the farmer, spoke softly to him. He stopped scrubbing but held the brush clenched in his hand on the floor in front of him as he mumbled a few words.

'It's not the German,' Kezia said. 'It's the boy. He's afraid for the boy.'

Turning to Sid, Luke said, 'Fetch the horse blanket from the barn.'

Returning his attention to Van Pelt, Luke spoke to Kezia. 'The Germans will never find out what really happened. Even if they find the body, they'll never know who killed him.'

'You don't understand,' she said. 'Herr Van Pelt's son killed this man. The boy has no mother. His father's afraid of what will become of him. In this kind of a world how can he raise Cornelius to become a man he can be proud of?'

'The boy's a blooming hero,' MacNeeley put in. 'What more does he want?'

'What can I tell him?' Luke asked Kezia.

147

'There's no good answer. He can only do the best he knows how.' Luke reached down and helped Van Pelt to his feet just as Sid returned with a tattered blanket.

Turning Van Pelt so he faced him, Luke said, 'We have to hide the German's body and his bicycle where they'll never be found. Where, tell me where?'

Kezia translated his words into Dutch. Van Pelt wiped his wet eyes with his sleeve and shook his head.

'We've no time,' Luke said urgently. 'We have to hide the body and leave before dawn.'

Van Pelt, standing with slumped shoulders listened to Kezia, shaking his head before she finished as though the disposal of the dead German didn't concern him.

Luke grasped the farmer's shoulders and shook him savagely. Van Pelt stared at him, fear creeping into his eyes. 'Cornelius,' Luke snapped. 'Think of the boy. Your son.'

Kezia's voice took on sharpness as she translated. Van Pelt blinked. Shaking off Luke's grasp, he pulled himself erect, looked down at the dead German, being rolled into the blanket by Sid and MacNeeley. He nodded. Luke thought he noticed the hint of a smile on Van Pelt's lips before he turned away, motioning for Luke to follow him.

'Sid,' Luke ordered, 'watch the road from

148

the front of the house. Mac, stay here.'

Luke and Kezia followed Van Pelt through one of the inner doors, stopping behind him in a rear hallway while he lighted a lantern. They went outside, crossed the courtyard and circled behind a pig sty and a chicken coop. When Van Pelt stopped at the rear of a shed, Luke smelled the sweet, nauseating odor of excrement.

Van Pelt placed his lantern on the ground and leaned forward to grasp a large metal ring. Luke gripped the ring and together they lifted a heavy cover and rolled it to one side. The fetid odor was overwhelming. Van Pelt, seemingly not bothered by the stench, spoke rapidly.

'He says this is the back of their privy,' Kezia told Luke. 'As you can see, or smell, he'll soon have to empty it or move the privy. He says he'll eventually move the privy so the German can remain undisturbed. He seems to feel this is the best place to hide the body. A most appropriate place, he says.'

'All right. Tell him we'll dump the body in here. And the bicycle. Sid can dismantle it and we'll lay the pieces on top of Fritz to weigh him down.'

Van Pelt spoke to Luke, laughing grimly.

'What did he say?' Luke asked.

'Nothing of importance. A local joke.'

'Tell me.'

'He said that with the German here, he'll think of him every time — ' She hesitated. 'Herr Van Pelt will remember him at least once a day.'

Luke smiled wryly as he gripped the Belgian's shoulder to let him know he understood. And approved.

While Sid disassembled the bicycle in the kitchen, MacNeeley carried the German's body, wrapped in the old blanket, to the privy and, after weighing the arms and legs, let it slide into the muck of the pit. They brought the bicycle parts from the house, shoved them down on the body, weighed down both bike and body with stones from a nearby crumbling wall. Then they eased the cover back on.

They trooped to a pump in the courtyard. Luke washed quickly. While Kezia pumped water for the other two men, he walked to the house. The sky to the east was a pale grayish yellow with the coming of the dawn.

Herr Van Pelt stood in the doorway.

'Cornelius,' Luke said. 'I'd like to see him.' he added in broken German.

Van Pelt led him to a bedroom where the boy lay with his eyes open, staring at the ceiling.

Summoning up his imperfect German,

150

Luke spoke to the boy. 'What you did was very brave. Do you understand me?' Cornelius nodded.

'You saved my life and the lives of my friends. You served your country well. You should be proud.' He reached down to touch the boy's forehead. 'If I ever have a son, I want him to be like you.'

He left the room with Van Pelt behind him. When he reached the outside door, the farmer touched his sleeve. 'Thank you,' he said in German.

Luke nodded. He'd only told the boy the truth.

When he returned to the pump, Kezia was washing while Sid and MacNeeley dried themselves off.

'Spotted a wagon in the barn,' Sid said. 'No horse but there's an old mule.'

'Sounds good. Hook up the mule.' As Sid and MacNeeley headed for the barn, Luke handed Kezia the towel. Their fingers met. He drew in his breath. She looked up at him, her face in the shadows. Without realizing what he meant to do, he bent and brushed his lips over hers.

Still looking at him, she backed away, her hand going to her mouth. He followed her, putting his hands on her shoulders.

'No.' She shook her head. 'Please don't. I

don't want you to.'

Luke didn't believe she meant it. Her quickened breathing told him another story.

'It's wrong,' she said. 'The time is wrong. The place is wrong.'

'Another time?' He let the question hang.

'No, I didn't mean that. You're confusing me.'

Since she hadn't tried to free herself, he pulled her closer, his mouth closing over hers in a real kiss. She didn't fight him, didn't resist. For a moment he thought he felt her respond but then she went limp, her lips motionless under his. He drew back, still holding her, stifling his urge to try to make her respond.

She broke free, walked past the black jut of the pump, stood looking away from him at the brightening sky.

'You wanted me to kiss you,' he said.

'You're wrong. Quite wrong.'

Coming up behind her, he put his arms about her waist and drew her back against him, excitement pulsing inside him. She made a muffled sound and he turned her toward him, saw she was crying and released her, his ardor dampened. He didn't know what to do or say.

'Why are you crying?' he asked.

She wiped her eyes. 'Because you're being

a fool. And because I'm acting even more like one than you are.' She swung abruptly away from him and ran toward the barn. He didn't follow.

Luke sighed, needing the comfort of a cigarette in the worst way. Walking slowly, he headed toward the barn. In the gathering light he noticed the red of a begonia bed and, somehow, the sight of the flowers startled him. As though flowers didn't belong here.

Kezia's right, he told himself. *I behaved like a fool.* A genuine jackass. He wondered what T.J. would have said.

'Some things are worth being a jackass about,' his father had told him once. 'A heap of money, for one. Women, for another.' T.J. spat tobacco juice into a brass spittoon. He corrected himself. 'A few women, that is.'

Luke smiled. T.J. would agree, he was sure, that Kezia was one of those few.

★　★　★

The ancient mule plodded south, reluctantly drawing the wagon along the road to Brussels. Herr Van Pelt, his son Cornelius beside him, sat holding the reins loosely in one hand. Although the sun barely topped a row of fountain-like elms to their left, the day was already warm, a July day in the middle of September.

The gates at the railroad crossing were down, barring their way, but, though Van Pelt could see for several kilometers in both directions, there was no sign of an approaching train. He looked to his right and left, searching for another road, a lane at least, but saw none.

As he neared the crossing, two German soldiers emerged from a hut next to the gate, a young private and an older sergeant. The young soldier, rifle slung on his shoulder approached the wagon. Van Pelt drew up and, without being asked, reached into his pocket and brought out his *carte d'identité*, a pass with his photograph and description issued to him by the German commander in Kapellen.

The private studied the card, muttering angrily to himself, and it took Van Pelt several seconds to realize the man's anger wasn't directed at him but at someone or something else. Looking past the young private he saw the sergeant start walking toward them, limping. Probably disabled at the front, Van Pelt told himself, and sent here to recuperate. When the German private handed Van Pelt his identity card, he carefully returned it to his wallet and picked up the reins. The private turned but the sergeant was blocking his way, pointing at the wagon.

'What does he carry, Schwartz?' the sergeant asked in German. His intonation, Van Pelt decided, was Prussian.

'A wagonload of potatoes,' Schwartz said somewhat sullenly.

The sergeant limped to the wagon and looked over the side at the potatoes. 'Search the peasant's wagon,' he ordered.

Private Schwartz flushed and for an instant Van Pelt thought he'd protest. He nodded curtly, however, and approached the wagon.

Van Pelt sucked in his breath. 'Sergeant,' he protested, 'as you can see, I have only potatoes. My son and I are taking them to the market in Brussels at the order of the German authorities in Kapellen. Brussels needs potatoes. This winter, they say, will be long and hard for all of us in Belgium.'

'The fault's your own,' the sergeant said. 'If you Belgians hadn't resisted our armies we would have thrown the English into the Channel and turned the flank of the French. I'd be in Paris now, not in this hole.'

'We didn't understand,' Van Pelt said, 'that your army came to Belgium to bring us German *kultur*. At the time we mistakenly thought you meant to kill us.'

The sergeant frowned as though uncertain how he should take Van Pelt's words. All at once the sergeant laughed, slapping his thigh. Still smiling, he turned to Private Schwartz who was watching from beside the wagon.

'Do as I said,' the sergeant told him. 'Search this good farmer's wagon.'

Private Schwartz clambered over the side and stood unsteadily atop the potatoes.

'He'll bruise them,' Van Pelt complained.

The sergeant shrugged. 'It is the war.'

Schwartz unhooked his bayonet from his belt and, after fastening it to the barrel of his rifle, poked among the potatoes. The sergeant limped to the rear of the wagon where he climbed onto one of the spokes of the wheel to watch the private.

'There,' he said, pointing to a higher pile of potatoes on the far side of the wagon bed. 'Search there.'

Cornelius, on his knees on the wagon seat, watching them, leaned forward as though to speak. Van Pelt placed his hand on his son's arm and the boy remained silent.

Private Schwartz thrust his bayonet into the pile, drawing it out with a potato impaled on the point.

'Now search there,' the sergeant said, pointing to the front of the wagon. 'Must I tell you everything?'

Again Schwartz, his face brick red, thrust the bayonet into the potatoes.

'Attack the potatoes until you strike wood,' the sergeant ordered.

'You'll ruin them,' Van Pelt said. 'I'll get next to nothing in *La Capitale.*'

'Which is more than you deserve.'

Schwartz probed among the potatoes, his bayonet thudding into the wagon bed on the sides, the front and the back. 'There's nothing hidden here,' he reported with a faint tinge of triumph in his voice. 'As he said, he carries only the potatoes.'

'Did you think I was smuggling a British army into Brussels under my potatoes?' Van Pelt asked.

Taking a handful of potatoes from the wagon, the sergeant stepped from the wheel to the road.

'Those are my potatoes,' Van Pelt said.

'This is your toll for the use of the road,' the sergeant told him. 'A word of warning. Your tongue will get you in trouble before many days are past. It's fortunate for you that I'm a man of the world.'

Van Pelt said nothing. He saw Schwartz, facing away from the sergeant, raise his eyebrows. The private leaped from the wagon to the ground.

Van Pelt looked at the sergeant. 'May I be on my way?' he asked.

'Proceed,' the sergeant told him. He tossed

one of the potatoes to Schwartz.

The private raised the crossing gate; Van Pelt flicked the reins. The mule turned to give him a reproachful look but then leaned into the harness and the wagon jounced across the single railroad track.

'The sergeant is a man of the world,' he murmured to Cornelius, 'who steals a poor farmer's potatoes.'

They drove into Brussels from the north with a strong wind at the backs and with dark clouds piled high in the sky behind them. Van Pelt headed toward the Old Town, once a great merchant city with seven routes leading from its toll gates, turning onto a side street a few blocks before reaching the Grand Palace. Brussels was quiet and somber, a city of black-garbed civilians hurrying about their business while German soldiers marched in the streets or, off-duty, sat in boisterous clusters in otherwise deserted cafés.

When he reached Ixelles, Van Pelt guided the mule across the tram tracks in the cobbled street to an alley between houses, turning in at an open gate and stopping in front of a stable. A boy ran from the rear of one of the houses, ignoring the sprinkles of rain. Nodding to Van Pelt and Cornelius, he opened the door to a barn smelling pungently of hay and horses.

Van Pelt waited until the boy closed the door behind them before he climbed down, took a lantern from a hook on his wagon and lit it. Finding a crowbar among the tools at the rear of the barn, he brought it back to the wagon. Cornelius was already watering the mule.

Placing the lantern on the floor, Van Pelt crawled under the wagon. He thrust the crowbar over his head, prying loose the end of a board. He yanked the board free and put it on the floor. After he'd pried loose a second board, MacNeeley pushed himself from the cramped crawl space beneath the false floor of the wagon followed by Kezia, Sid and Luke. They stood beside the wagon stretching and brushing off their clothes.

Van Pelt methodically replaced the boards, then drove off with Cornelius to deliver their potatoes and return home. The four waited, the rain drumming on the barn roof until, shortly after sunset, a bushily moustached Belgian, a man Van Pelt had referred to as the Walrus, led them to the main house, the Pension Pierard. Kezia, Luke noticed, avoided the Walrus, walking as far from him as she could. After eating *boudin-blanc* and *fritre*, sausage and hot, crisp french fries, they were being shown to their separate rooms when Kezia said to Luke, 'I'll contact Andre tomorrow.' Andre was their principal contact in Brussels.

He wished he'd had the chance to ask her why she avoided the Walrus although, come to think of it, the man did smell as though he hadn't washed in a year.

Luke bolted his door and walked to the window of his small bedroom, holding the curtain to one side to peer into the darkness, seeing only the rain slanting against the panes. The room looked and smelled foreign with its pervasive odor of horses and strange foods, its high, lumpy bed, its bare walls decorated only by a single picture of Jesus with a crown of thorns encircling his blood-red head. A light appeared in a window at right angles to his own. As Luke watched, a figure crossed between the candle and the gauze curtains. A woman's figure in a long white gown. Kezia. He waited but she didn't reappear.

Luke let his curtain fall. He stripped to his underwear and lay on top of the quilt on the bed. The night was warm, too warm. He laced his fingers behind his head and stared at the ceiling. Thunder rolled in the distance and when he closed his eyes the thunder became the roar of artillery and he heard the chatter of German machine-guns, felt his hands on Manion's lifeless body . . .

He woke up sweating. The room was still dark, the rain beating steadily on the roof overhead. He swung from the bed and crossed to the window. To his left, lightning flickered and thunder rumbled in the distance as the storm moved on. The window at right angles to his was dark.

Kezia.

He remembered the scent of her when he'd held her, the scent of flowers coming through the overlaying mud and dirt they'd acquired on their way to the farm. He remembered the feel of her lips under his, cool and tantalizing. He wanted her. Pulling open the casement window, he leaned out, feeling the sting of rain on his face. Her window, four feet away, was open slightly. He reached across, touched the narrow stone sill as the rain soaked his head and undershirt. The cold and wet failed to quench the fire in his blood.

Luke scrambled back into his bedroom. He pulled on his pants, crossed the room, unbolting and opening the door. He looked both ways along the hall. The house was dark, no one seemed to be astir. He slipped from his room and padded in bare feet down the hall, his hand feeling for the corner, finding it. He hurried down the adjoining hall to the first door. Kezia's door.

Luke turned the knob and pushed but, as

161

he'd expected, the door was locked. He tapped softly. Waited. Heard no sound from inside. He tapped again, a little louder. Waited.

'Who is it?' Kezia spoke from close to the door.

'Luke.'

The bolt rattled as it slid aside. She opened the door a crack, the light in his eyes making him blink. The door swung wider and she saw she held a candle, the light gleaming in her warm gray eyes. Her auburn hair, cut short, glowed, her nightgown, long and white, was the one he'd seen her in. She couldn't have brought it from England, they'd traveled too light.

Accepting what he chose to interpret as an invitation to enter, he stepped inside. She backed away, her gaze never leaving his, her expression unreadable. He reached behind him and closed the door. Advancing, he reached for the candle, took it from her and placed it on a table.

Putting his arms around her, he drew her to him. She made no attempt to resist. Or to help. There were, he saw, tears in her eyes.

'Why are you crying? There's no need to cry.'

'I should never have volunteered to come

with you,' she said. 'It was a mistake from the start. I should have known. I should have known.'

His lips sought hers but she turned her head away and he kissed her cheek, tasting her tears. Breaking away, she walked to the curtained window. He followed, stopped behind her.

'Should have known what?' he demanded. Could she mean she cared for him?

She said, 'That I'd feel so sorry for you, Luke.'

He blinked. 'Sorry?' he repeated. What was she talking about?

She sighed. 'I'm sorry for anybody who becomes involved with C. No one should. I shouldn't have. And you. I shouldn't have let you.'

'Let me? I don't know what you mean.'

She swung to face him, wiping at the tears on her cheeks with the back of her hand. 'Do you actually expect to get safely back to England?' she asked angrily.

'Of course. With some luck.'

She shook her head as though she thought him beyond hope, beyond saving. Suddenly she threw her arms around him, pressing her head to his chest. Confused, he held her awkwardly as his excitement rekindled. He laid his hand on the back of her head and caressed her hair, soft as silk under his fingers.

Kezia stepped back from him, took his hand in hers and led him to the narrow brass bed. Releasing him, she slid beneath the coverlet, looked up and held out her arms to him.

10

Luke stared down at Kezia, hardly believing she meant for him to join her in bed. It was an invitation he had no intention of refusing. He reached down to pull the cotton quilt back to uncover her.

'No,' she whispered, clutching it tightly about her. 'On top.'

'On top?' he echoed.

'Lay on top of the coverlet.'

Good God, was she taking up old-fashioned bundling with the quilt as a bundling board?

'If you find you can't get all you want of something,' T.J. used to say, 'take what you can get and wait awhile. More than likely the rest will come your way.'

T.J. hadn't been talking about women. Or had he? In his younger days, before he married Luke's mother, T.J. had a reputation as a ladies' man. When Luke heard of it years later, the stories seemed like ancient history, interesting in their way but not quite real. His father's advice, though, seemed appropriate at the moment.

Luke eased off his pants and stretched out

on the bed beside Kezia with the quilt between them. The candle chose that moment to gutter out. In the dark, he leaned to her, heard her soft breathing, found her lips with his and kissed her gently. Her lips yielded, responsive to his so he deepened the kiss. Her hand went to the nape of his neck, holding his head to her.

All too conscious of his arousal, he kept his body away from hers, not letting it touch her even through the coverlet, determined not to be rebuffed again. This time he'd let her call the shots. Her breathing quickened, her hands slid down his back and she strained toward him.

His tongue probed, tasting her lips until she turned her head away. Tamping down his excitement, he made no attempt to pursue her but lay propped on one elbow, peering at the white blur of her face. It was impossible to see her expression so he concentrated on the sound of the rain gusting against the window next to the bed to keep himself from reaching out for her.

He heard her sit up in the bed and mutter, 'Damn you.' Her tone was furious and, sensing she was about to slap him, he braced for the blow. Instead, she laid her hand against his cheek, the intended blow becoming a caress as her fingers roamed lightly down his cheek, found his lips and lingered. His tongue touched the tip of first one of her fingers, then another. She gasped with surprise and, he hoped, pleasure.

Kezia rolled away from him and stood on the floor on the far side of the bed. The only sound in the room was the steady beat of the rain. He pictured her tall, lovely body as he'd seen in the candlelight, curves and shadows only partly concealed by her white gown, and held his breath, waiting.

At last he murmured her name. 'Kezia.'

'I'm afraid,' she whispered.

'Don't be. There's no need to be afraid. I won't — '

He hesitated, searching for the words that would bring her back to him. 'I won't do anything you don't want me to.'

'That's why I'm so afraid,' she said, her voice pitched so low he could hardly hear her. 'Not of you, of myself.'

He let out his breath in surprise, in elation. Sliding across the bed, he stood up so close to her he could feel her warmth, but he didn't touch her. For long moments neither moved, neither spoke. His senses tingled with her nearness, he ached with his need for her.

Unable to wait any longer, he took her in his arms, his lips closing over hers as her hands gripped his back. Urgently, he pulled her closer, feeling the curved softness of her body through the fabric of her gown. Kezia's mouth opened to his, their tongues met, hers retreated shyly. She moaned, her arms tightening around him.

Clasped one to the other, they tumbled sideways onto the bed, Luke turning her so she fell beneath him. He yanked the pillow out from under her and flung it aside. His hand trailed down her side, over the sweet curve of her hip to her thigh, slid lower, searching for the hem of her gown. He touched her bare ankle, ran his fingers up beneath her nightdress. She began to tremble and jerked her head away, her teeth chattering.

At first he thought she was cold, realizing belatedly she was terrified. He removed his hand from the warm flesh of her lower leg, reassuringly caressing her through the fabric of her gown, rubbing her back in ever widening spirals.

'Darling Kezia,' he murmured, then paused, surprised at his words of affection.

She sighed, nestling closer to him. When her trembling lessened and finally stopped, he drew her closer, feeling oddly protective, wanting to shield her. But from what? Him? Herself? His cheek pillowed against her hair, he patted rather than caressing her back.

She murmured but, with her lips close against his bare shoulder, he couldn't make out her words. 'What?' he asked. 'What is it?'

'Why can't it always be like this?'

Unsure of exactly what she meant, he didn't ask, instead tried to reassure her by saying, 'It can be. I'll make it be. Somehow. Someday.'

He felt her shaking her head and added, 'I promise.'

And he'd keep that promise, he told himself. Kezia stirred emotions he'd never before felt for a woman. He wanted her desperately but at the same time wanted to keep her from all harm.

They lay quietly in each other's arms. As though they were in a cocoon, Luke thought, safe from the storm raging outside the house, from the war that had spread like a greater storm across Europe, from the uncertainties of a threatening future. Here they were warm and at peace.

Kezia stirred in his arms as though she'd dozed off and was now beginning to awaken. She turned onto her back and his never-quite-conquered desire flared. His arm slid up along her side to cup her breasts through the cloth of her gown. She shifted uneasily but didn't draw away. His hand drifted to the neck of her gown, his exploring fingers discovering a satin ribbon tied in a bow. Taking one end of the ribbon between his fingers, Luke pulled slowly and steadily until he felt the bow come undone.

Kezia's hand closed over his and he stopped, expecting her to push him away. Instead, she led his fingers to the opening in the top of her gown, led him beneath the soft fabric until his hand touched the warmth of her flesh.

He pushed the top of her gown to one side. She caressed the side of his face as he drew the cloth down and away from her breast. He leaned forward until he found her breast with his lips, her nipple rising and hardening under his tongue. Her arms closed around his neck, holding him to her. As his tongue circled her nipple, his mind whirled with the sweet scent of her, the demand of his arousal, his ever-increasing desire for her, his —

He raised his head from her breast, about to speak. But when he realized what he meant to say, he held.

'What is it?' she whispered.

The phrase that had made him draw back in astonishment couldn't be true. He'd wanted to tell her how much he desired her, how much he loved her. Love? He didn't believe love crept up on a man unawares. And he had never used the word lightly, to seduce a woman. Yet, if not love, what was it he felt for her?

She stiffened in his arms. 'Listen!' She whispered urgently.

He sat up, listening, heard footsteps on the stairs. Running footsteps. He was swinging his feet off the bed when the tapping came at the door. He grabbed his pants.

'Kezia.' Was the voice from the hall MacNeeley's?

His pants on, he started for the door but Kezia's hand gripped his arm.

'No,' she muttered. 'Not you.' He heard her pad across to the door.

'What is it?' she asked through the door.

'LeMur's here. Andre sent him.' Now Luke was sure it was MacNeeley. 'Something's gone wrong downstairs. I couldn't rouse Luke. I'll get Sid to keep trying.'

'Wait,' she said, but there was no reply.

Luke stepped past her, found the bolt, slid it free and started to ease the door open.

She gripped his arm again. 'Let me go first. They mustn't see you coming from my room.'

He didn't argue, she was right. 'You take them downstairs,' he said. 'I'll follow in a minute. Hurry.'

He heard a rustle of clothing — probably her robe — then she eased past him. Before she could open the door, he turned her toward him and kissed her, a quick hard kiss, then let her go.

She opened the door. More footsteps pounded up the stairs, a light wavered in the hall and a knocking came from around the turn in the corridor. From the door to his room. Shutting the door behind Kezia, he ran to her window and yanked it open. Climbing through, he stood on the narrow ledge in the darkness with the rain a monotonous drizzle on his face. Though he couldn't see for sure, he was positive he'd left his own window open. Without waiting to think, he leaped across the gap separating the windows, his momentum hurling him against the window frame. He stumbled backwards, twisted to one side, grasped the sill with one hand as he fell, whacking his arm on the ledge, his knees slamming into the brick on the side of the house.

Luke drew ragged breaths. As he pulled himself up, he heard a shout from the yard below him, from behind the house. Levering his body onto the ledge, he cast a quick look through the mist lightened by the coming of dawn and thought he saw a man running swiftly and silently. Edging himself forward, he fell into the room.

The knocking at his door was rapid,

insistent. 'Good God, Luke, wake up,' Sid called from the hall.

'Coming,' he answered. Standing, he thrust the wet curtain aside and looked from the open window toward the rear of the house. Saw nothing. Heard nothing. He could have sworn a man had shouted, that he'd seen a running figure near the stable.

'Luke!'

He limped across the room, cursing his bruised knees. Flinging open the door, he blinked in the light from Sid's lantern.

'You all right, governor?' Sid asked, glancing from Luke's damp hair to the dirt on the knees of his pants.

'I'm okay,' Luke told him. 'What's going on?'

'A bloke named LeMur's here. He's got the wind up. Thinks the bloody Huns are after him. You'd better come down. Take this. He handed Luke the lantern and headed toward the stairs.

Luke threw on clothes by the lantern's light. Once downstairs, he found them all in the main room, MacNeeley, Kezia in her robe, Sid, the Walrus and a man Luke had never seen before. LeMur. A tall, thin man wearing a wet black raincoat.

'M. LeMur came to warn us,' Kezia told Luke. 'There were arrests last night. Two of

173

our friends are prisoners of the Germans, another's dead. M. LeMur was away on an errand, stumbled on the raid when he returned, but managed to escape in the darkness.'

'I regret this exceedingly much,' LeMur said in English. 'I suspect those in St. Gilles with your Miss Cavell by this time may have said more than they should have said. Without knowing what they did. I do not blame them in the least. The Hun — '

'Were you followed?' Luke broke in, thinking of the running man in the courtyard. 'Did the Germans follow you?'

LeMur gestured emphatically. 'No, no, of a certainty they did not follow me. I was most careful. We all are safe for the present time. Tomorrow, who knows?' He shrugged.

'He thinks the Huns may force one of the prisoners they took last night to talk.' Kezia bit her lip. 'A man with a wife and children.'

'We can't stay here,' MacNeeley said. 'LeMur thinks he wasn't followed but how can he — or we — be sure?'

Luke nodded at Mac. 'Right.' Turning to Kezia, he asked, 'Is there another house where we can go?'

She looked at LeMur and the Belgian nodded.

'Get dressed,' Luke told her.

'We'll leave in five minutes,' Luke said as Kezia hurried from the room. 'Take everything we brought, don't leave a trace.' He glanced at the Walrus. 'You'll go with us? Guide us?'

'It's not so simple,' the Walrus said. 'I don't know this place you will go. I'll stay here, it's better that way.'

'No,' Luke said curtly, 'it won't be better.'

A pounding came from the front of the house. Shouts from the street outside. Commands. German voices. The pounding came again, the slamming of a rifle butt against the panels of the front door. Startled, they all froze for an instant. Luke's hand touched the revolver in the holster under his arm, wishing he hadn't left his old familiar Peacemaker in England.

'The back way,' the Walrus said. 'I'll show you.'

Kezia. Luke ran to the stairs and started up just as she appeared at the top once again dressed in a man's shirt and pants.

'The Germans are here,' he said as she ran down to join him.

Thinking again of the figure he'd seen as he leapt from one window to the other, Luke suddenly realized what the man had been doing. The pounding at the front was a ruse. The Huns wanted them to flee from the back of the house. They were being driven into a trap . . . just like the way he'd seen cowpunchers herd wild horses into a corral.

He raced through the house, Kezia at his heels, caught the others before they reached the back door. 'Not this way,' he said. 'I heard them in the back from my window. Didn't realize then — ' He broke off and grasped the Walrus' arm. 'There must be another way, another escape route.'

'The roof.'

'Good. Show us.'

They followed the short heavyset Belgian to the stairs, climbed one flight, climbed another to a dark and musty attic. Grunting, the Walrus lifted a large trunk onto the top of a still larger one, clambered to the top and unbolted and pushed open a trap door in the roof. Pale light outlined the rectangle. The Walrus put his head into the opening and looked in all directions before climbing out. He motioned to them to follow.

One by one they climbed onto the trunks and the Walrus pulled them through the opening to the steeply pitched roof on the side of the house. Kezia, ahead of Luke, hesitated before taking the Walrus' hand, finally letting him clasp it and help her up.

The sky was brightening behind the tower of a church in the distance, smoke curled

176

from a few of the multitude of chimneys and a cart rattled over the cobbles on the unseen streets below. There was no sign of the Germans.

The Walrus led them single file down to the roof's edge. He paused. The roof of the next house was a good five feet away and several feet lower. Crouching, the Walrus leaped, landing on hands and knees on the slates. MacNeeley and Sid followed, then Kezia, Luke behind her.

Luke climbed to where he could see over the roof's peak. The Brussels' skyline was etched against the dawn, towers, domes, slender belfries, gables decorated with stars, clusters of chimney pots. He glanced behind him. LeMur stood on the far side of the gap between the roofs staring down at the ground thirty feet below.

'Get your bloody ass across,' Sid urged in a stage whisper.

LeMur, obviously terrified, shook his head.

'Jump,' Luke muttered.

'*Sautes*,' the Walrus hissed.

'The Huns,' Kezia said softly.

LeMur stared at her, then retreated a few paces, ran forward with a shambling gait and jumped, his black-garbed arms fluttering like ineffectual wings. He landed on the roof's edge, clawed the air. Before anyone else could move, the Walrus leaped forward, reached out and grasped LeMur's arm, and hauled him onto the roof. His bulk hid massive strength.

A slate clattered to the gutter and fell over the side. Luke held his breath, waiting to hear it strike the street. There was no sound from below, none at all.

They hurried across the roof, crouching, stepped over to another, descended a ladder into an attic and climbed down narrow stairs. When a woman in a nightdress appeared in a doorway, the Walrus spoke rapidly to her under his breath. She drew back and eased the door shut. They reached the street, found it deserted. Again there were no Germans. Where the hell were they? Luke didn't like the set-up, not at all.

'We must separate,' the Walrus said. 'We are too many.'

'I'll take Sid and Mac with me,' Kezia said. 'M. LeMur must not be seen with any of us. He can meet us later.' LeMur dabbed at the sweat on his face, making Luke wonder if he'd be okay on his own.

'I am all right,' LeMur said as though sensing his hesitation. 'I am perfectly all right.' He walked away from them along the tree-lined avenue, his steps quick yet unsteady.

'The storeroom of the pipes,' the Walrus

said to Kezia as soon as LeMur was out of earshot. 'Do you know it?' When she nodded, he said, 'We will meet there.'

She glanced at Luke. He started to object but she shook her head almost imperceptibly. Flanked by MacNeeley and Sid, she walked away.

Luke wasn't happy about them splitting up but perhaps it was necessary. A group of two or three attracted less attention than one of five. At least it had stopped raining. The Walrus led Luke from the street into an alley, onto another parallel street, turned right down still another alley that took them to a narrow lane lined with shops.

Doors and windows were open, a fat old man vigorously wielded a broom to sweep the rain water from in front of his bakery shop into the gutter. A wagon rattled by on its way to the marketplace.

The Walrus slowed as they approached an intersection where five streets met, one a main thoroughfare with tram tracks running down its center. Two men sat on a bench in an island in the street, waiting. Here the shops, a butcher's, a funeral parlor, a grocery, a postal office, were shuttered. On reaching the intersection, the Walrus turned sharply right into a street without trees. The buildings were older wooden structures with the paint peeling from the signs over the shops. They followed an alley to a door at the rear of a ramshackle shed-like building. Taking a key from his pocket, the Walrus opened the door and stood aside while Luke entered. They were in a little-used storeroom where long sections of pipe lay piled on racks along the walls.

'We will wait,' the Walrus said.

Luke found a chair and sat in the shadows beside a murky window, facing the door. The Walrus leaned against a dust-covered counter, taking a cigarette from his pocket and lighting it. Luke's mouth watered at the tobacco scent. He could use a drag or two himself. But he said nothing, watching as the other man rubbed his hands on his pants as though to clean them.

'The way she acts,' the Walrus said, 'you'd think I was a leper.'

Luke knew he meant Kezia.

'They were savages,' the Walrus went on, 'and the only way to treat a savage is with force. You must make them fear you. You're an American, you had the red Indians to deal with, you must understand.'

'You were in America?' Luke asked.

'No, no, not American, I've never been to America. The Congo. I was a post commander in the Congo Free State for ten years.

An officer must do what's expected of him, you understand that.'

The Walrus fell silent, smoke from his cigarette curling above his head. God, the Congo, Luke thought. He'd read Roger Casement's reports from that private fiefdom of the king of Belgium where the natives harvested wild rubber to be processed into bicycle and automobile tires, toiling in the jungles to meet the ever rising quotas of Leopold's trading agents.

The *Force Publique*, recruited from the cannibals of Lualaba and led by Europeans like the Walrus, enforced the quotas. The soldiers were paid low salaries but received high commissions based on the amount of rubber collected by the natives in their districts.

To make sure the quotas were met, they took hostages, usually women and children, holding them in gangs with the emaciated women tied together by ropes around their necks. If hostages and flogging with the *chicotte*, a bullwhip, didn't bring results, the soldiers raided the villages, cutting off the heads and sexual parts of the men and hanging them on the village palisades, nailing the bodies of the women and children on the palisades in the form of a cross. Even more grisly, if possible, was the cutting off of hands.

When the rubber collection fell short, native hands were severed, at first from men killed in raids, later from living men and women. The soldiers presented baskets of severed hands to their post commanders in place of rubber. Soon the collection of hands was an end in itself, they were harvested just as the rubber had been and were used as a sort of jungle currency.

In the twenty years of Leopold's rule, five million people were killed in the Congo.

Luke grimaced. Fighting Indians in self-defense as his father had fought the Utes was one thing. This was different. No wonder Kezia —

Someone knocked. The Walrus crossed the room, put his eye to a crack in the door and murmured a word, listened, nodded, opened the door.

Kezia, Sid and MacNeeley came in. Kezia ignored the Walrus, smiled at Luke. Much as he wanted to jump up and wrap his arms about her, he forced himself to nod, saying nothing.

'This is the storehouse used by one of the men who was arrested last night,' the Walrus said, stubbing out his cigarette while Sid watched in envy. 'It will surely be searched in time.'

'I'll go to Andre,' Kezia told Luke. 'If it's

safe there, I'll come back for you.'

'Not alone,' Luke said, unwilling to let her out of his sight again. Actually he wanted them all to stay together.

'M. Reynaud,' she indicated the Walrus, 'must warn the others. He can't go with me.'

'I'll go with you,' MacNeeley offered before Luke could speak.

'I don't think — ' he began.

MacNeeley cut him off. 'Luke, you know French better than I do, almost as good as Kezia. You should stay here with Sid. Then each of us has a French speaker with us.'

On the surface what Mac said was reasonable. Yet it felt wrong. All wrong. The escape from the house had been too easy. He had the uneasy sense that the Huns were pushing and prodding them, forcing them to go where they, the Germans, wanted them to go. But why? He couldn't fathom why.

'Never split your forces,' T.J. had said more than once. 'I can't begin to count the expeditions on the plains that came to grief after they decided to split up.'

This is Belgium, not the American West, Luke told himself. *I'm a foreigner here and a damn amateur at espionage.* Could be the rules differ.

'All right, you go with Kezia,' he told MacNeeley reluctantly.

The Walrus cracked the door open, waited, slipped from the storeroom and was gone. After a few minutes Kezia followed with MacNeeley, leaving Luke alone with Sid.

'Something smells bloody rotten,' Sid said. 'I feel it in my bones.'

'I agree,' Luke said. 'But what? What's wrong?'

Sid shrugged.

Luke sighed, wishing to God he knew what to do.

11

Kezia had never known Brussels to be so hushed, the cobbles and sidewalks darkly wet, the September leaves on the trees washed clean by the rain. She glanced at MacNeeley walking beside her. There was a spring to his step she hadn't noticed before. Because Luke was no longer with them, thus making MacNeeley his own man? No, it was more than that, but what?

'Are you armed?' she asked.

'I'm carrying my Webley, of course.' He smiled, a charming smile, she admitted to herself. Yet the smile seemed false, not a smile from the heart but one ordered by the mind. 'Didn't Luke order us to take along everything we'd brought to Raynaud's house?'

'Yes, but if we're stopped — ' She paused. She'd given her revolver to the Herr Van Pelt back at the farm, rather than risk being caught with it.

He shrugged. 'It's a slight risk but a calculated one. We can't expect our good Belgian hosts to provide firearms as well as all the other help we're asking for, can we?'

She shook her head, still not satisfied. The issue wasn't the gun. No doubt Luke and Sid still carried theirs. And MacNeeley was right — they'd need them. At the same time, at any moment they could be stopped and searched. He seemed unconcerned about that possibility. She wished she had some of his coolness.

They turned onto the rue Ixelles as a yellow tram clanged past, the passengers staring straight ahead. Kezia stopped, pondering which route to take to Andre's. The city seemed so strange under German Occupation, the streets almost deserted, the few passersby preoccupied.

'How far is it to Andre's house?' MacNeeley asked.

'About two kilometers.'

'What's the address? I don't believe you've ever told me.'

She frowned. She hadn't told anyone. Though there seemed no reason not to divulge the address now that they were on their way to Andre's, she hesitated to tell him.

'The house is on the rue de la Culture,' she said slowly. 'I know the place by sight but I'm not sure of the number.' Why had she lied to him when she knew very well the number was 54? She couldn't explain her reluctance to trust him.

'The same street as Nurse Cavell's clinic.'

MacNeeley nodded as though satisfied.

'Yes, the same.' Her unease grew because he'd known the location of the clinic. Had it been mentioned in their briefing? She didn't think so.

Deciding to follow main thoroughfares, Kezia walked on. The city was different, she decided. Not the tree-lined streets nor the narrow-fronted houses, of course, the change was subtler, though no less evident. The entire atmosphere of the city had changed.

She remembered Brussels as a cosmopolitan city of charm, warmth and friendliness, of smiles and small courtesies. Now there was suspicion in the air, distrust. The Germans had accomplished one thing, she told herself. The Belgians, so often in conflict with one another to the point of civil war between the Walloon south and the Flemish north, had become indivisible in their hatred of the occupying Huns.

A flag emblazoned with the German imperial eagle hung limply from a staff in front of a three-story building ahead. Kezia couldn't help grimacing. As they neared the stairs beneath the flag, the front door opened and two German officers, lieutenant's and major's insignia on their collars, came out, pausing at the top of the steps to survey the

187

street before trotting in unison to the sidewalk.

Kezia drew in her breath as the Germans walked in their direction. Though a man's cap completely covered her hair, she wondered if they couldn't see through her masquerade as a male. Despite herself, she glanced at MacNeeley. He seemed unperturbed. His pace didn't falter and she had to walk rapidly to keep at his side.

The officers looked first at her, then at MacNeeley.

The taller of the two, the major, opened his mouth as though he meant to stop them and ask to see their identity cards. At that moment the major's companion said something Kezia couldn't hear, the major laughed as though at a risqué remark and the Germans walked on, the sound of their brown leather boots receding behind her. Kezia let out her breath in a sigh of relief.

'Those Germans certainly didn't faze you in the least,' she said.

MacNeeley shot her an appraising look. 'I do speak a bit of German, you know. I think I could have satisfied the blighters.'

Without an identity card? she asked herself. But she merely nodded, letting it drop, aware she was on edge. Ever since that night when she'd been in London during the

Zepp raid she'd not been herself, she'd been jumpy, ill-at-ease, suspicious.

'Damn you, Luke Ray,' she muttered, 'it's all your fault.'

'You said something?' MacNeeley asked.

'No, I was only thinking out loud.'

They walked on in silence. Without warning, children burst from a schoolyard gate, laughing as they chased one another, a teacher following them, scolding good-naturedly. A church bell chimed nine and, from afar, came the melody of a hymn played on a carillon. Ahead of them a gendarme walked to the center of an intersection, raising his hand to stop a single horse-drawn cab so the children could cross.

Number 54 rue de la Culture was on the other side of the street, a narrow two-story brown building with a multi-peaked roof, separated from its neighbors by vacant lots on both sides. The only windows appeared to be on the front of the house and all of them were closed despite the increasing heat of the day. A short flight of stone steps led to a roofed entrance and an imposing oak door.

'This way,' Kezia said, crossing the street with MacNeeley a pace behind. 'That's Andre's.'

From the corner of her eye she saw

189

MacNeeley nod. 'And the password?' he asked.

Again Kezia hesitated. Surely C had investigated MacNeeley up and down and sideways, she told herself, so there couldn't be even a shadow of a doubt about his loyalty. Yet, intuitively, without reason, she didn't trust him and she'd come to pay attention to her intuition. This time, though, she must be mistaken. Look what they'd already been through together.

'The password's 'The guns of Liège,' she told him.

'Ah, yes, the famous guns of Liège.'

She thought, as he must be doing, of the Belgian forts and their heroic, futile resistance to the onslaught of the German heavy artillery and the masses of German soldiers streaming triumphantly across the borders of neutral Belgium in the great flanking movement designed to sweep west to the English Channel as they engulfed the French armies.

Kezia crossed the last of the cobbles — their rounded surfaces were never meant for walking — and hurried along the sidewalk past a gnarled tree protected by a circle of iron fence. She approached the steps leading to Andre's house.

'Wait.' MacNeeley's hand closed on her

wrist, his fingers biting into her flesh. 'Keep walking,' he said urgently, 'and don't even glance at the house.'

When she tried to pull free, he tightened his grip. 'There's danger. Do as I say,' he ordered.

Wondering what he'd seen that she'd missed, she let him lead her along a fence paralleling stairs going down to the building's basement.

'What was it?' she asked in a low tone.

'Don't talk. Take my hand, be casual.'

His grip relaxed and his hand grasped hers as they strolled like lovers along the sidewalk in front of the lot next to the house. At the lot's rear, debris from a summer vegetable garden had been piled against a wooden fence. They walked past three other tall, narrow houses before MacNeeley directed her into an alleyway along the side of the last of the buildings, a constricted passage that led past small rear yards to a brick wall behind the houses on the next street. The alley was cool and sunless, shut in by tall buildings on both sides and the wall at the end. Except for the two barrels partly filled with rain-water, the alley was empty and quiet, the sounds of the city muted and distant behind her.

She pulled her hand from his. 'Why did

you take me here?'

'To show you why we couldn't go in the house.' MacNeeley smiled at her. 'I'm sorry I startled you back there on the street. I didn't mean to but I couldn't let you go inside. Or even appear to be thinking of going inside.'

'You still haven't told me what you saw. I don't appreciate riddles.' *Or men who talk in them.*

'Come.'

She followed him reluctantly deeper into the alley. When they reached the rear of the buildings, she saw a jumble of fences and sheds in the small rear yards.

'Look along there.' MacNeeley pointed. 'That's the rear of number fifty-four.'

'I don't see a thing.' Only the fences, the back porches, the shrubs and small trees. There was no sign of activity at Number 54 or at any of the other houses.

'Keep looking. You will.'

He shifted position until he stood directly in back of her and the hair on her nape rose. Dread swept over her, a fear that tingled a warning up her back, alerted all her senses. Resisting her almost uncontrollable impulse to whirl around, she held, her mind racing, seeking a way to distract him.

She heard a whisper of movement behind her. As though he'd raised his arms. She steeled herself not to flinch away from him and said, 'Perhaps it was one of the others you saw in fifty-four.' She fought to keep her voice level.

'The others?' She heard the interest in his voice.

'Yes, the others.' When she heard him step back she knew she'd found the key to her escape. Or was she imagining her danger? No, deep in her bones she knew it was real. 'They didn't tell you about the others while we were at Dover?' Kezia asked. 'No, of course they didn't. I wasn't to breathe a word about them until the time was right. Until now.' She bit her lip, hoping her lie sounded convincing.

What she'd said wasn't true. Though there was another group. Justin Graham was the one who'd revealed the plan to her. C certainly never intended her to reveal their presence to Luke Ray or any of his men. Even to save her life. She felt a sinking sensation in the pit of her stomach. She'd committed an unforgivable indiscretion. But, damn it, she was still alive.

Kezia turned slowly to find MacNeeley, his hands at his sides, looking expectantly at her. He smiled his charming, false smile. Had she imagined it all? Had her apprehension at being alone with this man she didn't trust led her to suspect that, as soon as he learned the password, he'd taken her into the this alley to kill her? So he could take her place and find Andre. But for what reason? Only one occurred to her.

'Tell me about these others,' MacNeeley said. 'Do you mean the Belgians who'll help us attack the prison?'

Without answering, she edged away until she was between MacNeeley and the street. Could she outrun him? When in doubt — attack.

'What did *you* see?' she countered. 'Why did you bring me here?'

'You should have told me of these others before. At the very least, you should have told Luke Ray. Or have you told him?'

She shook her head. He moved closer, as though daring her to flee. She'd measured the distance to the street with her gaze by now and decided it was too far. He'd catch her.

'Tell me who they are,' MacNeeley insisted.

She gazed at him, not responding.

Stalemate.

He grasped her upper arm, hard. Though his grip was painful, she refused to wince.

'Tell me,' he ordered, an angry flush rising to his cheeks.

She'd never before noticed how cold a blue his eyes were. She sensed he was capable of killing her without a second thought, without regret. Repressing a shudder at the thought that he almost had, she summoned up words. If she agreed the others were Belgian would he feel he didn't need any more information? What would happen to her then? She was afraid to risk it.

'They're not Belgian,' she admitted. 'They're English.' She knew she'd told him too much but she'd wanted to stay alive. Unless she meant to reveal everything, she'd have to concoct a believable lie. 'They're a backup group to yours,' she said. 'To transport you out of the country after the attack on St. Gilles.'

MacNeeley let go of her arm and nodded, seemingly satisfied. 'You should have told us about them before. C should have told the rest of us, not just you.'

When he saw she was still watching him, he added, 'You want to know why I avoided the house. Nothing specific, I had a hunch things weren't right. I thought if something was wrong we might get a clue to what it was from the rear of the house. It appears I shouldn't have acted on my hunch.'

Kezia knew he was lying but she nodded trying to look like a helpless woman seeking a man's advice. 'It's safe to go in then?'

'Do we have a choice?'

No more of a choice now than when you hurried me past the door into this alley. On the other hand, there was a slight possibility she was mistaken about MacNeeley.

Without another word, he led the way as they returned to the street and walked to Number 54. At the door, Kezia raised and lowered the brass knocker, the sound louder than she'd intended. A small opening in the door concealed by the carving of a rampant lion slid aside.

'What do you want?' a voice asked in French.

'The guns of Liège,' replied Kezia.

There was a pause followed by the rasp of a key turning. The door eased inward. Though not over 35, the heavy man in the doorway had already turned gray with whorls of thinning hair curling about his flushed face. His suit, a rumpled tweed, was stained by several dark spots that looked to be burn marks.

'I'm Andre,' he told them in English after giving the reply to the password.

When he turned, Kezia saw a scar running across his neck from below his ear to his Adam's apple. Sensing her gaze, he touched the scar lightly with his fingers.

The scar was Andre's memento of the siege of the twelve forts of Liège. In the two weeks' battle he'd been afraid and ashamed of his fear. He grew to accept it, was proud he'd been able to fight despite it. He seldom talked of the fighting, even in his thoughts those fourteen days were blurred, a series of vivid, unconnected episodes . . .

The cheers, the kisses, the mugs of beer thrust at him during the patriotic frenzy of the first days after the German Army crossed the frontier . . . the roads jammed by the mobilization . . . machine-guns headed for the front on carts pulled by dogs . . . the underground forts with only triangular mounds on the surface with their retractable gun turrets . . . a searchlight in a steel observation tower . . . the mounds surrounded by dry moats thirty feet deep . . . Germans storming the slopes below him, their dead piling in ridges . . . a second wave advancing shoulder to shoulder, line after line after line . . . a barricade of German dead so high his captain didn't know whether to fire through it or lead his men out to pull the bodies aside . . .

Snowy-haired General Leman ordering them to 'Hold to the end' . . . soldiers in British-style uniforms driving up to Leman's headquarters and asking to see the general . . . the general's aide shouting, 'They aren't English, they're Germans . . . the Germans' killing the aide only to be shot down themselves . . . '

The roar of German siege guns so large each had a crew of two hundred soldiers . . . the terror inside the fort as the shells fell with a screaming whistle . . . the explosions, the mutilated bodies, the ceiling collapsing around him, the fire, gas, the bedlam, like a scene from Hieronymous Bosch . . . the girder lacerating his neck . . . Alard, his comrade, screaming as he waited for the next shell to fall . . .

The surrender, his escape into the countryside, the Germans marching west weeks behind schedule, the same Germans who'd called them chocolate soldiers . . . the blinded Belgian sergeant saying 'We showed them what kind of chocolate soldiers we were, didn't we?' . . .

Suddenly conscious that the man and woman he'd let into the house were staring at him, Andre pulled himself together.

Kezia saw Andre shake his head, saw sanity return to his eyes. Without speaking, he led her and MacNeeley from room to room, there seemed to be almost no halls, finally taking them past a rectangular area of the carpet that was lighter than the rest. He paused momentarily and said, 'They took out the piano. In 1915, they steal pianos. In 1870, in France, they stole clocks. Perhaps there's hope for the Huns. They become more cultured as time passes.'

MacNeeley didn't seem to find the remark as amusing as she did. She wondered how she could manage to reveal her suspicions of him to Andre without alerting MacNeeley to what she was doing.

The smell of meat cooking made her stomach roil, reminding her how hungry she was. But she knew there was no time to eat. Andre opened a door and they entered a kitchen, a small room with a pot simmering on a wood stove to their left, a table covered with a floral oilcloth in front of them.

'My name — ' Kezia began.

'I know your name.' Andre looked from her to MacNeeley. 'I expected four men to be with you. I was told four.'

'The Germans raided M. Raynard's house,' she said. 'Two of our group are in hiding. The other was killed crossing the border.'

Andre nodded, his attention still focused on MacNeeley. 'You wait here,' he finally ordered, pointing at MacNeeley. 'You — ' he pointed at Kezia ' — are to come with me.'

She followed him through the kitchen, half-expecting MacNeeley to follow, despite the direct order to stay where he was. When he didn't, a weight lifted. After they entered an enclosed porch and the door closed behind them, she said, 'I don't trust the man I'm with. His name is MacNeeley.'

Andre looked at her without expression. After a moment he nodded, opened another door and murmured words she couldn't hear to a man peeling potatoes at a table in the back kitchen. The man rose, walked past them through the enclosed porch and opened the door to the main kitchen, leaning against the frame. Past him, Kezia could see MacNeeley seated at the table with a cup of coffee.

'This way,' Andre told Kezia. In a far corner of the porch, he lifted a trap door in the floor. Looking down Kezia saw ladder-like stairs leading into darkness. 'You first,' Andre said.

She climbed down backwards with Andre following her into the gloom. Her feet touched stone. She heard a muted thud as the door over her head closed, making the darkness complete. When Andre touched her arm, she started.

'This way,' he said, guiding her through what she thought must be a tunnel. After a time he stopped, saying, 'Wait.' She obeyed. A moment later a door opened ahead of her and, in the sudden glow of lamplight from the other side, she saw Andre in the doorway, motioning for her to go ahead of him.

She entered a low-ceilinged windowless room. In the meager light from a kerosene lamp on a bench against one wall, she noticed pipes over her head, a black giant of a furnace in front of her and, beyond the furnace, a bin holding a scant supply of coal.

While she wondered if they were even in the same house she'd entered, Andre latched the door behind them, walked past her to the far wall where he put his shoulder to the side of a high wooden cabinet that was empty except for two jars of preserves. He pushed the cabinet away from the wall. Bugs scurried away from the sudden light into crevices in the cement floor.

A wooden door was recessed in the wall behind the cabinet. Andre tapped once, then four times in quick succession. Kezia heard a bolt drawn. Andre pushed the door open and gestured to Kezia to go inside. Ducking her head, she entered. This time he didn't follow, instead he closed the door behind her, remaining on the other side.

The room she came into was lit by a single lamp on a table. A man stood beside the table smiling. 'Kezia,' Justin Graham said, 'Kezia, my darling.' He strode to her and took her in his arms. 'Thank God you're all right.'

12

Kezia kissed Justin quickly, then drew away. 'I didn't know whether you'd be here or not,' she said.

She watched him as he brought another chair to the table and held it while she sat down. Justin looked exactly as she remembered him, tall and blond, lean, the skilled athlete who'd always been looked up to by the others boys in his form. When he smiled at her, his blue eyes bright in the lamplight, she felt a pang she couldn't define. Sadness? Regret? Perhaps a touch of both.

He didn't join her at the table but paced. 'Our network in Belgium was crippled more severely than we thought.' He paused to sit on the edge of the table. 'Not only was Nurse Cavell imprisoned but the Countess and Philippe Baucq and a dozen or more of the others. We couldn't stay where we'd planned so I came here. The rest of my group is in hiding nearby.'

She opened her mouth to tell him about MacNeeley but held, conscious he was staring oddly at her.

'What is it?' she asked, removing her cap to

run her fingers through her hair.

'You've changed, Kezia.'

She touched her man's garb but he shook his head. 'It's not the clothes. I can't tell exactly what the difference is but you're not the same woman you were five months ago. At Southampton.'

'When we rowed up the river.' Even as she smiled, remembering, she realized that time seemed so far distant as to have taken place in another life.

'We stopped at the inn for strawberries with cream,' he went on. 'That was the day you convinced me we should wait until after the war before we married.'

'You agreed,' Kezia said, 'saying we shouldn't be like all the rest, rushing off to get married. Besides, you told me, the war would be over before too long. You gave it six months.'

'I've changed my mind,' Justin said, beginning to pace again.

'About the war?'

'That, too. Now I think it may last for years. In fact, I can't see the end. But what I meant is, I've changed my mind about getting married. We should have then, at Southampton.' He stopped beside her and took her hand in his.

Tears stung Kezia's eyes.

'We should have seized whatever little time we could,' he said. 'We can still do it. We can have so much more than we do. Before it's too late.'

Too late. The words echoed and reechoed in her head. Justin released her hand and stood staring down at her. 'The thing is, I don't believe I'll live to see the end of the war.'

She blinked the tears away. 'Nonsense, Justin. You're not Rupert Brooke, you mustn't think like him.'

'He was right wasn't he? He's dead, you know. I only met him the one time, at Antwerp, but I'll never forget him. Do you know what he said when the war started? 'Well, if Armageddon's on, I suppose one should be there.' Exactly what I felt.'

Kezia rose and put her arms around him, holding him as she might a child. When he kissed her, she made herself respond. Oh God, what had happened to her feelings for Justin? Impossible to have them dissolve into mere affection. She eased herself away.

'You don't like me to hold you?' he asked. 'You know I'd never insist on anything you didn't want. Wrongheaded though you often are.'

Annoyance shot through her. Why must he constantly criticize her? He always had, she realized now, but she'd ignored it before. Before she could control herself she snapped, 'You're such an honorable man.' Instantly she regretted the words. 'I'm sorry,' she murmured.

'So love has changed to kindliness, is that it?' Justin asked. 'Can I help being what I am — though honorable isn't the word I'd choose. I think I'm a damn fool to have let you get yourself into this. To let you work for C.'

'Let me? You had no choice.' Anger drove her forward. 'You really didn't have a say in the matter, did you? I'm the one who approached C, I'm the one who made the decision. I'm really much too independent a woman to suit you. You said it best, I'm wrongheaded in your eyes. And I always will be.'

He looked at her, slowly shaking his head. 'I think you should let me be the judge of what I want, Kezia. You're lovely. Intelligent. Capable. Though you're a damnably poor lawn tennis player.'

Hoping he was striving for a lighter note, Kezia swallowed her anger. She forced a smile. 'That's why you asked to be introduced, isn't it? You saw me playing at the Houghton's and knew you could beat me.'

'You know that wasn't the reason,' he said

softly. 'You were the most attractive, the most desirable woman I'd ever seen. You know I love you, Kezia.'

She put her hand to the side of his face. She did know. And yet . . .

All at once she recalled what she'd meant to tell him and shivered. Taking her hand away, she hugged herself. How could she have let herself be distracted by personal concerns?

'Are you all right?' The concern in Justin's voice failed to warm her.

'Do you know Byron MacNeeley?' she asked.

'MacNeeley? He's one of Luke Ray's group isn't he?'

Kezia nodded. 'I should have told you the minute I arrived. Do you know anything about him?'

Justin shook his head. 'What about him?'

'He's from Cornwall, an expert in demolition. I admit I didn't like the man from the first and so I'm afraid that might have clouded my judgment, making me mistrust him with no reason.'

Justin let out his breath as though in relief, surprising her. Had he suspected something different? Something more personal? She knew he was a jealous man. Without intending to, she thought of Luke and flushed.

'Tell me what happened,' Justin said sharply. 'From the time you left England with Ray's group.'

Without looking directly at him, she described crossing the border, told him about Manion's death, the German soldier killed at the farmhouse, their ride concealed under a wagon into Brussels. In greater detail she described their flight from Raynaud's house, the decision to split into two groups and MacNeeley's peculiar and, she felt, incriminating behavior when they first arrived at Andre's.

'You suspected he meant to kill you?' Justin asked when she told him how MacNeeley had led her into the alley.

'Not suspected. I was sure of it.'

'Yet he didn't. He didn't harm you in any way. I don't think I quite understand what you're trying to say.'

Kezia hesitated. She realized she'd have to confess everything and that she didn't want to. 'He didn't harm me because of what I told him. I shouldn't have, but I was afraid for my life. He was the last person I should have — '

'Stop. Tell me exactly what you said.'

She sighed. 'I told him there was another group on its way to Belgium. I know he believed the second group was from England even though I insisted they were Belgians.'

'You had no right.' Anger thickened Justin's voice.

'I'm aware of that. I told him it was backup group to the one he was in — Luke Ray's group.'

Silence hung between them, the weight of his disapproval seeming to press against her. She should look at him, she knew, but she didn't, afraid of what she'd read in his face.

'You were the only person who could link our two groups,' he said. 'No matter what the danger, you shouldn't have breathed a word. You know that. Or at least you should.'

Resenting the accusation in Justin's voice, she snapped, 'Of course I know that! MacNeeley would have killed me, I'm sure he would have, if I hadn't made him believe there was more to discover.'

'You've put us all in jeopardy. Worse, you've placed our mission in danger. Didn't C warn you? I know he did.'

She stared at him. Guilt mixed with fury made her erupt. 'You care more for your damn mission than — ' she paused, feeling even more in the wrong.

Justin grabbed her shoulders and shook her until her head bobbed. When he stopped, she staggered back, a hand up, afraid from the rage in his face that he meant to strike her.

He released her abruptly. 'Where is he, this MacNeeley?'

'Before I came down here I told Andre I didn't trust him. He sent a man to watch him. A short dark man.'

'Raoul, that's Raoul. He's one of the best, we don't have to worry about your Mr. MacNeeley running off as long as Raoul's looking after him.'

'I shouldn't have told MacNeeley,' Kezia admitted. 'I shouldn't have panicked.' She started to add that maybe Justin was right about her staying home knitting socks for the men in the trenches instead, but when she noticed the self-satisfied look on his face, the words stuck in her throat.

You're so smug, Justin Graham. As though you never made a mistake in your life.

'We'll have to make the best of a bad bargain,' he said, crossing the room to the low door leading from the chamber into the main cellar.

She followed, asking, 'What do you intend to do?'

'Deal with MacNeeley. You stay here.'

'I'd rather — '

He whirled on her. 'Do as I say!'

Damned if she was going to be ordered around like a pet dog. 'I have a right to know what you mean to do,' she said.

209

He shot her an exasperated look. 'I'll do what I have to do. Ouê mission is more important than me or MacNeeley or — ' He paused, then added, 'It's more important than you, Kezia.'

Something inside her protested. Was a mission more important than the lives of everyone involved in it? Justin certainly thought so. She feared she knew what he intended. 'You mean to kill him, don't you?' she whispered. 'Even though you're not sure I'm right about him.'

'We've no margin for error. MacNeeley knows my group exists. He's intimately acquainted with Luke Ray's group. He's too dangerous to live.'

'But he may not be what I think. Don't kill him without knowing.'

'I have to. We're not civilized men any longer. We're less and more. Beasts and gods.'

'Damn Rupert Brooke. You have to be sure.'

He turned on her, his voice rising. 'You weren't sure when you told him about my group, were you? So now I have to kill him and I jolly well will.'

He blamed her. Told her outright it was her fault that he had to kill a man who might be innocent. 'Don't do it!' she cried, grabbing his arm.

He shook her off, shoving her so that she stumbled and fell backwards. Sprawled on the dirt floor she stared up at him disbelievingly. This Justin was nobody she knew.

He started to duck under the lintel, stopped and came slowly back, reached down and pulled her to her feet. He tried to put his arm around her but she drew back.

'You must see it's what has to be done,' he said.

'I don't want you to kill him,' she said as reasonably as she could. 'Think what it will do to you, Justin. You'll never know whether or not you killed a man needlessly. And I'll always believe it was my fault that he died. That you killed him.'

'In war there's no fault, no blame. You did what you thought best. Now I intend to do what I think best. Stay here.'

She watched him duck through the doorway and disappear into the darkness of the cellar beyond. She waited, hand clenched against her mouth. He was wrong, wrong. And she would not be left behind. She hunched down to go into the cellar, walked past the furnace, threaded through the dark passage and climbed the ladder, finding the trapdoor open. Kezia climbed through to the enclosed rear porch, saw Justin talking to Andre in the kitchen, Andre gesturing with his hands as though uncertain. There was no sign of MacNeeley. When she entered the kitchen, Andre nodded to Justin and walked quickly from the room. Justin glanced at her, seemingly not surprised to see her.

'They're gone.' His voice was flat. 'Raoul and MacNeeley are gone.'

'Come here!' Andre's call from the front of the house carried urgency.

Justin strode through the rooms with Kezia at his heels. They found Andre in the entry holding a closet door open and peering into the dark interior.

'*Ce sont tout des barbares*,' Andre said, spitting out the words. '*Mais tous, tous*. All are barbarians.'

Justin put his hand on the Belgian's shoulder and when Andre stood aside, Justin knelt in front of him. Kezia tried to peer past the two men into the closet.

'What is it?' she asked.

Justin rose, looked at Andre and shook his head, turned to her. 'Raoul's dead. Broken neck, from the look of it.' Shocked, Kezia made an effort to push past him. 'There might be something I can do,' she said.

Justin stopped her. 'I know a dead man when I see one. There's nothing you or anyone else can do for Raoul.' He led her away from the closet. Looking back, he said to Andre, 'Make sure MacNeeley's not hiding in the house.'

'I doubt it but I will search. If I'm right and don't find him, we'll have to leave here, my friend. And quickly.' Nodding, Justin led Kezia into a small sitting room, taking a quick look around for possible hiding places.

'You don't think he's still in the house, do you?' she asked.

'No, he's gone. We'll never see your Mr. MacNeeley again.'

'Stop calling him mine!'

'Sorry. It appears your suspicion was justified. We'll have a visit from the Germans before too long, we can count on that.'

She drew in her breath, fear crowding in as she remembered Luke. 'What about Luke?' she demanded. 'Luke Ray and Sid. MacNeeley knows where they're hiding. We have to warn them before the Germans find them.'

'No, it's too risky. They'll have to fend for themselves.'

'I don't understand.' She stared at him, puzzled and concerned. 'The mission. If they're caught, how will you rescue Miss — ' She broke off, catching herself before saying Nurse Cavell's name. 'What chance does the mission have without them?'

'Every chance, Kezia. I thought C told you. Luke Ray and Sid and this MacNeeley weren't the real rescue mission. They've always been no more than decoys, intended to be caught unless they were incredibly lucky. Which they weren't. As a matter of fact they've had less luck than we thought possible.'

Kezia shook her head in dismay. In disbelief. 'C didn't tell me. He only said there were two groups. I wondered why he chose an American, chose Luke, but I never thought it was all a ruse. That they were considered expendable.' Her voice quivered on the last word.

'We have to let them take their chances, Ray and Sid.' He frowned. 'There's one thing I don't understand.'

She'd seen it, too. 'About MacNeeley,' she said. 'Why C picked MacNeeley.'

'It's unlikely C would have failed to uncover his other connections. C's nothing if not efficient. I wonder — ?'

'Would C have done that? Sent MacNeeley on the mission on purpose, knowing he was a German agent? Sent him to betray Luke and the others so you'd have a better chance to succeed.'

'I don't know, C's capable of everything and anything.' Justin urged her from the parlor. 'Talking won't help. We've got to find a safe place for you so we can get on with our job. I don't believe C ever intended for you to be captured so the best — '

'I'm as much a part of the mission as you are and I refuse to be set aside. But I thought perhaps we might have to give it up. Under the circumstances.'

He shook his head. 'We may be compromised but the Germans have no idea what our plans are. In fact, this may work out to our advantage.'

'You can't just leave Luke for the Germans to take. He'd be of help to you. Both he and Sid would.'

Andre came into the room, his face flushed and glistening with sweat. 'MacNeeley is not here,' he said. 'The house will tell the Huns nothing they don't already know.' He motioned with his head toward the rear. 'I have a buggy waiting. We should go at once.'

'Raoul?' Justin asked.

'What would you have me do? We must leave poor Raoul.'

'I suppose there's no choice,' Justin said. 'We're ready then. Come along, Kezia.'

He left the room with Andre, not looking back to see if she was following. Kezia's anger rose like a red mist and she had to fight back her impulse to shout that she wasn't a dog to call to heel. He could be so smug, so righteous, as though being male made him a

215

god. *You're beasts, not gods.*

For an instant she remembered watching him walk from the field after scoring the winning goal in the rugby match against Ireland, his fair face impassive, his head held high, while the cheers thundered around her, cheers for Justin Graham. How like a young god he looked. How her heart leaped, how proud she'd been.

At that moment, as she stood and cheered, warmed by the knowledge that he wanted *her*, she felt the first prickling of unease, wondering if this was the man she should marry. Did she really know him? He seemed a stranger, not the man she'd thought she was ready to live with for the rest of her life . . .

'Damn all men,' she muttered.

'Hurry, Kezia,' Justin called from the hall.

Placing a clamp on her anger, she pulled her cap from a pocket, tucked her hair under it and followed him into the dining room, through the kitchen and out the door at the rear of the house. Andre opened a gate in the fence, they crossed the alley and went through another fence gate into the rear yard of a house on another street. Taking a flagstone path that ran along the side of the building, they emerged onto the street. A boy of about fifteen sat in the driver's seat of a buggy drawn up beside the curb.

Andre climbed in, sitting next to the boy. Justin turned to Kezia to help her into the seat behind the driver. She turned away and walked briskly down the street. He strode after her and grasped her arm, stopping her. She tried to wrench free but couldn't.

'Where in the bloody hell do you think you're going?' he asked.

'To warn Luke and Sid.' She spoke between her teeth.

'The end result of that sort of madness will be to see you in the hands of the Germans.'

She turned on him. 'I must live with myself, whatever else happens. They deserve to be warned and I intend to do just that. I may have deceived Luke without realizing it but I refuse to desert him. Not when the fault's mine.'

'Oh God,' Justin said, letting go of her arm. 'Chaos results when you allow women in this sort of business. Men's business. Do what you think you must. I'll have no part in it, none at all.'

She walked on, increasing her pace as she crossed an intersecting street, glancing about for landmarks that would lead her to the plumber's storeroom where she'd last seen Luke, all the while fighting back tears of frustration and anger.

A horse clip-clopped behind her, overtaking her. At first she refused to look back but when she did she saw the buggy. The boy drew up a few feet in front of her and Justin reached down for her hand. Passersby stopped to stare.

'This foolishness has gone far enough,' Justin snapped. 'We'll see to it that your Sergeant Ray is warned.'

Mine? She shook her head. She didn't want any part of any man. 'I have your word?' she asked.

Justin's face reddened. Seeing he felt she impugned his honor with her question, in his eyes he'd already given his word, she stepped to the buggy and let him help her up beside him.

The boy flicked his whip and, in silence, they rattled over the cobbles, turned right, turned left and left again. She didn't recognize her surroundings and glanced at Justin. Was he trying to deceive her? At that moment the boy slowed and stopped the buggy.

'I will reconnoiter,' Andre said in a low voice. He jumped to the sidewalk and disappeared around the corner of a pharmacist's shop.

As they waited, Kezia looked at Justin from the corner of her eye. His face set, he stared

218

straight ahead, ignoring her, probably wishing he'd never met her. For that matter, she felt the same. He seemed a stranger to her, not the Justin she'd thought she knew.

'It is safe.' Andre's words startled Kezia. He'd returned without her being aware of his approach. Accepting the offer of his hand, she climbed down from the buggy, Justin behind her.

'No, wait here,' Andre told him, 'to make certain no one follows.'

Andre led her past the pharmacist's, along a narrow street of shops and cafés and around a corner. She recognized the dilapidated front of the pipe storehouse in front of her.

They walked along the alley to the door and threw it open. Kezia looked past Andre. Cobwebs hung from the ceiling and dust covered the pipes stored on shelves along the walls. There was no sign the storeroom had ever been used as a hiding place.

'As you can see,' Andre said, 'your friends are gone.' He crossed himself. 'God save them both.'

13

'When I joined this man's army,' Sid said, 'I didn't expect to have to march all the bloody way to Berlin. At least not in the middle of the bloody night. I can't see if I'm coming or goingô They're right when they say a Tommy gets more kicks in the ass than halfpence.'

'Why *did* you sign up, Sid?' MacNeeley asked. 'I don't recall you ever told us.'

MacNeeley's tone, Luke thought as he trudged along the dark country lane, was sharp and probing. Like a needle. He'd had no choice but to let Byron take temporary command, since he had no idea what to do next. But he didn't care for MacNeeley's attitude. He hadn't from the beginning, sensing the man was laying back, waiting for his chance to take over.

'I don't recall you ever asked,' Sid said, imitating Mac's precise speech. 'I've naught to be ashamed of, though there might be some who think different. I signed on to win an early release from the Liverpool Lockup. Where I happened to be incarcerated through a whim of fate.'

'What sort of whim of fate was that?' Luke asked.

'I was jailed because one Mr. Jeffrey Coleman ate an oyster that didn't agree with him.'

'You tried to poison the man?' Luke heard surprise in Mac's voice.

'You take me for a bloody murderer, do you? Me, who never harmed a soul in my life. Mr. Coleman was attending the annual banquet of the Thirty Year Service Organization of the employees of the Liverpool Water Works, he being a director of that organization, when he ate the oyster that roiled his stomach. Because of that oyster, the blighter left the dinner two hours early and that led to him and me meeting the way we did.'

Luke smiled as Sid paused. T.J. used to hesitate in the same way when he told a tale. Sometimes for effect. Sometimes because he was doing a little inventing to embroider his story.

'Unfortunately,' Sid went on, 'we met in his wife's boudoir.'

'I never took you for a cuckolder, Sid,' MacNeeley said.

'And, by God, I'm not.'

'Yet he found you with his wife,' Luke put in.

'Not likely,' Sid told them, 'seeing as how

221

she'd been dead for going on three years. Mr. Jeffrey Coleman was what you'd call sentimental and when his helpmeet passed on he took pains to keep her room just exactly as she'd left it when she passed on. He turned it into a blooming shrine, that's what he did.'

'Perhaps he hoped she'd signal him from the beyond,' Luke suggested, glancing around him in the darkness at the hedgerows on both sides of the lane and, to their right, at the grove of trees rising high above their heads. Moonlight glimmered through the haze in the east.

'If you'd heard the howl he let out when he happened on me,' Sid said, 'You'd've thought he'd stumbled on a ghost. But finding me instead didn't seem to relieve his mind in the least.'

'Of course,' MacNeeley said. 'I should have known. You were after her jewels, weren't you?'

'Didn't I mention that?' Sid asked innocently. 'What else would have brought me to his wife's boudoir? The end result of Mr. Coleman's stomach-ache was ten years in prison for yours truly.'

'That's a stiff sentence,' Luke said.

'My third offense. I could've gone to France instead of coming here except I was in Victoria Station when some of them came home after the Somme. They all had grins on their faces 'cause they were back in Blighty. Most of 'em anyway. Some didn't have enough of their faces left to grin with.' Sid stopped walking. 'I'm fagged,' he said. 'How much longer before we're there?'

'It can't be more than a kilometer from here,' MacNeeley said. 'Miss Faith's directions were none too precise. As I've told you.'

'I'm taking five,' Sid said, sitting on the grass at the edge of the lane.

Luke sat beside him and MacNeeley hunkered down, facing them both. Luke closed his eyes, feeling the dampness of the October wind blowing off the sea to the north. He had a chilling sensation he'd lost control, the same feeling he'd once had when his Bebe stalled, spun into a vrille and plunged toward the ground thousands of feet below. Trapped. Helpless. Desperate.

Luke forced his thoughts into order. The trouble was he was overtired and also didn't feel he was in charge of anything. A temporary condition. They'd reach the sanctuary before midnight, MacNeeley would make contact with the Belgians, and tomorrow they'd begin the final preparations for their assault on St. Gilles Prison. Up until now they'd had a run of bad luck, nothing worse. Their luck was bound to turn.

'What's that?' Sid asked.

Luke opened his eyes. He raised his head, listening and heard a faint drone to the east.

'A Hun airplane,' answered MacNeeley.

Luke frowned. The sound wasn't quite right for an airplane, it was too steady, too low-pitched. He knew that sound, that throaty hum, but couldn't place it. The drone grew louder and suddenly the snout of a Zeppelin thrust over the trees. They stared in awe at the huge silver airship gliding effortlessly less than a thousand feet above them, nose high as it climbed to begin its journey to England.

No lights showed on the lighter-than-air ship but, peering up, Luke made out the open control car hanging below the center of the craft, heard the steady drone of the five engines as they propelled the ship into the wind. Directly overhead now, the six-hundred-foot Zeppelin seemed to fill the sky from one horizon to the other.

The tail slid into view, ballasted with water tanks, its rudder and elevators guiding the Zeppelin. For a moment Luke imagined himself in the control car with the great hydrogen-filled ship above him, with seven thousand pounds of bombs in the racks beneath the superstructure, the wind cold on his face as the Zeppelin climbed toward its ceiling of 10,000 feet.

The Zeppelin, he realized, was a monstrous streamlined weapon of war, capable of spreading terror even more effectively than when it rained death from the sky. A relatively silent scourge which, despite its offensive arsenal, was defenseless, depending for survival on surprise and altitude, on the darkness of a new moon or the enshrouding secrecy of clouds.

The airship rose higher, its nose reaching toward the cloud cover in the west. The three men stood staring upward until the Zeppelin was a dark blur in the distance, until the sound of its engines could no longer be heard.

Luke rubbed the soreness at the back of his neck, speculating on where the ship was moored.

'Damn bloody Zepp,' Sid muttered.

'The hangar must be close by.' Luke looked to the east in the direction of the grove of trees where they'd first seen the airship. 'Her port can't be more than a mile — a bit over a kilometer — from here.'

'She has nothing to do with us,' MacNeeley said sharply. 'Let's get on with it. We've enough to worry about without concerning ourselves with Zepp hangars.'

Concealing his annoyance at the man's

225

assumption of authority, Luke, with a last glance to the east, followed him along the lane, Sid bringing up the rear. They soon left the hedgerows behind and came into flat, open country. The farmhouse, when they reached it ten minutes later, surprised him. Sid, too, if his indrawn breath meant anything.

The building, sheltered by tall trees, sat on a slight rise several hundred feet from the lane, a sprawling three-story house made of time-weathered brick. Large, with steep gabled roofs punctuated by chimneys, the structure seemed more like a displaced English country house than a building that belonged on a Belgian farm.

A sullen blond man answered MacNeeley's knock and, after a grunt of acknowledgment, led them through an entry hall and along a corridor to a room off the kitchen where he pulled down the shades on the windows before lighting the lamp on the table. Unlike other Belgians Luke had met, he made no attempt to effusively shake his hand.

'I'm Henrik,' he said, then gestured to the table.

'Sit. Katryn will bring the food.' He stared at each of them in turn before disappearing into the kitchen.

'That bloke'll know us again,' Sid muttered, seating himself.

Luke and MacNeeley followed suit. Luke blinked back sleep as he listened to the clatter of pans and smelled the rich aroma of meat and spices wafting from the kitchen. He couldn't decide whether he was more hungry or more sleepy.

A young woman appeared in the kitchen doorway carrying a steaming black kettle. Luke blinked again, suddenly wide-awake. Katryn was petite, scarcely more than five feet tall, her hair was long and blonde, her face fair, her eyes blue, her nose tilted slightly upward at the tip. Her blue gown, tied loosely, failed to hide the pleasing curves of her figure.

'Let me help you,' MacNeeley said, leaping to his feet a scant second before Luke would have done the same. He watched MacNeeley take the kettle from her, once again feeling the man was usurping what should be his place.

Katryn's startled smile was also warm as she nodded her thanks to MacNeeley before glancing around the room, looking briefly at Sid, her gaze lingering on Luke. He smiled and Katryn smiled back at him, revealing a hidden dimple.

'Katryn,' Hendrik said sharply from the

kitchen door, gesturing peremptorily to her.

She hurried into the kitchen, leaving Luke to wonder what the relationship between the two was. Man and wife? Somehow he didn't think so.

'This soup's a bit of all right,' Sid said.

Luke sipped the steaming liquid. It was delicious.

'They call it waterzooi,' MacNeeley said, 'chicken boiled with herbs. Usually it's made with fish but with the war . . . '

Katryn returned with three mugs. As she put Luke's in front of him, her breast brushed his arm. He looked quickly up at her and she drew away, the color rising to her face.

MacNeeley sipped his beer. '*Geuze*,' he said.

'This ain't too bloody bad,' Sid judged, 'for foreigners. I'd still rather pay my pence for a glass of Bass.'

'*Geuze* is part wheat, part barley,' MacNeeley said. 'Some claim it tastes almost like wine.'

'You know a lot about food,' Luke commented.

'One of my passions before the war.' MacNeeley nodded appreciatively. 'Hendrik's not a half bad cook, not bad at all.'

Sid lifted his mug. 'I'll drink to that.'

'They love good food here,' Mac went on.

'Where but in Brussels do you find streets named for artichokes, herring, butter, pheasants and cabbages? The list goes on and on. When you look at a map of the center of the city you think you're reading a menu.'

Katryn pushed open the kitchen door carrying plates, more tableware and a basket of bread. In her haste she dropped a knife on the floor.

'You must excuse my sister,' Hendrik said from the doorway, making no move to retrieve the knife or to help her. Luke jumped to his feet and picked up the knife, earning another smile from Katryn, a smile she took care to conceal from her brother.

Brother and sister, not man and wife. For some reason Luke was pleased this pretty girl wasn't married to a lout like Hendrik.

'The *civet* is excellent,' MacNeeley told Hendrik.

A slight smile flitted across the blond man's face and he sketched a bow before returning to the kitchen.

As he ate the hare soaked in wine, Luke watched for Katryn to come back but she didn't reappear. When they finished eating it was Hendrik who said, 'I will show you gentlemen to your rooms.'

MacNeeley remained seated. He was returning to Brussels immediately to try to regain contact with LeMur and, if possible, bring him to the farmhouse the next day.

I should be going instead. But he didn't know Brussels and MacNeeley did. A good commander sent qualified men; he didn't try to take over a task he wasn't suited for. And yet . . .

Luke dismissed his uneasiness, shook MacNeeley's hand and wished him, 'Good luck.'

'I envy you and Sid,' MacNeeley said, 'spending the night in feather beds.' When Luke walked to the door with him, he added, 'Pleasant dreams.'

Shutting the door behind him, Luke stood there a moment. He'd been right in his feeling that four of them shouldn't split up. Despite Mac's assurance that Kezia had been all right when he'd left her, Luke was concerned for her safety. She should be here, with him, where he could protect her.

He sighed and followed the waiting Hendrik up to the second floor and into a room opening off a hall to the left of the stairs. Sid's was the next room beyond.

Once alone, Luke examined his door, finding neither lock nor bolt. Frowning, he crossed to the double casement windows and looked out at the trees near the house and beyond to trees stretching away into darkness.

The moon shone palely through a thin cloud cover.

Despite the lack of a door lock, once he hit the bed he fell asleep at once . . .

The wind chilled his face as he walked through the field towards a woods. An odd noise alerted him and he pulled his scarf over his nose and mouth, hearing the hiss of escaping gas. Glancing up at the sky above the dark trees he saw nothing. A Tommy, his face flushed with excitement, ran from the woods, shouting as he passed, 'She's going down, she's going down'.

Luke looked up again and saw the great gray shape of a Zeppelin fill the sky. The airship, in trouble, tilted earthward, its nose only a few feet above the trees. He walked on rather than run away, determined not to show his fear. White light flashed silently, illuminating road and woods. He glanced up and back. The Zeppelin was engulfed in flame. The ship plunged down at him, seemed to seek him out. He raced away, stumbling in his haste, the heat of the fire searing his back. Pausing to swing around, he saw no doomed airship, there was nothing except for the flames enveloping him. He threw up his hands to protect his face . . .

Luke jerked awake abruptly. He sat up, shivering, still caught in the web of his nightmare. The flames had been so real he could hardly believe there was no fire. He licked dry lips.

A whisper of sound came from near the door. Suddenly alert, Luke thrust his hand beneath the pillow, his fingers closing on the butt of his revolver. He peered into the darkness. Saw a figure approaching him. He raised the gun, waiting.

The intruder paused in front of the windows and in the meager light of the moon he saw it was a woman dressed in flowing white. His breath caught. Kezia!

No, not her, he was in another place, this was another time. Katryn, that's who he saw. She glided toward the bed, leaned down and, in a quick fluid movement, raised her hands over her head. Her nightgown fell to the floor. Luke let out his breath, his heart thudding. Carefully, he eased back down on the bed.

Without a word, Katryn pulled the cover from Luke's body. Awkwardly, he shifted the Webley to his left hand, reached down on the far side of the bed and laid the gun on the wooden floor within reach. He wasn't sure anyone could be trusted, even a pretty girl apparently offering herself to him. Still, when she knelt on the bed beside him, her pale skin glowing in the faint light from the windows. Luke reached for her, his fingers touching the warmth of her bare arm.

She laughed throatily, pushing him back as he started to sit up. She leaned over him, her hair teasing his face, her lips closing on his as her bared breasts lightly touched his chest.

She kissed him hungrily, her lips demanding, her tongue probing between his teeth and into his mouth, meeting his. He felt a tingling on his leg and realized she was trailing her hand along his inner thigh. Arousal replaced caution. He took her into his arms, her body soft and pliant as he pulled her to him, but when he tried to roll on top of her, she put a restraining hand to his chest.

Her hand trailed down again, found the top of his underwear and slid inside, her fingers exploring, caressing him. His excitement rose. Her breathing quickened when her hand closed lightly, tantalizingly over his sex. He strained toward her, yanking off his underwear, tossing it to the floor.

Touching him gently with her fingertips, her hand slid along the length of his shaft, back and forth, back and forth, then left him without warning. She knelt above him, straddling his body. Leaning forward, she let one of her breasts caress his face lightly. He raised his head and circled her nipple with his tongue and she cried out in pleasure. He kissed her breasts one at a time, sucking her nipples into his mouth.

Katryn reached down and guided him into her warm wetness. She rose up, then lowered herself until he was sheathed entirely within her. Taking his hands, she guided them to her breasts, holding them there as she raised and lowered her hips in an ever increasing rhythm.

It flashed through him that he wasn't the first man she'd bedded and then he was beyond thought, his world exploding in flames. When he could think again, Katryn was rolling off him. She turned her back to him. Sated, his worries of a few hours before were forgotten, hidden by the gloss of passion. When Kezia crossed his mind, he felt a spurt of guilt.

Damn it, what else could he have done? Even T.J. hadn't been immune to the appeal of a pretty girl. Thinking of his father somehow reminded him of C, which made him remember he was in a strange country, surrounded by enemies. Easing his arm over the side of the bed, he collected the Webley and thrust it under his pillow again. Beside him, Katryn breathed deeply, apparently asleep.

He closed his eyes and once again he saw the Zeppelin looming over the trees, the great gray ship rising into the night sky. For an instant he caught his breath, thinking he was on the verge of a discovery, that some baffling puzzle was about to come clear to him, that there was a meaning in this fragment if a dream that he had never been able to grasp before.

As quickly as it had come, the knowledge fled, while at the same time the vision of the Zeppelin fled and Luke felt himself descending deeper and deeper into the oblivion of sleep.

A sound awakened him. As he glanced across the room, he heard his door click shut. Katryn? He reached out, found the bed empty, swung his feet to the floor and stood up. The first light of dawn paled the windows, the house was quiet. He donned his underwear and reached for his pants on the chair where he'd left them.

The pants were gone. What the hell? They're weren't on the floor or the bed. He slid the Webley into his hand, crossed to the door, eased it open and looked out. Saw a flash of movement at the far end of the hall to his left.

He padded down the corridor, stopping to listen outside the closed door where he'd heard movement. Inside the room, footsteps pattered across the floor. After a moment he eased the door open and peered inside.

Katryn, wearing her white nightgown, sat

with her back to him at a table where a lamp burned low. Careful to make no sound, he stepped into the bedroom. At first he couldn't tell what she was doing, but then he realized she held his pants on her lap and was systematically emptying the pockets and placing the contents on the table in front of her.

What else had he expected?

14

Staring at Katryn searching his pants pockets, Luke's first thought was that she was robbing him but almost immediately he discarded it. Surely she wouldn't risk discovery for a few francs. If not robbery, what? Was she working for the Germans, a double agent pretending to help the Allies while at the same time sending information to Berlin?

If she was, she'd find damned little by searching his clothing. Nothing that would help the Huns.

He took a step toward her, intending to surprise her, to force her to tell the truth. Had Belgians, French and English escapees stayed here, he wondered, only to be betrayed by Katryn? Would she talk? Probably not. Changing his mind about confronting her, he retreated into the corridor and closed her door.

In his own room he replaced the Webley under his pillow, then slid under the bed cover. He'd give Katryn five minutes to return his clothes. After less than half that time, the door opened and bare feet padded across the floor, pausing beside his chair before heading for the bed. He closed his eyes. He sensed Katryn leaning over him, felt a featherlike touch on his lips, then heard steps padding away. He slitted his eyes and saw her ease through his door, closing it behind her.

He sat up. Why the hell had she kissed him? A Judas kiss? He rose and pulled on his pants, finished dressing, holstered his Webley, went into the hall and tried the door of the next room. Unlocked. Once inside, he saw Sid's form outlined under the bedcover, heard the rasp of his breathing. Edging close to the bed, he recalled T.J.'s admonition: 'Never startle an armed man when you wake him unless you enjoy dodging .45's.'

'Sid,' he whispered. 'Sid, it's Luke. Wake up.'

Sid groaned.

'It's Luke. Are you awake?'

'Too bloody right,' Sid said plaintively, rising onto an elbow. 'Why'd you have to wake me? I was dreaming of this little French *mademoiselle*. 'Sid, she says to me — ''

'Not now,' Luke cut in. 'Listen. We've got trouble. Here's what I want you to do . . .'

As soon as he left Sid, Luke returned to his room and waited. Hearing a voice from the yard below, he looked from his windows and saw Hendrik leading a horse from the barn.

The smell of cooking drifted through the open window. The house was rousing to life. He shrugged. It might turn out to be helpful.

Luke glanced at his watch. Five minutes had passed. Going to the door, he eased it open and looked along the corridor. Empty. He walked to Katryn's bedroom, lifted the latch and pushed inward. It wouldn't budge. Damn, her door had a bolt and she'd used it. Katryn was still inside. Why hadn't he checked the door earlier? Now he'd have to play it by ear.

Returning to his own room, he paused, smelling smoke.

In the early morning light he saw gray tendrils curling along the hall toward him. Slipping into his own room, he left the door ajar. Though he expected the cry, Sid's shout still startled him.

'Fire! The bloody place is on fire!'

Luke waited.

'Fire!' Sid shouted again.

An answering shout came from below stairs. Footsteps raced along the hall and he saw Katryn hurry past his slightly open door carrying a small black notebook. He stepped into the hall and gazed after her. She wore a robe over her nightgown and he marveled at how small and fragile she seemed. No matter what their size, could any woman be trusted?

When she was out of sight, Luke turned and ran back along the hall. When the smoke billowed around him, he covered his face with his handkerchief, feeling his way along the hall with his other hand. Katryn's door stood open. He entered, shutting door behind him. Through a thin veil of smoke, he saw an open bottom drawer of a chest against the far wall. He crossed to the chest, knelt on the floor and probed inside. Nothing but feminine undergarments. Now. Rising, leaving the drawer as he'd found it, he returned to the door.

Hearing nothing, he left Katryn's bedroom, finding the smoke had eased. He ran down the rear stairs. Through the open back door he saw Sid in the yard throwing water from the bucket on a pile of smoldering rags.

'What the hell's going on?' Luke asked loudly as he came out of the house.

'I was cleaning my gun,' Sid said, 'and smoking the last of the fag Mac scrounged for me. How the hell was I to know those rags were there?'

A weak story but it would have to do.

Hendrik hurried toward them from the front of the house and, behind him, Luke saw the curtains of a window flick aside. Katryn. The curtains fell back into place. Sid repeated his story to Hendrik before hurrying to the pump for another pail of water. Hendrik, hands on hips, looked from the burned debris to the retreating Sid. Luke wondered if he bought the tale. He shrugged. What if he didn't? He wouldn't be likely to tumble to the reason Sid had started the blaze.

Ignoring Hendrik, Luke returned to his room and straightened his bed. If nothing else, the French Air Service had taught him to make a bed properly. As he finished the door opened and Sid slipped into the room.

'Time for chow, governor,' Sid told him.

'Are both of them downstairs?' Luke asked, sotto voce.

'Righto. In the kitchen.'

'Tell Hendrik I'm on my way. If he gets antsy, make sure you're the one who comes looking for me.'

Sid nodded. Luke followed him into the hall and watched him start down the stairs. Okay, get on with it, he told himself.

He walked quickly to Katryn's room and tried the door. Unlocked, it swung inward. No one was inside. Closing the door behind him, he started to bolt it and shook his head. A dead giveaway, trapping him inside, besides.

The bed was made, the curtains billowed inward from an open window. Crossing to the chest, Luke knelt and opened the bottom drawer. The underwear had been rearranged in neat piles. His fingers slipped underneath the silky garments, probing until he touched a hard surface. Thinking he heard a sound from the hall, he held, listening.

When the sound wasn't repeated, he pulled out his find — a book with a black cover, the one Katryn had saved from the fire. He stood and flipped through the pages. Most were blank. On the last few were listed names, addresses, dates and series of numbers. He slid the notebook into his pocket, bent and shut the drawer.

As Luke crossed the room, he stopped, staring at the door, sensing someone was outside, waiting in the hall, listening. He shook his head. Nobody was out there. Still, he hesitated.

He watched the latch slide up, slowly and silently. Luke stared at the moving latch for an instant before hurriedly glancing around the room. No place to hide. He stepped behind the door, sliding his Webley from the holster. The door swung a few inches open, then gradually opened wider. He tensed, gun at the ready.

Without warning the door swung back hard, slamming against him, smashing into his nose, the pain momentarily stunning him. By the time he recovered he was staring into the muzzle of a Mauser pistol gripped in both of Katryn's hands. He started to bring up his gun, saw her finger tighten on the trigger and held.

Katryn motioned with her head, telling him to drop his revolver. He opened his hand and let the gun fall to the floor, then took a step toward her. She took a step back, her blue eyes cold, her face set. He took another step. She fired, the roar filling the room. The shot zinged past his head and thudded into the wall.

He halted. Either it was a warning or she was a poor shot. If she'd meant to kill him and missed she'd fire again. He braced himself. She didn't pull the trigger, continuing to back steadily away from him, the muzzle of the gun never wavering.

Behind him, he heard two sets of footsteps on the stairs, the sound of a struggle, then silence. Katryn, now standing on a throw rug near the bed, stopped but continued to watch Luke warily. His nose throbbed and, when he licked the trickle on his upper lip, he tasted blood.

They both were listening, he knew, listening and waiting. Footsteps again, one man's. Katryn's gaze darted to the door. Luke dove forward, reaching not for Katryn, she was too far for him, but for the edge of the rug. He grasped the near end and yanked the rug to one side as her gun roared, missing him. Katryn stumbled backward, her arm striking the footboard of the bed. He leaped at her, his shoulder caught her waist-high. She gasped. His fingers closed on the wrist of her gun hand and he twisted. The Mauser spun away.

Luke dived for his Webley but before he reached it a shot thudded into the floor in front of him. Hendrik, pistol in hand, stood in the doorway. 'Leave the gun,' Hendrik ordered. 'Get to your feet.'

Luke obeyed, seeing Katryn stumble to her feet and cross to her brother, standing behind him. She pointed accusingly at Luke.

'What did you do to her?' Hendrik demanded. 'Why are you in her bedroom?'

Luke stared at him. Surely Hendrik didn't think he'd raped Katryn.

'Your hands,' Hendrik said. 'Place them behind your head. Now, tell me what you did to Katryn.'

'Nothing. Ask her. Nothing at all.'

'Asking will do no good when we both know she can't speak.'

Luke's gaze shifted to Katryn, realizing he'd never heard her utter a word. Sounds, yes, but no words. He was putting together a story that involved Katryn stealing from him when she slipped from behind her brother, hurried to the chest against the wall and opened the bottom drawer. He shrugged and abandoned the false tale.

Katryn searched the drawer, then turned and shook her head.

'You'll find the book in his lower right pocket,' Hendrik told her.

Luke glanced down and saw the telltale bulge of the notebook. When Katryn started toward him, he tensed, ready to make the most of any opportunity.

'No,' Hendrik told his sister. 'We'll get it later.'

After he was dead, Luke realized with a cold chill. Where the hell was Sid? What had Hendrik done with him? He glanced toward the door.

'Your friend fell when he was climbing the stairs. He'll recover. But too late to be of any help to you.' He smiled at Luke. 'Last year a Frenchman tried to take advantage of my sister, tried to force her because he knew she couldn't call for help. I caught him in time. I didn't kill him, I dealt with him in my own way. I swore that if I ever caught another bastard trying to take advantage of her, I'd kill him. And I intend to.'

Hendrik gestured with his pistol. 'Take off your clothes.'

'Go to hell.'

When Hendrick said nothing, Luke added, 'I was after the notebook, not your sister's virtue, as you know damn well. If you're going to shoot me, at least get it right.'

'I don't believe you. The notebook, yes, but also Katryn. I saw how you looked at her.'

The man was obsessed. No matter what his reason, though, Luke knew Hendrik would kill him.

'If you don't wish to remove your clothes now,' Hendrik said, 'I can take them off for you afterward. If that is what you prefer. Make your decision.'

Now or later was his choice.

'I'll take them off,' Luke told him. He sat on the bed and began unlacing his boots, slowly. At least his nose had stopped bleeding, for whatever that was worth. He couldn't help thinking God was punishing him for sleeping with Katryn, even though the seducing had come from her. His mother would have thought so. Not T.J., who must have bedded Linda May many times while he was still married to Luke's mother. No, that couldn't be right. T.J. hadn't known Linda May then. It hadn't been Linda May T.J. and his mother had been quarreling about.

'Faster.' Hendrik was watching him, the pistol steady. Luke dropped one boot to the floor, then the other. He began unbuttoning his shirt, eyeing Hendrik, then glancing at Katryn as she crossed the room, keeping well away from him, to pick up his Webley from the floor before retrieving her own Mauser. She placed the Webley on the chest, keeping the Mauser.

She looked from her brother to Luke and he saw she was breathing rapidly, her cheeks flushed. Perspiration beaded her forehead. This is how she must have looked the night before, when they made love. He realized she was anticipating seeing him naked. And then dead?

Luke tossed his jacket and shirt over the back of a chair and started unfastening his belt. He pretended to have trouble unfastening the buttons on the front of his pants.

'Faster, if you please,' Hendrik told him. 'And keep your eyes off Katryn. No one is allowed to touch her.' Recalling that the girl was far from being a virgin, was, in fact, a woman of no little experience, a suspicion took root in Luke. Someone had taught her and that someone could only be her brother. He stared at Hendrik, wanting to accuse him but knowing he'd die all the sooner if he did. Hendrik gestured impatiently with the pistol and Luke let his pants fall. He kicked them to one side.

Luke calculated the distance between himself and the blond man. Too far. Hendrik would get off two rounds, maybe three before Luke reached him. Katryn? She stood to one side and slightly behind her brother. Worse yet. If only he could lure one of them closer.

'Now the underwear,' Hendrik ordered.

Luke pulled his undershirt over his head. Debated whether to throw it at Hendrik in an attempt to distract him. No, he was grasping at straws.

The window? It was open. Luke resisted the impulse to glance that way, already aware the window was some six feet from him. He could hurl himself through the opening. His fall to the ground wouldn't be more than fifteen feet. If he made it without getting shot on the way.

Hendrik, as though anticipating him, stepped closer to the window. 'Don't,' he said. 'Take off your undershorts and get on the bed. On your hands and knees.'

Luke winced inwardly. He'd feared all along what Hendrik meant to do to him before he shot him. No damn way would he submit. He'd make the bastard kill him first.

He pulled off his undershorts and dropped them to the floor, naked except for his socks. He started to turn toward the bed, intending to leap for the window instead. He held for an instant to glance at Katryn. She was staring at him, her eyes glazed.

'Katryn,' he said softly.

'I warned you,' Hendrik snapped, aiming the pistol at his gut.

Luke poised himself to jump for the window, knowing he'd be dead before he reached it.

KA-BAM.

The roar of gunfire exploded in the room. Luke stiffened. He felt no pain. Nothing. He'd expected to feel pain when this moment came. Had Hendrik missed? He glanced at him. The blond man pitched face-first to the floor.

Luke's gaze shifted to Katryn. Had she shot her brother? She was backing away, her Mauser in her hand, staring at the door.

Luke swung around. MacNeeley stepped into the room, his revolver swinging from the dead Hendrik to aim at Katryn.

'No!' shouted Luke.

MacNeeley fired. Blood stained the white front of Katryn's dress. Hurled backwards, she slammed into the wall, her Mauser clattering to the floor. She slid downward until she was sitting on the floor, her mouth open as though to speak at last, her eyes open in the stare of death.

15

Luke and MacNeeley found Sid sprawled on the stairs and carried him to the front parlor where they laid him on a divan. Though unconscious, his breathing was steady and his color good. Luke, kneeling, saw a bruised swelling in Sid's reddish hair above his right ear.

MacNeeley went to the kitchen, returning with a damp cloth. As he bathed Sid's forehead, the injured man moaned. 'He'll come out of it in no time,' MacNeeley said. 'He's had a bad whack but I doubt if there's any real damage. Thank God. He'd be a problem for us otherwise.'

Luke watched MacNeeley wipe smudges from Sid's face with the cloth. 'You saved my life up there,' Luke told him. 'Not to mention a few vital appendages. There's no way to thank you.'

'You don't owe me,' MacNeeley replied, obviously uncomfortable. 'Aren't we comrades, all for one and one for all?'

'She wouldn't have shot me,' Luke went on, discovering with a small shock that he couldn't make himself say her name. In a way he mourned her, she'd been a victim all her life. He didn't like having a woman's blood on their hands.

'I couldn't take that chance,' MacNeeley said. 'In my experience, some women can prove deadlier than men. How could I tell which kind she was? There you were bare-ass naked and there the two of them were with their Mausers. We're better off with both of them dead.'

A cold-blooded bastard, MacNeeley. But that's what an agent operating in enemy territory ought to be, wasn't it? Quietly efficient, undeterred by false sympathy for the Germans, male or female, coldly calculating. Mac stood a better chance of surviving than he did.

Still, Luke wondered how the man managed to live with himself.

'There's blood on your shirt,' MacNeeley told him.

'My own.' Luke felt his sore nose gingerly. He'd washed his face but he hadn't noticed the stains on his shirt. Wanting no reminder of that grim scene upstairs, he picked up the damp cloth and scrubbed at his shirt.

'We'll have to dispose of the bodies.' Luke spoke as much to himself as to Mac, glancing from the window at the empty farmyard, the barn and the Belgian countryside stretching away to the horizon.

'From what I heard in Brussels last night, our late friend Hendrik won't be missed for some time. All in all, he wasn't an ingratiating sort of chap. What love he was capable of must have gone into his damn cooking. And then there were the scandalous whispers about him and his sister.'

Luke didn't want to think about it. 'What else did you find out?'

'Nothing good. Kezia's still all right, though it's not safe for us to try to contact her. It turns out that our *M.* LeMur is a prisoner of the Huns. Our Belgian apparatus has been crippled, all but destroyed, and the prison guards we were counting on to bring us the plans of St. Gilles are in hiding. Then there's the dynamite, my lovely dynamite. The entire cache of explosives was confiscated by the Germans.'

As he muttered, 'Damn,' it crossed Luke's mind that so much betrayal meant a leak somewhere but there was no point in discussing something they could do nothing about at the moment.

MacNeeley half-smiled. 'I know C must have given you an out,' he said. 'A contact to make in extremis. That's where we are, in extremis. We've reached the end of what we can do on our own. The time's come to ask for help. You've heard of the saying about there being old spies and bold spies but you rarely meet an old, bold spy.'

Luke shook his head. 'I was fed some hocus-pocus I can try as a last resort. I don't think we're to that point yet.'

'Good God, man, if not now, when? When we're sitting in our cells in St. Gilles waiting for the padre to come to pray for our immortal souls before they take us to the firing squad?'

Luke could feel himself digging his heels in, a trait that had driven his mother to distraction. Ever since he'd been a child, the more anyone tried to persuade him of what he should do, the more resistant he became. He couldn't help himself. Besides, he hated to admit failure.

Sid groaned. His eyes blinked open and he stared around him in confusion.

'Take it easy, old chap,' MacNeeley told him. 'Don't try to get up. Stay quiet and you'll soon be right as rain.'

Sid sighed and closed his eyes again.

'The three of us aren't helpless,' Luke said. 'We can reconnoiter the prison. Look for some other way to free Nurse Cavell.'

MacNeeley snorted. 'Without my explosives? Without any help from the Belgians?'

'After this, I'm not so sure I can trust a

Belgian. In any case, C didn't say it would be a cakewalk.'

'He didn't say he'd put a stubborn Yank madman in command, either.'

Luke clenched his fists, glaring at MacNeeley. He'd known all along that the man thought he should have been in charge. Damn it, C must have had a reason for choosing Luke Ray instead and he wasn't going to take guff from MacNeeley, even if the man had saved his life.

MacNeeley stared back at him for long moments, finally looking away. 'Sorry,' he muttered. 'I was out of step. We can't afford to quarrel. It's only that I thought the least we could do here at the dead end we're in was to sound an alarm. Perhaps they'd send the other group to help us.'

'The other group? What other group?'

'Before I left Kezia she told me about them so you don't have to pretend you don't know. The backup group that's somewhere in Brussels now. Who they are, how many they are, I haven't the foggiest. Why are you shaking your head? Surely they told you.'

'I never heard of a support unit.' Luke walked to the window and looked out to hide his confusion, his feeling of being betrayed. Could MacNeeley be lying? He brushed the thought aside. If he couldn't trust Mac, who could he trust? 'If C wanted us to know,' he said, 'he'd have told me.'

'Yet Kezia knew. And told me.'

Again Luke's suspicion flared. Why hadn't Kezia told him?

'Why wait until now to mention it?' he asked MacNeeley.

'I thought you knew. I thought you must have known.'

I didn't know shit. They didn't want me to for some reason. Rather than try to figure out why, he walked to the divan where Sid was sitting up with his head in his hands.

'That blighter gave me a God-awful thump,' Sid said. 'My head feels like the devil's in there driving his pitchfork into my brain. I saw the bastard come up behind me too bloody late to duck.' He glanced around. 'Where is he?'

'Hendrik and his sister are both dead,' Luke said. 'Mac saved us. We'd be six feet under by now if he hadn't come back in time.' Luke turned to MacNeeley, his mind made up. 'We're not in extremis,' he said flatly. 'Not yet. If there is another group, they damn well will have to find us. There'll be no asking for help unless and until I can't find any other way out. Understood?'

'Righto. But whatever we do, we'll have to do quickly. I found out something else while I was in the city. The trial of Edith Cavell begins today.'

★ ★ ★

The two men trudged along with their heads lowered against the cold October drizzle, the collars of their jackets up, their caps pulled low on their foreheads. Horse chestnut shells crunched under their feet.

They entered a spacious *place* in the ancient heart-shaped section of the city. A fountain dominated the square but no water burbled skyward and the water in the collecting pool was covered with a scum of dirt and dead leaves from the trees bordering the cobbled streets. Pigeons perched on the cornices of the structures on the four sides of the square, anonymous government buildings with entrances at the top of broad flights of stone stairs.

Luke glanced appraisingly at the German soldiers stationed in front of the buildings and at intervals on the streets leading into the square. They passed two of them, both young, both wet and no longer trying to hide their discomfiture as they huddled inside their greatcoats in the slow-falling rain. They wore the new steel helmets that were rapidly replacing the old leather ones.

These Germans, Luke realized, as he recollected the English research he'd done on the country when he knew he was going there, were only the latest in a long line of invaders. Belgium, a country the size of Maryland, had been a battleground for centuries, at least since Julius Caesar led his legions to the North Sea. Charlemagne ruled here, and Spain, France and Holland. Napoleon conquered the country only to be finally beaten twelve miles south of Brussels at Waterloo. Then, in 1830, Belgium became a free nation, her independence guaranteed. Until the Germans marched across her borders in 1914.

Luke turned to MacNeeley. 'You're sure of the time?' he asked.

'Ten o'clock,' Mac told him. 'The Germans are as punctual as Big Ben. They'll arrive here in the square at ten or a few minutes after. The session in the chamber starts at ten-thirty.'

Luke grunted, resisting the urge to thrust his hands deep in his pockets. The Belgians on the nearby streets didn't seem to do that. A bell pealed above him and he looked up at the clock in a spired tower. Ten. The bell tolled and he counted under his breath, 'Eight, nine, ten.' The bell fell silent, leaving the trace of an echo in the damp air. The

German soldiers around the square, he noticed, had straightened, become alert.

'There you are,' MacNeeley stopped, indicated the way they'd come.

A staff car. A black sedan, drove slowly into the place from the sidestreet they'd just crossed. Two flags emblazoned with the German imperial eagle hung damply from small staffs mounted on the front fenders, making Luke, just for a moment, nostalgic for the United States eagle emblems, similar and yet so different from the German ones.

The three German *landwehr* soldiers in the car, one driver and two men in the seat behind, sat stiffly erect. One of the soldiers glanced to his right, caught Luke's gaze and stared directly at him. Luke stared back, his face expressionless, then looked away. As the car drove past, he judged its speed at fifteen miles an hour.

Another long black car followed, then another and another, each a duplicate of the first except that they carried Belgian civilians, both men and women, riding with their German guards. Some of the prisoners stared straight ahead while others looked with fixed, hopeless eyes through the rain-streaked windows at the buildings around the *place*. A very few actually gazed at the few onlookers, perhaps hoping to catch a glimpse of a loved one.

'Here we are.' MacNeeley touched Luke's arm. 'This must be the car.'

The black sedan was identical to those that had preceded it. Two German non-coms in front, a third stiffly erect in the back seat. The woman sat beside the soldier in the rear. Dressed in a dark blue coat and wearing a blue hat, she appeared small next to her German guard. Small and middle-aged. Her face was set, expressionless. As the car passed Luke, her eyes found his. To his surprise her mouth opened as though she was about to speak. Then the car was past him and Luke was staring not at her but at the small oval rear window.

He'd recognized her, of course, from the many photographs shown him at Boling Hall. She looked older than he'd expected but then many of the photos had been taken years before. For some reason he'd expected her to be wearing her nurse's uniform, perhaps because he knew that Germans were impressed by uniforms. Maybe they hadn't let her. After all, she was their prisoner. She'd seemed resigned, ready to endure whatever fate held in store for her. Serene was the word that came to him. She looked like a woman who'd made her peace with God.

The last car in the procession drove by, its tires jouncing over the wet cobbles. After it was gone, Luke and MacNeeley crossed the street and walked slowly around the fountain under the dripping chestnut trees.

'You saw her, of course,' Mac said.

Luke nodded.

'Are you satisfied that it's her?'

'I'm sure of it,' Luke said. He lowered his already low voice. 'Nurse Cavell was the woman in the next to last car.'

'Her trial in the Senate chamber will last another day, or it could be two. General von Sauberzweig has brought *Kriegsgerichtsrat* Stober to Brussels to prosecute the case. He's certain to make a show of it.'

'And after the trial?'

'I'd estimate there'll be at least a week before the verdict's announced.'

'That means we have nine days'

'No more. Stober's expected to ask for a sentence of death for most of those tried. Including her. On the grounds that many brave soldiers have died as a result of their so-called plot.'

Luke looked back across the square. The staff cars had left but the German soldiers still manned their posts in the drizzle. Luke felt a sense of unreality . . . that this wasn't happening. He shook his head.

'Was I right,' MacNeeley asked, 'when I said there were possibilities here if we could only discover how to take advantage of them?'

Luke frowned. 'They say Germans follow orders implicitly. Without question.'

'That's true, they're good soldiers. I had some dealings with Germans before the war when I bicycled in the Black Forest near Stuttgart. It was there I learned to speak the language without an accent. They're stolid for the most part. Perfectionists. They lack a sense of humor. I suspect they don't have much imagination.'

'We'll go back and talk it over with Sid,' Luke said. 'He can help us get whatever we might need. In his own way.' He paused, then added, 'You were right about the possibilities.'

* * *

The rain ended in the night and the next day was clear and cool, the sky a deep October blue. On the last stroke of ten the caravan of prisoners on its way from St. Gilles to the Senate Chamber entered the *place* with the flags on the sedans snapping in the breeze. German soldiers jogged crisply into position to stop traffic from entering the square from cross streets.

An old man waited impatiently on the curb as the first car went by. After the second German car passed, he limped into the street as though to cross. His head jerked up as the next sedan bore down on him. He stopped, undecided, before limping back to the curb. A German soldier in the car glared at him, waved him back.

The old man held a brown paper sack clutched in his right hand. Before the procession he'd been taking crumbs from the sack and scattering them for the pigeons. The birds still scurried to and fro on the pavement a few feet behind him, pecking at the last of the bread.

More long black cars passed the old man. He measured their speed and the distance between them with his eyes, waiting for a chance to cross. A hundred feet farther along the street a Flemish farmer, sturdy, broad-faced, sat placidly on the seat of his wagon, the reins held loosely in one hand, also waiting. There were several other wagons on the perimeter of the *place*, a few buggies, but the only automobiles were the black staff cars making their way like a funeral procession toward the nearby Senate Chamber.

The next to last car turned into the *place*. For a moment the old man peered at the blue-coated woman in the back, then looked

262

away. After her car was well beyond him, he again limped from the curb into the street. The final car bore down on him. He hesitated as he had before, as though uncertain whether to risk hurrying across in front of the car or to retreat. He clutched his sack in both hands. At the last moment he limped ahead and safely reached the other side.

There was a sharp explosion followed by a loud whistle. Pigeons flapped into the air, calling in alarm. Another explosion. The rearmost German car veered right, toward the curb. The driver gripped the wheel with one hand, braked and stopped. The sergeant at his side threw open the door and sprang to the street a Mauser carbine in his hand. The other cars in the procession, unaware of what was happening behind them, drove slowly on.

The sergeant who had leaped to the pavement shouted to the driver, pointing at the car's wheels. Two tires were flat, the left front and the right rear. The driver opened his door and stood, hands on hips, as he stared at the damage.

Farther along the street, the horse hitched to the farmer's wagon whinnied, reared and bolted. The farmer stood, calling to the animal and tugging on the reins. The wagon clattered into the street in front of the car transporting the English nurse. The driver braked. Too late. The car skidded and slammed into the side of the wagon.

The wagon tilted onto its side, the horse broke free and trotted, wild-eyed, nostrils flaring, over the cobbles. Steam plumed from the car's radiator. The guard in the front passenger seat sprang from the car with his carbine in one hand. Leaping from his tilted wagon, the farmer ran. The guard raised his carbine, calling to him to halt, lowering his gun when the farmer disappeared between two buildings. Whistles shrilled around the square.

A staff car glided from a side street, carefully skirted the car with the two flat tires and slowed as it came to the nurse's car. A German lieutenant leaped from the front before the car was fully stopped, ran to the rear of his car and yanked open the door. Pointing into the car, he shouted to the guard with the carbine. *'Los bringen sie hier rein!'*

The German in the rear of Nurse Cavell's car opened his door, ran around the back of the car and opened the door on the far side. He gestured to the middle-aged woman in blue. She hesitated before stepping into the street. The guard ran up, took her by the arm and shoved her into the newly arrived car, climbing in after her. The lieutenant slammed the door shut and joined the driver in the front. The car accelerated.

The other staff cars had driven from the *place*. The lieutenant's car followed their route until, where the procession had turned right, it veered left, speeding up. '*He! Wo fahrt ihr hin?*' the guard in the rear shouted. The lieutenant turned and rested the barrel of his Mauser on the back of his seat. The car screeched to a halt. '*Raus!*' he ordered. '*Lass dein Gewehr liegen!*'

The guard stared at him.

'*Tu was ich sage,*' the lieutenant repeated. His finger tightened on the trigger.

The soldier placed his carbine on the seat, got out of the car and shut the door.

MacNeeley turned to Luke, who was driving. 'I make a rather convincing Hun lieutenant, don't you — ' He stopped. Luke, paying no attention to him, was staring at the middle-aged woman in the rear seat.

'There's Sid.' MacNeeley pointed.

Luke turned in his seat and shifted gears, accelerated, slowed and stopped beside the old man. The limp was gone as Sid climbed into the rear of the car. Again Luke sped away. He was about to turn from the square when MacNeeley put a hand on his arm, shouting, 'No!'

The street was blocked by a German staff car. Luke swung left. Whistles shrilled and men shouted behind him. Armed soldiers, led by an officer waving them forward with his Mauser, ran past the fountain toward them.

Luke squealed his tires as he sped to the next intersection street. He braked. Damn. Another black car blocked the exit. He heard the rear door open behind him. He twisted around in time to see the blue-coated woman jump from the car, pitch forward and fall to the pavement on her hands and knees.

Sid scrambled across the rear seat to the open door. 'I'll get her,' he said.

'No.' Luke reached back and grabbed Sid's wrist. 'Let her go.'

Sid stared at him, shrugged, shut the door. Luke swung the car left once more, racing past horse chestnut trees, past steps leading to stone buildings with gilded gables. The next street was blocked by rifle-bearing Germans in position behind a two-car barricade. Again Luke braked. The car swerved to a stop.

'That alley.' MacNeeley pointed.

The narrow passageway led between two massive buildings. It appeared to end at a brick wall.

'It's a dead end,' Luke said.

'No,' MacNeeley insisted. 'There's a turn before the wall. Trust me.'

The soldiers had spread out and were

closing in on them from both sides and the rear, holding their fire as though meaning to take them alive.

Luke swung the car into the alley. He braked as he neared the wall. Let out his breath. The alley turned sharply right. Luke skidded into the turn. Stared. A car was bearing down on them, its black bulk filling the alley. Germans leaned from the car's windows. Pistol shots snapped. The windshield in front of Luke shattered in a burst of glass. Flying shards stung his cheeks. He pressed down on the gas, raced at the other car.

Just as he'd challenged the Fokker. Only here there was no place to turn.

For an instant he wondered who the woman they'd taken from the German car had been. Of one thing he was certain. She wasn't Edith Cavell.

16

'Hang on!' Luke shouted. 'We're gonna hit 'em hard.' The approaching German car screeched to a halt, skidding sideways to block the alley. Luke braked and his car slowed. He saw four German soldiers in the other car. One threw open the door and poised to leap to the pavement.

Luke accelerated, his motor sputtered, the car lurched. Damn, the engine was dying on him. Suddenly the car rallied, shot ahead. He glimpsed the startled faces of the Germans. The cars met with a jarring crash. Metal clanged to the stone street. Steam and smoke rose from the hoods of both cars.

'Over the top,' Luke shouted.

He shoved open his door. Scrambled into the alley with his Webley in his hand. He fired. The German car's windshield starred. A soldier screamed in pain. Another shouted orders. Black smoke obscured the German car. MacNeeley fired from the far side of the alley. A German bullet smacked the wall beside Luke's head and whined away. Tendrils of flame snaked from the hood of the car. More smoke billowed upward. Flames exploded in a searing fireball above Luke's head.

Luke, hand raised to shield his face, ran to the rear of the car, put his foot on the fender and threw himself onto the roof, rolling across the top and dropping on his feet on the other side. MacNeeley followed, clambering between the spare tire mounted at the car's rear and the brick wall of the building.

They ran deeper into the alley, fearing another explosion. As soon as he was away from the heat, Luke swung around. A German ran toward him from the burning car, carbine in one hand. Luke fired two rounds. The German stopped as though he'd hit an invisible wall. Crumpled backward to the cobbles.

The car was blazing along its entire length. Where were the other Germans? Where was Sid?

'What happened to Sid?' he asked Mac-Neeley. 'Did you see Sid?'

MacNeeley shook his head.

Luke sprinted toward the burning car. Shots barked above the crackle of flames. Heat seared his face, forcing him to slow. Footsteps pounded behind him and Mac-Neeley grabbed his arm.

'We don't have time,' MacNeeley shouted.

Luke shook him off and started forward.

T.J. wouldn't abandon a comrade in trouble. The flames, he thought, were lessening, the smoke thinning. But the heat was so intense he couldn't reach the car.

'Sid!' he shouted. 'Sid!'

He thought he heard an answering shout mingled with the roar of the fire. Through gaps in the flames he saw a figure limping away from him on the other side of the wrecked cars. Sid, it was Sid retreating along the alley, his limp real now, not assumed. Luke couldn't see any of the Germans.

Sid tried to open the doors along the side of the alley. Without success. A car careered around the sharp right turn, headed for Sid. Luke heard the slap of shots. He fired at the car, knowing the range was too great. He glanced to where he'd last seen Sid. He was gone. Germans piled from the car, two running into an open door on the side of the alley, three others trotting toward the burning car.

Two shots cracked from behind Luke. He turned and saw MacNeeley reloading his Mauser.

'Let's get the hell out of here,' MacNeeley called.

Luke glanced to where he'd last seen Sid.

'We can't help the poor bastard now,' Mac pointed out. He was right, Luke admitted.

Reluctantly. They had to think about saving their own hides.

They jogged down the alley with their German boots clicking on the cobbles and slowed when they came to a street. Luke noted a crèche built into the corner of one of the buildings. From high above his head the Virgin Mary, hands outstretched, looked down. Miraculously, the street was empty.

'This way,' MacNeeley said, turning to the right. Luke hesitated. That direction would take them farther from Sid and closer to the square, to the Germans. 'We'll never find Sid,' MacNeeley added. 'I know that area back there, it's a regular rabbit warren.'

Then maybe the Germans wouldn't find Sid either.

'This way,' Mac repeated. 'Hurry.'

Luke followed. MacNeeley holstered his pistol and Luke did the same. Two old priests rode by on bicycles with the skirts of their cassocks flapping about their knees. All at once MacNeeley slowed, put out his hand in warning. Luke also slowed to a walk, brushing his pants and straightening the jacket of his German uniform.

Moments later two German non-coms walked toward them, saluted. MacNeeley and Luke returned the salutes. Mac pointed back the way they'd come and issued crisp orders.

Luke's German was good enough to understand Mac was telling the soldiers there was a
fire that they must investigate. At once.

The two non-coms trotted past them down
the street. Without a question. Without
hesitating.

'One of the many pleasures of being an
officer in the Imperial German Army,'
MacNeeley said as they walked quickly on.
'You never have to explain yourself.'

'If we can bluff those two,' Luke said, 'we
can bluff others. We can — '

'We can't go back,' MacNeeley told him.
'They'll have our descriptions by now. We'd
best get rid of these uniforms. Sid's on his
own. He's used to being in tight corners.'

True. But in Sid's other tight corners he'd
been in a country where they spoke his
language. MacNeeley was right, though.
Much as he hated leaving Sid, they couldn't
go back. He realized, not for the first time,
that he liked Sid, felt closer to him than he
did to MacNeeley, who'd saved his life.

'That wasn't Nurse Cavell in the staff car,'
Luke said. 'She was dressed the same but she
was a younger woman.'

MacNeeley stared at him. 'Are you sure?'
His tone was skeptical.

'The Huns brought in a ringer. They're on
to us.'

'No, they couldn't be. If she wasn't Miss Cavell, then they were just being cautious.'

Luke shook his head. 'It's more than that.'

'They do seem to be checkmating us at every turn,' MacNeeley agreed. 'Sometimes I have a feeling that they know what we have in mind before we do ourselves.'

Luke glanced at the other man. Mac had echoed his own thoughts. He knew what MacNeeley was driving at.

'T. J., that's my father, always said a man branded himself a coward by asking for help too soon,' Luke said. 'And showed he was a fool if he didn't ask once he knew he was in over his head. What I'm saying is the time's come for us to play our last card.'

MacNeeley nodded. 'I'll volunteer to make the contact.' Luke shook his head. 'You can't. It has to be me. And I have to go alone.'

★ ★ ★

Luke Ray left the Grande Place and walked along the rue de L'Étuve wearing a nondescript gray coat that had a black band around its left arm. A folded newspaper protruded from his left pocket and he carried a brown leatherbound book in his right hand. Centimes and francs jingled in his pocket. He paused briefly on a corner in front of a lace

273

and linen shop, raising his eyebrows as he saw, for the first time, what he'd been told was the most famous statue in Brussels, the *Mannekin Pis*.

'This charmingly outrageous statue,' he remembered his guidebook declaring, 'is know as the city's 'Oldest Inhabitant.' His origin is a mystery though it is certain that a similar figure molded in sugar and emitting rose water was a much admired centerpiece at one of the banquets of Philip the Good, the present bronze sculpture is the work of the seventeenth century craftsman, Duquesnoy.'

The statue was of a naked boy urinating.

Luke shook his head. He could imagine the reaction if European visitors had come upon a similar statue among T.J.'s collection of artworks on the grounds of the Denver estate. They'd snicker behind their hands, calling T.J. crude and vulgar, an American barbarian.

But here in the Old World, a pissing boy in a public square was a part of history, an amusing and sophisticated work of art. Any Yankee who might disagree obviously lacked cultivation, wasn't a true citizen of the world. You couldn't win for losing in Europe, Americans always got the short end of the stick.

The only time Europeans appreciate us is when they have to flee for home with the

274

soldiers of a king or czar or kaiser in hot pursuit. Then the Statue of Liberty looked mighty good. To hell with them. Let them fight their own wars, we'll stay on our side of the Atlantic, thank you.

Yet *he* hadn't, had he?

He looked around him at the fountain, the iron grillwork in front of the shops, the gilded grandeur of Brussels and wondered what he was doing here.

Ah, well, there was more to Europe than the *Mannekin Pis*.

After walking past a street market he came to the Boulevard de Waterloo. Glancing at his wristwatch, he saw it was ten minutes to four. He was early. Luke sat on a bench to kill time. At the stroke of four, he looked to his right. The street was empty. A few minutes later a horse-drawn yellow tram appeared. Luke stood as the tram slowed to a stop, stepped aboard and paid his fare.

Though the car was nearly full, he found a seat by himself near the rear. He unfolded his newspaper and placed it on his lap. The bell clanged and the tram rattled up the hill as Luke surreptitiously studied his fellow passengers. He didn't know where the contact would be made or by whom, he only knew the time, between four and five.

An old gentleman seated near the front, an

unlit pipe in his mouth, had looked up at him as he boarded the tram. Was he the one he sought? Or was it the pretty young girl sitting across from him? Perhaps he wouldn't be approached this time. Perhaps later. Perhaps tomorrow. The day after? Not at all? The Belgian organization had, after all, been decimated.

Looking from the woman, he saw a tall woman walking away from him past a statue of a bearded knight on horseback. Kezia! He half-rose, his paper falling to the floor, intending to leap from the moving tram, run and overtake her. The other passengers stared. The woman on the street turned to cross an intersection and, seeing her sharp-featured face, he realized it wasn't Kezia after all.

God, he thought as he retrieved his paper and settled back in his seat, how he wanted to see her again! MacNeeley had claimed he'd left her with an Englishman whose name he didn't know. Where was she now? In England? Or was she still in Brussels? Luke gazed, unseeing, at the headlines on the newspaper on his lap. He wasn't a religious man but he closed his eyes and murmured a prayer for Kezia. And for Sid. Wherever they were.

The Boulevard de Waterloo became the

Boulevard du Regent on the uphill side of the Palais du Roi. When the name of the thoroughfare changed once more to the Boulevard Bischoffsheim, Luke walked to the open platform to the rear of the tram to get off. The conductor offered him a transfer. Luke started to refuse but thought better of it. No one had told him but maybe he'd need the transfer to make the contact. To be safe, he took the yellow slip of paper and thrust it in his pocket.

He walked back along the tram route for a few hundred feet to the park where he strolled under the elms and beeches to the first of the lake-fountains. No one seemed to pay the slightest attention to him. He glanced at his watch. Eight minutes before five.

Eight more minutes. Luke walked to the second pool and circled it, walking deliberately. A bespectacled elderly man sat on a bench reading a newspaper. A nursemaid in uniform pushed a black-hooded baby carriage, two boys played follow-the-leader, balancing precariously on the edge of the pool. The second boy faltered on the edge as Luke passed and he reached to steady the kid who smiled shyly at him before trailing the leader again.

No one appeared to notice him. By the time he completed his circle of the pool, it was well past five. Luke shrugged. There was nothing for it but to wait another day. He left the park and walked to his right on the rue Royale. A tram clattered toward him from higher on the hill.

He signaled the tram with his book, climbing aboard as soon as it stopped. About to pay the two-franc fare, he remembered the transfer. After fumbling in his coat pocket, he brought forth the yellow paper and returned it, shaking his head. Luke couldn't follow all of the man's voluble French but his meaning was clear. The transfer wasn't valid on this route. Luke paid the fare and made his way to a seat in the middle of the car. Crumpling the transfer, he was about to toss it to the floor when he frowned, hesitating, he thrust it into his book.

A few minutes later, under cover of the book, he smoothed out the paper. The front was unremarkable, a list of tram stops followed by numbers. As soon as he turned the transfer over he saw the address printed neatly in pencil on the back. An address on the Avenue Louise.

'You're one stupid bastard.' Without realizing it, he'd had the address ever since leaving the first tram. And he'd almost thrown it away.

Closing his eyes, he pictured the street map

he'd memorized in England. The Avenue Louise led southeast from the center of Brussels, near the Palace of Justice, toward Namur. The Porte Louise, at the head of the avenue, must have been one of the original gates of the city.

Luke left the tram and, after carefully destroying the transfer, walked in the darkening late afternoon to the Avenue Louise, a street of balconies decorated with black iron grillwork, of small shops, of crèches containing statues of saints set high in the corners of the buildings. He noted the house numbers, walking more than a mile before finding the one he wanted. He passed by it on the opposite side of the street, without pausing.

It was, he noted, in the middle of a row of attached houses, all narrow, all two stories, each painted a different pastel shade. The rendezvous house was a pale green. For no good reason, he remembered a Chinese cook his parents once had, a man with a pigtail who'd fascinated him as a child. Among other oddments he'd learned from the cook, was that green, in China, was an unlucky color.

But not in Brussels, of course. Still, he couldn't shake off a feeling of unease as he walked on to the end of the next block. He paused there as though to get his bearing, glancing unobtrusively around. There were no vehicles on the road at the moment and only a few people afoot — on his side of the street a middle-aged woman and a half-grown girl walking a dog, on the opposite side an elderly gentleman tapping his way slowly along with a white cane. Blind.

Good, he hadn't been followed. Crossing at the intersection, he made his way back to the green row house and knocked on the door. There was no answer. He knocked again, louder, and was ready to knock a third time when he heard steps inside. A stout middle-aged woman looked up at him from the interior darkness. Luke got an impression of graying blonde hair, thin lips, an aquiline nose.

'I've come to see the nightingales,' he said in French. The woman turned her head so her left ear was toward him. 'Don't whisper, young man,' she said.

'I have come to see the nightingales,' Luke repeated, louder, involuntarily glancing around. The blind man was tapping his way past. No one else was in sight. Or hearing, he hoped. To him, his voice sounded loud enough to wake the dead.

'Ah,' she said, opening the door wider, 'if you will please come in.' She led Luke to a sitting room whose tables and shelves were cluttered with knick-knacks. 'I am *Madame de Ligne*,' she said.

Luke bowed. He saw no reason to give a name, nor did she seem to expect him to.

'Alas, I have no nightingales to show you,' *Mme*. de Ligne said. 'However I have birds of other species. Do you have a message for me?'

Luke took a pencil stub from his pocket and wrote around the edges of one of the pages from his book, tore out the page and handed it to her.

'Make two copies, if you please.'

Luke wrote the short coded message again, on another page of the book and tore that one out. After feeling the pages, she nodded, saying, 'Thin enough.'

Mme. de Ligne folded both the pages and put them in the pocket of her black dress. 'If you will come with me,' she said.

Luke followed her from the sitting room to the rear of the house, puzzling over her comment about the thinness of the pages.

'With all their modern inventions,' she said as she started to climb a narrow stairs, 'they still come to me, don't they? They have their telephones and their telegraphs and their wireless and still they come to me. Their tricks, so ingenious, so easy to detect. Messages in rosaries, in matchboxes, in cigarettes, in tubes in the windpipes of corpses, inside artificial eyes.'

Dumbfounded, Luke could think of nothing to say. The windpipes of corpses?

'If only I had been at Messina in Italy,' she said, stopping at the top of the flight to catch her breath.

'Messina?' Luke repeated. 'In Italy?'

'Of course Messina is in Italy. It's a port in the toe of the boot. Don't you young people pay attention to what's going on in the world about you? If I or someone with beauties like mine had been at Messina a year ago, the whole course of this terrible war would have been different. The history of the world would have been changed. For the better. All that you young people care about is your own pleasure. Surely you've heard of the *Goeben* and the *Breslau*.'

The names had a familiar ring. 'They're German ships, aren't they?' Luke asked. He forgot to speak loud enough, so had to repeat his question.

'Of course they're German ships. They were a year ago and they are today. If I had been at Messina when those ships recoaled, I could have warned the British garrison at Malta. The Mediterranean Fleet would have found and sunk those two Hun ships. So the *Goeben* would never have reached the

Dardanelles, Turkey would have stayed neutral at the worst or entered the war on our side at the best. The British landing at Gallipoli wouldn't have been necessary. The Russians would have been supplied with arms through the Black Sea and Czar Nicolas would be leading his armies into East Prussia today instead of being threatened by a revolution. The entire war would have been changed if only I had been at Messina.'

'I'm sure it would have,' Luke said politely.

'And I'm certain you don't have the faintest glimmering of what I'm talking about.' *Mme*. de Ligne turned, unlocked and opened a door. Stairs led up into darkness. Luke followed her to another door at the top of the steps, waiting while she opened it and walked after her onto the flat roof of the house.

She crossed the roof on planks to a large wooden loft. Following her inside, Luke saw a wire cage no larger than a closet with several pigeons perched on shelves along the walls.

'Ah, my beautiful babies,' she crooned. 'These are all I have left. The Germans forbid us to keep them. Don't you find them beautiful, young man?'

He was about to agree — the birds were bolder looking than the pigeons he'd seen around the fountains — when he checked himself. Why lie? 'I'm sure you find them so,' he said diplomatically.

'True. Very true. I have the honor of being a former president of the Société Columbophile of Brussels,' she told him proudly. Taking a capsule from her pocket, she inserted his message and put it in her pocket. She opened a door in the cage, she lunged, caught one of the birds with her right hand, smoothed its gray feathers with her left.

'This is Mercury,' she said. 'Two years ago he won the Concourse National in record time.'

'The Concourse is a race?'

'Of course it's a race. Five hundred miles, from Toulouse to Brussels. The race was held every year since 1881. Until the war. Ah, but we are great pigeon fanciers here in Belgium, always have been, always will be. You can have your modern inventions. They'll never be a match for a well-trained racing pigeon.'

Holding Mercury in one hand, she fastened the capsule to his leg with an elastic band. Going to the roof edge, she threw the bird into the air. Luke watched him climb, then circle twice before flying into the west. For a moment he thought of his Bebe and wished he, not Mercury, was flying.

'That was beautiful,' he said appreciatively. 'Seeing him fly.'

She smiled at him for the first time. 'His flight will be as true as an arrow's. But there are dangers, such as hawks. So, just in case . . . '

She placed the copy of the message in another capsule, selected a plumper, purplish-gray bird and fastened the capsule to his leg. 'All right Ulysses,' she said, releasing the pigeon. 'Fly well.'

The bird circled, orienting himself, Luke realized, and flew west. He watched Ulysses until he was a speck against the orange of the evening sky.

'I begin training them when they're twenty-eight days old,' *Mme*. de Ligne said. 'I teach them to enter the loft, to exercise, to return home from a mile away, ten miles, five hundred miles. Farther.'

'What brings them back?'

'They return for two reasons. Pigeons, after all, aren't that much different from men. If you think about it, young man, I suspect you can tell me what brings them back.' They paused at the door leading from the roof to the house. Now the second of the homing pigeons was no longer visible in the darkening sky.

'Hunger?' Luke guessed.

'Yes, that's one of the attractions of the home loft. But, perhaps not really the strongest.'

'A mate?'

'Very good, very good indeed. The young aren't as hopeless when it comes to brains as I'd thought.'

They descended the stairs to the sitting room.

'When shall I return for my answer?' Luke asked.

'You will not return, we won't see one another again. You will hear in good time and in the same manner as you learned of my address. What way that is I do not know and do not wish to know.'

'Before I leave, I must tell you there is trouble here in Brussels. Many of your colleagues have been arrested. Perhaps you have heard this.'

'I have no contact with any colleagues, I am merely the message sender,' she said. 'No one bothers me.'

He hoped she was right.

Ten minutes after Luke left *Mme.* de Ligne, a car pulled up in front of the house on the Avenue Louise. Four German soldiers hurried up the steps, forcing their way inside. Two of the soldiers arrested *Mme.* de Ligne and drove off. Two remained behind, one on the first floor to intercept human visitors, the other to be ready to greet airborne couriers.

17

The sun was down. The faint glow of the street lamps on the Avenue Louise did little to dispel the darkness that gathered beneath the bare beeches and crouched between the gray buildings. Luke's footsteps echoed in the emptiness. The street was deserted although it was still three hours to curfew.

The feeling of unease that had come over him just before he entered *Mme*. de Ligne's house returned twofold, causing him to glance right and left, searching for eyes watching from the shadows. He should feel satisfied. Relieved. He'd done what he could, now everything depended on the two homing pigeons winging west to England. And on C. He might have a reply as early as tomorrow.

Yet he couldn't shake the sense something was wrong, had been wrong ever since they'd returned to Brussels.

Once more he pictured the middle-aged woman in the blue hat and coat riding in the black car to the Senate Chamber — the real Edith Cavell, the woman whose serenity had told him she'd made her peace with God. He'd come so close to rescuing her.

Thinking about the fiasco, he felt guilty, as though he should have anticipated a ringer. Yet how could he have? The day before, when he'd seen the real Nurse Cavell, he and MacNeeley could do nothing, not with the two of them against thousands and no concrete plan.

T.J. would have said — Luke frowned. What would his father have said. He didn't know. T.J.'s past advice refused to surface.

Maybe 'Two against thousands sounds like mighty fair odds as long as you and me are the two.' No, the words were false, too full of vain braggadocio. T.J. had never given him pie-in-the-sky advice; his father had always been a realist.

'T.J.,' Luke said aloud as though trying to conjure up his father's ghost. He heard nothing except the dying whisper of his own voice.

'T.J.,' he repeated. Again there was silence and a blankness in his mind.

Luke walked on, faster, hastening to return to the cellar room where he and MacNeeley had sheltered the night before. He turned off the Avenue Louise and followed a black fence for a block before going left on the first cross street. The safe house was in the middle of the block on the other side of the street.

He started to cross when he heard hooves on the cobbles behind him. Luke retreated to the sidewalk and went on, glancing at the cab as it passed. A German officer, his waxed mustaches curled and shiny, sat in the lighted interior with a pretty dark-haired young woman whose hands fluttered as she talked. The officer put back his head and laughed. Luke stared after the cab. Anger replaced his sense of foreboding, a seething, unreasonable fury. He ran after the cab, meaning to yank open the door and drag the German to the pavement where he'd pound him senseless with his fists.

He saw haloes of street lights ahead. Somehow the lights reminded him of the staring eyes of the shell-shocked *poilus* in the hospital and a shred of reason returned to him. Slowing to a stop, he clenched his fists at his sides, breathing hard as he called in his rage. *Careful. Don't lose control. You're not a mental case. Never!*

In his rage he'd run past the house so he retraced his steps and was about to climb the stairs when he noticed the drawn shade on the window to the right of the door. Danger. He hesitated, then walked on. He was almost to the corner when he heard MacNeeley's voice from the darkness.

'Luke.'

He slowed. Glanced about. Saw no one, nothing.

'Luke.' A form appeared at the top of shadowed steps leading down to a basement entrance. MacNeeley.

'Don't stop,' MacNeeley said, joining him, walking beside him.

'What happened?' Luke asked in a whisper.

'I don't know.' MacNeeley touched Luke's arm to guide him into a side street. 'A courier came. His message got the Belgians' wind up. They made me get out.'

The hair on Luke's neck prickled, his sense of danger stronger than ever. Ahead of them he saw the glow of lamps where the street looped around a fountain. He was about to warn MacNeeley they shouldn't chance the light when twin beams of headlights appeared from the darkness to the rear of the circle. Swept across the fountain as the car turned and raced toward them.

Luke was already edging up against a metal fence bordering the sidewalk when MacNeeley muttered, 'Huns.'

He crouched down immediately, MacNeeley beside him.

The car slowed to a halt, headlights on, illuminating the dark figures of soldiers forming a skirmish line across the street. They advanced, rifles ready.

Luke looked behind him. Two pairs of headlights approached slowly, the cars side by side, blocking the street. He drew his revolver, aware that MacNeeley was doing the same.

'Halt!' The command was in German.

Luke was certain they hadn't been seen. Yet.

'There's a side street a few yards further on,' MacNeeley whispered. 'I'll draw their fire.'

'No.' Luke reached for his arm but MacNeeley was already springing to his feet. He sprinted ahead toward the circle. His revolver flashed.

Luke ran after him, heard shouts from behind, saw darkness to his right. The cross street. He shook his head. He'd be damned if he'd leave MacNeeley. Turning in a crouch, he fired at the headlights. One blinked out and he grunted with satisfaction. Swinging around, he saw MacNeeley a few feet ahead outlined in the glare of a car's lights, saw the revolver in his raised hand. MacNeeley shouted in German, words Luke didn't know. Rifle fire crackled in a fusillade of yellow flame.

MacNeeley staggered. Fell. A German shouted in triumph.

Luke sprinted ahead. MacNeeley's dark

form lay huddled on the cobbles. As Luke knelt, a bullet ricocheted from the paving stones at his feet. He rolled MacNeeley over, saw his blank, staring eyes and blood staining his jacket. If he expected to get away, he had no time to check for a heartbeat — but he didn't need to. There was nothing he could do for MacNeeley. Ever again.

Damn. He fired blindly once, twice, at the twin headlights. Crouching, he turned and ran to his left into the side street. Shots cracked from behind him, the bullets high and harmless. He ran through the darkness without turning, gulping air into his lungs. Figuring they'd expect him to zigzag, he didn't.

At last he slowed and listened. When he heard no pursuing footsteps and no car engines, he flattened himself against a building and looked back.

The scene was framed between the trunks and branches of two trees on opposite sides of the far end of the street. A tableau lit by the headlights of black staff cars in the wings. German soldiers with spiked helmets and greatcoats stood over MacNeeley's huddled body.

As Luke watched, the tableau dissolved into action. A squad of soldiers trotted along the street toward him. Others lifted MacNeeley's body and carried it from sight. Two cars backed, turned and drove off.

Luke eased away from the wall and ran on, swung right, left, right again until he could no longer hear the voices of the Germans or the sound of their cars. He slowed to a walk. He'd have to find shelter, somewhere to hide until the time came to make contact with C.

MacNeeley was dead. The poor bastard. He'd never liked the man; he'd been too smooth, too clever. Yet Mac had saved his life not once but twice. And died in the doing. Luke raised his hand to his cap in a silent salute.

★　★　★

Three days later, Luke sat in the tram, staring from the window as the horse-drawn vehicle made its way up the long hill of the Boulevard de Napoleon. When it reached the top, he would get out, as he'd done for the past two days, and walk in the Parc de Bruxelles on the far side of the Royal Place. Two days of waiting for a message that didn't come. His initial anticipation had settled into the boredom of routine.

Even the people on the benches had begun to look familiar to him. The elderly man, for instance, must come and sit on that same bench every day. Perhaps he was bored, too.

Through the window he saw a woman walking along a street leading away from the boulevard. Luke drew in his breath. Kezia, it was Kezia. He shook his head. How many times in the last few days had he glimpsed a woman and thought for a pulse-pounding moment that it was Kezia. Only to be disappointed.

The woman turned to cross a street. He stared. It *was* Kezia! There was no question of it, she was a block away, walking toward the tram. He yanked the cord, the bell rang and he hurried to the rear of the car. When the tram slowed, he leaped off.

He looked along the side street but didn't see her. Kezia was gone. He pushed past the Belgians waiting patiently to board the tram. Stopped. She was sitting on a bench throwing crumbs to pigeons that strutted to and fro on the sidewalk in front of her. When Luke neared she looked up and smiled, getting to her feet.

He reached for her, wanting, needing to kiss her but she put her hands in front of her, warding him off. Warning him off.

'Shall we walk?' she asked, not looking at him.

Anger threaded through his delight and

relief at seeing her. Had he turned into a leper overnight? He fell into step beside her, walking rapidly. She matched his stride. 'MacNeeley's dead,' he said bluntly. 'The Huns killed him three days ago.'

'Dead?' she echoed. 'I can't believe that.'

He slowed to stare at her.

'We heard the shooting,' she went on. 'Are you quite sure, are you positive he's dead.'

'I saw him shot, saw the blood, his staring eyes.'

'Did you check for a heartbeat?'

Luke stopped and gazed at her in disbelief. 'Why the inquisition? Do you think I'm lying?'

'Of course not. But please answer me. Did you check for a heartbeat?'

'I didn't have time. But dead is dead, Kezia. I'm absolutely certain he was. Is.'

After a glance around them, she resumed walking. 'MacNeeley saved my life,' he added as he walked at her side. 'He died saving my life. I misjudged the man.'

She shot him a puzzled look. 'Misjudged him how?'

He shrugged. 'I guess what I'm trying to say is that I didn't like him.' As he spoke he recalled that she'd never liked MacNeeley either. He wondered briefly if anyone had. They walked in silence as they climbed the hill to the Royal Palace. He had so many things to tell her but their exchange so far kept him from saying anything.

'And Sid?' she asked finally.

'Probably a prisoner. If not dead. If, by some lucky chance the Germans don't have him, he's gone to ground. He was wounded when we ambushed the motorcade on its way to the Chamber. To save, as it turned out, a ringer.'

'We heard about that, too. We were afraid you'd spoiled everything but now we think it will turn out all right.'

His anger began to escalate. What was she saying? Who did she mean by we?

'I don't know what the hell you're talking about,' he said. 'Who's we?'

'We'll sit over there in the park,' she said. 'I was sent here to tell you the truth, Luke. It's time you knew everything.'

'Past time, you mean,' he muttered. He didn't relish being treated as though he were a naughty boy. Spoiled everything? By trying to do what he'd been sent to do?

'You should have been told in the beginning,' she went on. 'Before you left England. Evidently that's not C's way.'

'Why not send one of the others from the 'we' I'm supposed to know nothing about?' he growled. 'Why you? Because they thought

I'd be more likely to believe Kezia Faith?'

She hesitated only a moment. 'Yes, that was one of the reasons. And, of course, you know me — the others are strangers.' Her voice softened. 'I wanted to come, asked to come. Besides, I'm not as important in their scheme of things as the men. I'm expendable. We have that in common.'

'That's one damn fool way to try to win my confidence. Informing me I'm expendable. That it doesn't matter to C whether I live or die. Let me tell you something. It matters to me. It happens to matter a hell of a lot to me.'

'Luke.' She stopped walking and he couldn't keep himself from staring at her, at her auburn hair, at her eyes, usually so cold, brimming now with unshed tears. His heart lurched. As long as he lived he'd never forget how she looked at this moment.

'Luke,' she said again, 'listen to me. Listen hard. I do care what happens to you. I happen to care very much.'

She slipped her hand into his and, as they resumed walking, pressed his arm against the warmth of her body.

'You care?' he asked.

'Of course I do. But — '

'There's always a but, isn't there.'

'I've told you before. What we're doing is more important than how I feel. We have a job to do. For England.'

'Nothing is more important than how you feel about me. Or how I feel about you. To hell with England. As far as I'm concerned, England can — ' He paused, felt his color rising.

'You don't mean that,' Kezia said softly. 'The Huns raped Belgium. Sank the *Lusitania*. Used poison gas.'

Luke winced, remembering a blind *poilu* he'd met in hospital. 'The last thing I saw was so beautiful,' the Frenchman had told him, 'the green clouds drifting across the No-Man's-Land at Ypres. The green clouds of death . . . '

'Green,' the pigtailed cook had said in his sing-song voice. 'Bring no luck. Bad.'

He suddenly wondered if *Mme*. de Ligne in her house painted green was all right. No one else connected with him seemed to be.

'Let's get on with it,' Luke said, shaking off his morbid thoughts. 'What do you and your friends want me to do?'

Kezia led him from the street to an isolated bench near a calm pool in the park and they sat side by side. Water suddenly jetted high into the air, sparkling in the sun as it fell in foaming white cascades into the pool below.

Luke leaned to Kezia, kissing her as he'd longed to do all along. She responded, her lips parting, her eyes closing, her hand rising to the nape of his neck to hold him to her. But all too soon she opened her eyes, stiffened, and drew away.

'I've come from Justin,' she told him.

'Justin who?'

'Justin Graham.' She glanced at him as though the name should mean something to him. Evidently she saw that it didn't because she continued. 'From what you've hinted, I suspected that MacNeeley told you about the second group.'

'He said you told him there was one.' Despite himself, his voice was accusing.

'I was more or less forced to. But I didn't tell him everything. In any case, Justin's the leader. He's in Brussels. You've been placed under his command.'

Luke fought down his resentment. He hadn't done so damn well, had he? Lost all his men. Maybe he needed to follow rather than lead. When he looked at Kezia he saw her eyes had turned cold again. Her hand touched her hair, smoothing it as though being with him was making her nervous.

She doesn't want to be here, he decided. She didn't ask to come, they made her.

'Who the hell is Justin Graham?' He watched her closely, waiting for her response. He didn't trust her, couldn't trust her, she was hiding something. He never should have trusted her. There was no one he could trust. Hadn't been since T.J. died.

'Justin Graham is a very capable English officer.' Kezia's tone was precise but flat, as though she was reciting vital signs from a hospital chart. 'He was awarded the DSC early on. He played rugby for England before the war. At one time we were engaged to be married. It was because of Justin that I went to work for C.'

Luke homed in on the one statement that mattered the most to him. 'And now? You and this Graham?'

'We're good friends. I'm very fond of him but I don't intend to marry him, if that's what you mean.'

'Why are you telling me this? You didn't have to. And don't say it was because I asked.'

'I — ' She paused as a middle-aged man wearing a bowler hat and carrying a briefcase passed their bench. When he was out of earshot, she said, 'I told you I came here to tell you the truth. I want you to believe me, Luke. Now you must listen carefully because what I'm going to say next is important, more important than any feelings of mine. Or yours.'

'Is that what your good friend Justin Graham told you to say?'

She glared at him. 'Stop that!' Kezia took a deep breath and let it out slowly, obviously trying to calm herself.

Luke felt a tad ashamed but at the same time he didn't intend to be taken in by anyone, ever again. 'I'm listening,' he muttered.

'In this work, I admit it's hard to tell where deception ends and truth begins,' she said. 'After a while you don't recognize the truth. It's as though you lived all your life in a house of mirrors showing you either tall and thin or short and fat. The first time you see yourself in a true mirror you don't believe what you are.'

He found himself wanting to believe her and hardened his heart. 'You told MacNeeley about the second group after you'd lied to me about it. Is that supposed to make me trust what you tell me now?'

'I never lied to you.' Her voice rose and she glanced around before continuing in a lower tone. 'Because at the time I was afraid of him, I told MacNeeley a part of the truth.'

'Afraid of him? Why?'

'Since you're sure he's dead, it doesn't matter. He didn't hear the whole truth, only a part of it.' She gazed steadily at him, her eyes no longer cold but not warm, either. Businesslike. 'This is important. You must tell me the truth. Where did you stay the last three nights?'

'In a *pension* near the marketplace in the old city.'

'At MacNeeley's suggestion? Did he give you the address before you saw him shot?'

Luke shook his head, 'Mac had nothing to do with it. I found the *pension* on my own. They didn't question my papers. So far no one's shown any curiosity about me. Why the questions about MacNeeley?'

She shrugged. 'Just being careful.'

'You never did trust him did you?'

'How can I trust a man I don't know?'

'Yet you're telling me you believe I know you well enough to trust you.'

'That's different.' She took his hand in both of hers. 'I think we do know one another well enough. Don't we, Luke?'

He didn't answer directly. 'Mac saved my life. Not once but twice.'

'I could very well be wrong about him,' she admitted. 'I've been wrong about other things in the past, myself included. How I felt, the life I thought I wanted.' She frowned. 'That has nothing to do with this. MacNeeley frightened me.' She closed her eyes briefly, making Luke wonder what the hell Mac had done to her.

Before he could ask her, she said, 'I asked

you a question, Luke. You haven't answered me.'

He had to trust her. There was no one else left to trust. 'I'll give it to you straight,' he said. 'I'll trust you. With my life. If you lie to me now I'll never believe you again. Never. About anything.'

She drew in her breath and, as she let it out in a sigh, she let go of his hand. 'Fair enough.' After a pause she went on again as though by rote. 'There were always two groups, yours and Justin Graham's. While you were coming to Brussels by way of Holland, he was coming by sea. Yours was the decoy group, his the real one. You were to create the diversion that would make it possible for him to accomplish the mission.'

Luke glanced around and lowered his voice. 'To rescue Nurse Cavell.'

Kezia shook her head. Speaking so softly he had to lean closer to hear her, she said, 'The entire scheme for rescuing Edith Cavell was the diversion. The Huns were led to think she was your objective. And the objective of the second group as well. We've succeeded in making them believe it. Helped by your attack on the convoy of prisoners. Which wasn't planned. The Germans have increased their guard at Gilles because they still expect us to try to free Miss Cavell. Giving us the opportunity to go after our real objective.'

Luke had difficulty swallowing the notion that no one intended to rescue Miss Cavell. It seemed cruel and heartless to abandon her to her fate. Which is what would happen if Kezia was telling the truth. Since he'd promised to trust her, he put aside his doubts and asked, 'What is the objective then?'

Kezia's voice dropped still lower. He was so close to her now an observer — though he didn't see any — would have taken them for lovers exchanging sweet nothings.

'The Zeppelin hangars,' she whispered. 'The civilians in London are frightened. They're demanding that the War Ministry bring aeroplanes home from France to defend the cities. Some have already been flown back from the front. Where they're desperately needed. C was ordered to strike at the Zeppelins by raiding their bases in Belgium. Other groups like yours and Justin's have been sent behind the lines. Bombers will attack the Zepps at the bases in Germany.'

Luke's flash of memory about the great gray airship floating above the trees as he and the other two men made their way to Hendrik's farm was obliterated by a vision of the middle-aged woman in the German staff car, Nurse Cavell on her way to face her accusers. He remembered how she'd looked directly at him. 'You're abandoning Miss Cavell. Washing your hands of her.'

Kezia sighed. 'The Germans would be mad to execute her. Think how the world would view such barbaric treatment of a woman, a nurse whose mission in life is to help others. C expects she'll be given a sentence of not more than ten years in a German prison and, since the war will be over sooner than that, she won't have to serve a full term.'

Luke frowned. 'The Germans are a cruel and stubborn people. How can C be sure? How can anyone be sure what they might do?'

'It's not as though she was an agent sent here as a spy. And, don't forget, she *is* a woman.'

He hadn't forgotten. As he wondered if C could possibly be right, his anger at the man boiled over. 'C should have told me the truth,' he said bitterly.

'What good would it have done? If you and your men didn't know, then none of you could give anything away under duress. Or by being careless. You may not like C, few do, but he wouldn't be where he is if his missions weren't successful. He knows what he's about.'

'I wonder,' Luke said. 'I wonder if any of us do. Don't you wonder sometimes?'

Kezia shook her head. 'I don't let myself. I believe in C. He's in a position to do more than we, as individuals, ever could. He knows what the Huns are thinking, what they're planning, not only because of his agents but because he knows how the Huns think. We have to trust him, Luke.'

Because C thinks like a Hun, a highly intelligent, coldly calculating Hun, Luke thought but didn't say. 'I've heard a lot about trust today,' he told Kezia.

'And?'

'And nothing. I haven't folded, have I? I'm still in the game. To the end. What does your Justin Graham want from me? Tell him I'll do what's necessary.'

'Good.' She practically spat the word at him. 'You men,' she snapped. ''My Luke Ray. My Justin Graham.' Neither of you are mine, do you hear? Neither! Nor am I yours.'

Luke gazed at her in surprise. After a moment a slow smile curled his lip. So Graham didn't like him any better than he liked Graham, sight unseen. The man must see him as a rival. He liked that.

'Stop smirking,' Kezia ordered. 'I can't bear smug men.'

Luke wiped away the smile. 'When do I meet my new leader?

She frowned at him before answering. 'I'm

to take you to him tomorrow. He'll be the one to tell you what he wants but I can say this much.' Down went her voice again. When he leaned in he caught the scent of lilies of the valley and, for a moment, was back in her bed in the Walrus' house. 'Are you listening?' she asked.

He nodded.

'There'll be an attack on the Zeppelin hangars north of Brussels. I don't know where exactly because I haven't been told. There was another question I was to ask you? You've handled explosives?'

'Some. When I worked summers in the Colorado mines before the war. That was MacNeeley's job, as you know. Tell Graham I can do what's needed. Whatever that is.'

'He'll tell you himself tomorrow,' she said, rising. 'Be here at this place. The same time.' She walked away from the bench, hesitated, turned and ran back. Leaning over Luke, she kissed him. 'Oh, Luke, Luke,' she said. The words were more a plea for understanding than an endearment.

She walked swiftly away along the path leading from the park without turning around again. Luke stared after her, shaking his head. He didn't know if she'd lied to him or not. Lies of omission, certainly. He was certain she hadn't told him everything. And maybe not the unvarnished truth about Graham. Nor about their mission.

Something was awry. Smelled, in fact, to high heaven. He didn't have an inkling as to what it was. And, even if he did, there was nothing he could do about it. At least not yet.

He wished to hell he knew where Sid was. He could use an ally.

But, damn, trust her or not, it had been wonderful to see Kezia again, to kiss her, to feel her response, if only momentary. He might not understand her but he sure as hell wanted her.

18

Luke hunkered down on wet leaves and peered into the driving rain toward where he knew the bridge must be. He'd hidden his poor excuse for a horse some distance away. He hadn't expected the rain, the skies had been clear when he'd boarded the train at the Gare du Nord to travel north from Brussels. When he left the second class coach at Vilvoorde fifteen minutes later, clouds were gathering in the west. Now it was pouring.

He pulled Lundi's coat higher around his neck, the gesture more from habit than for protection since the coat had been soaked through a few minutes after he'd put it on. Besides the coat, Lundi had given him a spavined horse, dynamite stolen from a *Wehrmacht* storehouse, caps, wires and a plunger.

When he'd said goodbye to the little Belgian, Lundi had shaken his hand, wished him luck and walked away into the slanting rain, leaving Luke on his own. Lundi had a habit of glancing over his shoulder as though he heard footsteps overtaking him. Ever since leaving him, Luke had resisted the urge to look back.

To hell with Lundi. To hell with Justin Graham. As for C — hell was too good for him.

Luke shielded his eyes with his hand. Saw nothing except the night's enclosing darkness. Like an undertone beneath the beat of the rain on the leaves he heard the murmur of the river to his right. Graham had claimed the bridge was guarded by a single sentry. Luke meant to reconnoiter, find out for himself.

Graham was a smooth bastard, you had to give him that. Bland as a tall glass of water. A bit too pretty for Luke, he didn't take to men with such looks. And too patronizing by half. Probably tough, too, though, under all that highfalutin English manner of his. The real trouble, Luke admitted ruefully, was that he could see why Kezia had taken a liking to the Englishman. A liking? She'd meant to marry him.

Luke took off his dark coat and used it to cover the wooden box, then pushed the explosives deeper into the concealing under-growth. Reaching up, he grasped a branch and bent it to the ground, twisting until he heard it snap.

He pictured the map of the area in his mind, the river to his right, the road passing the German barracks on the way to the aerodrome on his left. A hundred yards ahead of him the river swung gently left and, fifty yards on, the road crossed it on the timber bridge. When the attack on the hangars began, German reinforcements would be sent along this road, across this bridge.

Except that by the time the Huns reached the river, Luke would have demolished the bridge. He was certain he could handle the demolition, dynamite being one of the least sophisticated explosives. He'd used it often in the mines. The hardest part would be to evade the Germans long enough to get the job done.

Leaving the broken branch on the path, Luke walked into the full force of the rain. Trees, he knew from the detailed map, grew along both sides of the river, flanking the corridor of trees was farmland. Across the road on Luke's side of the bridge a lane led between pillars to what had been the country home of a Brussels doctor, an estate commandeered by the Germans and used as an officers club.

Luke slowed as the sound of the river increased. Trees rose darkly on both sides of him. He stepped into nothingness, threw himself backwards and sat down hard on the muddy bank. The river surged by a few feet below him. After removing his boots and stuffing his socks inside them in what would probably prove to be a vain attempt to keep them dry, he slid on his stomach feet-first from the bank into the water.

The bottom was muck, he shivered as the cold water reached his thighs. As he waded downstream the bottom mud clung to his feet. The current pushed him forward as though it wanted to hurry him to the bridge. Rain stung his cheeks. Floating debris struck the backs of his legs before floating free. The only good thing, he figured, was that he'd be unlikely to set off hidden trip wires with the river running so rapidly.

He slogged ahead, keeping close to the bank. There was only the night and the rain and the river. Nothing else. When the rain suddenly lessened and the night became even darker, he realized he must be under the bridge. He heard the tattoo of the rain above his head and nodded.

He was under the bridge all right. Just where he needed to be. Justin Graham had shown him a photograph of the bridge taken before the war, not a good picture for the scene was slightly out-of-focus, but good enough. The old bridge, built of timbers, was substantial. One lane wide, about thirty feet long, the span was supported by two massive timbers at its center, one on each side, the timbers embedded in concrete piers and reinforced by heavy wooden supports. Piece of cake to destroy once he had the dynamite in place.

Luke pulled himself from the water onto the bank beneath the bridge, straining to hear above the murmur of the river and the drum of the rain. No tramp of feet, no sound of voices. The bridge appeared vulnerable to demolition. He debated whether to return upstream at once for the explosives or to explore further.

There'd been too many unwelcome surprises lately.

Better make sure. He angled from under the bridge, crawling up the slippery grass slope until he lay beside a roadway. Still he didn't see or hear anything alarming. If there was a guard, as Graham had said, he was keeping himself dry. Luke slid down the back and lowered himself into the river. After wading upstream along the water's edge, he turned and allowed the current to push him back to the bridge.

His arm struck concrete. He grasped the rough surface with both hands and levered himself onto a platform. Reaching out, he touched one of the timbers of the central support and nodded. This is where he'd secure the dynamite. Again he lowered himself into the river and edged over until he came to the bank.

The storm, by driving the guard to shelter, had made his job easy. Too easy. If something you really wanted came too easily, you'd have to pay sooner or later. Bitter experience was teaching him to be leery of situations like this.

He slogged upstream, climbed out, put on his socks and boots, then located the broken limb that led him to his cache. He returned to the bridge on foot, carrying the box of explosives, slipping and sliding on the muddy bank, stopping every few moments to look, like Lundi, over his shoulder and to listen. Once there, he flattened himself onto the bridge on his stomach and edged along with the box of dynamite on his back until he reached the middle.

Climbing down, he located the center supports and lashed the sticks of dynamite where the supports met the underside of the bridge, then disposed of the box by allowing it to float downstream with the other debris. He anchored the fuse wire on a rock at the bottom of the river before leading it upstream underwater to the bank where he connected it to the plunger. Dripping water and shivering, Luke opened a waterproofed leather sack that had been fastened to his belt. Carefully, not allowing any light to escape, he peered at the illuminated dial of his watch. It lacked five minutes to midnight.

Graham's attack on the hangars would begin in a little over an hour, at one. He was to blow the bridge at ten minutes past one or at the first sign of unusual German activity, whichever came first, return to the horse he'd concealed in the trees upstream, and make his way to the rendezvous house in Brussels. God and the Huns willing.

His main problem now, soaking wet as he was, had to do with keeping from freezing until the time came to act. What he'd give for a set of warm dry clothes. He hunched down out of the wind with his back against the trunk of a tree, hugging himself as he shivered and waited. The rain fell steadily, the river surged below him. Despite his soggy discomfort he began to doze.

Before he fell into a deep sleep, all hell broke loose, jerking him awake. A star shell broke over his head. Luke stared up through the tree branches at the white light. German voices shouted near the bridge. Squinting, Luke saw soldiers run from the trees a quarter mile upriver while others trotted across the bridge to fan out between the road and the riverbank. He was caught between the jaws of a closing trap.

Luke swore, scrambled to his feet. A

second shell burst above him as the first dimmed and went out. Luke gripped the handle of the plunger and shoved down. He looked toward the bridge, expecting to see the blast hurl the center of the span skyward, scattering timber fragments into the river. Nothing happened. There was no explosion. He yanked up on the plunger and shoved down again. Nothing, nothing at all. Frantically he checked the wiring in the light of the flare. All connections had been properly made, all were secure. Either the damn Huns had spotted him and cut the wires or he'd been betrayed. He lifted the plunger box in both hands and hurled it from him into the river.

The light from the star shell faded. A German voice called orders from the darkness a few feet away. He understood enough to realize they hadn't yet spotted his exact location. Luke ran along the bank, heading upriver, slipping and falling into mud, pushing himself up and running again. Footsteps thudded behind him. He found the broken limb where he'd hidden the dynamite, ran on to the grove where he'd picketed his horse.

He slowed when he neared the first of the trees, sensing danger. He no longer heard any footsteps behind him but he feared danger ahead, feared betrayal, so he held, huddled against the bole of a tree, waiting. A guttural voice shouted from the direction of the road and he thought he heard the rumble of trucks above the whisper of the rain. Without looking at his watch, he was sure it was not yet one and he wondered what Justin Graham's fate had been at the hangars.

The woods loomed black above him. A horse whinnied off to his right. Luke parted branches and pushed ahead. Had they found the horse? Unlikely they'd stumble on the animal yet he had to be sure. A hand closed on his shoulder and he spun around. He ducked, struck upward with his fist into a man's midsection. His attacker gasped, backing away. Luke followed, winced as a kick caught his shin. Grunting like an animal, the man charged. Luke stepped aside, brought his fist down on the back of the man's head. Heard him go down. Luke turned and ran. The whinnying horse had been a trap. He pushed through underbrush, branches whipping his face. Heard the panting breath of the German behind him. Luke darted to his right, stopped, crouched in the darkness. Footsteps pounded past and faded in the night.

He plunged blindly into the woods. His shoulder struck a tree and he bit back a grunt of pain. He slowed and turned right, making for the road, for where he thought the road must be. A light flared overhead, another star shell. He stopped, remaining motionless, still under the cover of the trees. Through the branches he saw, ahead of him, a truck rumbling slowly along the road in the direction of the bridge. Four German soldiers trudged through the mud in its wake.

The light dimmed and died. Luke walked quickly from the trees, climbed into and out of a ditch and up to the sparsely graveled roadbed. He turned away from the bridge and ran all out, striving to put as much distance between him and the Germans before the next star shell.

When the flare exploded in the sky above him, he saw, through the slanting rain, a mass of trees to his left, a barricade less than fifty feet ahead of him manned by at least three Germans. Luke threw himself from the road, rolling and sliding down a muddy bank until he lay in rainwater at the bottom of a deep ditch. Peering out, he saw a crouching German trotting toward him from the barricade, his coat dark with rain. The flare went out.

Something touched his arm. He drew in his breath, his hand closing on the butt of his revolver.

'Luke? Luke?' It was a woman's voice. 'It's Kezia.'

'I'll be goddamned,' he muttered. 'What the hell are you doing here?'

'Don't talk. Follow me.'

He trailed her through reeds in water that was ankle-deep. Up a low bank into the shelter of the woods. Light glowed in the sky behind them but when Luke looked back he could see nothing through the trees. Kezia, he saw, wore men's clothing. There were no sounds of pursuit. Yet.

'I couldn't find you in the rain. At the bridge,' Kezia said in a low tone. 'It's so dark. I've been looking for a good half hour. Longer. I left the horses near here. Somewhere.'

He still couldn't believe she was really with him.

As the light faded, she pushed branches aside. 'Here.' She took his hand and guided it to a tether. 'This one. She's yours.'

He untied the horse and, putting his foot in the stirrup, swung into the saddle, aware Kezia was capable of fending for herself. Her voice came from the darkness ahead of him. 'I'll walk the horses to the road. Beyond the barricade.'

Luke stifled his instinctive protest. At the moment there was nothing to be gained by opposing her. She knew the way and he didn't.

Soaked, he huddled in the saddle, his thoughts as bleak as the weather. The attack on the aerodrome must have failed, the Zepps were unharmed, able to fly again, to kill again. He'd failed. Worst of all, Graham had to risk Kezia to bring him back to Brussels. He cursed the rain, Justin Graham, the Huns. Himself. And C.

Kezia walked through the woods for what he estimated to be ten minutes before she led the two horses onto a road. 'This is a different road,' she told him after she mounted. 'With luck they won't look for us here.'

Luck. They hadn't much of it.

Though the rain had lessened, the darkness forced them to ride at a walk. They passed through a small village, quiet and deserted, and into the countryside again where trees lined both sides of the roadway. They'd seen no one, heard no one since leaving the bridge. It was almost as though the road was closed. Sensing danger, Luke reined in. 'Stop,' he whispered. Kezia pulled up beside him. 'Listen' he urged.

After a time she said in a low tone, 'I don't hear anything.'

'I thought I heard voices,' he told her.

'Let's wait a while longer.'

In the misty drizzle they strained to hear.

A motor coughed to life ahead of them. Lights blazed, momentarily blinding Luke. When his vision cleared he saw a wooden barricade, a motorcar with headlights on, German soldiers, an officer pointing at them with a riding crop. 'Follow me,' Luke called to Kezia. 'Over the barricade. It's the only way.'

He dug his heels into his horse's flanks. The mare trotted forward toward the lights. Luke unholstered his pistol, fired at the soldiers near the barricade, than slammed the butt of the gun against the mare's side. She broke into a gallop. Luke glanced behind him, saw Kezia following. Gaining on him.

Fire flashed from both sides of the barricade. He heard the pop-pop-pop of rifle fire. Of mausers. The plank barricade was at least three feet high. The mare pounded toward it with Luke's head against her mane. Hooves thundered.

'Over the top!' he shouted. 'Now, damn it. Over the top!'

The mare seemed to hesitate for an instant that stretched into eternity. Then he felt her gather herself for the jump. She leaped high and well but one of her rear hoofs caught the top plank with a thud, knocking it loose. When the mare hit the road, she stumbled, recovered and galloped on. Over his shoulder, Luke saw Kezia's mount clear the barricade and race past a black car. Wild shots followed them into the darkness.

Luke slowed. 'Wait,' he called to Kezia as she passed him. He heard her horse slow, stop, return.

'They'll be after us,' she said.

'Yes, in that car we saw.' He dismounted and handed Kezia the mare's reins. 'Lead her off the road. Get both of the horses well into the trees. Out of sight. Now.'

For a moment he thought she meant to protest, then she turned and led the two horses into the rainy darkness. Luke crouched in the ditch bordering the road. Headlight beams knifed toward him. As he'd suspected, they'd turned the car around and were accelerating toward him. He steadied his gun hand, revolver at the ready.

The car sped close, almost on him, mist swirling past its headlights, the car blacker than the misty night. He meant to hit the tires, a trick shot under the best conditions. He could miss, his shots would tell the Huns where he was hiding.

The car roared past. Shaking his head, Luke lowered his Webley, holstered the gun unfired. He climbed from the ditch and hurried into the woods. 'Kezia?' he said.

'Here.'

'Do you know this area? Other roads? The way to Brussels?'

'There's a crossroads a half kilometer on,' she said. 'I know the way from there.'

She led the horses onto the road and they mounted, urging the horses into a fast trot. They reached the crossroads without seeing the German car and turned to left. At the next road, they turned again, zigzagging on toward Brussels.

'I'm told that at night the Huns tend to stay to the main thoroughfares,' she said after a time.

Luke hoped she was right. By now they rode along a muddy lane, the tired, dispirited horses plodding forward with their heads down. Luke knew exactly how the animals felt. The rain had almost stopped, the sky lightening even though there was no moon to be seen. He guessed it must be around four, maybe a tad earlier.

'I gather the raid on the hangars failed,' he said. Kezia didn't answer. He looked at her, saw she was staring straight ahead. The man's jacket she wore was as soaked as his and some of her hair was straggling wetly out from under her cap. She sat heavily on her horse as though either unused to riding or exhausted.

'Do you know whether or not the raid failed?' he asked. Kezia sighed.

'There was no raid on the Zeppelin hangars. No such raid was ever planned except as a diversion tactic. You became the diversion instead. This was all necessary because MacNeeley was a traitor. A double agent. There's no question of it. MacNeeley killed one of our Belgians the day I took him to Justin. He knew I'd become suspicious of him and would report it to my contact.

'He killed Raoul and escaped, going directly back to you and Sid, as we later realized. We knew he must think you could lead him to the other group so Justin decided to use you as well. He suspected MacNeeley had the Germans watching your every move so he used you to lead them to the hangars, made them think the attack would come there. That's the truth.'

The truth or another truth? Or another lie. Luke was too tired to care. His scratchy throat warned him he was more than likely coming down with a cold. It was just too much trouble to get upset. All he wanted was to find a warm bed, crawl into it and sleep forever.

They rode in silence until Kezia finally

said, 'You don't seem surprised.'

'I'm not surprised. Nothing surprises me any more.'

'Luke.' She reined in her horse but he rode on, ignoring her. 'Luke,' she said again but he didn't slow or look back. She hurried after him until she was riding beside him once more.

'They went into St. Gilles tonight,' she told him. 'They planned to make the attempt to rescue Miss Cavell a little after one.'

He said nothing, letting the words fall like bricks on his head.

'You probably think Justin sent me after you,' she said. 'He didn't. He doesn't know. I came on my own, without telling him. Which probably means I'll never make a good agent. I don't follow orders any too well.'

He supposed he should be cheered because she'd come to warn him, to help him on her own. Either his utter fatigue or his utter disgust with the entire mission, or both, prevented him. He couldn't even dredge up any kind of appropriate remark.

'The least you could do,' she said, 'would be to tell me you're glad I came. I did bring the extra horse, after all.'

'She's an improvement over the one Lundi gave me,' he admitted.

'I did what I had to do,' Kezia said. 'You

see that, don't you?'

Though he heard the tiny quaver in her voice, he said nothing more, urging the mare ahead. She followed him along the muddy track. The mud changed to cobbles and they were in the city.

There was no answer to Kezia's knock on the door of the rendezvous house. Luke tried the door, found it unlocked and let himself in. They walked in darkness along a corridor toward a partly closed door to a lighted room in the rear. Luke took Kezia's arm, eased past her with his revolver in his hand and pushed the door open.

'Andre!' Kezia exclaimed, staring past him to the man sitting at a kitchen table with an empty glass in his hand, a whisky bottle in front of him.

The balding Belgian didn't turn; he continued to stare at the light from an overhead lamp reflecting from his glass. Kezia pushed past Luke and ran to him. 'Andre,' she demanded, 'where are they? What happened?'

'The Huns were ready for them.' Andre's voice was slurred. 'The Walrus is dead, three of the English are dead, two are missing. Prisoners in St. Gilles.'

'Justin? What about Justin?'

'One of the two prisoners,' Andre said.

Kezia's hand went to her mouth. Luke nodded. *Graham was a cocky bastard. What could you expect?* He took the bottle, raised it to his lips and drank, feeling the fiery liquid warm his stomach, if not his heart.

He sat the bottle on the table and spoke to Andre, his own words startling him. 'I'm going in after those two, Graham and the other. And you're going to help me.'

19

The whisky seemed to have cleared Luke's head enough so he could think again. He glanced at Kezia, sitting across from him at the table and asked, 'How did Graham get into St. Gilles?'

'I don't know,' Kezia answered. 'You'll have to ask him.' She nodded at Andre who was returning to the room carrying three mugs of coffee. He sat them on the table, slid into a chair, picked up his mug, and took a sip of the steaming coffee.

Luke did the same. Laced with chicory but welcome all the same. 'Andre, who got Graham into the prison?'

'A man called Nicolas guided them,' replied Andre. 'That's not his real name, of course, any more than mine is Andre. He's one of us, has been from the beginning.'

'Do you still trust him after what happened to Graham's group?'

'When the Huns marched through his village last year,' Andre said, 'they were fired on by *francs tireurs*, civilian snipers. At least the Huns claimed they were. Forty civilians were marched into the village square and executed. Nicolas lost his mother, his father and his younger brother. He's the only one of his family who survived.'

Luke no longer trusted anyone's reasons. 'He may have made a deal with the Germans,' he pointed out. 'His life in exchange for services to be performed later.'

Andre put his mug down and studied Luke. 'It surprises me that an American should be such a cynic, M. Ray. Still, Nicolas is not like most. Who would be after such a tragedy? But he'll go to his grave hating the German barbarians.'

Which wouldn't preclude him working for them in exchange for his life, Luke thought. He shook his head. Maybe he was becoming too cynical. 'Nicolas is a guard at St. Gilles?'

'No, never. The Germans would be fools to have a man like him working at the prison. Nicolas lives in the underground, beneath the city. He has friends among the wardens, the Belgians who still work in the prison, so he's able to get in and out of St. Gilles without the Germans knowing. Nicolas guided M. Graham and his friends into the prison, left them there.'

'And they never came out,' Luke said.

'You have no idea what happened inside?' Kezia asked Andre. She had, Luke noted, scarcely touched her coffee.

Andre shook his head. 'None. Only what I've told you, that M. Graham and one other Englishman are held prisoner in St. Gilles itself. The others are dead. The Walrus is dead. He died heroically, sacrificed himself. One never knows. Who would have thought he'd end his life in that way? Perhaps he's cleansed himself of all that happened in Africa.'

'How do you know as much as you do?' Luke asked.

'Nicolas was told this when he returned to lead them from the prison. And he told me.'

'Nicolas will take me inside?'

'Us,' Kezia put in. 'I'm going with you.'

'Perhaps it can be arranged.' Andre leaned forward with elbows on the table and his chin resting on his clasped hands. 'But think. Last night six men went into St. Gilles and none have returned. Four never will, they are dead. And now you wish to go in alone. You're not only a cynic, M. Ray, you are a madman as well. Is it you have a wish to die?'

''Half joy of life and half readiness to die,'' Kezia murmured as if to herself. Fixing her gaze on Luke, she told him, 'You're not going into St. Gilles without me.'

Luke raised his hand, seeing alarm leap into her eyes. Did she think he was the kind of man who struck women? He brought his fist down hard on the table. The mugs of coffee jumped.

'I've listened to you for the last time,' he said. 'I don't intend to, ever again. Is that clear?'

Kezia drew back as though he actually had hit her. She opened her mouth, held, her face reddened. Without speaking she stood and half-walked, half-ran from the room.

'You're quite right,' Andre said quietly. 'St. Gilles is no place for a woman. Even one with such spirit.'

'Can arrangements be made for me to go to the prison tomorrow night?' Luke asked.

Andre nodded.

'I'll need to know the layout of the prison. The location of the guards. Are there plans?'

'You can have them now. *M.* Graham used such plans and left a set concealed here in this house. You'll find them quite complete.'

'I'll need a guard's uniform,' Luke added. 'One that fits.'

'It is no problem. But I caution you, Graham's men wore them.' Andre raised his hands in a Gallic gesture of despair. 'To no avail.'

'I'll need identification,' Luke went on. 'To get me past the Germans inside the prison.'

'To have suitable documents prepared in a day's time will be difficult.'

'I've seen copies of *Belgique Libre*,' Luke said. 'Somebody's got a printing press.'

'They move about to avoid capture. One week the paper is prepared here, the next week on the other side of the city. I'll see that an identity card is arranged, M. Ray. By tomorrow night.'

Luke finished his coffee and set his mug on the table. 'Is it true a man named MacNeeley killed one of our Belgians?' he asked.

Andre scowled. 'Raoul was my friend. A true comrade. His neck was snapped by that monster as though poor Raoul was no more than a cat he wished to dispose of. If the Germans hadn't shot him first, something I do not understand, I would have searched until I found M. MacNeeley and I would have killed him.'

Luke didn't understand it either and he was too tired to make sense of it. At least Kezia hadn't been lying about Mac murdering Raoul. He rose. 'I can't think of anything else I'll need,' he told Andre. 'Except to get some sleep. I'll be up by noon.'

'May I make a request?' Andre asked.

Luke nodded.

'I'd truly like to go with you into St. Gilles. In part I blame myself for what happened to M. Graham and the others. They were, they are my comrades, I should like to do what I can to free those who are left.'

Luke smiled wryly. 'Perhaps you're the one with a wish for death.'

'Not at all. There are few things in this world a man would stand ready to give his life for. I'd give mine to free Belgium from the Boche.'

'In the West we'd say you were a good man to ride the river with, Andre.'

'I do not understand.'

'In the old days in Texas, the times before the first of the great cattle drives north to the railroads, the cattle wintered in the brush along the rivers. It took a good man to rout them out for the spring branding.'

Andre nodded doubtfully.

'But I'm going into St. Gilles alone,' Luke said. 'You can help by leading me to Nicolas and then seeing that Miss Faith gets safely to Holland. Will you do that?'

'Of a certainty, *mon capitaine*. Always assuming it is possible to persuade her to go. I will do my best to keep her safe.'

As Luke started away from the table, Andre rose, came around and clasped him in his arms. Luke, embarrassed, stood with his arms at his sides. Andre released him, turned away and left the room, muttering about bed coverings but not before Luke saw the tears in his eyes.

The next evening, Luke, dressed in a blue guard's uniform and wearing a kepi, followed Andre from a rear door of the house into the Brussels night. He'd not seen Kezia since she'd stormed away from him the previous night. He'd thought she might appear before he left to renew her pleas to accompany him or at least to wish him luck. She hadn't.

Luke glanced up at the myriad of stars, breathed deeply of the clear, cool air, savoring the pleasure of being alive. He and Andre followed an alley, crossed a darkened thoroughfare, walked rapidly down another alley. Andre stopped beside the blank brick wall of what Luke took to be a factory.

'This way,' Andre said, unlocking a chained gate. Luke stepped past him and waited while Andre snapped the padlock shut behind them.

The night darkened. Luke looked up and saw hazy clouds drifting from west to east to cover the stars. If it rained again tonight, at least he'd be inside.

'Hurry,' Andre urged.

They passed outbuildings, empty and unused, and piles of huge wooden cartons stretching row on row into the darkness. Luke stumbled, saw that they'd reached a railroad spur. They followed the track with their footsteps crunching on the gravel roadbed. Another track arced away from them. Glancing behind him, Luke saw only the looming blackness of the factory buildings. When he looked ahead again, Andre was gone.

'I'm here.' The Belgian's voice came from the darkness. Luke followed him along a fence that ran beside a shed. Andre stopped, took keys from his pocket and unlocked a door, motioning Luke inside. In the shed, Luke felt a wooden floor beneath his feet. Andre closed the door. A match flared and Luke watched the other man kneel to light a lantern. The shed, he saw, had no windows. Andre stood, lifted another lantern from a hook on the wall, lighted its wick and handed the lantern to Luke.

Again Andre knelt on the wide, rough-hewn floorboards, fitting his fingers into one of the larger cracks and lifting. Beneath this trapdoor was a round metal cover, two feet across, a ring in its center.

'Help me,' Andre said.

Together they grasped the ring and lifted, straining as they raised the heavy door and shifted it to one side. When Andre held his lantern over the opening, Luke saw metal rungs descending into darkness.

'You first,' Andre told him.

Luke stared down, hesitating. *Not afraid of the dark, are you?* This no different than descending into the bowels of a mine, after all. Dismissing his apprehension, he picked up his lantern and climbed down the ladder. His feet touched a solid surface and he stepped away from the ladder to watch Andre, lantern in hand, begin his descent.

'Take this,' Andre said after climbing down several steps. He handed Luke his lantern, then reached up and, with much grunting and obvious effort, closed the cover over the hole. As Andre climbed down to join him, Luke raised both lanterns and looked around.

He was at one side of a large chamber from which four black-mouthed tunnels led away in front of him and behind him, to his right and left. The chamber walls and floor were moisture-darkened stones but Luke could hear no sound of running water. The air, though stagnant and heavy with dampness, carried none of the sweetish, pungent odor of waste he'd expected.

'These aren't the sewers,' he said to Andre.

'No, not here, though some of the tunnels lead to them.' Andre took back his lantern and led Luke into the tunnel beside the ladder from the surface. The light from the two lanterns threw their shadows on the walls in wavering phantasmagorias. Their footsteps echoed mournfully in the emptiness, accompanied by intermittent scurrying sounds. 'Rats,' Andre muttered. 'They live in the sewers.'

Luke grimaced. Rats flourished worldwide. After a moment he heard the insistent murmur of water far ahead of them.

'The River Senne flows through Brussels,' Andre told him. 'Forty or fifty years ago the waters were vaulted over and the city was built above them. The sound you hear is the river.'

The tunnel widened and they entered another chamber where the ceiling was lost in the darkness high above them. Part of old machines lay rusting on the stone floor, huge cogged wheels, pistons and cams, empty iron frames, strands of wire as thick as a man's arm.

Andre slowed, holding his lantern first to one side and then to the other until he came to a pyramid of discarded metal castings. With a nod, he walked between two rows of corroded iron pipes to a corridor that zigzagged into darkness. Water oozed from the ceiling and slid down a slimy wall in front of them. Andre placed his lantern on the floor, grasped a sheet of metal resting against the wall and shifted it to one side, revealing a metal door studded with boltheads and pockmarked by rust.

Andre took a small section of pipe from the floor and tapped three times on the door. He waited, then tapped three times again. The door swung open. Luke peered into a long narrow room, cell-like in its austerity, his gaze drawn to the flame of a candle on the table.

'This is Nicolas.' Andre took Luke's arm and urged him into the room. He made no attempt to introduce him.

Luke made out the tall figure of a man standing beside the table. At first he thought Nicolas' hair and short pointed beard were black but when Andre shifted his lantern, he realized they were a dark red. Nicolas bowed to Luke, grasped his left hand in his, more a gesture than a shaking of hands. He motioned to the two men to chairs at the table. Luke shifted his shoulders, as though trying to rid himself of unease. He was here, he was going on.

Nicolas disappeared into the darkness at the far end of the room, returning with a bottle of wine and three stemmed glasses, all clutched awkwardly in his left hand. The left sleeve of Nicolas' old-fashioned frock coat was of normal length but his right sleeve had been cut off slightly below his shoulder to reveal the stump of his right arm.

He placed the glasses on the table, thumbed the cork from the bottle and poured the dark red wine. The three men, standing, raised their glasses.

'To our destinies.' Nicolas proposed the toast in perfect English, surprising Luke.

'To victory over the Hun,' Andre said.

They looked expectantly at Luke. He raised his glass. 'To truth,' he said. 'To truth and freedom.'

The wine was sweet and warm. Too sweet for Luke's taste but a welcome glow spread through him after the first few sips and he drained his glass. Nicolas watched him over the rim of his glass through green eyes set close together. Remarkably close together.

'It don't make any real sense when you come right down to it,' T.J. had said, 'but I know from experience that when you meet a man with eyes set close together you'd best keep your hand on your wallet. Never trust him any farther than you can throw him.'

They set their glasses on the table, Luke hoping he wouldn't be expected to drink another glass. He needed all the wits he had about him tonight.

'Thank you for bringing him to me.' Nicolas' words were an odd dismissal, but one all the same. 'Pray for me as I'll be praying for you.'

With no one praying for Luke Ray? The man who probably needed it the most.

Andre looked from Nicolas to Luke and, for a moment, he seemed about to speak. Instead, he turned without a word. When he was at the door, Luke said, 'Wait,' and strode to him. Keeping his back to Nicolas, he handed the black notebook he'd taken from Katryn's bedroom. Up until now the notebook had never left his person. MacNeeley hadn't known he had it, no one did. Luke trusted no one fully but it made little sense to carry the damn thing into a German stronghold.

'Take this,' he said in a low tone. 'Two people died trying to keep it from me.'

Andre riffled through the pages and stared up at Luke. 'Code,' he half-whispered. 'Could it be the names of German sympathizers?' He stuffed the notebook into a pocket and touched his fingers to his cap, saluting Luke, then walked, lantern in hand, through the door into the maze of tunnels. Nicolas came up to Luke and placed his left hand on Luke's shoulder. His face, Luke noted, was pale, almost ashen. Did he never leave his lair beneath the city and venture into the sun?

'Have you prepared yourself?' Nicolas asked. 'Your person. Your soul.'

'I'm as ready as I'll ever be.'

It was Nicolas who seemed unprepared, Luke thought. The other man appeared to carry no weapon. His black hat and black frock coat make him look like someone from another place, another time. If anything, they reminded Luke of the flamboyant dress of a Mississippi riverboat gambler.

'Come with me, then,' Nicolas said, 'into this, my domain.'

Luke took his lantern from the floor and followed the other man from the room. He no longer felt uneasy, the warmth from the wine had dissipated his apprehension.

Nicolas walked swiftly and quietly, showing no hesitation despite the subterranean gloom, striding ahead as though he knew every twist and turn of this underground labyrinth by heart.

Though he made an attempt to memorize all the turns, Luke hoped he wouldn't have to negotiate the maze by himself. Hearing a hiss like the sound of a snake poised to strike, he tensed and held, raising his lantern. A huge corroded pipe ran head-high along the wall beside him, the escaping steam hissing as it sent puffs of vapor up toward the unseen roof of the tunnel.

He hurried to catch up to Nicolas. As they walked on, the sound of running water became louder. Nicolas stooped to enter a low, narrow passageway with Luke a step behind. The passage broadened, opening into what seemed, in the lantern's feeble circle of light, a limitless chamber. Nicolas advanced a few steps before he held out his hand. Luke stopped beside him, staring down at the dark surface of what he knew must be the Senne. Though the water flowed swiftly, the river was smooth, unruffled by currents or eddies.

'We must cross the river,' Nicolas told him.

They climbed down slippery steps to a stone pier beside which a raft was moored to a ring in a black timber protruding from the water. Nicolas held the raft against the stones while Luke boarded, then untied the mooring line with his one hand and stepped gracefully aboard. Taking a long pole from the boat's deck, he thrust it deep into the water and pushed the raft into the river.

Nicolas' one arm, Luke realized, must be incredibly powerful for the raft shot swiftly out into the stream. Luke's lantern created a pale dome of light around them, a light encompassed on all sides by the hovering gloom of the tunnel and the greater darkness of the river. Behind Luke, the dock was soon lost to view, while ahead of him he saw only a distant indistinct shore.

They floated on, drifting now, seemingly without direction or purpose, on a timeless river with no yesterday and no tomorrow. Luke shuddered involuntarily, feeling a loss that was no less wrenching for being undefined.

He knew how Theodore Roosevelt must have felt on that St. Valentine's Day more than thirty years before when his wife, Alice, only twenty-two, and his mother, Martha, both died within a few hours of one another.

He knew how his mother must have felt when T.J. left, the sense of loss, the hurt that made her refuse to speak his name, ever, until the day he died.

The raft thudded against stone, the lashed timbers quivering beneath Luke's feet, the jar banishing his gloomy reverie. Nicolas laid his pole on the deck and secured the mooring line to a large ring embedded in one of the dock's great stones.

They walked away from the river and down a broad stone staircase with the sound of the river coming from above them. Sweat gathered on Luke's forehead. The effect of the wine, he supposed. Oddly, the glass he'd taken hadn't caused any light-headedness, instead, for some reason, his perceptions had become sharper, more distinct.

Odors he didn't recognize teased the edges of his memory. A fetid smell forced him to pinch his nose shut with his fingers for a moment or two. The smell of decay was soon left behind, replaced by — ? He shook his head. No, impossible. It couldn't be the aromatic scent of pines.

'Sometimes,' Nicolas said, 'odors become imprisoned here beneath the city. They linger in crevices, in the still air, for years and years. Perhaps for all time. There. Do you recognize that scent?'

Luke could have sworn he caught the faint perfume of lilacs, so well remembered from his childhood. He shook his head in disbelief.

'Lilacs,' Nicolas said. 'I've never noticed that smell before. It must have to do with you.'

Nicolas stopped in front of a metal door with a narrow grilled aperture in the top. removing a loop of keys from inside his frock coat. The key he chose turned noiselessly in the lock and the door opened without a creak. Nicolas locked it behind them before leading Luke up a curving flight of stairs.

In the corridor at the top, voices clamored behind the walls. Luke heard murmurs of conversation, moans of pain. A woman keened, her voice rising and falling in sorrowful lament. A man laughed gleefully. The laughter went on and on becoming a maniacal scream of despair and lost hope.

Oil lamps in brackets glowed from high on

the walls so Luke left his lantern in a recess. He saw thin, skeletal-like hands reaching through barred windows. At the far end of another corridor hung a huge man-sized cage and he blinked, thinking for a moment he saw faces from the past drifting before him. Manion. Katryn. Hendrik. The German who'd leaped, burning, from the staff car. The dead. Those who'd died because of him.

'We can't linger here,' Nicolas told him. 'You'll have time enough for that another day.'

He'd spoken in French and Luke wasn't sure he'd understood him right. His words didn't seem to make sense. They climbed steps and the voices faded. After they passed through another doorway the corridor became cleaner, brighter. The sharp smell of disinfectant rose above other odors, not quite obliterating the scent of urine and stale sweat. Hospital smells, human smells. Metal doors were spaced at regular intervals on both sides.

'Wait here,' Nicolas ordered, walking past Luke and turning down a side passage. Luke waited only a moment before striding to the corner but Nicolas was already out of sight.

'*M.* Ray.'

Luke spun around. A guard, his uniform and kepi identical to Luke's, stood watching him warily. A Belgian because his accent wasn't German. He was a short, pudgy man, his cheeks pale, his small mustache a dash punctuating an otherwise unremarkable face.

'You were told I was coming?' Luke asked in French.

'I was.'

'I have questions,' Luke began.

'Not now, later. Now you must come with me.'

The guard turned and Luke fell into step a few paces behind him, reflecting that he always seemed to be following people he didn't quit trust. He tensed, gearing himself to ready for anything, from anywhere. They entered an intersecting corridor, turned right, then left. Luke, staring warily about, fingered the butt of his holstered revolver. The guard stopped in front of a door very much like the others, unfastened a key from his belt and handed it to Luke, nodding to the door.

Luke shook his head, not liking the situation. The guard gestured to him, then to the door.

Was it possible he'd been led to Graham's cell. Again the feeling it was too easy snaked through Luke. He stared down at the key. Open the damn door, he told himself. You've come this far unmolested, open the door.

Luke inserted the key. It turned easily in the lock. He removed it and pushed the door

346

open, staring inside. The cell was small, sparsely furnished with a table, two chairs and a cot. A crucifix hung on the hall. A man sat at the table, his hand over his face.

Not Graham, Luke knew immediately, even though he couldn't see the man's face. The other Englishman? He took a step toward him, then heard footsteps behind him. He swung around. Two German soldiers, pistols drawn, were approaching, one from the right, one from the left. Luke stepped into the cell, shutting and locking the door behind him. A futile gesture, he knew, but it would buy time.

When he turned, the man at the table had dropped his hand and was looking and smiling at Luke.

'Welcome to St. Gilles,' Byron MacNeeley said.

20

Luke Ray, dressed in a gray inmate's uniform, sat on the edge of his cot with his head in his hands. His cell, two feet by six, was unlighted and without windows, the only illumination from the oil lamps in the corridor, their wavering lights seeping in around the metal door. He guessed it was early in the afternoon of the day following his capture.

MacNeeley. After they'd locked Luke in this cell, it had occurred to him sometime between waking and sleeping, that the reason he hadn't seen MacNeeley's face among his vision of the dead in that hellish underground Nicolas had led him through was because MacNeeley was still alive. Too bad he hadn't realized that earlier.

Sid's face hadn't been among the dead, either. He hoped that was significant. Providing anything he'd seen in that eerie trip had been real.

The damn cell was real enough. Luke closed his eyes, recreating in his mind the plan to St. Gilles Prison. Confident he knew the approximate location of his cell, he pictured the long corridors leading to other tiers of cells, to the assembly hall, to the kitchens on the floor below and the administrative offices and cells above.

A key turned in the lock. Luke glanced up. The door opened and a rectangle of light fell across the floor. He blinked. Two German guards entered the cell and positioned themselves on either side of the door. Byron MacNeeley walked between them and stood looking down at Luke.

'The prison commandant,' he said, looking over Luke's head, 'has asked me to bring you to the assembly hall. An event will take place there shortly that he wishes you and the two Englishmen to see.

When Luke stood, MacNeeley refused to meet his gaze.

The other man, Luke realized with surprise, was strangely ill-at-ease. He was no longer the cock of the walk of the day before who had welcomed Luke to St. Gilles and made him his prisoner. MacNeeley obviously didn't like what he was about to do.

They walked from the cell with MacNeeley at Luke's side and the two German guards a few paces behind. The prison corridors were long and dim, the tiers of cells smelling of man and decay. And despair. MacNeeley led the way through an open double door into the rear of a large room that was empty except for row upon row of wooden benches.

'You're to sit there.' MacNeeley gestured to the last row.

Luke sat down while MacNeeley and the Germans remained standing behind him. He heard footsteps and turned as Justin Graham, dressed in prisoner gray, came into the assembly hall. Seeing Luke, Graham paused for a beat, staring, recovering in time to wink before he was seated at the other end of the rear row. Another Englishman, one Luke had never seen before, was led into the hall and seated a short distance to Luke's left. The man was short, perhaps five-six, with a brown mustache and a round, almost cherubic, face. Like Luke, the two Englishmen were each guarded by two Germans.

Luke closed his eyes, picturing the plan of the prison in his mind, particularly the labyrinth of corridors leading from the hall. Voices intruded and he opened his eyes. Prisoners, both men and women, were being herded into the front of the hall, their guards seating them in the first three rows of benches. Edith Cavell was one of the last to enter. Although flanked by guards, she seemed alone, as though separated from the Germans and from her fellow prisoners as well.

They sat, waiting thirty or thirty-five in all.

No one spoke. A German lieutenant walked from near the door to the front of the room. The officer, tall with blond hair, stood flicking a riding crop against the side of his trousers. 'Ladies and gentlemen,' he said in heavily accented French, 'I have the great honor to present to you the *Auditeur Militaire, Kriegsgerichtsrat* Stoeber.'

Stoeber, elegant, brisk, cheerful-looking, strode into the room followed by four men.

'That's his interpreter just behind him,' MacNeeley said sotto voce from in back of Luke. 'Then the prison commandant. Next the chaplain. And Herr Stoeber's aide.'

Luke gave no sign he heard.

The aide reached into a portfolio, removed several papers and handed them to Stoeber.

The room was silent, expectant. When Stoeber took the papers and held them in front of him there was a rustle as the prisoners drew closer to one another.

The interpreter cleared his throat. 'The *Auditeur Militaire*,' he said, 'will now pronounce the judgment of the court.'

Stoeber read the first name, his voice seeming over-loud in the hush of the hall. He spoke with a flourish, pronouncing each syllable with emphasis, as though he saw himself speaking to history rather than to the defendants.

'Five years at hard labor,' he pronounced.

The sentences followed the names, one after the other.

'Ten years at hard labor.'

'Five years at hard labor.'

'Philippe Baucq.' Stoeber paused. '*Todesstrafe*,' he intoned. There was a whisper of indrawn breaths. The death penalty.

Luke leaned forward. Enraged. Helpless. Which, he was sure, was what the German commandant had intended when he'd had him brought here.

'Louis Severin. *Todesstrafe*.'

'*Mlle*. Louise Thuliez. *Todesstrafe*.'

Luke's mission, all he had done, all he had tried to do, had led here to St. Gilles, to this moment in the prison assembly hall.

'Countess de Belleveille. *Todesstrafe*.'

To failure. It didn't help that Justin Graham had also failed. That C had failed. *He* had failed. Luke Ray.

'Edith Cavell,' Stoeber said. In the pause after the reading of the name, Luke glanced at the English nurse. She sat staring ahead, her face impassive.

'*Todesstrafe*.' Stoeber said.

Luke thought he saw Nurse Cavell's mouth tighten when she heard the verdict of death but, from where he sat at the rear of the hall, he couldn't be sure. He clenched his fists in frustrated anger. He'd never hated the Huns as much as he did at this moment.

He didn't doubt that he, Graham and the other Englishman would receive short shrift from their captors. Death by firing squad was an inevitable verdict for them. But he'd never really believed they would kill a nurse, a woman.

When the reading of the sentences ended, Luke saw one of the Belgian prisoners approach Edith Cavell and speak softly to her. She shook her head as she answered him, her features calm, fatalistic. Luke couldn't hear what she said. The guards hurried their charges from the hall, the prisoners appearing stunned, shocked by the severity of their sentences. Each walked as if in a trance, unresisting yet undaunted, not speaking, as though now the only meaningful communication would be with God.

When the hall cleared, MacNeeley said, 'Now it's back to your cell, old chap.'

Trying to sound like an Englishman to the last. The duplicitous bastard. Though he hadn't recognized it as falseness then, from the beginning something about MacNeeley had set Luke's teeth on edge. He realized now Byron MacNeeley had been too English to be real. Strange that C hadn't sensed it.

A guard's rifle butt prodded Luke to his

feet. He walked from the hall with MacNeeley falling into step beside him, the guards behind them, the two Englishmen and their guards following.

'Hun bastards.' Luke spoke under his breath so only MacNeeley heard. 'Condemning a woman to die. Barbarians.'

'She's a spy, you know that.' MacNeeley's voice was defensive, almost apologetic. 'She concealed English and French soldiers and sent them on to Holland. From there they went back to their units to fight.'

'She was a nurse, not a spy. Nurses are trained to save lives, to help the injured, the victims, not the conquerors. She was doing what she had to do. I'd have done the same. I'll bet even you would have, MacNeeley.'

'The verdict of the court was entirely correct,' MacNeeley said stiffly.

Luke grunted his disgust, saying nothing. The only sound in the corridor was the thud of boots on the stone pavement.

'The verdict was proper,' MacNeeley repeated. When Luke still said nothing, he went on. 'She was guilty of the charges brought against her. There's no question of that. Even you must agree.'

'Bullshit.' As he spat out the word, Luke glanced about, matching the intersecting corridors to those on the plan of the first

354

floor of St. Gilles Prison. The stairs they were passing led to an upper tier of cells. The next passageway was a blind alley housing a series of interrogation rooms. If he got the chance —

'I'm a fair-minded sort of bloke,' MacNeeley said. 'I'll admit to you that the sentence was a miscalculation. Completely proper, but a mistake. I so advised the commandant.'

'Obviously your opinion doesn't carry much weight,' Luke said.

MacNeeley shrugged. After a pause, he said, 'I've spent many, many years living among the English and the Cornish. I've lived half my life in Blighty. I know the ways of the English, how they think, how they react. I told the commandant that these sentences, particularly Miss Cavell's, will only make the English fight harder. Unfortunately, he wouldn't listen to me.'

MacNeeley had slowed his pace as he talked. One of the guards behind him muttered.

'*Sich Geduld*,' MacNeeley snapped. His demand for patience silenced the guard.

'I explained to Herr Bergen, the prison commandant,' he said to Luke, 'that the English war lords would like nothing better than to have the German Army execute *Fraulein* Cavell. 'What a perfect way for us to create a martyr for them,' I told him, 'where none now exists.''

'You sure didn't tell him,' Luke observed.

The next side corridor led to a stairs in the lower depths. To make a run for it would be suicide. But better than facing a firing squad. If only he had an edge, an advantage. If only there was some way to distract the guards.

'The commandant has no authority over the executions, of course,' MacNeeley said. 'He refused my request to carry my protest to a higher command. 'Herr Stoeber,' I informed him, is a modern day Pontius Pilate. If Pilate had sentenced Jesus to a few years at hard labor that would have been the last the world would have heard of the man — assuming, of course, Jesus *was* no more than a man. Instead, Pilate crucified him. We all know which of them gained the greater victory.' Again my argument fell on deaf ears.'

'You were right,' Luke said.

'*Sich be-eilen*,' the guard said to MacNeeley. 'Hurry.'

MacNeeley swung around and confronted the German, glaring at him. '*Halt de Mund!*' he shouted.

The second guard stepped between the two men. Beyond them Luke saw Graham, the other Englishman and their guards stop, confused. This was the moment he'd been waiting for.

'Graham!' Luke called. He stepped behind the second guard, yanked the man's Mauser from its holster and slid off the safety. The guard whirled, the butt of his rifle swinging up. Luke fired. The German grunted and staggered away, a dark blotch staining his chest.

'Don't be a fool,' MacNeeley shouted at Luke. 'You're only their pawn.'

Luke swung the Mauser to MacNeeley while wondering what he'd meant. He fired just as MacNeeley flung himself to the floor and rolled away. He found Graham at his side. Unarmed. A guard fired, the sound thunderous in the passageway. The bullet ricocheted harmlessly from the rock walls.

'The first passage,' Luke told Graham, 'Run.'

Graham sprinted past him. Luke fired again, saw the first guard, the one MacNeeley had told to shut up, pitch forward, his rifle clattering on the stone. The other Englishman dashed toward Luke. A guard grabbed his arm, swinging him about. Luke fired, deliberately high, afraid of hitting the Englishman.

Pistol shots flashed and roared. The Englishman broke free and ran. Luke knelt beside one wall of the corridor, firing past him.

'Good God,' the Englishman gasped as he neared Luke. 'Good God.'

'Into the first passage,' Luke told him.

The Englishman stumbled and pitched forward, dropping to his knees beside Luke as another round hit him in the back. Luke grasped the man's shoulder. The Englishman stared at Luke, mouth open, blood trickling down his chin.

'What's your name?' Luke asked, firing past the man's shoulder.

'Kingman,' the Englishman whispered. His eyes closed and he died in Luke's arms.

Luke eased Kingman to the stones, turned and sprinted away from the Germans. The corridor was acrid with the smell of burnt powder. Two shots thundered from behind. Graham ran beside him, grabbed his arm.

'The passage,' Graham shouted in his ear. 'You've gone by it. It's behind you. Run!'

Luke ran with him into the dark mouth of the side passage. Two more shots slammed from behind them. Shouts and curses followed them. Moans of the wounded. Boots pounded over the stones.

Luke stopped, turning and running back to the passage entrance. A German stood an arm's length from him. The guard stared, raised his pistol. Luke fired, point-blank. The German grunted, hung motionless for an instant, collapsed. Lay sprawled on the stone floor, groaning. Luke stepped into the main corridor, firing back along it. A man screamed in pain. Luke nodded in satisfaction. A bullet zinged past him.

'The bloody gun's empty,' Graham said loudly. 'Your gun.'

Luke looked down and pulled the trigger. Heard nothing, felt no recoil. He hurled the pistol into the corridor at the advancing Germans. 'Bastards!' he shouted. 'Goddamn bastards!'

Graham yanked at his arm, forcing Luke to turn.

Panting, he let Graham pull him into the dark passageway and then ran alongside him, stumbling in the gloom.

'I'll kill them,' he shouted at Graham. 'All of them.'

'Where does this bloody tunnel go?' Graham asked.

'With my bare hands if I have to.' Luke could feel the blood throbbing in his temples. His heart pounded. 'Kill them, kill them, kill them.'

Graham gripped his shoulder and pushed him against the wall, his face inches from Luke's. 'The tunnel.' Luke felt Graham's spittle on his cheek. 'Where does it go? You said take this passageway. Where does it go, damn it.'

'The tunnel?' What the hell was Graham talking about?

Graham slapped him hard across the face. Luke rubbed his stinging cheek, staring at Graham.

'You said take the first passageway,' his tone patient but harried. 'This tunnel.'

Luke heard a confusion of running footfalls from the way they'd come. Heard shouts. Remembered.

'This way,' he told Graham who released him immediately. Luke trotted forward. The stairway should be no more than a few yards from here. He slowed, looking right and left, saw a patch of wall darker than the rest. He reached to touch the darkness and his hand groped into emptiness. He sighed with relief.

'This is it,' he told Graham.

'Thank God.'

With his fingertips gliding along one wall, Luke ran down the stairs with Graham a step behind him. The sounds of pursuit faded. Whistles shrilled from above and behind them. Ahead of them was silence.

Without warning, Luke stumbled and plunged forward, falling to his knees. The bottom of the stairs. Graham knelt at his side.

'All right, old chap?' he asked.

'You're talking like that bastard MacNeeley,' Luke growled. Sitting up, he saw a dim stationary light in the tunnel ahead of them.

'Martin Kingman,' Graham said. 'What happened to Kingman?'

'He's dead.'

Graham sighed. Luke pushed himself to his feet and looked around as he once more pictured the plan of the prison.

'St. Gilles will be an armed camp within the hour,' Graham said. 'Do you know a way out?'

'The way I came in. The same way you came in. On the river under the city. The door can't be more than a hundred feet from here.'

'You've done your home study better than I.'

Limping, Luke walked ahead. Two turns to the right, followed by one to the left should get them to the entrance to the underground. He turned right, turned right again.

A German guard blocked their way. Both men stepped back in surprise. The German raised his pistol. Luke hurled himself forward, his shoulder struck the guard's chest and sent him staggering back. The Mauser thundered, deafening Luke, but missing. Still charging, he curled his leg behind the guard's and pushed. As the German fell to the floor he brought the Mauser up holding it in front of him with both hands. Luke stared into the black bore of the barrel.

Graham's foot lashed out, kicked the pistol, sending it flying against the wall. The German cried out, clutching his wrist, hunching backward across the stone floor with Graham advancing warily on him. Luke groped along the floor in the darkness. His fingers closed on the gun.

'Get out the way,' he shouted at Graham. The Englishman flattened himself against the wall.

The German pushed himself to his feet, raising his hands high over his head. Luke fired. The German screamed and sat down hard, staring at the dark stain on the leg of his trousers a few inches below his crotch.

Luke skirted the fallen guard. He'd meant to kill them all. Why had he lowered his gun at the last moment?

He led Graham along the corridor and to the left. The door was where he'd remembered. Locked. He fired into the lock, yanked on the handle. The lock held. He fired again. Shook the door. To no avail.

'Here,' Graham said. 'Let me.'

Holding the Mauser at an angle, he fired into the lock. Pulled the handle toward him. Reluctantly, the door swung open.

'I left my lantern near here,' Luke said.

'Can you light it? Have you a match? I don't.'

'The hell with it.' Luke dismissed the lantern.

They groped into the darkness. Heard the river murmuring to them, tried to walk toward the sound but found their way barred by slimy stone walls. After ten minutes Luke admitted he was lost.

'I get the feeling we've been wandering around in circles,' Graham said as they sat on a damp stone step. 'We'd best find one wall and follow it.'

Recalling all the twists and turns when he was led to the prison, Luke was none too sure following a wall would get them anywhere. He was about to say so when he spotted something. 'Look,' he said to Graham.

A light bobbed in the distance. As they watched, it came toward them. They crept back into the concealing darkness, the Mauser in Graham's hand. As the light came nearer they saw what appeared to be two men, the smaller one carrying a lantern.

'By God,' Graham said, 'it's that Nicolas fellow. But who's that with him?'

Luke smiled and started forward. 'Kezia,' he called softly. 'It's Luke.'

She put the lantern on the ground. With a

cry she ran and threw her arms around him. Luke held her close for a long moment before he eased away. 'Graham's with me,' he told her. 'Kingman's dead.'

She turned to Graham, taking his hand in hers. 'Thank God you're both safe,' she said.

'Did you bring weapons?' Luke asked.

'Two pistols.'

'We've got to go back to St. Gilles,' Luke said. 'We won't get another chance to save Miss Cavell.'

Kezia and Graham stared at him.

'We wouldn't get more than ten feet inside the prison,' Graham said. 'Not alive. They're waiting for us.'

'We have to go back,' Luke said. 'It's why we came.'

'No. Luke.' Kezia put a hand on his arm. 'That's over and done with as far as we're concerned. There's no chance now. It's too late.'

'We'll be lucky to get out of Brussels alive as it is,' Graham said. 'Besides, I was told they'd moved Miss Cavell to a new cell. They intend to execute her early tomorrow morning.'

'You're lying,' Luke said. 'They haven't moved her.'

Graham grasped the front of Luke's shirt.

'Listen, you crazy berserker, I am not a liar. Take it back.'

Nicolas didn't move, watching them with a slight smile on his face. It was Kezia who stepped between them.

'Justin! Luke! There's no time for this. We have to hurry.'

Graham released Luke.

Kezia said, 'Take my hand, Luke. Come with me.'

Luke looked back the way they'd come. It *was* over. The mission, yes, but more than that. It was as though a door had closed and been locked behind him, a door through which he could never return, a door shutting off his past.

He swung on his heel and, though not taking her hand, joined Kezia and Graham, following Nicolas to the underground river, the raft, and a passageway to the surface.

21

Shortly before two in the morning on October 12, 1915, guards led Edith Cavell and Philippe Baucq into a courtyard where two hundred and fifty German troops stood at attention. *Auditeur Militaire* Stoeber climbed the steps of a platform and faced the ranks of soldiers.

'Comrades!' Philippe Baucq cried. 'In the presence of death we are all comrades — '

A gag silenced him.

Stoeber read the sentences of death, his words repeated tonelessly by an interpreter. The firing squad, he told them, should have no hesitation about executing a woman because of the heinous nature of the crimes she had committed against the German nation.

Pastor le Seur held Edith Cavell's hand as he repeated, in English, the Grace of the Anglican Church. Miss Cavell pressed his hand and said, 'Ask Mr. Gahan to tell my loved ones that my soul, I believe, is safe and that I am glad to die for my country.'

Father Leyendecker murmured final words of comfort to Philippe Baucq as Pastor le

Seur led Edith Cavell to the execution post. A German soldier bound her loosely, facing the post, and bandaged her tear-filled eyes.

Father Leyendecker still spoke quietly to Philippe Baucq. At last the Catholic priest sighed and walked away from the condemned man. Soldiers escorted Baucq to a second execution post. He refused to be blindfolded. His gag was removed.

The two firing squads, eight soldiers in each, took their positions six paces from the condemned. A German officer shouted a command. Two salvos rang out.

Philippe Baucq pitched forward calling, 'Vive le Belgique.'

'My eyes were fixed exclusively on Miss Cavell,' Pastor le Seur reported later, 'and what I saw was terrible. With a face streaming blood — one shot had gone through her forehead — she had sunk down forward, but three times had seemed to raise herself up without a sound. I ran forward with the medical man but he was right when he stated these were merely reflex movements as bullet holes as large as a fist, in her back, proved that she was killed immediately.'

★　★　★

They drove north from Brussels on the Vilvoorde road, Andre and Kezia in the front of the canopied four-seater rig, Luke and Justin in the rear.

Luke held his watch — left with Andre before his jaunt into the prison — a few inches from his eyes. 'Ten minutes past two,' he said.

The night breeze rustled through the autumn branches of the trees over their heads like a sigh.

'It's all over, then,' Graham said.

Kezia whispered, 'Dear God, oh dear God.' She bowed her head.

'Men are barbarians,' Andre muttered as he urged the horse on. 'The nations of the world seek to outdo one another in their barbarity. Once it was the Spanish, at another time the French or the English.'

'The English?' Graham's tone showed his objection.

'The English. And not only because they burned Joan of Arc at the stake. But this is the century of the German barbarians, the Huns. We'll never forget. Never forgive.'

Graham looked behind them and cursed under his breath. Luke glanced back and saw two pairs of lights in the distance.

'Motor vehicles,' Graham said. 'They're about a mile behind us and gaining.'

'It was too good to last,' Andre said.

He slowed the rig. There was darkness to their right, a scattering of faint lights far to the left.

'Why do you slow?' Kezia asked. 'They'll overtake us all the sooner.'

'The Germans are known to have a checkpoint on the Vilvoorde Road near here.' Andre brought the rig to a stop. 'Look for yourselves.'

Ahead of them dark figures warmed themselves around an ill-concealed fire. Andre climbed to the ground, hurried to the horse and led him off the road to the west. Luke jumped from the rig and walked beside the Belgian.

'The road to Wolvertem's on the far side of this field,' Andre said before Luke had a chance to speak. 'From there we can take the Antwerp road to the north.'

'And the other way? We just passed a road to the east. Where does it go?'

'To Malsbroek and beyond. The German aerodrome's near there, the barracks, the Zeppelin hangars.'

'They wouldn't expect us to go that way,' Luke said.

'And for good reason, my friend. The Germans patrol that area in force.'

Graham joined them, 'This isn't the best

of times to hold a debate, is it now?' he asked.

'The German aerodrome's the other way, to the east,' Luke told him. 'Near where I tried to blow the bridge. How far are we from the front?'

'From Ypres? Forty miles, maybe fifty at the most.'

'I see.' Graham hesitated only a moment. 'Can you handle one of those Hun aircraft? Can you get her off the ground? And down again all in one piece?'

'I can fly anything if I get a fair chance at it.' Luke knew he sounded more confident than he felt. But what the hell, he *was* a good pilot. 'They're built pretty much the same as ours,' he went on. 'I've handled the controls of a German plane before.' And so he had. At the airfield, after an Albatross was forced down behind French lines.

'Can you get us to the aerodrome?' Graham asked Andre. 'Close to it, at least?'

The Belgian, reins in his hands, stared from Graham to Luke and back. Behind them Luke heard the motor vehicles, saw the beams of their headlights touching the trees along the road.

'You English are as mad as the Americans.' Andre shrugged. 'As mad as we Belgians.' He brushed past them and clambered onto the rig. 'Hurry,' he called. 'We have little time. Hurry, hurry.'

Luke and Graham leaped into the rig as Andre swung the horse back onto the road, calling to the animal and cracking his whip. The lights of the two cars appeared and reappeared though trees like a warning message flashed in code. Andre drove toward the cars, the horse's hooves pounding on the dirt, the rig creaking as it swung from side to side.

The rig veered abruptly to the left, forcing Luke to grasp the rail at his side. The headlights were lost behind the trees as they raced onto the darkness of a side road. Looking back, Luke saw the lights of the cars pause at the fork, swing their way, following them.

'They're onto us,' he called.

Andre cracked the whip. They careered through a black tunnel of trees whose branches met over their heads. The road turned, they left the trees and saw stars overhead.

'On the left,' Andre shouted over his shoulder. 'The aerodrome.'

Luke saw a dark huddle of buildings, saw the dim glow of blue lights. He leaned forward. 'The aerodrome,' he shouted. 'Describe it.'

'They've changed it,' Andre shouted back. 'Last summer the aerodrome was a sod field with a road on this side, this road, a road on the other side. The sheds are ahead of us, the sheds for the aeroplanes. The barracks are on the other side. The Zeppelin hangars are beyond the other road. Two or three miles from here.'

'The field,' Luke told him. 'Drop us near the field.' He saw Andre nod. They raced on, the rig swaying from side to side, the two cars gaining on them. Andre slowed the rig, stopped.

'Here,' he said. 'The field's to your left. Past the fence.'

Kezia leaped from the front of the rig, Luke and Graham vaulted from the rear. Luke ran forward and clasped Andre's hand. 'Good luck,' he said.

'Go with God,' the Belgian replied softly.

Luke turned but couldn't see the others at first.

'Here,' Kezia whispered.

Luke slid down a low embankment in the direction of her voice. A hand found his, Kezia's hand, and pulled him deeper into the darkness.

'*Viva la Belgique!*' Andre shouted as the rig rattled away.

The first of the two cars braked into the

turn, skidded, recovered, its headlight beams sweeping over their heads, finding the surface of the road again. The lights pinpointed the black rig. A shot snapped from the car. The second car braked, lights swinging above them. Dust swirled behind the cars. Another shot cracked followed by a volley of four or five.

Luke drew his pistol. A hand gripped his arm.

'Don't be a fool,' Graham told him. 'If anybody can make it alone, Andre can.'

Luke holstered the pistol, knowing that Graham was right. Andre was eminently capable. And a shot from here would tell the Germans they'd bailed out of the rig. He followed the Englishman up the far side of the ditch to the edge of what appeared to be an unfenced field, Kezia on his heels. They hurried forward, crouching, with Graham in the lead.

Graham's hand stopped Luke. 'The fence,' he warned in a whisper. 'Get down, you'll see it better.'

Luke knelt, made out a network of posts and barbed wire.

'I'll have a go at it,' Graham said.

The Englishman took a pair of cutters from his belt and crawled forward, Luke and Kezia behind him, snipping the wire as he went, the click of the cutting muted by his gloves. Graham was damn good at it, Luke admitted. Good or not, it took them all of twenty minutes to reach the far side of the wire barricade.

Luke knelt beside Graham. 'Did you ever see such a beautiful sight?' he whispered, gazing ahead.

A row of monoplanes stretched away on the field ahead of them. Fokkers. Kezia's cautionary hand touched his arm. A figure loomed in the darkness, helmeted, rifle slung over one shoulder. The German sentry walked slowly past, between them and the field, disappearing to their left.

'I'll reconnoiter,' Luke said. 'Wait here.'

He slipped into the darkness, keeping in the shadows of the Fokkers as long as he could. Luckily, the crescent moon he'd seen earlier was obscured by clouds at the moment. He walked ahead, the wind in his face, pacing the distance. After two hundred yards without reaching the far end of the field and without meeting another German, he returned to the row of Fokkers.

A door rumbled open. Luke held, listening, watching.

He saw a biplane being rolled slowly from the hangar across the field and, after a few moments, made out the shapes of the men, mechanics probably, who were pushing it. The plane came to a stop and the mechanics walked away in the direction of the hangar.

'Ray.' Graham's voice. 'What's going on out there?

'They're getting a biplane ready for a dawn patrol. She looks like an LVG. Reconnaissance. Bombing, too. She's a two-seater. This is the best chance we're likely to get.'

'What do you want us to do?'

'Kezia, you get in the rear cockpit,' Luke ordered. 'Graham, go to the front of the plane and grab hold of the propeller. When I give the word, rotate the prop two times. To prime her. Let me know when you're done. When I tell you, snap down hard on the prop. Okay? If she starts, get in the rear cockpit with Kezia. If she doesn't start, we go through the routine again.'

'Righto.'

The German mechanics had disappeared into the hangar. 'Let's go,' Luke said.

They trotted at a crouch across the open field. Luke noted protuberances beneath the LVG's lower wing. When he reached the plane, he looked and found three bombs mounted on the wing on each side of the fuselage.

Climbing onto the wing, he swung his leg into the cockpit. With both hands on the padded sides, he raised himself up and then lowered his body into the cockpit. He breathed in the odors of gasoline and castor oil and gave a sigh of contentment. He was where he belonged, he was home.

Lighting one match after another, he studied the interior of the cockpit, found the stick, rudder bar, ignition switch and fuel cock. He puzzled over a lever that appeared to have been newly mounted. Placing his feet on the rudder bar, he kicked sharply right and then left, heard the cables squeak as they pulled the rudder on the tail from side to side. He pushed the stick forward and pulled it back. Again he heard the squeaking as the elevator dropped and rose.

'Turn her over,' he ordered Graham.

Graham's whisper came a few minutes later from the front of the airplane. 'Ready.'

Luke lit another match. The ignition was off, the fuel cock on. He flipped the ignition switch to on. 'Now,' he called.

He heard the snap of the propeller. The primed engine exploded into life, sending smoke belching back toward him from the cowling. The engine coughed before settling into a steady, high-pitched roar. Graham ran around the end of the wing toward the rear cockpit.

God! He'd forgotten to tell him to take the

chocks from under the wheels. Luke stood, the plane vibrating under him. As he was about to climb to the wing, Graham saw him. Luke waved, pointing beneath the fuselage.

'The chocks!' he shouted, trying to make himself hear above the roar.

Graham stared at him, finally nodding, kneeling and crawling under the wing. Luke glanced past the LVG's tail at the hangar, saw a rectangle of light framing the closed door but nothing more. The LVG jounced ahead over the grass — the chocks were gone.

Luke looked back and saw Graham climb into the rear cockpit, squeezing in beside Kezia, the LVG's single machine-gun tilting rakishly skyward on the fuselage behind him. Graham called to him but his voice was lost in the roar of the plane. He raised his hand, thumbs up.

Luke settled into the cockpit and turned the plane into the wind, heading away from the hangars onto the open field. He kept the stick forward as the LVG accelerated. He felt the tail lift from the grass and he eased the stick gently back. The plane refused to rise. He eased the stick further back. Heavily, reluctantly, the LVG rose from the ground. Luke saw the blackness of trees ahead. He pulled back on the stick, held his breath as he risked stalling. The trees loomed nearer,

nearer, suddenly dropped away beneath the plane.

He let out his breath in a slow whistle of relief. He gained altitude with the eastern horizon glowing faintly to his right. Luke looked back and saw Graham raise both arms triumphantly. Luke looked below. The aerodrome was dark, there was no sign of German pursuit. Thank God.

He climbed into the dark early morning sky, swung the LVG to the west of south toward the Channel. Despite the wind screen in front of his cockpit, the cold air stung his face and neck. He slapped his hands together and then against his thighs for warmth. His air speed, at a guess, was 60 m.p.h. In less than an hour, then, he'd reach the German lines and cross No-Man's-Land into France.

Gently, he tilted the plane to the right, looked down, tilted to the left, looked down on the other side. The terrain below was dark. He searched the sky ahead of him to the west, to his sides, behind and above. As far as he could tell, there were no other planes aloft, the sky was clear except for a cloud in the northwest several miles off his right wing.

He glanced at the cloud, large and black in the gray light of the pre-dawn, thinking there was something strange about it, something wrong. His attention caught, he studied the cloud and a tingle coursed up his spine. The cloud was floating serenely toward him. Not remarkable in itself except that it sailed against the wind.

Not a cloud, then, an airship. A Zeppelin.

He turned, waved his hand. When Graham waved acknowledgment, Luke pointed to the Zeppelin bearing down on them from the direction of the Channel. He thought he saw Graham nod. Luke pulled back on the stick and the LVG climbed slowly. When he reached Zeppelin's altitude he realized the airship was beginning its descent for a landing. A machine-gun chattered behind him.

Luke whirled. Graham waved to him, kept the gun pointing toward the Zeppelin and pressed off another burst.

Luke leveled off, ranging the LVG along the side of the Zeppelin. The airship, more than twenty times as long as his plane, slid soundlessly past. Graham fired in short bursts. Tracers streamed into the Zepp's cloth superstructure. Luke braced himself, fearing that at two hundred yards they were too close to avoid being blasted to eternity in the explosion of the hydrogen-filled ship.

Nothing happened, nothing at all. The

LVG roared past the elevators and rudders of the Zeppelin, the airship sailing serenely away from him. Luke climbed and veered to his right as he turned to follow. He'd make another run alongside, give Graham another shot at the airship. He flew above the Zeppelin to avoid machine-guns mounted in the control car and suspended from the underside of the ship.

The LVG slowly overtook the descending Zeppelin. When the plane was above the airship's tail section, Luke pressed his rudder with his foot to turn the LVG to the right, eased the stick forward to fly along the airship's side for another machine-gun run.

Tat-tat-tat-tat.

Luke jerked his head to look behind him. Two single winged planes dived from above, the lead plane's guns winking fire from between its propeller. Luke pulled back, climbing steeply, the Zeppelin falling away below. The Fokkers swept past beneath him, Graham firing at them, his tracers curving behind the Germans.

The LVG struggled to gain altitude. She was too heavy. The bombs. Luke remembered the lever at the side of the cockpit, the lever he hadn't recognized. The lever must activate the bomb release. He yanked the lever back, pushed it forward, felt the plane leap upward as the bombs fell free. He pulled back on the stick, climbing.

German machine-gun fire sputtered from behind him. Graham's gun answered. The range was too great, Luke knew. He meant to gain as much altitude as he could, aware the LVG had a higher ceiling than the Fokkers. But the pursuit planes were faster, too fast. They'd overtake him before he'd climbed another thousand feet.

All hell broke loose below and behind him. A wall of orange flame shot skyward. A massive explosion hurled the LVG up and onto its side, the aircraft rocking in the shock waves. Luke fought the rudder and the stick, leveled the plane. The engine sputtered, caught again. Heat seared Luke's cheeks and he choked on acrid fumes.

Looking down, he stared in awe at the Zeppelin. At what had been the Zeppelin. Flames engulfed her top rear as the tail sank earthward. The Fokkers were gone, consumed in the fiery death of the airship. The bombs had done what machine-gun fire had failed to do.

Tail-first, the Zeppelin settled lower as the fire swept amidships, the flames blinding, the heat intense. Below the Zeppelin, a pale eerie light from the burning ship showed

Luke fields, woods, a road running to the north.

He pulled back on the stick and the LVG responded, the heat from the doomed airship diminishing as he climbed. Once more he swung the plane to the southwest, flying toward France and home.

22

Luke flew at five thousand feet with a sky a pale blue vault above him and sun a red disc rising to his left. He grinned. Two Fokkers and a Zeppelin! Exuberant, he pounded his fist on the padded front of the cockpit. He was triumphant. Invincible. It was as though the hand of God had helped him strike his enemies from the sky.

The word Graham had called him in St. Gilles came back to him. Berserker. His mother was Scandinavian. Maybe he had inherited a tad of Viking blood at that. And maybe he had gone over the line, gone a little mad in the prison. Graham had certainly thought so.

By God, but the two of them made a good team. He thought Graham felt the same. They might not ever be friends but they did damn well as battle comrades.

Below him the brown October fields of Flanders undulated southward until they merged with the morning mist along the horizon. He passed high above a woods, flew over a Flemish village untouched by war. The LVG purred and Luke dipped his wings and looked behind him, wanting to share his joy. He saw Graham staring raptly over one side of the rear cockpit, Kezia over the other.

The terrain changed gradually. The next village had no church, or so he thought until he saw a sheared-off tower, only then realized that the surrounding houses were no longer homes but empty roofless shells. He followed a road from the ruined village that had been cratered by artillery fire, a road repaired only to be cratered again, the fields on both sides littered with the debris of war: wagons, trucks, shattered .75's.

The last of the woods disappeared beneath him. Now the landscape was barren, stark, the few remaining trees shorn of limbs, the ground scarred by the precise zigzags of the German rear trenches and the haphazard craters left by the seeking shells. He flew above an observation balloon and thought he saw the German observer wave at him. At the LVG. The scenes of war below him had eaten away at his elation until none remained. Edith Cavell was dead. He'd failed her, failed Manion and Sid — how he wished he knew Sid's fate. What had MacNeeley shouted at him, there in the prison? That he was a pawn. He hadn't understood then but he did now.

All along he'd been unawares, an ingenuous fool, he'd allowed MacNeeley to manipulate him, permitted MacNeeley to deceive him. And the bastard may well be still alive — he didn't think he'd killed him.

MacNeeley hadn't been the only one. Kezia and Graham also had their chance at playing him for the fool. But he could forgive them, especially Graham, a man to admire. Kezia — well, he didn't want to think about her just now.

How C must have laughed to himself at the brash young American who thought he knew so much. And who, in reality, knew so little. The perfect pawn, yes he'd been that.

His anger rose until he tasted bile. The deceit had come from one source. C. Once you let a man walk all over you, T.J. often said, you're branded as a coward. You have to get your own back. Make the bastard pay. Unsure whether or not his father had actually said all that, Luke shook his head, smiling grimly. It didn't matter. He intended to make C pay. Major bloody Cunningham, as Sid would have called him, was going to regret casting Luke Ray in the role of a fool.

Far to the east two Fokkers patrolled behind the German lines. Luke ignored them. The trenches slid below his biplane, the bunkers, the machine-gun nests, the barbed wire entanglements of No-Man's-Land. He flew over the first of the French lines. A machine-gun flashed off to his left.

He pictured a *poilu* cranking his field telephone to report a single LVG flying into France. In a few minutes aviators would strap themselves into their Morane-Saulniers and their Nieuport Bebes and roar into the sky, ready to do battle.

By that time, God willing, he'd be safely on the ground. He eased the stick forward, searching the countryside ahead of him. There, that field should do. He flew low over the stubble, looking for ditches and stumps of trees. Seeing none, he brought the plane around into the wind.

'Hang on!' he shouted over his shoulder.

As the ground rose to meet him, he switched off, gliding down with the wind cold on his face. Off to his right he glimpsed a French *poilu* running along the side of a road.

The soldier looked up, knelt, raised his rifle to his shoulder. Fired and fired again. Luke paid him no heed. Hitting a moving plane from the ground with a rifle was a ten thousand to one shot.

His wheels touched and the LVG bounced into the air. Again the wheels came down, held, the plane jouncing across the field. Luke saw the dark line of a ditch in front of him, braced himself. The LVG had no brakes. The

386

plane slowed, its wheels dropped into the ditch, the nose tilted forward and the LVG slammed to a stop, quivered and righted itself once more. They were down. All in one piece.

Luke unstrapped, grasped the sides of the cockpit with both hands and levered his body up. Swinging a leg over the side, he climbed to the lower wing and looked behind him. He froze. Kezia sat unmoving in the rear cockpit, her eyes wide, her mouth working. Graham was slumped beside her with only the back of his head visible above the cockpit's rim. 'He's — ' Kezia closed her eyes. Opened them and made another attempt. 'He's — ' She gagged, retched, turned her head to spew vomit over the side of the plane.

Luke gently lifted Graham's head. The *poilu's* bullet had entered his right eye. The ten thousand-to-one-shot. Blood from the wound was smeared on his face, had streaked his blond hair with red, one of his eyes was a black hole that stared lifelessly at Luke.

Shit. Poor Graham. The best ones always seemed to be the ones to die. Luke released his hold and Graham's head fell forward once again.

Gagging, Luke turned away. He took several deep breaths, letting them out slowly until he was in control of his stomach. He looked across Graham's shoulders at Kezia who sat with her eyes shut, her hand covering her mouth. 'We've got to get you out of there,' Luke said.

Reaching awkwardly across Graham, he gripped Kezia under the arms, lifted. He couldn't budge her, she was wedged too tightly between the dead man and the side of the cockpit. Knowing he was being irrational, he felt angry at Graham for putting Kezia through this hell.

'You'll have to help me,' he told her. When she didn't answer, he shook her. 'Help me!' he cried.

She opened her eyes, looked at him and nodded. Raising her hands, she put them on the rim of the cockpit. Luke yanked up, felt her strain to help, her body pulled free and she fell into his arms. Staggering back, he grabbed a strut to keep from falling off the wing. He lifted her legs from the cockpit, lowered her to the ground and released his hold. She sank to her knees on the brown grass. He jumped down beside her.

She was bent over, arms supporting her as she retched, choked, began to cough. Luke knelt facing her and, wanting to comfort her, reached out and raised her enough so he could draw her into his arms. She clung to him as her coughing subsided, her fingers digging into his back. Then she began to sob, pushed away from him and stumbled to her feet. Turning to the plane, Kezia pounded the fuselage with her fists. 'Damn you all,' she said brokenly. 'Goddamn you all to hell.'

She rested her head on the side of the airplane, sobbing quietly. Luke watched, anguished, wanting to comfort her without knowing how, afraid his touch was the last thing she wanted to feel. At last Kezia stepped away from the plane, shaking her head as though silently admonishing herself, and turned to face him. Her cheeks were tear-stained, her eyes darkened by surrounding shadows.

'I'm perfectly all right now,' she said stiffly. He realized she was anything but. Still, he didn't argue.

He took her hand and led her from the plane. Turning, he laid his free hand on the Mauser at his belt, intending to put a round into the LVG's gas tank, light the escaping fuel and make a funeral pyre of the airplane. That's the way a warrior should leave this earth, consumed in flames, not left to decay in a hole in the raw wet earth.

A man shouted behind him. Luke swung around. Three rifle-carrying *poilus* trotted across the field toward the aircraft. His hand left the pistol, he dropped Kezia's hand and raised both his over his head.

'Raise your hands,' he told Kezia.

She glanced from him to the advancing *poilus* and did as he said. Together, hands held high, they walked away from the plane to meet the French soldiers.

* * *

The truck laboring up the hill was actually little more than a large automobile with a truck-bed replacing the back seats and equipped with four rear wheels instead of two. Its canvas top had been folded forward over the cab, revealing the three coffins containing the bodies of Captain Justin Graham, Lieutenant James Laurie, and Lieutenant Holden Morefield. A five-man British Army burial party marched behind the truck while at the rear of the small procession a chaplain rode in a staff sedan with Luke and Kezia.

The truck stopped at the beginning of the loop where the dirt road ended in a circle around an ancient oak. Four soldiers lifted Graham's coffin from the truck and carried it to the first of three open graves, lowering it to the ground beside a mound of dark earth.

'This is truly a lovely spot,' Chaplain Miles said to Kezia as they followed the burial party. He was a small pudgy-cheeked man whose slick hair glistened in the sunlight. 'As you can see, he'll be near the top of the hill where there's a splendid view of the fields and the village. Why, there's even a stone bench under the oak where you can sit when you visit.'

Kezia glanced at Luke, a plea in her eyes.

'Perhaps we ought to start,' Luke suggested.

'As you wish.'

The chaplain nodded to the officer in charge of the burial party and, at his command, the soldiers lowered the coffin into the waiting earth. Chaplain Miles read the burial service, prayed, then sprinkled dirt onto the coffin while the soldiers watched, their faces impassive, as though they were bored by the monotonous sameness of death.

'Fire!' Three rifles flashed above the grave.

'Fire!'

'Fire!'

As the echoes died away, the chaplain approached Luke. 'I suspect the young lady's not feeling quite up to snuff,' he said. 'Perhaps you should take her to the village. Just be sure to send the car back for me.'

Luke looked down at the gaping grave.

'Don't be concerned,' Chaplain Miles told him. 'All three will be made presentable later today. The fatigue detail was delayed and won't be able to get here until this afternoon. There *is* a war on, after all.' He touched his lips lightly with his fingertips. 'I do suggest you accompany the young lady back to Abbeville.'

The chaplain squeezed Luke's arm before following the burial party to the truck for the next coffin. Kezia, dressed all in black, black dress, black hat, black veil, ignored him as she walked to the foot of Justin's Graham's grave. She lifted her veil and looked down at the earth scattered on the top of the bare wood of the coffin. Luke went to her side.

'The padre's an ass,' he said, 'but that doesn't mean he's not right. We ought to go back.'

'Not yet,' Kezia said softly. 'Justin deserves more than this. He wasn't religious, not in the usual way. But he loved England . . . and life . . . and ritual. Justin would have wanted something more. I'd like to say a few words to him, for him. There's a poem he used to quote. By Rupert Brooke. He was a great admirer of Brooke, you know. Even before he met him during the fighting at Antwerp.'

'I'll wait for you by the car,' he said, thinking she wanted to be alone.

'No, don't leave. I want you here. Justin would have wanted you here.'

Luke bowed his head.

'If I should die — ' Kezia paused and drew a long, shuddering breath. She began again.

'If I should die, think only this of me:
That there's some corner of a foreign field
That is forever England. There shall be
In that rich earth a richer dust concealed;
A dust that England bore, shaped, made aware,
Gave, once, her flowers to love, her ways to roam,
A body of England's breathing English air,
Washed by the rivers, blest by the suns of home.'

Kezia picked up a handful of dirt and, leaning forward, threw it gently into the grave. She took Luke's arm and started to walk away with him.

'Wait here,' he said halting. He disengaged his arm and turned back, knowing he had a farewell to say.

Standing over the grave, he heard an airplane, a Bebe by the sound of it, and looked up. 'There's where you belong,' he told Justin Graham. 'Not in the ground but up there, among the clouds where warriors go when they die.' He saluted, still looking up rather than into the dank hole.

He did not observe the ritual of tossing dirt on the coffin but walked slowly back to where Kezia waited.

'He's not in there, you know,' he told her. She nodded.

They walked on in silence. Finally she said, 'You're not to worry about me, Luke. It's just that it's all so damn senseless. The war. The killing. I've known that from the beginning, of course, but knowing a thing and understanding it with your heart and soul are different. I'll be all right. I'll do my patchwork, that's what I'm good at. Perhaps in the long run it does more good than harm, who's to say?'

He wondered what she meant but by then they'd reached the car and so he didn't ask. He'd find out in time, he suspected.

★   ★   ★

That night Luke took a bottle of the local red wine to his room on the second floor of the inn at Abbeville. The air was warm, the beginning of what would be an Indian Summer back home, so he opened the window and looked across the lawn, half expecting to see fireflies winking their messages of long ago. The night, though, remained dark. In any case this was October, not July. And it was France, not Colorado.

After undressing, he sat on the edge of the bed in the dark, letting a breeze cool his naked body as he sipped the wine. He was tired and wanted to sleep but he was afraid he'd lie awake as he had the last two nights, not finding sleep until after he heard the church bells toll three. Though he longed for sleep, he feared the dreams, dreams haunted by too many phantoms of too many men who'd died before they'd had a chance to live.

He sighed, wondering if the time would ever be right for him and Kezia. She intended to leave for Paris on the morning train but she'd been vague about what she meant to do after that. His own plans were firm: Return to England and find C. And when he did? He wasn't sure how he'd kill the man, but kill him he would.

What was the motto in the German War Book? 'Cunning and violence.' He meant to adopt it as his own.

There was a tapping on the door. Pulling a robe around him, Luke crossed the room and eased the door open.

'Kezia.' His voice rose in happy surprise.

Her auburn hair had grown, flowing onto the shoulders of her white nightgown. When he stepped aside to let her walk past him, the scent of lilies of the valley surrounded him. She'd never seemed more beautiful, more desirable.

'What a wonderful breeze.' Kezia went to the window and gazed into the night as though trying to hide her face from him. What was she afraid he might see there?

'I couldn't sleep,' she told him. 'Last night, when I finally did fall asleep, I dreamed someone was knocking on my door. When I opened it, Justin was standing there staring at me out of his one eye, not speaking but still pleading with me to help him. I took his arm but found no substance. He vanished before my eyes. And then I knew there was nothing I could do to help him, then or ever. Nothing in the world.'

Luke crossed the room to stand behind her, his hands lightly touching her upper arms. She trembled and he let his hands fall to his sides, thinking he'd frightened her. She turned to him, her gaze meeting his, and she put her arms around him, drawing him to her.

'I want you to hold me,' she whispered. 'I want you to take me in your arms and hold me as close as you possibly can.'

He held her to him. The feel of her softness, the scent of her, the sound of her rapid breathing all excited him while at the same time he was brushed by sadness, a sense of loss. As though at this moment Kezia, coming to him for comfort and not for love, was as far away from him, as inaccessible as she'd ever been.

He'd never met a woman so difficult to understand. All his previous experience with them had been of the yes-I-will or the no-I-won't variety and he'd tended to prefer the yes types. He'd never been sure with Kezia whether she wanted him or not. He did know he'd never be able to forget her. Tonight, if she needed comfort from him, comfort she'd have, and never mind what he wanted.

Luke put his arm beneath her legs, lifted her, carried her across the room and placed her gently on the bed. He flung off his robe and lay beside her. When he took her into his arms she tensed, the length of her body becoming rigid against his nakedness.

'Ssh,' he said softly, 'it's all right.' He stroked her hair, nestling his lips in its warm fullness, murmuring her name, and after a time she sighed and relaxed in his arms. When her breathing deepened, he thought she'd fallen asleep.

'Luke?' she whispered. 'Are you awake?'

He nodded against her hair.

'I need you, Luke. I have for a very long time. But I was afraid. I still am but now is the right time.' She sat up and slowly drew her gown over her head. The faint light from the window glowed on her skin.

He needed no urging. They came together tentatively at first, then with a desperate need, their hesitant exploring caresses leading to a frenzied passion. She was eager, yet not experienced, ardent without seeming to know exactly what to do. It drove him so wild with desire that when they joined, he realized, far too late to turn back, that this was her first time.

For some reason he'd thought that she and Justin must have made love. But perhaps he'd been too much the proper Englishman.

Luke wasn't either proper or English and so he took the innocent passion she offered and gave her himself, body, heart and soul, in return.

With her, he thought, it was as wonderful as flying. Later, holding her lightly, reluctant to let her go, he listened to a church bell toll in the distance. 'I didn't understand what you wanted,' he said softly. 'Not at first.'

'I didn't want you at first,' she told him. 'Not in that way. At the same time, I knew it would be wonderful. With you.' She leaned away from him and rose on one elbow. 'Isn't this where we both have a cigarette?'

Grinning, Luke sat up, took the pack of Players from the table, lit two cigarettes and handed her one.

Kezia propped herself against the head-board, pulling the sheet up to cover her nakedness. 'I'm taking the train to Paris in the morning,' she told him. 'To be assigned to a field hospital. If they'll have me.'

'Thank God,' he said. 'I was afraid you might have another assignment from C.'

'This isn't,' she assured him.

'Do you have to go so soon? We could have a week here, maybe longer, just the two of us. Don't you think we deserve it?'

'Don't tempt me, Luke. You have from the beginning, you know. I've never met a man quite like you. Just when I feel I know exactly how you'll behave, you go off on another tangent. You're totally unpredictable. Which is why you're alive and I am, too.'

'You said you were afraid.'

'It's the damn war. There's little place for the feeling I have for you during a time like this. It must wait. But I couldn't, not entirely. I needed to share this with you, at least.'

He raised her hand to his lips. 'You're like no other woman,' he said. 'You confound me.'

She smiled. 'Good.' Her smile faded and she sighed. 'But I still have to leave on the train tomorrow, I'd feel guilty if I kept on enjoying myself while so many boys were being killed.' She sat upright, heedless of the sheet falling from her breasts. 'The damn generals,' she said. 'They pore over their maps in their French chateaus miles behind the lines, order the boys over the tops, watch them being slaughtered, thousands killed for an advance of a few hundred feet, and the next week the generals do the same thing, order another attack, create another debacle. The Somme, Ypres, Verdun, Gallipoli. Why won't someone say, 'Enough, you've killed enough men'?'

'We'll never win until we break the stalemate in France,' Luke said. 'These generals are probably still fighting the last war's battles. They don't know what to do when they're faced with hundreds of miles of fortified trenches.'

'Can't they see they're destroying an entire generation? I suppose if my father were alive today, he'd be the same.'

'Your father?'

'The Boer War. He was killed at Magersfontein. I never really knew him. He gave me my name and little else.'

'You should be glad you're not in the generals' shoes,' Luke said.

She spoke as if she hadn't heard him. 'The day's coming when there'll be no more killing, when we'll see an end to wars. We'll bring the change, women will. Not men.' She leaned over him and stubbed out her cigarette in the ashtray on the table.

Luke curbed his flare of desire at the brush of her breasts against him, aware she wasn't in the mood to make love again.

'Soon women will have the vote,' she said, 'not only in England but in the States, eventually all over the civilized world. When women have the power, they won't be like men, they won't think of themselves as English or American or German or French, they'll be women first, mothers and wives with sons and husbands. Only women can stop the slaughter and bring peace to the world.'

She might be right about women getting the vote but she hadn't faced the fact that getting the vote didn't mean women would vote for women when they got it. Luke sat up and put out his own cigarette. All of the accumulated weariness of the last few days swept over him. He closed his eyes and sighed, wanting nothing more than to lie with her next to him and fall asleep.

But Kezia, he realized, was bent on bringing peace to the world. A noble objective, one he approved of, if only she wouldn't choose this particular time to expound on it.

'You don't think women will ever be in control, do you?' she asked.

He felt suddenly very old. Kezia seemed so young. 'There has to be a change,' he said carefully. 'The world can't go on like this with a war every twenty or thirty years. Wars could end the way you say, I suppose. But, no, I don't believe they will.'

This war would end, he told himself, only after his countrymen came in on the side of the Allies. As Theodore Roosevelt was urging them to do. The country needed him, a leader, in the White House, not a vacillating college professor.

Kezia stood up, found her nightgown on the floor and pulled it over her head. When Luke took her in his arms she clung to him, the war and everything else forgotten.

'Let this be our goodbye.' She kissed him for long moments. Tenderly. 'Don't come to see me off tomorrow,' she said. 'Please don't come.'

★　★　★

The next morning Luke arrived at the station just as the whistle shrilled and the coach doors banged shut. He ran along the platform, pushed past a porter wearing a blue smock, searched the windows. Steam billowed from the locomotive ahead of him and the carriages jerked into motion. He found her in the most forward coach, wearing the black dress and hat of the day before. He called her name and she saw him, smiled, struggled to open the window without success. A *poilu* reached past her, yanked the window up and she put her head out, leaning toward Luke.

'I'm glad you came,' she said. 'Despite what I told you last night.'

Luke, walking beside the slow-moving train, reached up and took her hand. She was so beautiful, looked so fragile when she wore black. She was anything but fragile, though. One of the things he'd learned to admire about her was that, though utterly feminine, she could act as swiftly and as competently as any man when it was necessary.

Kezia was unique.

She leaned down, kissed him. The train gathered speed and he had to trot to keep up to her window.

'Come visit me if you can,' she said. 'The Red Cross in Paris will know where I am. I thought, I even planned last night to be an end but I think now it might be a beginning. I want to see you again.'

'There'll never be an end between us.' His own words startled him.

She smiled. 'I expect I'll hate it, patching up the boys so they can go back into the lines but that's what I do best. Patch.'

'Not patch,' he said. 'Heal.'

He ran beside the rattling train, watching Kezia, memorizing how she looked, all the while knowing the end of the platform was close at hand.

'I don't want to say goodbye,' she cried.

'Not for us. We'll say *au revoir*,' he told her. He wanted to add more. That he loved her? He couldn't, unsure what love was. Seeing the end of the platform, he stopped, calling, 'We *will* meet again,' not knowing if she heard him.

The train bearing Kezia away from him sped down the track, faster and faster. He stood at the end of the platform feeling lost, repeating her name over and over. No one paid him any heed. War was a time of partings.

When the train disappeared in the hazy distance, he squared his shoulders and strode from the station. Kezia was gone and there was work to do. He had unfinished work to do.

By the time he retrieved his belongings from the inn, he'd stowed Kezia away carefully in his mind and began concentrating on C.

23

At four o'clock on a sunlit November afternoon, a lorry braked to a stop between the pillars at the entrance to Boling Hall. The driver handed identification papers to the British Army guard who, after examining them, shook his head. The driver opened the door of his cab and got out, his voice rising in indignation, his finger jabbing at the papers in the guard's hand.

The guard glanced behind him to the stone gatehouse, gestured with his hand and a second uniformed sentry joined them, smoothing papers on the lorry's fender and studying them. A constable on a bicycle pedaled toward the entrance along a Coventry road. As he swung left past the lorry and between the pillars he raised his hand to salute the two guards.

After a perfunctory glance, the first guard waved the constable into the estate.

With the gravel crunching beneath his tires, Luke pedaled past rhododendrons, entered the woods, and climbed a low hill. When he could no longer see the gatehouse, he dismounted and pushed his bike into the trees, leaving it concealed behind bushes.

Knowing he had an hour and a half before sunset, Luke walked deeper into the woods until he saw an oak that had been shattered in a lightning storm. Slowing, he studied the ground, smiling when he spotted the wire just where it had been three months before.

Stepping over the wire, he advanced cautiously until he was able to see the sweeping lawns of the estate between the trunks of the trees. Using elbows and knees, he crawled to the edge of the undergrowth behind the main house, fifty feet from the first of the outbuildings. A porch protruded toward him from the rear of the house, its roof a deck enclosed by an elaborately latticed balustrade. Above the deck, the roofs angled upward, their steep slopes interrupted here and there by squat brick chimneys.

All was as he remembered it. Or almost. A slight difference nagged him but he was unable to put his finger on what it was.

As he watched from his hiding place, the light of the setting sun struck the upper window, touching them with an orange flame. Remembering the exploding Zeppelin, he blinked and glanced away. When he looked back the glow was gone. Though the house appeared deserted, he knew C was there. In fact, he was scheduled to have an interview with C in less than twenty-four hours. An interview that would never take place. By the next day one of them perhaps both of them, would be dead. His fingers touched the Webley in his shoulder holster.

Luke was ready to retreat deeper into the woods to wait for darkness when C walked around the corner of the house carrying a bushel basket in front of him. Though casually dressed in a tweed jacket and plus fours, C looked much the same as Luke remembered him, dignified and urbane, a country squire. Luke wondered if C was a man unaffected by remorse, a man who never thought of those he'd sent to their deaths.

C shifted the basket so he held it against his side with one hand while he opened the door to a potting shed with the other. He disappeared inside, leaving the door open. Disdaining concealment, Luke stood and walked quickly across the lawn to the shed. He paused in the doorway, drawing his Webley.

C stood with his back to Luke. He had put the basket on a table and was taking bulbs from it and laying them on racks along the far wall. When he finished, he turned. The almost imperceptible widening of his eyes was his only indication of surprise. Luke was disappointed that C showed no sign of fear.

'I didn't expect you until tomorrow.' C smiled as though genuinely amused. 'Nor did I expect you to arrive in this quite remarkable costume. I'm not sure you'd make a very convincing constable, Mr. Ray.'

Luke shrugged. 'I've come to kill you, C,' he said.

'In cold blood? You know I don't carry a firearm.'

'In cold blood.'

'I almost admire your rashness. But at least you've proved me correct. I thought you were the man for Brussels, I told Asberry so at the time. I was right.'

'You sent me to Belgium to be killed,' Luke said. 'We were decoys, bait to be fed to the Huns in the hope that Graham would succeed.'

'I prefer to call your group a diversion rather than a decoy. Battles are fought using diversions, demonstrations we used to call them, wars are won with them. Even savages such as your red Indians know and use the advantages of diversions. Nothing may be gained immediately and a few men or even a few hundred men may be lost, I give you that, but each well-planed ploy brings the eventual victory that much nearer.'

Words, nothing more. Another diversion, another demonstration. C would soon find out he was on to him. That words wouldn't help.

'You told us we were being sent to rescue Miss Cavell,' Luke said, 'that we were the ones who'd bring her out of Belgium.'

'You don't mind if I smoke, do you?' Luke's finger tightened on the trigger, relaxing his grip only when C placed the pipe he'd removed from his pocket in his mouth and lit it.

'I'm disappointed,' C said. 'You're talking like an adolescent, Sergeant Ray, a young man who still believes everything must be fair and above-board. I'd hoped your experiences would have helped mature you.' Pipe smoke drifted above Luke's head. 'Of course I didn't warn you. If you'd known, in time the Germans would have known as well. No matter what you think, you'd have been less than totally enthusiastic in carrying out your assignment.'

'The Germans would have found out from MacNeeley, wouldn't they? You knew he was a traitor when you sent him with us. At the end, he called me a pawn. He was right.'

'If there was a pawn, he was Byron MacNeeley,' C. said. 'We've known the truth about him for some years, ever since we discovered a German message center in London during the coronation of George the

Fifth. Mr. MacNeeley's still among the living by the way. Bad luck. Still, from my point of view, it does seem as though he might have deliberately provided you with the opportunity to use your considerable skills in effecting that escape from St. Gilles.'

Luke frowned, momentarily distracted. Deliberately? That traitor MacNeeley? He found he couldn't dismiss the possibility.

C took a drag on his pipe and removed it to expel the smoke. 'The Chinese warn me I must be careful who we save from death because they believe one becomes responsible for that person. I understand MacNeeley saved your life at least once before the prison episode.'

'MacNeeley's not Chinese.'

Ignoring that observation, C said, 'One question, Sergeant. A matter of professional curiosity. Could you and Graham have accomplished the mission? Could you have rescued Nurse Cavell if you'd had surprise working for you?'

'Surprise was what we needed most and had the least of. MacNeeley aside, the Huns seemed to know what we were planning almost before we did.'

'You haven't answered my question.'

'The answer's yes. We could have pulled it off. With any luck at all.'

'You do seem to possess that rare commodity when you're not operating under a handicap. Luck. A Fokker and a Zeppelin in one fell swoop. Plus bringing in an LVG for us to examine.'

'Two Fokkers and a Zeppelin,' Luke corrected. 'Not confirmed but I know they went down.'

'Ah, two Fokkers then.' C pointed the stem of his pipe at Luke. 'Let me tell you about Justin Graham's mission,' he said. 'You seem to suggest that we favored him. A childish idea, you'll have to admit. Let me tell you something you obviously don't know. Graham's mission was never intended to succeed.'

'Never intended — ?' Luke stared at him. 'I don't know what you're talking about.'

'Graham was as much of a diversion, decoy if you insist, as you were. The Huns knew he was on his way to Belgium, knew his time of arrival, what he intended to do and how he intended going about doing it.'

Luke shook his head in disbelief.

'Are you still so naive?' C asked. 'Can't you see that our organization never intended to rescue Miss Cavell? We wanted to give Lord Kitchener the impression that we'd made every possible attempt so we dispatched not

411

one but two rescue missions to Belgium, penetrated the defenses of St. Gilles and so forth and so forth. Our object was to make the Hun believe Miss Cavell was more important to us than she actually was.'

'She was important!'

'You see, we've convinced you. What was she? An obscure English nurse captured in occupied Belgium. She mattered for little as long as she lived. If we'd accomplished the rescue, we'd have had an overnight sensation, a three-day wonder. The way it turned out — helped, of course, by the remarkable stupidity of the Huns — we've been blessed with a martyr.'

C sucked on his pipe again. 'Do you realize the value of an honest-to-God martyr? The whole world's outraged, especially your American compatriots with their innate sympathy for the lone woman in distress. A heritage from your frontier past. From what I've read, I pity the desperado who kills a woman. The wrath of every red-blooded man in the West is automatically directed against him.'

'I can't believe you wanted the Germans to kill her,' Luke said, considerably disturbed. 'The most lowdown, horse-stealing bush-whacker wouldn't think that way. Even the Huns wouldn't.'

'Remember that the woman you're defending so earnestly was guilty as charged. She did help our soldiers return to our lines where they fought again, killed Germans again. More than a hundred returned because of Miss Cavell. The proof of the pudding's in the eating. Consider what's happened since Miss Cavell's execution. Enlistments have soared. If the government insists on a volunteer army, we must have enlistments and Miss Cavell's death gave us thousands more than we had any right to expect.

'Much more importantly, consider the effect on the United States. When we're in a position to look back at our leisure, two events will be seen as having propelled your country into this conflict — the sinking of the *Lusitania* and the execution of Edith Cavell. The Germans seem intent on proving they're the beasts our propaganda paints them as being.'

'You're taking a big chance, C. What's to prevent me from telling the American papers what you've told me?'

'Even if your story managed to reach print, how many would believe you? Think about it. You, a veteran of over a year's fighting in France, a hero, yes, but one who's obviously shell-shocked, turning him into a renegade who forced an entrance here at Boling Hall

413

disguised as a member of the constabulary, a man who blames himself for the death of his comrade, Justin Graham, a man so deranged that he came here threatening to kill his superior officer.'

C looked steadily at Luke. 'How did you picture the English before you had occasion to deal with us? Fair play, a stiff upper lip, good sportsmanship, 'well done, old chap.' That's how your countrymen view us. How can you expect them to believe we English would fight a war in the manner you're suggesting? Your story wouldn't wash. Especially considering the kind of man your father was. Like father, like son, I believe the adage goes.'

T.J.? What did C know of T.J.? Luke glanced down at the revolver in his hand. Suddenly the gun seemed heavy. He gripped his right wrist with this left hand for support. 'What does my father have to do with it?' he demanded.

'Perhaps a great deal. We *are* thorough, we English, even though all of us may not be the best of sportsmen. I had an exceptionally complete dossier prepared on one T.J. Ray, deceased. The results were most revealing.'

'You had no right.' Luke snapped.

'I had every right. You don't seem to understand that the war takes precedence

414

over everything, over you, over me, over Justin Graham, even over Miss Edith Cavell. We're trying to save civilization as we know it, at least for another thirty years or so.' He puffed serenely on his pipe. 'Do you want me to tell you what I found out about your father? Or are you afraid to hear the truth?'

'Go ahead, tell me.' Luke spoke through his teeth. 'Whatever you say, I won't believe. You've spun a web of lies ever since you first had Sid lure me in here.'

'You're perfectly free to believe any truth you're unable to face.' C's lips tightened in an almost smile. 'These are the highlights of what our American operatives discovered about Mr. Theodore Joseph Ray. First, he murdered four or five red Indians, the number's debatable, to secure the property they'd been given in perpetuity by the United States government. I believe they were known as Utes and lived in a territory called Colorado. Your father's motivation for killing them was to secure the mineral rights to their land.'

'Utes might have been killed fighting the prospectors,' Luke conceded. 'Damn it, Colorado was the frontier. You had to fight for what you got.'

'I'm afraid these Utes were murdered rather cold-bloodedly, Mr. Ray.' C traced a

Roman numeral II with his pipe. 'Second, when your father suffered financial reverses after the price of silver fell rather precipitously, he stole a considerable sum of money from the firm controlled by him and his partner, a Mr. Irvine, blaming the partner for the loss. Irvine later committed suicide rather than go to jail for your father's crime.'

'That's a lie! Irvine stole the money. He was convicted by a Denver court.'

'On perjured testimony paid for by your father.' C paused. 'Third, your father became romantically involved with a Colorado woman, a Mrs. Linda May Lowe. This led to Mrs. Lowe's divorce following a rather sensational trial, recorded by the newspapers in some detail. Your father subsequently divorced and married this woman.'

Luke's heart had begun to pound. 'My father didn't take up with Linda May until after he divorced my mother.'

'No, before, as the Denver newspapers give clear evidence. You might want to look up the event — it's there in cold print.'

Luke felt as though C had hit him in the gut. Bile rose to his throat. He swallowed, fighting down nausea. He shook his head stubbornly but in his heart he knew that C told the truth. All the gossip he'd heard as a child, all the stories about his father he'd squirreled away in a dark corner of his childish mind, swept out like evil ghosts. Again he saw the hunting lodge his father had taken him to, saw the bunk where he supposedly lay asleep, heard his father laugh as he described to the other men at the lodge how he'd massacred the Utes.

Luke recalled covering his ears when his mother's angry voice floated up the stairs to his bedroom as she accused his father of being a coward to let Irvine face jail for a crime he hadn't committed. Her words echoed in his mind. 'Being a thief is shameful enough,' she'd cried. 'But to allow an innocent man to suffer — '

He shook his head violently, thrusting away the unwelcome memories, but unable to avoid the truth that had seeped in. T.J. wasn't the father he'd looked up to and admired all his life. What was he then? Just a murderer, a betrayer? Luke took a deep breath. No, not just those things. His father had been only a man, better than some, worse than others. A man who did his best most of the time, did what he thought he had to do, a man driven by ambition and dreams and lust. As every man is. Imperfect.

'May I suggest that you didn't come here to kill me?'

C spoke quietly but his voice startled Luke.

'You actually came intending to kill your father for what he did to you and your mother.'

'That's — ' Luke had to clear his throat ' — a lot of hogwash.'

'Why don't you put away that firearm?' C suggested.

Luke stared at the gun, now pointing at the floor of the potting shed. All the anger and hate had drained from him. He despised C but he no longer wanted to kill him. He slid the revolver into its holster beneath his jacket.

'Now then,' C said, putting his hand on Luke's arm.

'Let me present the proposal I intended to mention to you at tomorrow's meeting.'

Luke drew his arm away.

'You don't have to give me an answer immediately,' C told him, 'but I'd like you to consider what I have to say, consider it most carefully. You may or may not know that Tony Fokker's perfected a device that allows Hun machine-guns to fire through the revolving propellers of their aircraft. Our planes, equipped with bullet deflectors and what have you, are no longer a match for them.'

He was right about that, Luke thought.

C put his dead pipe in his pocket. 'What we need,' he said, 'is a man with an aviator's skills to obtain one of those improved

Fokkers so we can duplicate its firing mechanism.'

'So you want someone to go behind the German lines and steal a Fokker.'

'Precisely. Who would be better equipped for the assignment than yourself? Think about it. The result of such an endeavor, if it was successful, would be of inestimable value to our cause.'

Luke shook his head. 'No. I don't want any part of you or your mission.'

'Don't be hasty. That's one of your faults, you know, not pausing to think ahead. In this business one must plan most carefully.' C walked ahead of Luke through the open door of the shed into the waning sunlight. 'Speaking of planning,' he said, 'there's something I want to show you.' C raised his right hand above his head. 'If you'd glance to the roof of the porch.'

A man holding a rifle stood up behind the latticed balustrade. The latticework was new, he realized, it was the one detail that he hadn't been able to pinpoint when he was surveying the house.

'Thank you, Jenkins,' C called. 'I won't be needing you any more today.' He looked at Luke. 'You see, we suspected your intentions ever since you arrived back in England. I let you enter the grounds, made certain I'd be available for our unscheduled interview. Naturally I took certain precautions. If I judged you were becoming too dangerous, Jenkins would have killed you.'

Luke gazed steadily at the older man. 'Someday,' he said, 'I will kill you. I don't know when, but I will.'

'I have no doubt but that you may try.' Again C put his hand on Luke's arm, leading him along the side of the house. 'In the meantime, consider my offer concerning the Fokkers and their machine-guns.'

'Go to hell.' Luke strode ahead toward the gravel drive.

'Wait. I'm afraid your bicycle's on its way back to the police. If you won't go to Germany for me, at least accept my offer of transport to London.' He signaled with his raised hand. 'Here we are.'

A uniformed chauffeur drove a sedan slowly along the drive, stopping in front of Luke.

Luke shrugged. 'Why not?' He opened the back door and got in.

'You know where to find me if you change your mind,' C said.

Luke didn't answer and he didn't look back as they drove under the trees and were waved past the gatehouse.

'Where to, governor?' the driver asked

when they neared the main road.

'Take me to — ' Luke paused. That voice was familiar. 'Haven't I met you somewhere?' he asked.

'You may have, governor.' The driver stopped the car and turned. Luke saw the scarred face, the startlingly blue eyes.

'Sid! Good God, man, I never expected to see you again.' Luke leaned forward and grasped Sid's shoulder.

'Did you think I couldn't stay out of the clutches of the Boches? For all their guns, the bloody Huns aren't any harder to give the slip to than London bobbies. Takes experience is all, which I got. A Belgian took me in, bandaged up my leg and got me to the border and here I am, hardly the worse for wear.'

'Good for him.'

'Her,' Sid said and winked.

Luke grinned. 'I'm damn glad you got here in one piece.'

'C told me about the Fokkers,' Sid said. 'The blooming planes with the guns that shoot through their props. No cakewalk, making off with one of those buggers. Might be a lark, though.'

'I'd hardly call it a lark,' Luke said, sitting back.

He wondered if it could be done. The new planes would be well guarded, unlike the

LVG at the aerodrome north of Brussels.

'You know how it is,' Sid said. 'An old lag like me gets what you call antsy sitting around with his hands in his own pockets instead of picking someone else's. That's why I broke one of my rules for staying alive. I volunteered to go with you to get us a Fokker.'

Luke stared at him. 'I thought you'd earned your parole by going on the Brussels mission.'

'You're one hundred percent correct. Brussels was for yours truly.' Sid cleared his throat, obviously embarrassed. 'The Fokker one's for old Blighty. I never was much at waving the flag but war's war. We owe the Huns one for what they did to Miss Cavell. Besides, I like working for C, the old bastard. He don't just sit on his ass, he gets the job done. One way or another. Like another gentleman I could mention.'

Luke raised his eyebrows inquiringly.

'A certain Yank sergeant. Served with him on the Brussels caper.'

'Me? Like C? You're loco.'

Sid shrugged, turned to face the windshield, put the car in gear and drove slowly along the Coventry road. 'Where to, governor?' he asked.

Luke's sigh was dragged up from the soles

of his boots. He didn't have a choice. Not because of Sid, though meeting up with Sid had cleared his mind so he could put his own problems aside and look at the bigger picture. He had no choice because he was Luke Ray. He had work to do. Maybe he was more like C than he realized. He hoped to hell not.

'Turn back,' he told Sid. 'I forgot something at the Hall.'

'Whatever you say, governor.' Sid swung the car around, drove through the gates, parked in front of the main house.

'I'll be back shortly,' Luke told him.

'No need to hurry,' Sid said. 'I've got my fags.'

Luke rang the bell and was ushered into the drawing room. C, who'd been looking from the window, turned and raised his eyebrows.

'I've changed my mind,' Luke said in a rush. 'I'll take the Fokker job. Me and Sid.'

'Good.' C walked toward him. 'Will you have a drink to seal the bargain?'

Why not? 'Don't mind if I do,' Luke said.

'Scotch and water. Am I right?'

Luke nodded. Of course he was right. The bloody bugger was always right, damn him.

'Naturally you'll be briefed here,' C said, 'but I believe I forgot to mention that you'll be getting a second briefing in Paris.'

Luke blinked, staring at C's back as the wily old devil walked toward a table. C couldn't possibly know about Kezia. About him and Kezia. Or could he?

Whether C knew or not, Luke suddenly realized how desperately he needed the chance to see Kezia again. To be with her. To find out just what it was he felt for her? He half-smiled. That, too.

C gestured to Luke and he saw that the table already contained two glasses. Filled glasses.

'As you can see, I've already poured the drinks,' C said.

The bastard knew I'd come back. He started to curse, shrugged and laughed aloud. He walked over, picked up his glass, raised it in silent salute to the conniving son-of-a-bitch and drank.

The whisky warmed his gut, but, more importantly, the thought of Paris and Kezia warmed his heart. War was one thing, love another. If it *was* love. He damn well meant to find out.